The Clifford Affair

A Chief Inspector Pointer Mystery

By A. E. Fielding

Originally published in 1937

The Clifford Affair

© 2014 Resurrected Press
www.ResurrectedPress.com

Published by Intrepid Ink, LLC

Intrepid Ink, LLC provides full publishing services to authors of fiction and non-fiction books, eBooks and websites. From editing to formatting, to publishing, to marketing, Intrepid Ink gets your creative works into the hands of the people who want to read them.
Find out more at www.IntrepidInk.com.

ISBN 13: 978-1-937022-72-3

Printed in the United States of America

Other Resurrected Press Books in *The Chief Inspector Pointer Mystery* Series

RESURRECTED PRESS CLASSIC MYSTERY CATALOGUE

Journeys into Mystery
Travel and Mystery in a More Elegant Time

The Edwardian Detectives
Literary Sleuths of the Edwardian Era

Gems of Mystery
Lost Jewels from a More Elegant Age

Anne Austin
One Drop of Blood
The Black Pigeon
Murder at Bridge

E. C. Bentley
Trent's Last Case: The Woman in Black

Ernest Bramah
Max Carrados Resurrected:
The Detective Stories of Max Carrados

Agatha Christie
The Secret Adversary
The Mysterious Affair at Styles

Octavus Roy Cohen
Midnight

Freeman Wills Croft
The Ponson Case
The Pit Prop Syndicate

J. S. Fletcher
The Herapath Property
The Rayner-Slade Amalgamation
The Chestermarke Instinct
The Paradise Mystery
Dead Men's Money
The Middle of Things
Ravensdene Court
Scarhaven Keep
The Orange-Yellow Diamond
The Middle Temple Murder
The Tallyrand Maxim
The Borough Treasurer
In the Mayor's Parlour
The Saftey Pin

R. Austin Freeman
*The Mystery of 31 New Inn from the Dr. Thorndyke
Series*
*John Thorndyke's Cases from the Dr. Thorndyke
Series*
The Red Thumb Mark from The Dr. Thorndyke Series
The Eye of Osiris from The Dr. Thorndyke Series
A Silent Witness from the Dr. John Thorndyke Series
The Cat's Eye from the Dr. John Thorndyke Series
*Helen Vardon's Confession: A Dr. John Thorndyke
Story*
As a Thief in the Night: A Dr. John Thorndyke Story
*Mr. Pottermack's Oversight: A Dr. John Thorndyke
Story*
*Dr. Thorndyke Intervenes: A Dr. John Thorndyke
Story*
The Singing Bone: The Adventures of Dr. Thorndyke
The Stoneware Monkey: A Dr. John Thorndyke Story
*The Great Portrait Mystery, and Other Stories: A
Collection of Dr. John Thorndyke and Other Stories*
The Penrose Mystery: A Dr. John Thorndyke Story
The Uttermost Farthing: A Savant's Vendetta

Arthur Griffiths
The Passenger From Calais
The Rome Express

Fergus Hume
The Mystery of a Hansom Cab
The Green Mummy
The Silent House
The Secret Passage

Edgar Jepson
The Loudwater Mystery

A. E. W. Mason
At the Villa Rose

A. A. Milne
The Red House Mystery

Baroness Emma Orczy
The Old Man in the Corner

Edgar Allan Poe
The Detective Stories of Edgar Allan Poe

Arthur J. Rees
The Hampstead Mystery
The Shrieking Pit
The Hand In The Dark
The Moon Rock
The Mystery of the Downs

Mary Roberts Rinehart
Sight Unseen and The Confession

Dorothy L. Sayers
Whose Body?

Sir William Magnay
The Hunt Ball Mystery

Mabel and Paul Thorne
The Sheridan Road Mystery

Louis Tracy
The Strange Case of Mortimer Fenley
The Albert Gate Mystery
The Bartlett Mystery
The Postmaster's Daughter
The House of Peril
The Sandling Case: What Would You Have Done?

Charles Edmonds Walk
The Paternoster Ruby

John R. Watson
The Mystery of the Downs
The Hampstead Mystery

Edgar Wallace
The Daffodil Mystery
The Crimson Circle

Carolyn Wells
Vicky Van
The Man Who Fell Through the Earth
In the Onyx Lobby
Raspberry Jam
The Clue
The Room with the Tassels
The Vanishing of Betty Varian
The Mystery Girl
The White Alley
The Curved Blades
Anybody but Anne

FOREWORD

The period between the First and Second World Wars has rightly been called the "Golden Age of British Mysteries." It was during this period that Agatha Christie, Dorothy L. Sayers, and Margery Allingham first turned their pens to crime. On the male side, the era saw such writers as Anthony Berkeley, John Dickson Carr, and Freeman Wills Crofts join the ranks of writers of detective fiction. The genre was immensely popular at the time on both sides of the Atlantic, and by the end of the 1930's one out of every four novels published in Britain was a mystery.

While Agatha Christie and a few of her peers have remained popular and in print to this day, the same cannot be said of all the authors of this period. With so many mysteries published in the period, it is inevitable that many of them would become obscure or worse, forgotten, often with no justification than changing public tastes. The case of Archibald Fielding is one such, an author, who though popular enough to have a career spanning two decades and more than two dozen mysteries has become such a cipher that his, or as seems more likely, her real identity has become as much a mystery as the books themselves.

While the identity of the author may forever remain an unsolved puzzle, there are some facts that may be inferred from the texts. It is likely that the author had an upbringing and education typical of the British upper middle class in the period before the Great War with all that implies; a familiarity with the classics, the arts, and music, a working knowledge of French, an appreciation of the finer things in life. The author has also traveled abroad, primarily in the south of France, but probably to Belgium, Spain, and Italy as well, as portions of several of the books are set in those locales.

The books attributed to Archibald Fielding, A. E. Fielding, or Archibald E. Fielding, are quintessential Golden Age British mysteries. They include all the attributes, the country houses, the tangled webs of relationships, the somewhat feckless cast of characters who seem to have nothing better to do with themselves than to murder or be murdered. Their focus is on a middle class and upper class struggling to find themselves in the new realities of the post war era while still trying to live the lifestyle of the Edwardian era. Things are never as they seem, red herrings are distributed liberally through the pages as are the clues that will ultimately lead to the solution of "the puzzle," for the British mysteries of this period are centered on the puzzle element which both the reader and the detective must solve before the last page.

A majority of the Fielding mysteries involve the character of Chief Inspector Pointer. Unlike the eccentric Belgian Hercule Poirot, the flamboyant Lord Peter Wimsey, or the somewhat mysterious Albert Campion, Pointer is merely a competent, sometimes clever, occasionally intuitive policeman. And unlike, as with Inspector French in the stories of Freeman Wills Croft, the emphasis is on the mystery itself, not the process of detection.

Pointer is nearly as much of a mystery as the author. Very little of his personal life is revealed in the books. He is described as being vaguely of Scottish ancestry. He is well read and educated, though his duties at Scotland Yard prevent him from enjoying those pursuits. His success as a detective depends on his willingness to "suspect everyone" and to not being tied to any one theory. He is fluent in French and familiar with that country. He is, at least in the first book, unmarried, sharing lodgings with a bookbinder named O'Connor, in much the manner of Holmes and Watson, though O'Connor disappears in the subsequent volumes.

While the early books fall plainly in the "humdrum" school with Pointer appearing almost immediately and much of story revolving on the business of tracking down various clues, the later novels are much more concerned with the lives of the characters surrounding the mystery. Pointer is much less center stage, often arriving instead at mid-book to clean up the pieces and insure that the guilty do not escape justice. It is, perhaps, this lack of focus on the detective, which has caused the works of Fielding to fade away while the likes of Poirot seem to attract the interest of each new generation.

One intriguing feature of the Pointer mysteries is that they all involve an unexpected twist at the end, wherein the mystery finally solved is not the mystery invoked at the beginning of the book. I leave it to the reader to judge whether Fielding is "playing by the rules" in this, but it does keep the books interesting up to the last chapter.

The Clifford Affair is the fourth mystery in the series involving Chief Inspector Pointer. In it, Pointer finds himself with a headless corpse. This presents him with some serious difficulties. Not only is the identity of the victim in doubt, but the cause of death, which presumably involved the head, has vanished along with that portion of the body. To this, is added a possible diplomatic complication, as certain clues would seem to point to an infamous Basque Anarchist as either the victim, or possibly the murderer. This latter dimension to the plot shows that international terrorism is not just a recent phenomenon.

Despite their obscurity, the mysteries of Archibald Fielding, whoever he or she might have been, are well written, well crafted examples of the form, worthy of the interest of the fans of the genre. It is with pleasure, then, that Resurrected Press presents this new edition of *The Clifford Affair* and others in the series to its readers.

About the Author

The identity of the author is as much a mystery as the plots of the novels. Two dozen novels were published from 1924 to 1944 as by Archibald Fielding, A. E. Fielding, or Archibald E. Fielding, yet the only clue as to the real author is a comment by the American publishers, H.C. Kinsey Co. that A. E. Fielding was in reality a "middle-aged English woman by the name of Dorothy Feilding whose peacetime address is Sheffield Terrace, Kensington, London, and who enjoys gardening." Research on the part of John Herrington has uncovered a person by that name living at 2 Sheffield Terrace from 1932-1936. She appears to have moved to Islington in 1937 after which she disappears. To complicate things, some have attributed the authorship to Lady Dorothy Mary Evelyn Moore nee Feilding (1889-1935), however, a grandson of Lady Dorothy denied any family knowledge of such authorship. The archivist at Collins, the British publisher, reports that any records of A. Fielding were presumably lost during WWII. Birthdates have been given variously as 1884, 1889, and 1900. Unless new information comes to light, it would appear that the real authorship must remain a mystery.

Greg Fowlkes
Editor-In-Chief
Resurrected Press
www.ResurrectedPress.com

CHAPTER ONE

The Assistant Commissioner of New Scotland Yard listened for a moment at one of his telephones, told the man at the other end, it happened to be Superintendent Maybrick of Hampstead, to hold on a moment, and sent one of his constable-clerks in search of Chief Inspector Pointer.

It was then just a little before nine of a Tuesday morning. A tall, lithe, lean young man came in with a step that suggested the kilt and the springing heather.

"Look here, Pointer. Suppose you hand over the reins of that case you're on to Clark. He can carry on all right now. Superintendent Maybrick of Hampstead wants help. Or rather, I think he needs it. He's just been called in to a horrid mess, a murder, in one of the flats in his district. From certain things he thinks it's an anarchist plot gone wrong, 'biter bit' sort of thing," Major Pelham said vaguely; "he's got into touch with the Foreign Office already. So by this time there's sure to be some F.O. man sprinting along to have a first look. Go and see what you think of it, will you? If it isn't a foreign spy job, then it should be a fine problem for you to solve. Here's the address." He handed a chit to the Chief Inspector, who left the room with his swift, unhurried stride that covered such an amazing amount of ground.

Pointer drove to the place mentioned—a large block of flats with a view over Hampstead Heath.

The head porter, after a keen glance at the Chief Inspector when the latter asked for "Mr. Maybrick," saluted, and took him up in the lift. The only information which he volunteered was that none of the residents had an idea of what had happened.

"These are all service flats, sir, and news gets around terrible fast unless one's very careful. As a rule illnesses are 'maternity cases' when possible. Deaths are 'measles' to account for the body being took away, but murder—the owners haven't given instructions about that. Not yet." The porter stopped the lift at the third floor, and stepped forward to ring the bell of a flat marked fourteen, which had no card in the little glass case beside the door. Pointer stopped him.

"A moment!" His eye ran over the door and mat and landing, as well as up and down the staircases. Then he nodded. The porter rang. The door opened an inch. The Superintendent inside, in plain clothes too, inspected them both cautiously, then he stood back and Pointer entered.

Maybrick saluted. He was one of Pointer's many policeman admirers. What a pity, he thought, that there was nothing here for the Chief Inspector to get his teeth into, those teeth that never let go.

"A moment!" Pointer said again, as he switched on the light and gave one swift glance around the square hall, a glance that nothing visible escaped. Then he nodded.

"Now lead the way."

"Shall I tell you first what I know, sir?"

"Not if any one from the Foreign Office is on the trail," Pointer said promptly. "They're quick workers. And I like to have my clues untouched, as far as may be."

"No one's come yet, sir. Not even the doctor. And the clues aren't ones that can be disarranged." Maybrick was about to expand into detail, but Pointer stopped him.

"Then this way, sir." Maybrick led down to a door at the farther end of a little passage. Pointer stepped into a tiled bathroom. In the bath-tub—it was not a pleasant sight—lay a man's body, stripped and headless.

"Where's his head?"

"Not on the premises, sir. Gone. Like his clothes. All gone."

Pointer knelt down in the doorway and looked sideways across the floor.

"Rubber-soled shoes. Man's heel marks. Apparently only one pair. What's that?" He advanced now, and bent to a tiny splash of something white on the tiles under the raised china bath.

"Powder they use to clean the tub, sir. Shall I tell you what the head porter"

Again Pointer stopped him.

"Has the body been touched by any one, as far as you know?"

"No, sir. Not the kind of thing to get touched by any sensible man."

"Have you photographed it?"

"Films are being developed at the station now."

Pointer lifted each of the hands in turn.

They were slender, beautiful hands, that looked as though they would be clever at whatever they did. Hard work had never been asked of them.

"Wore a ring on the middle finger of the right hand. Broad, thick ring. Signet ring very likely. Cigarette smoker. Gentleman certainly from the care of the whole body."

There were no marks of blood-stained hands either on the bath, or on the fitted basin beside it, or on any of the taps, nor finger prints of any kind.

Pointer stepped on into a bedroom opening out of the bath-room. Then he returned to Maybrick.

"We can wash our hands in the bedroom. The basin in there's not even been dusted. This one has been used."

A ring came at the door. Maybrick answered it. A small, quick-stepping, alert-eyed, gray-bearded man stepped into the flat. He was of the type to pass easily for English in England, French in France, Spanish, or Eastern, according to where he was met. "Many-tongued Tindall," a great international sleuth or sleuther of

sleuths, was an amateur. A man of means attached to the
Foreign Office, when he was not on loan to the Home
Office. In manner he was very quiet, in speech very
direct.

"I've come to see if the dead man's one of our birds,"
he said, after shaking hands with Pointer. "But you
here?" He eyed the Chief Inspector with mock distrust.
"No poaching, you know!"

For a second Tindall too stood looking about him with
swift, piercing glances.

"Now for the story"—he turned to the Superintendent.
First eyes, then ears, was Pointer's way. But Tindall was
as high in his branch as Pointer was in the C.I.D., and
was, moreover, a much older man. So Maybrick led them
into the drawing-room, where the dust lay thick, and
where the blinds still shut out the daylight.

The story, as known to Maybrick, was exceedingly
simple. The flat belonged to a Mr. Marshall, a senior
clerk at Lloyds, who, as usual, wished to let it furnished
while he was away on a four weeks' holiday. He had left
last Thursday. On Friday, about six, a man had
presented himself to the head porter with a view card
from the house agents, which gave his name as a
Monsieur Tourcoin. The flat was shown him, and a little
later the head porter was informed over the telephone by
the agents that Mr. Tourcoin had taken the flat for a
friend, a Captain Brown. Captain Brown would "take
possession" on Tuesday or Wednesday.

On Monday evening something went wrong with the
lock of an upstairs flat. The porter thought it a good
opportunity, when the locksmith arrived this morning, to
have him run his eye over the front door of Number
Fourteen as well. Mr. Marshall had complained of its not
always catching properly when hastily shut. He also
remembered a difficulty with Marshall's bathroom bolt,
and took the man in there first. He had his own pass-key,
of course.

"They didn't stay to look at any bolts," Maybrick said dryly. "Nasty sight that body in there. They rushed to the telephone and called us in."

"What body in where?" Tindall asked impatiently. He was taken to see it. His face paled as he looked carefully at it and at the room.

"Horrible!" he muttered. "Horrible!"

He turned to Maybrick.

"What made you 'phone to us—made you think the crime political?"

"This, sir." Maybrick passed into a sitting-room, which, like the bedroom, opened out of the bathroom. He pointed to a newspaper on the table. It was a _Times_ of Friday, heavily scored at a few passages. Maybrick pointed to these. Tindall read aloud:—

"_Anti-royalist plot suspected in Madrid._ I see he's underscored that _'suspected.'_ What's this next? _King Alfonso's yacht Esmeralda to be ready by a certain date._ A question mark is pencilled beside the date. Indeed! Indeed! And here's something about King Boris's coming trip to Sofia heavily marked at the side. Except for that last, the items are only Spanish. . . ." Tindall perched on a chair in a way that suggested flight rather than rest.

"Man's clothes missing. . . . Papers in them gone too, of course. . . . Head taken away. . . . Identity to be concealed, or— Anything else made you think the murder political beyond the marked paper, Superintendent?"

"These." Maybrick lifted up the waste-paper basket. "I screwed them up as nearly as possible as I found them. They're funny reading together with those bits in the paper and that dead body!"

In the basket lay what looked like two crinkly eggs. They were wads of paper that had been crushed into little balls. Opened out, they showed as two sheets of plain letter-paper, headed with the address of the flat. On each were some lines of writing in a pointed, very sloping, foreign hand. The first ran:—

"You have betrayed the change in the crew of the _Esmeralda._ But I give you one chance to explain. Come here to-night and clear yourself if you can. If not—"

The rest of the sheet was blank. Apparently this draft had not pleased the writer. It had been screwed up and tossed away. The second was a complete note. It ran:—

"You are a traitor, but I give you one more chance to explain why you have not carried out the orders I gave you at _Iguski Aide._ Take it. Or it will be the end. Come to this address tonight. If you do not come you know the penalty. Expect it without mercy."

The last two sentences had been scratched out. There was no signature, but a little drawing of the outline of a house with a V inside.

"That scratched out bit about the penalty is why he copied out the note and threw this away," Maybrick explained like a showman.

Tindall's eyes were shining. He stroked his beard with a hand that quivered a little.

"These settle it." He spoke calmly but with the calm of one who forces a layer of composure over a seething mass of red-hot feeling.

"It _was_ a political crime! Or an act of justice, if you will."

"You know what that signature stands for?" The Chief Inspector's tone made the remark a statement, not a question.

"The V within the outline of a house? Etcheverrey, Pointer. Yes. Etcheverrey, the great anarchist. Or rather anti-royalist agitator."

Pointer said nothing. Maybrick gave a cluck of delighted amazement. The police of every country knew, and were on the hunt for that name, that man.

"That's his secret signature," Tindall went on. "Only used to his own men. Only known to us at the F.O. And

Iguski Aide!—'Sunny Corner'! That's Etcheverrey's well-hidden Basque refuge, deep in the heart of some Pyrenees ravine, not yet located. The mere name is only known to a chosen and picked few among his followers. We at the F.O. have only just—only _just_ learnt it."

"He's French, isn't he?" Maybrick asked.

"Officially, yes. But there's not a drop of French blood in his veins. Basque father. Catalan mother. Speaks all languages. Brains of the devil. And up till now his luck."

"Do you think Etcheverrey's the killer, or the killed here, sir?" Maybrick asked again.

"The killed. The dead man," Tindall said, after a moment's deep thought. "Etcheverrey would have taken those scraps of paper away. His slayer is not identified by them. I think that the tables were turned on the Basque for the first —and last—time in his life, by the man he summoned here. And I can make a good guess at that man's name. You know my slogan." He turned to Pointer. "What the brain can't see, the eyes can't either. Eyes won't solve this problem. Not even yours. Now what has cost Etcheverrey his head, literally is, I think, his last break."

"His attempt on the Shah of Persia?" Maybrick knew every one of Etcheverrey's unsuccessful efforts by heart. "Pretty near thing for the Shah!"

"And for Etcheverrey," Tindall threw in grimly. "He was all but caught. As it was, they got a good view of him. The only time he's been really seen. And since then there's a fine price on his head at Ispahan. On the real, solid head. Duly delivered. That's why the descriptions we get from there are so vague. All we know of his appearance is that he has unusually small feet, and really beautiful hands."

"First thing I noticed about the corpse." Maybrick was sorting his notes. "Here it is. Par seven."

"Yes," Tindall was talking half under his breath, "Mirza Khan is over here, we know. He's the Shah's secret agent. It's his head or Etcheverrey's, I understand.

We know that Etcheverrey is in London again. Sir Edward Clifford rather inclines to the belief that he's been here for years, carefully hidden in some commonplace identity, and that he only leaves London for some swift flight and one of his lightning efforts, and then comes back again and takes up his seemingly everyday existence. I don't agree with him, but that's Sir Edward's view."

Sir Edward Clifford was Permanent Under Secretary of State for Foreign Affairs.

"Every man jack of us has been living on a volcano, with the King of Spain on his way here next month." Maybrick drew a deep breath. "Etcheverrey nearly got him in Spain last year," Tindall went on, "just as he had a hard try for our Prince of Wales in South America." He was examining the room carefully as he talked. There was little to discover. A smallish, still damp splotch of blood on the thick carpet near a little table on which stood a reading-lamp. A few drops of blood had dried on the wooden edge of the table. Smaller ones yet were found on the parchment lamp-shade, and a hint of a trickle down one leg of the arm-chair standing near.

"There's been no struggle?" Tindall looked at Pointer.

"No sign of any," Pointer said cautiously.

"Just so. Yet the man summoned by such a letter as that would have been on the alert and would have struggled. Etcheverrey, on the other hand, would not dream that the tables could be turned on him. He was either shot, or more probably slogged on the head. Dragged to the tub, beheaded, and the head's now on its way to distant Ispahan in the care of that good old hater, Mirza Khan. But all that's for me to find out."

"Well, sir," Maybrick slipped a band over his bulging note-book, "as you're quite sure that the murder was political, I hand it over to you."

The Superintendent was aware that he had done very well. But he knew when he was out of his depth. Nor had he any intention of wasting his time over a case of which the honours would all go to the Foreign Office. They had their own men. It was all very well for the Chief Inspector, who had already, young though he was, risen so high, but he, Maybrick, had more paying matters from the point of view of promotion waiting for him at his police station. And so with a salute, he passed from the scene—to his never dying regret.

"Now for the porters," Tindall continued, when the two were alone. They learnt nothing which could explain the crime itself from them, though they gained a clear idea of how the flat could have been entered and left by any one unobserved. The building had several lifts, the corner ones being automatic and worked by the residents. There were many staircases. There was a restaurant on the ground floor open to the public. There were billiard rooms and reading rooms.

The estate agent for whom they telephoned repeated in fuller detail what Maybrick had already told them about the taking of the flat. Monsieur Tourcoin had paid for the four weeks in twenty-four one-pound notes, and the transaction had been completed on the spot.

"No references asked for?"

"Not in a case of this kind. A furnished flat let for a month. The porters here keep their eyes open. And undesirable people would be asked to leave at once. We find that simpler and better than bothering with references," the house-agent explained.

"Now as to this Mr. Marshall"

"We know all about Mr. Marshall. Our firm has known him and his parents, they lived in one of our houses, for twenty years. Just as we've known the head porter here about that long. There's nothing wrong with Mr. Marshall, I'll go bail, any more than there is with Soulyby, the head porter."

"How did this Mr. Tourcoin learn of the flat?" Pointer asked. . .

"Saw our advertisement in the paper, I suppose."

"When was it advertised?"

"Friday morning for the first time."

"And the paper?"

"_The Times._"

"And he spoke broken English," Tindall murmured.

The agent laughed. "Rather!" He gave them a very good copy of the man's accent.

"On leaving he nipped into a taxi which some one was just paying off, and called to the chauffeur. 'To the station of Charing Cross. Arrest yourself there for one little minute while I learn what time train for Paris he start.' The driver winked, and said he'd arrest himself all right if need be."

"What clothes was the man wearing?" Pointer asked.

"Motor cap—he apologised very civilly for keeping it on, but he had a bad attack of head neuralgia—big brown and orange check motoring coat. That's all I remember."

"Young man?"

The agent thought so, but as he had seen many men yesterday afternoon he could not be quite sure. The whole affair was so small compared with most of their business that he had not paid much attention.

"Do you remember his hands, when he signed those papers," Pointer went on, "were they large hands?"

The estate agent could not remember anything about them. More details of the conversation were asked, and as far as possible, given. Then the agent took his leave—a very agitated leave.

The head porter had not noticed the appearance of the M. Tourcoin to whom he had shown the flat, except that the man wore a motoring ulster of orange and brown tweed, and a brown silk scarf. He had an impression of a young man, but as he had already on Friday afternoon shown the flat to several friends of Mr. Marshall's, he could not even be sure of that. .

The man had barely glanced over the flat.

"I never thought he meant what he said about taking it, but within half an hour the agents phoned up to me that the flat was gone. Taken by the monseer for a month. As to seeing him again—not unless that's him in there. But the chap I showed the flat to, looked a bigger chap. Bigger and brawnier, though I never saw his face. Not to see it."

"Was he smoking?" Pointer asked.

"Yes, sir. Briarwood pipe. One of these new comfort pipes."

"What kind of tobacco? Any kind you knew?"

"Yes, sir." It was a kind that the head porter particularly liked when he could afford it. A well-known British make. "I says to myself," the man went on, "France is all very well for wines, but when it comes to pipes and baccy—there's nothing like us!"

"Umph," Tindall murmured, when the two were alone. "Tourcoin takes the flat for a Captain Brown. He or this captain Brown can be seen; in it therefore. If need be. One of the two is Etcheverrey. Almost certainly he would be Brown. The Unseen. Now is Tourcoin the man to whom the summoning letters were sent? Is he the man who killed Etcheverrey? Is he, in fact, Mirza Khan, who speaks French—and English too for that matter—like a Frenchman?" There was a short silence broken by the Chief Inspector, who had been standing looking down at the toes of his shoes, hands loosely clasped behind him. He looked up now.

"Those papers found in the basket"—he spoke thoughtfully—"are they in Etcheverrey's writing?"

"He had some thirty different kinds of writing."

"And on the blotter," Pointer went on musingly, "there are no marks except from the two notes we found torn up. . . ."

"None. Why should there be?" Tindall asked, with a faint smile. "You police always want so much for your money."

There was another pause. Tindall eyed Pointer whimsically. Pointer looked back at him with his tranquil, steady gaze. The detective officer had fine dark gray eyes, pleasant, though at times rather enigmatic in expression.

"To stake the effect of a political crime would be a capital red herring, wouldn't it, to drag across the trail of a private murder."

Tindall smiled still more. A smile of real amusement at the doubt on his own reading of the case from a man young enough to be his son.

"We're like two Harley Street specialists, Pointer," he said good-humouredly, "each reading a case according to his own special lines. I say heart. You say liver. You're welcome to treat the case for liver, of course. But it's a heart case. Believe me, it's heart. In other words, I've been studying Etcheverrey so long that I have no hesitation in saying that this murder belongs to me. Don't waste your valuable time in hunting for this poor chap's head. I see that search being organised already."

Pointer laughed a little. Tindall was right. He was already charting his course.

"It's on its way to distant Ispahan," Tindall continued. "Pity Mirza Khan has such a start. Well, he knows my methods. They're lazy, compared with yours, but they're quick."

"They often lead to splendid results," Pointer said honestly. In what might be called society crimes, thefts, stolen letters, the finer shade of blackmail, Tindall had done wonders, besides winning many a triumph in his own field—the political field.

"I leave the details of the flat to you." Tindall despised hunting for clues. "The exact spot where the murder was committed . . . which way the man faced . . . and so on."

Pointer nodded, let him out of the flat, telephoned to Scotland Yard for their expert locksmith, and then rang for the head porter. That worthy was asked to institute a sort of house-clearing. Fortunately he was at one with the Scotland Yard officer in wanting to make sure that the missing head was not hidden somewhere on any premises for which he was responsible.

"I'll see to my part of it. Every nook shall be turned out. Every cupboard moved, or I'll know the reason why," Soulyby promised, "and every parcel opened."

"As soon as the doctor has examined the body we shall have a rough idea of about what time the murder was committed. As it is, we know that it must have taken place between seven on Friday evening, and eight this morning. Ask cautiously about whether any one was seen coming into, or going out of, this flat during that time."

Pointer dismissed him and telephoned to Lloyds. Marshall had been with them for fifteen years, he learnt. Came straight from London University. His present address was Bastia in Corsica. But as he had spoken of mules and guides. . . . Yes, the man answering the telephone was a friend of his and quite willing to act as his reference if necessary. The firm would act as another. But he believed the flat was taken. The inquiry was about Marshall's furnished flat, of course?

"Just so," Pointer murmured, as he turned away. "Of course!"

He now began his own patient investigations. The bathtubs, he had learnt, were cleaned with Sapolio. The little smear of white under this one seemed to him to be plaster. He scraped it into a stoppered bottle and labelled it before putting it into his attache case. Then he bent over some marks on the tiled floor—marks such as a dull lead pencil might make if it had been rubbed with a broad, circular motion over the spot. Pointer decided that a tin had been placed there, and been pressed hard down while it was moved round and round.

Then he turned his attention to the fitted basin beside the bath. The taps had been turned off and on with a towel he thought. Unfortunately the hall porter could not say, nor could the housekeeper, how many towels had been left in the warm cupboard just by the basin. Pointer looked about him for a pail. But failing that, he took a bronze jar from the living-room and set it beneath the basin. With a spanner he unscrewed the trap in the outflow pipe, and let the contents run into his receptacle. A thickish, reddish mixture came out. Ammonia told him that the reddish colour was blood, the whitish part he took to be more plaster. It looked to him as though the murderer or murderers had washed their hands here. He bottled some of this mixture too, and turned away after replacing the fixture. He started on the bedroom. Here he found nothing except proofs that the room had not been used last night. He passed on to the sitting-room. At that moment the doctor arrived.

"Going to have your work cut out this time, Chief Inspector," he 'grunted. "Even you must be up a tree with this body."

"Any help to give me?"

"The man was probably about forty. Good condition. Nails show he's had no operations, is no victim of any chronic disease. A gentleman, I take it."

"And the head was severed?"

"With two or three hard, downward blows." He gave some medical details. "As to whether the man was dead or alive first—can't be sure till I've examined the lungs, but probably dead."

"Had the man who cut off the head any knowledge of anatomy?"

"None whatever. A sixteenth of an inch lower would have made the job half as easy again. Tremendous violence was used. Must have been a strong chap, and used something on which he got a good purchase which had a very firm edge."

"How long would it have taken, do you think?"

"To cut off the head?" The doctor meditated. "About fifteen minutes, I should say."

"And the death occurred, at a rough guess?"

"Some time last night, I should judge. That cut's about twelve hours old. Certainly not more."

He left at that, and Pointer went on with his work. There were no signs of any bullet having entered a wall or piece of furniture. Nor did the man seem to have been shot in a line with any of the windows, supposing him to have been shot—as Pointer did, partly from the size of the blood stain, chiefly from the fact that the chair down which a rivulet of blood had run was the only one in the room that had a very high, spreading back. It was the last kind of a chair to choose had a blow been intended.

Feeling the carpet, going by the stain, Pointer replaced the chair as it had probably stood. The bedroom door was to one side and a little behind it—an ideal position for a shot. This bedroom door had odd pin-marks in the wood near the handle, two on one side, two on the other, about the same distance apart.

Pointer finally decided that a strip of some thin but strong material such as tape had been fastened with drawing pins taut across the tongue, so as to prevent the rather noisy latch from acting, and let the door be opened by a touch, though it might looked closed.

He drew the curtains and switched on the lights. The side of the door that interested him was then thrown into deep shadow by a Chinese lacquer cabinet. So that, provided that the strip had been white, for the door was white, it might pass undetected by a casual glance, or by a short-sighted person. Pointer thought this last idea very probable. It explained the otherwise venturesome silencing of the door, it was borne out by the position of the reading-lamp that had been drawn to the extreme edge of the little table, and close against the left side of the chair.

Pointer stared at the pin marks. To him they were a very odd detail, one that was quite out of keeping with the rest of the crime as known so far. Primarily they showed that the man who had been murdered was evidently not hard of hearing, since they spelled care that no snap of the catch could be heard. But they meant more than that. Those pin-pricks meant a quick job. Just as they showed that probably there had been no sounds—music, talk—during which the cautious opening of the door could pass unnoticed. It looked as though the victim had been alone. But alone or not. Etcheverrey must be always on the alert, ever suspicious. A man wanted by the police of all the world, a man with a price on his head, a man who had never yet been caught, would not have let any door pass uninvestigated, let alone one that stood half in shadow. Incongruous in any case, the tape seemed to Pointer doubly so in connection with the much sought-for, wily Basque.

It came to this, he thought, if Etcheverrey had been the man in the flat, he could have taken sufficient time to silence that door in some better way than by means of a hastily fastened-on strip. If the man was not Etcheverrey, then the anarchist would have noticed it.

A search found a bath mat in a hall cupboard. Where, apparently, a loop of tape had been sewn on, now only an end dangled; a roughly cut-off end, cut with a knife, not scissors. The piece that remained was the width indicated by the pin pricks. So the murderer had not come provided with tape. He found a few drawing-pins in a drawer which left just such marks as those on the door. Pointer again tested each object in the room. But still only the carpet, the chair, the table edge, and the lamp-shade showed marks of blood. On none of these, moreover, had there been any effort to clean away the marks. As for the crumpled papers in the waste-paper basket, of which, each promising the other photographic copy, Tindall had kept one, and Pointer one, the Chief Inspector found a few more sheets in a drawer. It looked as though they had been left there by Marshall. The writing had been done with a pointed fountain pen, which, like the ink—Pointer intended to have the latter tested at the Yard—seemed of quite an ordinary kind.

The lock expert arrived from the Yard at this point. A close scrutiny of the Yale lock now taken off the front door told him that though it was old and badly in need of new springs—failing entirely to catch now and then—yet it had not been forced, or picked, or opened with any other but its own rightful key. The house agent had said that he had handed Marshall's two keys to Monsieur Tourcoin.

The ambulance arrived and the body was taken away. Pointer went back to the bath and scrutinised the bottom. With what had those two deep gashes been made? The flat had no kitchen. No suitable knife or weapon hung on any of its walls.

CHAPTER TWO

Pointer strolled down all the stairs and let himself up and down in all the lifts. Finally he stopped beside a couple of workmen who were doing some plastering on the ground floor, near the foot of the stairs that led up to Number Fourteen. He had noticed the bags and the tools when he arrived just now.

"I borrowed some of your plaster last night," he said pleasantly, "how much do I owe you for what I used?"

"That's all right, sir," one of the men said civilly, "me and my mate was just saying that one of the porters must have done it. Quarter of a bag, wasn't it, sir. If you like to call it a shilling, that'll be all right."

Pointer liked a half-crown better, and so apparently did the men.

"Hope I cleaned the spade off all right," Pointer chatted on, lighting a cigarette. A cigarette which he took care not to inhale.

"Lord, sir, there wasn't no call to clean it that-away! Staggered Jim here it did to see it cleaned up. We only uses it for mixin'. Why, you sharpened the thing, didn't you?"

"No. Not beyond cleaning it." Pointer's cigarette was in his hand. He flicked its ash over the handle and stood lookingdown at it while talking. The ash, "finger-print cigarette" ash, showed no marks except those of a gloved hand. The workmen had not touched it. So some one had scraped it and cleaned it since they had used it last.

And, according to the men, some one had sharpened it as certainly as was quite sharp enough now to have done what Pointer believed it had done. A couple of blows from it would account for the marks on the bottom of the tub.

The murderer must have found his grisly task lightened unexpectedly by the implements left in the building. Or had "Tourcoin" noticed them, and laid his plan accordingly?

"I think I put everything back as it was," he said again; "messy work, plastering. When you aren't used to it. Miss anything else?"

"Nothing, sir."

But Pointer seemed still uncertain.

"Let me see . . . didn't I take a tin?" He was thinking of the marks on the bathroom tiles.

"That old tin isn't no loss, sir. You're more than welcome to it. We found it on the dust-bin, and was going to throw it out again when we was finished."

"Still," Pointer reminded them, "a tin comes in handy, I expect. What size is it? I borrowed another from one of the porters."

"Seven pound biscuit tin, sir. Stove in a bit at one side. It comes in handy for plaster we've sieved and don't want to use immediate, as you say, sir. But there's no hurry!"

"I'll send it down. Did I take its lid too?" he asked, peering about him.

He was told that he must have, as the lid was kept on the box.

Pointer tipped them, "in case the tin shouldn't turn up," and went slowly out of the building, an hour after he had first entered it.

If Tindall was right, and the body found was that of Etcheverrey, then, as far as he was concerned, the case was over. Some Special Branch man at the Yard would be told off to assist the Foreign Office, and Pointer would take up another tangle. But was it Etcheverrey? Was it "political" at all?

Very great care had been taken to dispose of all personal effects. Nothing but those scraps of paper in the basket had been left to tell who the man was. And, supposing the scraps of paper to have been faked, then no clew whatever had been left. For the flat was a furnished flat, shedding no light on the character of its present occupier. As far as identity went, if the papers in the basket were what the Force calls "offers," a trail laid to deceive, then it was as if the police had found a body stripped, and without a head, lying in an empty room.

Each great case, and Pointer nowadays was concerned only with great cases, groups its facts in such a different way from any other, that it becomes an entirely new problem. Pointer had never had one like this before, where all the usual means of identification of murdered man and missile used had been taken away. Of course Tindall might be right. Probably he was. But supposing he were not, how the dickens was he, Pointer, to find out who the man had been? And above all, who the murderer had been? Somewhere there was a weak spot in the crime. There always was. There always would be. Where was it in this case?

The detective officer's every nerve tautened at the idea of a murderer escaping. Pointer never saw his work as a game of brains against brains, where, provided only that the one move was cleverer than the other, it ought to win. He was a soldier, fighting a ceaseless battle where no quarter could be asked or given. The battle of light against darkness. Right against Wrong. If the other side won, it would be all up with the world. Pointer had never failed the side of justice yet. He would not fail it now, if he could help it.

But could he help it? Tindall was working at the case from his end. Pointer was not sure that he wanted to follow the other's track. He must make his own path therefore. If Tindall were right, the Chief Inspector's road and that of the F.O. man would meet in due course, like the two ends of a well-dug tunnel.

He went up to his rooms at Scotland Yard and did some telephoning. By that time the analyst's report on the bottles which had been sent in was ready. One contained nothing but plaster mixed with water. The plaster was a very coarse kind used by plumbers for certain face-work. The other contained the same plaster, some water, and a mixture of blood.

Pointer walked up and down his room. He was not the Chief Inspector now, but a man who had committed a murder; a man to whom it was absolutely vital that the corpse should not be recognised, or that the weapon used should not be identified. Pointer had an open mind as to which of the two reasons compelled the taking away of the head. The clothes might have been taken for the purpose of confusing the issue.

"Yes," he murmured to himself, "I've put the head in a biscuit tin, mixed and poured in plaster to keep it from rolling around, and now what?"

In the absence of all known hiding-places, he finally, after a short chat over the wire with the Home Office, sent a coded message to every post office throughout the United Kingdom that all wrongly-addressed or uncalled-for parcels were to be reported to him at once. He thought it very possible that the murdered man's clothes, and the towels used by his murderer, had been made into small, convenient parcels, and sent to various fictitious names and non-existent streets in some home-town. Abroad would be out of the question.

All omnibus headquarters, taxi stands, garages, and railway stations were warned to keep an eye out for similar but unmarked parcels which either had been left in vehicles some time last night or might be left in the near future.

Similar instructions reached the L.C.C. dustmen and all parcel deposit offices. The river police were not forgotten. They had found nothing so far which could interest Pointer, but they promised to be even more on the alert than usual, if possible. Then he telephoned to the police surgeon who had first seen the body. He learnt that nothing had been found to explain the cause of death. There were no signs of a struggle. Death had been absolutely instantaneous. The doctor thought that a bullet through the head would account for the facts. "But, of course, as Mr. Tindall suggests, a blow might be equally swift." At any rate, the head had been certainly severed after death. But not long after it. The death itself had taken place somewhere around midnight on Monday night. Pointer put down the telephone and went to the mortuary chapel, a grimly sanitary place.

The finger prints had already been taken, and definitely not identified at Scotland Yard, as those of any known criminal.

Flashed by wireless photographs to the continent, the same answer had come from each capital in turn. So the body was still nameless. And as long as it remained so, the murderer was safe.

Pointer looked the body over very carefully yet once again. Especially the beautifully shaped hands. Hands that in life must surely have done many things well. In whose life? What things had they done?

As he studied them, he remembered their quick examination by the doctor. He knew that on the arrival of an unconscious patient at any hospital, the medical men run their eyes over the nails for any trace of recent operations, illnesses, chronic complaints, or even nerve shocks. Pointer, calling in a constable to help him, scraped the inside of each well-kept nail with his penknife on to a small glass slide. Having carefully covered and marked each slide, he took them back with him to the Yard. There the slides were examined. The result was handed to him almost immediately.

Both hands showed fluff of white paper made from esparto grass of a kind that is usually only sold for very superior typewriting purposes. One nail had lightly scraped a sheet of carbon paper. One—the first of the right hand—showed traces of sugar.

In other words, the dead man was almost certainly a writer, or a typist. But probably a writer who was only in occasional contact with sheets of carbon paper. He might be a secretary. He might be a clerk. But the nails of the feet showed that he had last worn black socks of a most expensive silk. That suggested not a clerk. The sugar on the right hand suggested an investigating finger among lumps in the sugar bowl, which in its turn suggested the free and easy ways of a man's own home. Probably his after-dinner coffee. No china had been used in the flat where the body was found. No sugar-basin filled there. The complete picture as filled in by the police surgeon's and the analyst's reports and Pointer's own reading of the room in which he believed the murder to have taken place, was that of a well-to-do author, possibly a journalist, one used to sudden alarms, who, after his dinner at home, had gone out unsuspectingly to meet his terrible death. A writer of about forty years of age, in good health and circumstances. Not blind, for he had probably drawn that reading lamp towards him, but very likely short-sighted, for he had drawn it close. Not deaf, as the muffled door showed.

Pointer took a turn around his room. It was a step fo ward. But it looked like being the last step for the moment. Unless— Pointer stared at his shoe-tips. Then he went back to the mortuary chapel.

There was a tiny scar on the sole of one foot, such as might clinch an identification but not suggest one. He studied it afresh. No, that would not help him. There was nothing peculiar about that tiny mark. Again he picked up the hands, looked at the uncalloused palms. The man was no sportsman. Not a hard spot anywhere. Surely there was more to be learned. But how? The hands were the only chance. The only possible chance. . . .

The lines on the palms were singularly clear, and not at all like his own. Apart from palmistry in the sense of prophecy, of charlatanry, some people claimed that you could tell a person's character, even their profession, from the lines in their hands.

Pointer thought of Astra. The police knew all about her.

Astra was the professional name of an American, a Mrs. Jansen, who had amazed London by her skill in reading the character of men and women from their hands. She was no teller of fortunes. But she did tell what lay dormant, or wrongly applied. Parents brought her their children in large numbers, and Astra would examine the little palms, and then give the parents a very truthful, sometimes appallingly truthful, list of their drawbacks and their talents. She would proceed to point out that this must be encouraged, that repressed. In what the child should succeed, in what he was bound to fail. With elder people she was as forthright. "Your gifts are these—your bad qualities this and that." Astra was amazingly honest, and amazingly right. She was no pessimist. "Change your life, use your gifts, keep under the evil in you, and the lines will surely change," was her sermon. "Each of us is our own enemy. Fight that enemy." And she would give clear particulars as to where and how that fight should begin.

The two police inspectors who had been sent to test her, for you must not prophesy for money in England, had come back genuinely impressed. She had not prophesied, but she had hit off each man's character very neatly. Pointer had not much hope in the issue of any interview with her, but she might classify these hands still more narrowly than the microscope had done, and the microscope's testimony would serve to check her statements, if indeed she made any.

He took very careful imprints of the palms on tablets of thick, warmed, modelling wax, brushing a little red powder over them to bring out the lines. He wrapped each tablet in paraffin paper and fastened them side by side in his case. Then he telephoned from a call office for an appointment in the name of Yardly, an immediate appointment. As it was not yet twelve, he was successful. He drove to a house in Sloane Street, and was shown into a cubicle. Mrs. Jansen's clients did not see each other. After a few minutes waiting he was taken into a cheerful room, where, in a window sat a well-dressed woman with a thick mop of curly gray hair held back by combs. A pleasant, keen pair of eyes looked up. A pleasant, firm hand shook his.

Pointer took a seat facing the light, laying his lean brown fingers on two black velvet cushions. He would try her first with his own hands. Her reading of them might end the interview—probably would.

With a magnifying glass the American bent over them, turning them now and then. She nodded her head finally as if satisfied.

"I wish all the hands that have lain there were as pleasant reading," she said, slipping the glass back into its case. "They are the hands of one who, in any walk of life, would go to the top. Your chief characteristic is love of justice. Your dominant quality, penetration."

She went on to give an extraordinary accurate analysis of the Chief Inspector's character. Pointer, who was a thoroughly nice fellow, and very unassuming, actually blushed at the flattering picture drawn.

"I wonder if you can guess the nature of my work? my trade? or my profession?" he said, when she had done. "Or isn't that a fair question?"

"It's a difficult one. But sometimes I hit the nail on the head. I should say that law in some form was your branch. You could be a barrister and a great one—you could be great in any branch that you took up—only that the gift of a flow of words isn't yours. Nor have you that kind of personal magnetism. The friends you win are won by your character. Also, I don't think that you work for money. I mean, I don't think that your income depends on your work. So not a barrister. . . . You're too young to be a judge. Solicitor? . . . No, not solicitor. As I said when I read your hands, you deal with tremendously important issues. Your life is very varied, yet not by your own choosing. The decisions you make are important ones. You're used to constant calls on your physical courage.

Used to it, and are going to have plenty more of it. ... I should think the army but for—" She bent closer.

"You know, if you were older and had an ecclesiastical bent, from certain things in your hand I should guess you some Superior in the Jesuit Order. Even Vicar-General . . ."

This did amuse Pointer. He showed it. But it gave him little hope of any good issue from this wildest of forlorn ventures for a Scotland Yard man.

"It's nearer the mark than you think," Mrs. Jansen said shrewdly. "It would have suited one side of your character very well. By your laugh I see that you're not even a Roman Catholic. Then what about—" She frowned, gazing at the erect figure sitting so easily in the chair. Pointer could not slouch.

"Law . . . danger . . . executive ability," she murmured "Police! And since your hands show that you are a man doing work that thoroughly suits your talents, I should say some big man at Scotland Yard. How about the C.I.D.?"

She leant back and looked up inquiringly. Pointer gave a nod.

"You've hit it, and very clever of you indeed! You did that so neatly that I wonder what you'll make of the owner of these hands." He laid down his tablets. "It's to be paid for as a separate visit, of course. Do your best with them, won't you."

She glanced at the tablets. Then she looked a little vexed.

"Really, Mr.—eh—" She paused. "I know the Assistant Commissioner by sight. Are you the Commissioner?"

"No, no! I'm from the ranks. But you were saying?"

"If you take the trouble to glance through my book on Practical Cheirography, you'll see those palms analysed in Chapter Ten. Mr. Julian Clifford kindly let me use his hands in my chapter on authors."

Pointer felt as though he had had a severe punch. For Julian Clifford was England's greatest living author.

"Are you quite sure these tablets are imprints of Julian Clifford's hands?" he asked tranquilly.

"Oh, quite! His are as unforgettable, as unmistakable, as Sarah Bernhardt's. See. Here they are!" She drew a book from under the table and opened it at a couple of plates. Pointer's head was all astir. But he scrutinised them through her magnifying glass. The illustrations seemed identical with his tablets, even to a slight enlargement of the top joint of the left forefinger.

He thanked her and prepared to go. She stopped him with an exclamation. She was bending over his tablets with her glass.

"These were not taken from the hands of a living man! Julian Clifford must be dead!"

"What an idea!" he scoffed.

"A true one! There's a lack of spring, of elasticity about them that's unmistakable. Julian Clifford dead! What a loss to the world! Was it in some accident?"

There was a pause. Mrs. Jansen's reputation was that of an absolutely trustworthy woman. Besides, her face vouched for her. Or rather, her aura. That immense, impalpable Something, woven of our thoughts, our desires, that surrounds each one of us, that never leaves us, that perhaps is most truly "us"—_En nefss_, as the Arabs call it—having its own way of making itself felt, its own warnings, its own dislikes, attractions, and guarantees.

"I wanted you to help us identify a body," he said simply. "Apparently you have. I wonder if there is anything more you can tell me—about Mr. Clifford, I mean."

She interrupted him.

"That's no good with me,—I've seen your palms, remember—I mean that air of a child asking to be helped over the crossing. Besides, why are you here? You weren't in the least interested in your own character. You were keenly interested in those tablets. I don't think it's merely the identification"—her eyes widened—"has something—something criminal—happened to Mr. Clifford? Has he been—killed?" she asked in a low, horrified voice.

"And supposing something 'wrong' has happened to him, Mrs. Jansen?" He gave her back a long, steady stare. "Mind you, all this is in strictest confidence. I'm Chief Inspector Pointer of New Scotland Yard. Of the C.I.D. The whole of this conversation, of my inquiries, must be kept absolutely to yourself, just as the Yard will treat anything you tell me about Mr. Clifford as confidential. Why did the idea come so quickly to you that his death may be due to a crime? You have more to go on than merely my coming to see you."

She looked at him over her horn spectacles for all the world like a modern witch.

"Mr. Clifford came to see me himself a week ago last Thursday," she said finally. "He wanted to know whether I would look in his hands and tell him if any danger threatened him. He was kind enough to say that I had impressed him as truthful when I took the photographs of his hands for my book two years ago. I had only seen him that once before. In Cannes."

"And you?"

"I told him that that was out of my line. Nor could any one have answered that question for him. His hands only showed character and talents. . . . That sort of thing. There are people whose hands do record events. . . . His didn't. Events outside him didn't enter into Julian Clifford. What mattered to him came always from within. Death, for instance, wasn't marked on his palms. Death means very little to him. His personality was quite distinct from his body. With some people it is bound up in it. Even a toothache is marked on their palms."

"What did you tell him? May I know?"

"I told him just that. He seemed rather disappointed. He asked me to look again. 'I'm on the eve of something—well—important.' He hesitated before using that word. I thought he chose it finally rather as a cloak. I don't think 'important' was the word he would have used in writing."

"You think Clifford the man was not so honest as Clifford the writer?"

She did not reply for a moment. Then:—

"I have an idea that he was undecided about something. Or perhaps hesitating before doing something would be a better word."

Again there was a silence.

"Is that all you can tell me about him?"

"Everything," she said, with a frank look into the detective-officer's face.

Pointer stared at his shoes.

"Mrs. Jansen, I wish you'd tell me Mr. Clifford's weak points—as you see them. Suppose something untoward has happened to him. Something that needs investigation. As a rule a man's good qualities don't lead to that necessity. Was there anything in Julian Clifford's character—as shown in his hands—that could have brought about, or led to, or explain—sudden death? Mind you, I ask this in strictest confidence."

She nodded gravely.

"In strictest confidence," she repeated, "nothing in his hands could explain any end other than a happy and honoured one. His was a fine character, noble and generous. He had faults, of course. There was a certain ruthlessness where his work was concerned. He would have sacrificed his all on that altar . . . unconsciously or even consciously."

Still Pointer looked at his shoes.

"Was he a man of high morality, would you say?"

"I don't think he had ever been tempted. He was fastidious by temperament, and his wealth made high standards fairly easy." Mrs. Jansen rose. "And that, Mr. Chief Inspector, is all I can tell you. Mr. Clifford sat a moment there in that chair you're in, peering at his own palms. He was very short-sighted. Then he looked at me half in vexation as he got up. 'What did the ancients do when the oracle wouldn't oracle?' And with that he said good-bye."

"Can I call upon you, in case of need, to identify the hands from which I took these wax impressions as those of Julian Clifford?" Pointer asked, rising.

"I will identify them any time, any where, as his. Hands are to me what faces are to most people—the things I go by."

Pointer paid the moderate fees and drove off. His whole being was in a turmoil under his quiet exterior. Julian Clifford, the great author, younger brother of Sir Edward Clifford of the Foreign Office, to be that headless trunk!

Back at Scotland Yard, within half an hour, the plates in Mrs. Jansen's book were enlarged and compared with quickly-taken photographs of the dead man's palms. Again they seemed to be identical. Every whorl and loop, which showed in both tallied.

Pointer meanwhile looked up Clifford's town address. It was given as Thornbush, Hampstead. A moment more, and he was asking over the telephone if he could speak to Mr. Clifford—Mr. Julian Clifford.

"Mr. Clifford is away, sir," a servant's voice answered.

"Away!" Pointer's tone marked incredulous surprise. "But he had an appointment with the Home Secretary at eleven!"

"He's not here, sir."

"But surely he gave you a message, or a letter when he left? It's Mr. Marbury of the Home Office who is speaking."

Pointer's tone suggested that Mr. Marbury was not accustomed to be slighted.

"I'll inquire, sir," a crushed voice replied.

There was a pause, then the voice came again, very apologetically.

"No, sir. No message was left. Mr. Clifford left early this morning before any one was up."

"Most extraordinary!" Mr. Marbury said stiffly. "I think I'll call and see some one about the matter." He hung up.

So Julian Clifford was supposed to have left his home before any one was up. That probably meant that he had not been seen since last night. Since last night, when a murder had been committed in Heath Mansions.

What about Julian Clifford's brother! He might have some information. But an inquiry at the Foreign Office for Sir Edward told Pointer that the brother was not in town. A few questions to his valet in Pont Street added the information that Sir Edward had left town yesterday, Monday, evening after dining with his brother, Mr. Julian Clifford, at the latter's house. He had gone to his cottage in Surrey, a peaceful spot where the telephone was not.

Pointer opened his _Who's Who._ He reviewed the well-known facts of the novelist and playwright's life. Clifford was a little under forty-five, the younger son of the late Sir James Clifford of Clifford's Bank, long since incorporated in one of the big general banks; he had had a brilliant career at Eton and Oxford, and was the author of an imposing array of novels, poetry, plays, and serious works. He had been twice married, the first time to Catherine Haslar, daughter of Sir William Haslar, High Commissioner of Australia, and, some years after her death, to Alison Willoughby, daughter of Mr. Willoughby of Sefton Park. Clifford had no children.

That was all very well as far as it went. But again it did not go far.

Pointer smoothed his crisp hair which always looked as though it would curl if it dared. Then he pressed a bell. Could Mr. Ward come to his room at once? Apparently Mr. Ward could, for in another moment there appeared in the door a vision to delight a tailor's eye. Ward, sartorially speaking, was It, even in a royal group. His quaint pen-name adorned many a weekly paper. Always up-to-date, invariably correct in all his reports, for two hours of every week-day Ward occupied a small room in one wing next to the Assistant Commissioner's.

"About Julian Clifford—not his literary side, I suppose? Just so. A description of his appearance? Especially of his face?"

Ward gave a very good pen-picture of the great man, after which he repeated briefly what Pointer already knew about Clifford's family.

"Present wife had intended to become a Pusey Sister. Changed her mind and took to divining rods and crystal balls instead. Is on the committees of all the spook societies. People say she's a wonderful clairvoyante. But then they always do say that if the person concerned talks enough to enough people. She usually carries a crystal ball around with her in her bag."

"Supposing," Pointer began, lighting his pipe—that beloved pipe of his which he always denied himself while on the scene of a crime—it might blot out other scents. "Supposing, Mr. Ward, that Julian Clifford had suddenly disappeared from his circle, where would you look for him first?"

"I hardly know. Clifford does this sort of thing every now and then, you know, when he wants some new material for a book. But he always returns to the surface within a week or a month."

"But supposing you had reason to think that something had happened to him—that something was wrong with his disappearance this time?"

"Good God!" Ward's light manner dropped from him. "You don't mean to tell me, Chief Inspector, that anything serious has happened to Julian Clifford?"

Pointer nodded. "I do." He did not insult Scotland Yard nor Ward, by asking him to regard that as confidential. Everything that was said within these walls was always confidential to the men considered sufficiently trustworthy to be consulted there.

"You mean that he's—dead?" Ward asked in a hushed voice. "You think there's been foul play?" He spoke in the tone of a man who asks a monstrous question. "I'm sorry to say that I'm sure of it. And so, I want you to think whether you've ever heard any talk, any hint, anything that could explain his murder." Pointer gave the few terrible facts. Ward felt that headless body as an additional horror.

"Incredible!" he murmured. "No I know nothing whatever that can explain this crime. It must have been the work of a maniac."

"He was a wealthy man, I always understood?" Pointer asked.

"A very wealthy man apart from his literary work. And a quite sufficiently wealthy man apart from his private fortune."

"Who are the inmates of his household, not counting servants, do you know?" was the next question.

Ward had often been the guest of the Cliffords.

"All of them beyond suspicion. First there's Adrian Hobbs. He's Mrs. Clifford's cousin, and acts as Clifford's literary agent. Clever chap. Thoroughly good business man. Really he's wasted in his present surroundings. Hobbs ought to 've started life with half a crown and a huckster's barrow."

"Straightforward?"

"Perfectly, I should say. That is—eh, well—of course, he's a good business man, as I told you."

Both smiled.

"What's he like to look at?"

"Big, powerful build. Heavyweight." Ward described Hobbs' looks. "Then there's Clifford's regular secretary. A poor fellow who lost his memory during the war. Blown up once too often. Just at the end too. Hard lines, eh? Name of Newman. Clifford ran across him at a base hospital, and gave him a try. He's very good indeed, I believe."

Again, at Pointer's request, he gave a snapshot of the secretary's appearance. Slim, but very strong, he thought him.

"How do these two men and Mrs. Clifford get on? You say they both live with the Cliffords?"

"She bores her cousin, Hobbs, stiff. And I think she secretly bores Newman too. Though he's a chap of whom it's very difficult to know what he thinks."

"Were the Cliffords attached to each other?"

"As far as I know, very much so. But of course—there's that talk about Mrs. Orr, the Merry Widow."

"Widow? Grass or sod, as the Americans say."

Ward laughed. "Oh, a genuine widow. As though you hadn't heard of the beautiful Mrs. Orr. As beautiful and far swifter than the latest eight-cylinder. Julian Clifford is supposed to be—was supposed to be—putting her in his next novel. All I know is he's been haunting her society lately. In season and out of season."

"And what does Mrs. Clifford say to the hauntings? Hasn't she tried to lay the spirit?"

"Mrs. Clifford is quite unperturbed, apparently. She goes on smiling her faint smiles and dreaming her dreams, and hearing her voices and seeing her visions in her crystal. She's one of the few women who haven't begun to cold-shoulder Mrs. Orr of late. Rather the other way."

"More friendly than usual?"

"I saw them driving in the park together only last Friday. Never saw that before."

Pointer hurried off. It was one o'clock. Gossip, even very revelant gossip, must wait until he knew whether it were really wanted or not.

CHAPTER THREE

An elderly-looking, round-shouldered man, whose stoop took from his real height, walked up to the gates of Thornbush half an hour later.

Pointer had looked out the hours of postal deliveries. He had timed himself so as to be on the drive when a postman overtook him. He turned.

"Any letters for me—Marbury?" he asked pleasantly. "And I'll take on any for the household at the same time."

The postman thanked him, told him there were none for him, and handed him four for the house.

Though Pointer looked a typical civil servant from his neatly-trimmed beard to his neatly-adjusted spats, he knocked at the front door with the four letters—three for Julian Clifford, Esq., and one for Mrs. Clifford—in his pocket. He might re-post them after the briefest of delays—or he might not.

"I telephoned to Mr. Clifford just now, and was told that he is not at his home." The very way in which Pointer felt for his card-case suggested near sight and a certain precise fussiness.

"Mr. Clifford is away, sir. But will you see Mr. Hobbs? Mr. Hobbs said he particularly wanted to see you, sir." The butler led the caller into a room near by. A young man rose civilly.

"Mr. Marbury? From the Home Office?"

"I called to inquire why Mr. Clifford failed to keep an appointment he had this morning with the Home Secretary. Can I see him a moment? The matter is connected with the Metropolitan Special Constabulary Reserve, and is very urgent. We are drawing up our lists."

Hobbs seemed puzzled. "Did Mr. Clifford have an appointment? I think there's some mistake."

"Exactly!" Pointer broke in. "I'm sure there is. Kindly let me know where I can reach him on the 'phone."

Hobbs stroked his smooth black hair. Then he stroked his smooth blue chin.

The Chief Inspector was by nature and training a remarkably astute reader of faces, but he was looking at one now which—like his own—hid completely the character behind it. Like himself, Adrian Hobbs looked about thirty, more or less. Like himself, too, he suggested an out-of-door man. Like himself, Hobbs was exceedingly neat in appearance. From his hair to his well-shod feet he satisfied the most fastidious eye. His mind, again like Pointer's, was clearly a tidy mind. But beyond that even Pointer could not size him up. The eyes were large and wide apart. Were they frank or merely bold? The nose was long. Was it predatory or merely self-assertive? Was the large mouth frank? Or was there something just a shade sinister to it when he smiled?

"I really can't understand it," Hobbs said finally. "I had no idea that Mr. Clifford took any interest in the matter—"

"That is precisely why I must trouble you for his address. Or a telephone number that will reach him," Pointer again put in swiftly.

"Sorry," Hobbs smiled slightly, "impossible to give you either. Mr. Clifford has gone off in search of local colour, and where he gets it is always his own closely-kept secret. He left no address. He never does. In good time—a day, a week, two weeks—he'll be back."

"But a man doesn't make an appointment a week ahead with the Home Secretary and not keep it!" Pointer ejaculated," in the tone of a man whose patience is wearing thin.

The truism seemed to worry Hobbs. He nodded, but said nothing.

"I feel sure that he has left some word with some one. He must have!" Pointer urged.

"Mr. Clifford's engagement-book shows nothing for this morning," Hobbs said finally.

"When did he leave?"

"This morning. I got down to breakfast to find that he was gone. There was a note for me to say that he had left to explore some Chinese haunts. Liverpool rather than London, I fancy."

"Incredible!" Pointer murmured. "But"—an idea seemed to strike him—"would you ask Mrs. Clifford to spare me a few minutes? I must try and get this straightened out."

"Do you mind seeing if Mrs. Clifford's in the garden?" Hobbs turned to another man who was writing at the farther end of the large room where he and Pointer were talking. A man whom Pointer knew, by Ward's description, to be Newman, Julian Clifford's private secretary, and whom he had been secretly watching. The Chief Inspector had purposely lowered his voice so that what he was saying should only be partly audible to Newman. He noticed the intent look on the secretary's face, not when he entered the room, but when he spoke of Julian Clifford in a purposely raised voice. The look that came then, was that of a man straining his ears. Ordinary curiosity might explain this with many men. But Pointer did not think that curiosity was a trait of the dark young man with the close-shut mouth, and the deep-set, reserved eyes. Newman's ordinary interest, or he misread him greatly, was concentrated in some inner life of his own. A life so interesting in its close seclusion that he lived there almost exclusively. True, he would, he must, come out into some other court for business purposes, to buy and sell. The many who penetrated thus far, might indeed think that they had the run of all that there was to the man. But Pointer felt sure that there would be walled courtyard within walled courtyard and lock after lock behind which the real man stood on guard.

"Perhaps I'd better go myself," Hobbs said, after a second.

Alone in the room, Pointer thought over the two men, especially the secretary. There were great potentialities in that face. Newman had lost his memory in the last year of the war, Ward had said. But was the face at which the detective officer had just glanced, so apparently casually, the face of one with no memory reaching back beyond 1918?

Pointer had seen men who had lost all recollection of their lives up to a certain point. In the eyes of each had been a look impossible to forget or mistake. A piteous, searching look. The look of those who feel that they are the consequences of days that they cannot remember, that in their characters they are reaping what, as far as their surface intelligence is concerned, they have not sown. But Newman, strange though the effect was that he produced on Pointer's keen scrutiny, had not that look. Those watchful eyes . . . the iron reserve of the face. . . . Nothing could give that last but year on year of rigorous self-control. A self-control that was never set aside for a moment. Great business men sometimes have it, statesmen occasionally. Pointer had invariably seen it on those privileged to attend on royalties.

His thoughts passed on to the effect which his questions about Clifford had had on the men. Hobbs, Clifford's literary agent, had shown no emotion. But Newman? Newman was startled. Pointer knew that as well as though he had been one of these modern instruments which record heart beats. The man's rigid, sudden immobility had but one cause.

Yet, though Pointer could jump to conclusions when he could alter them, he was a very wary man when, as here, his conclusions were fundamental—were the basis on which he must build.

At that moment the door opened. Though Pointer did not know it, it was Julian Clifford's librarian who now looked in. A young man called Richard Straight, who, wandering rather aimlessly about the house, collecting missing volumes from library sets, had just met Hobbs.

He had turned and stared after the literary agent. Hobbs' face was strangely set. Straight promptly popped his head into the room which the other had just left. He saw nothing to explain Hobbs' look. A stout, elderly man was trying to disentangle his glasses from his watch-chain. At sight of the librarian, the elderly caller rose.

"Mr. Newman, isn't it?"

"No." Straight came on into the room. "No, but can I be of any use? I'm the new librarian here. Very new, I'm afraid. I only arrived yesterday—from Melbourne."

"I called," Pointer explained wearily, "on a very urgent matter. I must get into touch with Mr. Clifford. I'm from the Home Office, I should mention, and Mr. Clifford was due at a meeting to discuss the lists of the Metropolitan Special Reserve Constabulary. We want him on the committee." He looked questioningly at Straight, who looked questioningly back at him. "Mr. Clifford is absent, it seems. The Home Secretary is waiting!" Pointer's tone was inimitable as he pronounced those five words.

"Where is Mr. Clifford?" Pointer went on irritably, "kindly let me have his address, and I will do what I can to straighten out this most deplorable mistake."

"I haven't it," Straight said promptly. "Mr. Clifford apparently never leaves it when he goes off to collect new material for his work. He only left this morning."

"This morning!" Pointer's tone suggested that here was indeed the last straw. "Why, the appointment was for today!"

Straight merely smiled and shook his head, as though to say that he was not responsible for his employer's habits.

Hobbs returned. He shot a swift glance from Straight to Pointer. An inquiring glance.

"Mrs. Clifford knows no more than I do, but if you feel that you would like to see her, she is willing to give you a few moments, Mr. Marbury."

Hobbs showed Pointer into a large quiet room with bookshelves shoulder-high running around it. A big writing table stood by one window. A Koran stand, various old carved reading-desks, and lecterns, and broad tables such as architects use, were here and there. It was Clifford's own room, and admirably suited to its purpose of writing. The men stood desultorily talking of the weather, which, after having given a selection of winter airs for the past week, had remembered that July was the tune which it was booked to play, and seemed at last endeavouring to provide something suitable.

After a minute or two the door opened. Pointer had never seen any one quite like Alison Clifford. He had expected beauty, for Julian Clifford had written of many a lovely heroine. But this was not beauty as he understood it.

She was very tall, very slender, and very pale. Lint-white the short, soft hair, so fine that, as she turned to shut the door, it stirred above her head like thistledown. With every movement, with her very breathing, it seemed to rise and fall like the hair of a spirit. Her skin was white too. White and smooth, with a sheen as of a lily's petals. Even her lips were but a hint of colour. Her eyes were a clear aquamarine, veiled by lashes so white that they looked as though thickly floured. Something about the face made the Chief Inspector think of a face seen under water, or through a veil.

Pointer explained again about the meeting at the Home Secretary's.

"So sorry to disturb you, Mrs. Clifford, but I thought that perhaps you might remember some trifle which would help to locate Mr. Clifford—"

Mrs. Clifford regretted that she could be of no use. "My husband often disappears for a short time. Generally, of course, he lets me know where he will be, but not always. And I'm afraid he has a very poor memory for engagements."

"Sometimes he's writing, or dictating, and gets to a passage which needs local knowledge," Hobbs put in, "when he'll stop, think a moment, and without a word leave the room, take down his hat and topcoat, and be off. To return with the necessary information and atmosphere perhaps after a week."

Mrs. Clifford smiled acquiescence. "I'm afraid we must possess our souls in patience. He left me a note saying that he might be delayed until Friday."

"Delayed?" Pointer wondered at that word.

"I've heard, of course, of your wonderful powers," he went on politely. "Couldn't you ascertain by means of them where Mr. Clifford really is?" It was a test question. What would the woman's reply be?

"I've been watching him in my crystal off and on all morning," she said at once, smiling faintly with down-dropped lids—lids so thin that Pointer could see the colour of the iris through them.

Even as she spoke she touched the antique silver clasp of a small black velvet bag beside her. Within it Pointer saw a ball of what looked like glass. Bending lower she looked into it. He watched her. Seen like this, with the light on her silvery hair and amber frock, he saw her charm for the first time. There was something very alluring about the picture which she made. She looked like a tree sprite talking for a few moments to a mortal.

"There he is now!" she exclaimed suddenly. "I can always get results quicker if I am with some one who wants to see what I do. Yes, there he is!"

She half turned a shoulder so that both Pointer and Hobbs could look. Pointer saw but the shifting light beautifully reflected in the ball. Hobbs had stalked to the window, and stood with his back to the room, disapproval in every line of his body.

"What is Mr. Clifford doing? Where is he?" Marbury asked, gaping. Was the faint smile that curved her pale mouth mischievous or malicious?

"I'm afraid there's no address given in a crystal. I only see a street ... a very winding street. . . ." She was staring into the ball with what looked like concentrated attention, turning it now and then in its nest of velvet.

"Gables," she went on, "built like steps running up into heaven, are on both sides of him. Now he's lighting a cigarette. He's pulled out his watch. Now he's gone!"

"Gables built like steps running up into heaven?" Pointer echoed. "What sort of houses would they be on?"

Mrs. Clifford shot Hobbs a glance from under her lids as she shut her velvet bag. Pointer fancied that she regretted those words, and hoped that her cousin had not heard them.

"Oh, just irregular gables," she said hurriedly.

"Wonderful!" Marbury fairly gaped; "really wonderful! Thank you so much. And when Mr. Clifford returns, will you ask him to have a message sent me? We may clear up the mystery then. For I confess I find Mr. Clifford's unexpected absence a mystery."

His rather yellow eyeballs—there are drops, very beneficial to the eye, which yellow the balls for the rest of the day—turned vaguely towards the figure of a young woman who had just sauntered down the gravel path towards them past their window. At his words, spoken very clearly, even though in Marbury's little staccato voice, it stopped with the small head a little forward on the long neck, the large eyes glancing into the room at Mrs. Clifford—at Hobbs—at their visitor. Dwelling on each in turn for a length of time that meant uneasiness to Pointer. By what, or by whom, was the uneasiness caused?

"Is that Miss Clifford?" Marbury asked, taking a step towards her, "perhaps she—"

"There is no Miss Clifford," Alison said, while the girl outside stood still. No one made any move towards mentioning her name.

"What! No help towards solving the puzzle of where Mr. Clifford is! Dear, dear!"

Mr. Marbury dropped first one glove then the other. The girl outside in the garden had stiffened where she stood. Now she passed on.

"That's a Miss Haslar, a niece of Mr. Clifford's," Hobbs said quickly, and turned towards the door.

Diana Haslar walked on as though deep in thought—unpleasant thought. Tall and slender, she looked a mere girl, but she was close on thirty. She had a fascinating rather than a pretty face. There were subtle lines in it. There was both mockery and mischief in her smile. And her large eyes looked as though few things would escape them. Had there been a greater warmth in it, her face would have been more universal in its charm. Yet there were hints of fire in the tawny eyes, in the beautiful lustre of her close-clipped, wavy hair, in some tones of her rather deep voice. At last, still apparently lost in thought, still unpleasant thought, she stepped into one of the rooms, and laid a hand on the young librarian's shoulder.

Richard Straight, as he had told Marbury, had only landed yesterday from Australia. He had been head librarian in a large Melbourne civic library. Julian Clifford had met him while on a world's lecturing tour, and had been struck with his original views on how private libraries should be, and could be, run. On his return, the author had offered him the post of his librarian. A small position, but one that could bring Straight into contact with many people worth meeting. Straight had thought it over for a month, and finally accepted it. Had he known what Diana Haslar carefully did not tell him until his decision was made, that the great writer was a connection of hers, Straight would not have hesitated for a day. He had been a constant visitor at the big Haslar house in Melbourne. A friend of Arnold Haslar's, it was not his fault if he was not by this time his brother-in-law. As it was, he still hoped to win Diana.

"Dick!"—the two were about the same age, and Christian names come easily in Australia—"tear yourself away from first editions, isn't a man from the Home Office the same as from the police?"

Richard Straight tore himself away from books very promptly at the tone in which that question was put. He looked at her in surprise.

"You'll be had up for slandering the Force if you mean that benevolent old dear in the morning-room. He certainly can't be the same as a policeman. Why?"

Diana seated herself on the table and ruffled the pages of a book in a way to set a conscientious librarian's teeth on edge. Dick did not seem to mind.

"He came about Uncle Julian. ... I heard him say his absence was a mystery. . . ."

"Well?" Dick asked easily.

Diana looked at him a moment in silence. Then she turned away. Straight knew that a door had been gently shut in his face.

"How do you think you're going to like your work at Thornbush?" she asked, after a moment.

"I think I'm going to like it very much here." This was high praise from Straight. He was an ugly, clever-looking young man with a certain air of quiet self-possession. An air which still annoyed Diana Haslar exceedingly at times. "I should like any place where I could be near you," he added rather fatuously. .

She gave him a rallying smile.

"Any place? I really can't imagine your liking any place, Dick. You're rather a particular young man. Besides, when Uncle Julian has finished his Life of my grandfather, I'm off. It's only the fact I can check the family dates better than any one else can that keeps me here, though I like the work." She finished thoughtfully with a certain critical note in her voice.

"But not the house?" he asked, quickly looking up.

"We're so frank 'down under,'" she said a little wistfully, "dreadfully frank, you used to think when you first came out. And Thornbush—" She seemed to seek for the right word.

"Thornbush isn't?"

"Not frank. No. Not lately. I seem to be always interrupting people in most private conversations. I think I shall be glad when the Life is finished and I'm free once more. Though I love being with Uncle Julian."

"He's a splendid chap, isn't he!" Straight said warmly. "His welcome to me was kindness itself."

"He is kind. Yet he can be hard. When it's a question of his work."

Again there was a tone to her voice that intrigued him. Straight was fond of conundrums.

"Your uncle said in the notes he left each of us this morning that he had gone for local colour. Is it possible that you think 'local colour' should be spelled Mazod Orr?"

This time it was Diana's expression that puzzled Straight as she looked at him. She was far too modern a young woman to be shocked at the suggestion. Yet there was a something in her eye. . . -

"I see that Arnold has been repeating the silly tittle-tattle which is going the round in some quarters," she said scornfully." Why, Alison and Mazod Orr are tremendous friends —she is seeing her off herself for Paris this morning."

There was a pause.

"And how's Arnold?" Straight asked; "was it anything serious?" The name of Mrs. Orr had suggested that of Arnold Haslar to him, for Diana's brother was madly in love with the widow. Straight knew that Diana had had a telephone message early this morning that had made her hurry home, a message about Arnold having been found beside his breakfast table in a state verging on collapse.

"The doctor says it's trying to be 'flu. I wanted to stay, but Arnold's not to see any one. If he remains in bed and keeps absolutely quiet, the doctor thinks he may escape and be up to-morrow."

"Odd if Arnold should catch 'flu," Straight thought. "He always seemed to be immune. He looked all right last night."

"The doctor says he must have had a shock of some kind, or some great excitement. Do you know of anything?" She looked at Straight rather narrowly. He did not, and said so.

"Must have happened when he was called out of town last night," he suggested. "It was a business call, he told me, else we had planned to celebrate my arrival, as you know, by some crimson paint. If it isn't due to business worry, then it may be remorse at his having cut me dead this morning. Absolutely dead."

"Where was this?" she asked sceptically.

"Just outside a huge building on the corner of a main road near here. I got lost trying to take an after-breakfast stroll."

"Heath Mansions." Diana tapped her fingers on the table restlessly. "He didn't see you evidently," she went on in a rather absent-minded, ruminative voice.

"That's just it," he retorted. "Arnold shouldn't moon by daylight. I waved a friendly paw, and he fled as though it held a writ. Probably he was feeling ill. He looked perfectly ghastly."

Once more an odd look crossed Diana's face.

"And he left you early last night?" she asked, as though worried by that fact.

"Nearly as soon as I got there," Straight said, with a smile. "But in response to a telephone call, which made it less of a snub direct."

She did not smile. A silence fell on the room.

Suddenly Diana drew back farther into the shadow. Newman, her uncle's secretary, was walking past the open window outside. He looked up. Their eyes, his and hers, met. Newman's cigarette-case dropped with a sharp tinkle, as though something in her glance had startled him. He retrieved it instantly, and passing on, lit a cigarette rather hastily.

His movements were singularly free from hurry, as a rule. Like his face, they suggested plenty of reserve power. There was something foreign about his appearance: a little in his easy grace, more in his seldom-seen, faintly ironic, smile, most of all in the melancholy of his dark, brooding eyes, which rarely looked up. Newman had a habit of carrying on a whole conversation with his eyes on his cigarette, or looking out of the window. In build he was exceptionally lean and lithe, with small, strong bones.

"I must ask Newman about the Spanish books," Straight murmured. "Mr. Clifford told me in that talk we had last night after dinner, that he's making himself into quite an authority on Spain."

Diana said nothing.

"Mr. Clifford seemed to think him very clever, but—"

Then Straight too decided to say no more.

"Oh, he is!" Diana spoke with a certain grimness, "so clever that one wonders why he remains content with life at Thornbush year after year. There's some reason why he refuses every offer, and he's had some good ones. Just as there's some reason why he cultivates Arnold as he does. Mr. Newman does nothing without a reason."

Diana spoke half under her breath.

"You sound afraid of him!" Straight gave her a very sharp glance.

Diana's laugh failed to achieve carelessness.

"I loathe him. I can't think why he should try so tremendously to ingratiate himself with Arnold, who, unfortunately, has taken the most tremendous fancy to him."

"Perhaps the fact that Arnold's your only brother," Dick suggested.

"Mr. Newman and I feel alike about each other," Diana said shortly, "mutual dislike. On my side, distrust as well. Profound distrust."

"I must keep out of his way," Straight said lightly.

"Oh, he won't bother you! You're of no importance to him. There's nothing to be gained by cultivating you"— she flushed at her own rudeness and added hastily, "except the best of pals. And possibly Mr. Newman may scent the rising man in you that you are, Dick. However, even so, you'll be safe. I can't imagine any one pulling the wool over your eyes."

"I'm done brown quite often," he murmured sadly.

"Not you!" she scoffed. "I always know that if ever any of us gets into a hole you'll get us out.' She bit her lip, as though the words had slipped out. "Edward Clifford thinks the paper you sent in to the Libraries Association a masterpiece. He said he was going to keep an eye on you."

"A benevolent or a watchful eye?"

Both laughed. Straight looked down into her face not so far below his own.

"Were you pleased?" he asked abruptly.

"For your sake—very much." She laughed again, but Straight did not laugh back.

"Can't you manage to love me, Diana?" he asked, with a sudden passion in his voice.

"I thought we talked that over in Melbourne." She turned away, not shyly—Diana was never shy—but with something almost of impatience in her big eyes.

"Love!" she repeated under her breath. "Who does love, really? What is it? How does it come? How do you know when it's real, when it's not? I like you, Dick. I respect your character immensely"

"Then give me a chance! Give me a try-out!" he urged again.

Diana only shook her head. . .

"I'll make you love me"—he spoke as though taking a vow unto himself—"with the real love The love that stands by a man when all else drops away. You have it in you, that I'll swear. You _could_ love, Diana!"

Diana was very pale.

"Not with the love that calls the world well lost." There was a note of contempt in her voice. Was it for herself? or for the subject of their talk? It was hard to tell with Diana.

"I haven't that in me. For your own sake, make no mistake! But apart from that, I could be a good helper to an ambitious, rising man. If ever I do agree to marry any one, I'll back him up well."

"But you won't agree to marry—any one—now?" Straight asked in his usual, rather measured voice.

"Not yet. Perhaps I shall never have any better answer. It won't be any loss, believe me. I'm not deep. I'm shallow. Shallow, and pleasure-loving, and greedy for good things." Her tone was trivial again. "And now, let's talk of something else. I mean it." Her eyes warned him not to press her for the present.

"Well, then, let us discuss whether the Foreign Office secret-service men will catch that chap Sir Edward talked about so much yesterday at dinner. The anarchist with the odd name . . ." Straight looked to Diana to help him out. She did not glance up.

"Et—Etch— Sounds as if I were sneezing!" he said crossly. "Etche— What was it?"

She made no suggestion.

The door opened. A girl looked in. It was Maud Gillingham, a great admirer of Alison Clifford's.

"Di—but how white you are! Or is it that frock? Mrs. Clifford has a message for you. A very important one. She's out in the garden."

Maud Gillingham slid an arm through Diana's, and the two sauntered out on to the lawn to where, under a cedar tree, Mrs. Clifford lay in a long garden-chair looking more like the sketch of a woman than actual flesh and blood. She lifted her strange aquamarine eyes as the two came up to her.

"I have a message for you from your grandfather, Diana." She spoke as casually as though she had just met the dead man in the street. "From Sir William Haslar. It spelled itself out on my Ouija board. I would have sent for you at once, only some tiresome person came in about an appointment of Julian's. . . . But this message—'Tell Day' it began. Evidently you are Day."

Diana started. That was her grandfather's name for her, not heard for many a long year, and certainly not known to Alison Clifford.

". . . not to mind whatever it is that you are minding," Mrs. Clifford went on. "That it will all come right. That he could see the end, and it will all come right."

She signalled to Newman, who was standing watching them, to come closer.

"Come along, Maud!" Diana turned to the girl beside her, "let's take a stroll around the rosary. You know"— Diana began when they were out of earshot—"there are times when I can't bear Alison. Spiritualists can be so smug, and generally are!"

"It's like talking to a woman from Mars sometimes," Maud agreed, "but she can be wonderful. With Mr. Newman, for instance. But I forgot—you don't like your uncle's secretary."

"I'm sorry for him," Diana said rather reluctantly.

Maud Gillingham nodded. "Naturally. Anybody would have to be sorry for a man who lost his memory in the war. But instead of pitying him, as we all do, Mrs. Clifford makes him feel that what he's lost is so tiny a thing in the immensity of our eternal life that it really isn't worth while fretting over."

"Yet don't you think she'd fret if she lost her memory?" Diana checked herself. "Maud, I never can quite make up my mind about Alison. Is she posing, or is she quite sincere?"

"Heavens, Di, if she weren't sincere she'd have to be an utter liar. Surely you don't think that of her?" Maud was aghast. She was an honest soul who knew no half-tones. You were white or you were black to Maud.

"N—no. No, of course I don't think that." Diana spoke rather as though dropping a trap-door on something within herself that wanted to peep out. "No, of course not. Every one knows that Alison, however mistaken, has a beautiful mind. But that message from my grandfather . . ." There was a pause.

"_Did_ he call you Day?" Maud asked curiously.

"He did. But . . ." There was another pause. "This message from him for me: Maud, doesn't it ever strike you that Alison always gets the messages from the other world that she wants to get? Hears the things she wants to hear?"

Maud reflected a moment.

"I think there's more than that in it, Di. Oh, much more! Look at this last Saturday afternoon. But I don't think you were in the room. Mrs. Orr was here, and was scoffing as usual in her laughing way at something I said about Mrs. Clifford's powers. But I stuck to it that she could 'see'—sometimes—with her hands. Mrs. Orr whipped out a letter from her bag, folded it, and held it folded on Mrs. Clifford's knee, and said, 'Read this, then, Alison darling.' And she did! Mrs. Clifford did! She pressed her hands hard down on the letter and read out a whole sentence. 'If you keep your end up, no one will suspect us.' She would have gone on, only Mrs. Orr put the letter back into her bag. It was from a friend on her honeymoon. Even she looked startled. And no wonder! If that wasn't white magic, what is?"

Now Diana had been in the room; had heard and watched the whole strange little scene. But what had struck her most had been Julian Clifford's face as his wife began slowly— laboriously—like some one reading a distant signpost, to almost spell out the words. If Mazod Orr had looked startled, so had he. Diana thought that his hand had palpably twitched to snatch the envelope with its contents from under his wife's fingers. He and Mrs. Orr had drifted on into his study to look at some new prints which he had bought, and Diana saw again Mrs. Clifford's equable smile as she looked after them. Yet there had been a new element in her expression. Diana's perceptions were very quick. In Alison Clifford's eyes was a look almost of sarcasm. It was the smile with which skill might watch transparent make-believe through which it sees absolutely, but from which, for reasons of its own, it prefers not to tear the cloak away. It was not an unkind smile—Alison never looked unkind—but it had made Diana wonder. The two girls were back again by the cedar tree now. Mrs. Clifford was talking to Newman.

"But even so, why not let me get into touch with your forgotten memories? They're not important, but still, why not have them? I might be able to lift the veil for you."

Newman flicked the ash off his cigarette with an impatient gesture which had something almost of contempt in it. There was a certain haughty, hawk-like look about his whole face.

"I'd rather not. Thank you immensely for caring, Mrs. Clifford. But I have a very definite feeling against having the veil lifted that way. Your powers are very wonderful, but something tells me, warns me, if you like, not to use them for this purpose."

Diana gave him a long, long look. It amounted to a stare.

"I should never be able to resist the chance if I were you!" panted Maud.

"You mean if I were _you_," Newman said looking at her under his heavy, brooding lids—lids that lifted slowly. There was something watchful about his gaze always—not suspicious—just watchful.

Dick Straight joined the group, and when they moved towards the house, sauntered after them with the secretary, of whom he asked a question or two about a couple of old Spanish works on the shelves. They were soon discussing Spanish bindings, and Straight found that his companion was indeed well up in the subject. Diana passed them again.

"I'm off to see how Arnold is, though he hates me to fuss over him." She made her remark exclusively to Dick Straight.

"Interesting girl, Miss Haslar," Dick said casually as she walked on.

"Most girls are," was the equally casual reply. Newman's dark eyes glanced for the barest second at Straight's face; that face was not usually considered a tell-tale one, yet Dick felt certain that the man beside him was aware from it of the state of affairs between himself and Diana.

Straight took an instant dislike to the man.

"Dago blood of some sort," he told himself, as Newman left him with a civil excuse, and turned off into the hall.

CHAPTER FOUR

Pointer meanwhile, on his way back to Scotland Yard, had opened the four letters handed him by the postman on the Thornbush drive. The three to Mr. Clifford could have no possible connection with the case. The letter to Mrs. Clifford was different. It was from town, dated yesterday, and ran,

"Dear Alison,—A linelette to say that should you be asked questions, be sure you know nothing. Remember we count on you to put people off. Miles off. Till tomorrow morning.

"In great haste,
"Mazod Orr."

That letter was put back in the Chief Inspector's letter-case. The others were fastened up and dropped in the nearest box.

"We count on you to put people off," he murmured. "Not always so easy, my lady!"

Back at New Scotland Yard, during a belated lightning lunch, Pointer asked Mr. Ward to be good enough to come into his room again for a moment.

"Ever heard of Mr. Clifford's new librarian? A young man called Straight?" he asked briskly.

"Librarian? I thought Newman had that job. But as Hobbs is going for a six months' big game shoot in the autumn, I suppose he's going off duty now—he has some private means, as well as a whacking salary and commission—the new librarian may be a sort of stop-gap. First I've heard of him."

"And who could a tall young woman be with handsome, rather bitter eyes, and a face that should be beautiful but isn't. She looks a lot younger than her years, I fancy." Pointer went on to describe her colouring. He wanted to verify the name that Hobbs had murmured. "I have a snapshot of her in my glove button, but I can't develop it for the moment."

Pointer's glove stud, a thickish stud, furnished a complete minute roll of films, and was a perfect tiny camera by the touch of a nail on the edge.

"That'll be Miss Haslar, Clifford's niece. She's helping Mr. Clifford with his Life of her grandfather, Sir William Haslar."

"Very fond of gossip, isn't she?"

"Diana Haslar? Not half as fond of it as I am," chuckled Ward. "No, she's rather a high-brow."

"Is she attached to her uncle? Mr. Clifford would only be her uncle by marriage, of course."

"Worshipped him. Absolutely worshipped him."

"Is Mr. Arnold Haslar an electrical engineer in a big way, the head of the Wellwyn Company of Melbourne, a relative of hers?"

"Only brother. Only relative, as far as I know. Her father's dead."

"And this brother, was he by way of worshipping Mr. Julian Clifford too?"

"Until he and the widow got so friendly. Mrs. Orr is absolutely ripping, you know. If rumour tells the truth she has ripped through a good deal in a fairly short time, but she's connected with all the peerage that counts, royal god-mother, and so on. So what would you? It'll take a lot to sink her little boat definitely. Haslar is tremendously in love with her. He's of no family, but he's wealthy. She can't do better. Wonder is, she can do as well. For he's the last chap to stand some things. Yet they say it's she who's lately holding off. No one can understand it. Clifford's interest is purely academic. She's a type to him. That's all. But why Mazod the Fair should be apparently turning Haslar down is the mystery. Clifford can't marry her even if he wanted to, which he doesn't. Haslar wants to. Unless she tries him too far. He's not the sort to make a good dupe. The woman can't have lost her very alert wits. . . ." Ward ruminated over the problem.

"What sort of man is this Arnold Haslar?" Pointer finally asked.

Ward pondered.

"Well, not the sort of chap I should select with whom to wipe the floor. Not without a tussle. All correct to the outward eye, of course. But there's wild blood in his background. Botany Bay, in fact. Not for anything terrific. Well-deserved manslaughter we should call it nowadays—at least I should." Ward corrected himself hastily. He and the Chief Inspector had crossed swords on that point before. "You know the retort his grandpa made when Lord Boodle wrote an article during the last election hinting at his family's past? Old Sir William, as he was later, wrote back that it was quite true. His ancestor had been deported for not enduring what his, the honourable writer's, ancestor had been ennobled for standing. To any one who knew the Boodle pedigree it was a bit sledge-hammer, but very amusing. Australia crowed."

"So that there's ill-feeling between him and Clifford over Mrs. Orr?" Pointer repeated meditatively.

Ward nodded. "Said to be."

"Does Miss Haslar know of the attachment between her brother and Mrs. Orr?" This Ward did not know, but he felt certain that if she did so, Diana would very much object.

Pointer stood with bent head, hands deep in his pockets, eyes on his shoes. It was a favourite position of his when deep in thought.

"What about Sir Edward Clifford, Mr. Julian Clifford's brother? What is his reputation among his own set?"

"None better," was the expected reply. "A stickler for conventions, but that's all to the good in a man of his position."

"Were the two brothers on friendly terms?"

"On the very best. Always. Even though both wanted to marry the same young woman, and though Julian Clifford carried off the prize, it made no difference in their friendship. I'm speaking of the present Mrs. Clifford."

And that finished Ward's information.

Pointer pressed a knob. A light shone out on the table of one of his constable clerks in the next room. The man came in.

"Get me the address of the Wellwyn Company's London warehouse. Find out if it has any others in Great Britain."

In a few minutes Pointer had an address in Thames Street. The only warehouse, or office, of the great Australian firm in the United Kingdom.

To it Inspector Watts was sent, to find out by dexterous questions whether any parcel or package had arrived there since last night, except such as were to be handled and opened in the usual way of trade.

Next, a woman detective was sent to call on Mrs. Orr for a subscription to a quite genuine orphanage, and incidentally to find out from whoever would be in the house where that lady had been last night.

That done, an inquiry was put through to Mr. Arnold Haslar at his office in Thames Street. Warehouse and office were in the same building. The inquiry was intended to lead up to a polite request to allow Mr. Marbury to come and see him with a view to adding his name to the same M.S.C. Reserve in which, apparently, Mr. Julian Clifford had been so interested. Pointer learnt that Mr. Haslar had not been at his office all day—that he was down with influenza. And from the butler at his house in Hampstead, Pointer heard that complete quiet had been ordered him and a day in bed. Yes, the attack had been very sudden. Mr. Haslar had been all right yesterday. He had come down ill this morning. This morning! Pointer was interested. So much so that a plain clothes man was despatched to keep an unobtrusive eye on the invalid's house. And an order was left that the telephones of it and of Mrs. Orr's house, and of Thornbush were to be all connected with New Scotland Yard.

As for Thornbush, just a little over an hour after Mr. Marbury left it, a red-haired, very freckled, lantern-jawed man from the gas company was knocking at the back door. They were installing meters farther down. Something had blown out. The pipes here must be looked to, or there might be trouble. The butler was dazed by a string of the latest bye-laws—so Pointer called them— rattled off at top speed, and promptly let the man make a tour of inspection.

The gas man was very thorough, even though he worked amazingly swiftly. Every cupboard was opened and swiftly scanned. The top glanced over. Every movable article was lifted quickly. Pointer had found out at the Yard, before he started, the average weight of a dead man's head. He had had that weight dropped into a seven-pound biscuit tin, filled with plaster of Paris, and lifted the whole several times, registering the weight.

He found few packages or parcels at Thornbush heavy enough for what he wanted. These few were carefully inspected. He even took one swift turn over the roof. besides being keenly on the watch for biscuit tins ostensibly filled with plaster, he kept a look-out for weapons of any kind. He drew a blank in both respects. But within ten minutes he found what he was primarily after. Finger-prints on a dozen articles of Julian Clifford's were unmistakably the finger-prints of the man in the mortuary.

Pointer was outwardly unmoved, but his pulses beat quicker. He had won the first round. In vain had the head of the murdered man been cut off, the clothes taken away.

No longer could a doubter say that the man whose hands Mrs. Jansen had photographed at Cannes, and the man who had come to her office in town, though he called himself Julian Clifford, might be an impostor. Here was the proof that the author and the murdered man were one and the same.

As for the rest, neither Clifford's room, nor his wife's, nor Hobbs', had anything important to tell the Chief Inspector. Nor, strictly speaking, had Newman's. Yet in one way the secretary's room interested Pointer greatly. Newman had lived many years now with Clifford, yet the bedroom and his working room were as bare of personal effects as hotel rooms. There was not so much as a calendar which seemed the personal choice of the secretary. The only books were from a circulating library unless they belonged to Clifford.

Pointer stood looking about him, his bag of tools in his hand—intentionally bare. Intentionally devoid of all marks of individuality was his verdict. Nothing here to help any detective. Choice or necessity? Newman was a conundrum.

A chat in the kitchen told Pointer that Mr. and Mrs. Clifford were considered a most devoted couple by their servants, aid that the latter were not in the least surprised at only one more of their master's many short disappearances.

"It's just his way," one maid said airily. "He goes off like that, all of a sudden, when he gets fed up with writing. Mr. Trimble here he says that Mr. Clifford goes to find out more to write about, but is that likely?"

A few questions about last night, when the gas man thought that he had seen Mr. and Mrs. Clifford at a restaurant in company with Sir Edward Clifford, told Pointer that the dinner at Thornbush, where Edward Clifford and Maud Gillingham had been the only guests, had been a cheery meal; that the two guests had each left immediately after the meal, and that as far as the servants went, Mr. Clifford had not been seen after the butler took him in a glass of iced barley water about ten. Mr. Clifford had told him that "that was all"—his usual words of dismissal for the night. Back on his Yard-bound 'bus, Pointer thought over the household —over Julian Clifford, who had gone to Astra's to have his fortune told, as he might have gone to a gipsy.

He had gone recently. And he had asked the palmist to tell him if danger was marked in his hands. A strange question from a man who apparently within the month had passed to where that word has no more meaning.

Yet if it was his body that Pointer had seen, as the Chief Inspector believed that it was, he had not investigated that flat. He did not seem to have noticed the fastened back lock of that door. It looked as though he had had a definite idea of where the danger lay, and did not expect it to meet him elsewhere.

What was the best course now? Open or secret?

As a rule, an inquirer in a murder benefited by the rare chance of the murderer thinking his crime was still undetected. But here? Dared Pointer let him think himself safe? If that cut-off head was cut off with the idea of blocking the investigation, then it and those carefully laid trails of the Basque anarchist looked, Pointer believed, as though some thing was brewing which the knowledge of Clifford's death would spoil. Some business seemed to be on hand which must stop if it were known who it was that on this last night had been lured to a strange address, there murdered, and stripped and beheaded. They might not all belong together—the murder, the beheading, the stripping. But some vital necessity must have ruled to make a man risk any, or all, of them. No one goes to such terrible lengths unless driven. What was it which necessitated, perhaps the killing of Julian Clifford, but certainly the remaining unknown of the fact that it was he who had been killed?

Back at Scotland Yard, he arranged for a couple of his men to be installed in a road-mender's hut just outside Thornbush—men who understood tapping a telephone wire. They were instructed to do as little damage as possible with the maximum amount of effect. The point was that one or other was to be permanently on guard. And a message was sent to the police stations concerned which would be passed on at once to every constable on his beat, that any oddity noticed at the houses where lived Sir Edward Clifford, Mrs. Orr, Arnold Haslar, and Julian Clifford was to be at once reported directly to the Chief Inspector at New Scotland Yard.

Then he went swiftly to the Assistant Commissioner's rooms. Tindall, to whom he had telephoned, was just entering. Without a word, Pointer laid before the two men a sheet of paper with some red finger-prints on it. He had obtained them by dropping collodium in thin films over the fingerprints on a metal tube of tooth-paste in Clifford's dressing-room, then carefully peeling them off one by one when set, leaving them awhile in a red-tinted hardening solution, and finally pressing each carefully out on to unglazed paper.

"You agree that they're the same as these?" he asked.

"These" were prints taken from the hands of the dead man, and enlarged on squared paper.

"They're identical," Tindall agreed, after very carefully comparing the two. Major Pelham said the same, and the Assistant Commissioner was an authority on finger-prints.

"How on earth—where—whose?" Tindall was all but inarticulate.

"I got these red prints from marks on Mr. Julian Clifford's tube of tooth paste. Equally clear are those there taken off a lamp switch beside his bed. The tube of tooth-paste I have with me. And here's some of Mr. Clifford's manuscript paper. It's esparto grass paper. In other words I'm sorry to say that the murdered man in Heath Mansions is Mr. Julian Clifford the well-known author." Pointer detailed the somewhat odd steps of his investigations.

"Sir Edward's brother!" Tindall murmured, as one half stupefied. There was a long silence. Tindall strode to the window and back. Then he wheeled.

"These prints, of course, absolutely settle the question. So Etcheverrey was the killer this time, and not the killed! But why should Etcheverrey kill Julian Clifford? What took Clifford into that most dangerous man's inner circle? However, let me congratulate you, Chief Inspector. This was good work. Marvellously good. Considering how you at the Yard are so bound by red tape. You need a royal warrant or an Act of Parliament before you dare step an inch off the beaten track. With us, of course, it's different. But frankly, I can't think how you get the results that you do."

"We have to rely more on routine," Pointer agreed sadly, and let it go at that, while Major Pelham wrestled with a refractory cough.

Tindall bent over the finger-prints again.

"And to think of a Scotland Yard man going to a palmist!" he all but chuckled.

"Astra isn't what's generally meant by that word, or we wouldn't let her alone as we do," the Assistant Commissioner reminded him. "She's not a fortune-teller."

"It was a most amazing piece of luck that she had photographed Clifford's hands," Tindall said almost grudgingly.

Pointer nodded. It was.

"It wasn't good luck that made the Chief Inspector go to her," Pelham pointed out.

"What would you have done if she'd never seen Clifford?" the Foreign Office man asked with real curiosity.

"I think she might have been as good at placing him, or his interests, as she was with mine. I tried her with my own hands first. If so, what with her suggestions, and the clue furnished by his fingernails, I think we should have run him to earth in time."

"I wish you were wrong for once," Tindall pushed the sheets of prints away. He spoke with genuine emotion. "Quite apart from my having been a little off the true, I wish with all my heart that you were wrong. Why, his coming novel is said to be one of the finest things even Julian Clifford has ever done! It's not finished yet. I must be the one to break the news to Sir Edward, of course." Suddenly he straightened. "I wonder! Is he the link between Julian Clifford and the Basque? There's no man keener on having Etcheverrey caught than our Chief. And there is a great resemblance between the brothers. But first of all, I must hurry to the French Embassy." He glanced at his watch. "Four o'clock. I've been there until now. Etcheverrey—"

Pelham stopped him.

"Just a moment, Tindall. We must lay this before the Commissioner. I've told him the facts as far as they went."

He took the two into another room. The prints were laid before an elderly, shrewd-faced man with singularly steady, piercing blue eyes.

"You think, Tindall, that Julian Clifford may have been killed because of Sir Edward's inquiries, or because the younger was mistaken for the elder brother?" General Brownlow asked finally.

"I can see no other possible link. No other gap to cross such a bridge as that between a Basque revolutionary and Julian Clifford."

Tindall looked at Pointer. All three looked at Pointer, who looked at his shoe-tips.

A silence fell on the room. Then General Brownlow spoke.

"I don't for a moment doubt your result, Chief Inspector. None of us do, or can. But it rests for identification of the body only on palm and finger-prints. Juries and coroners don't like that kind of evidence. We must go step by step. I think we must keep back from the public our belief, our certainty rather, that the murdered man is Julian Clifford until we get the usual proof. I mean until we get the actual head. As to the family—that must, of course, depend on what Sir Edward says; or on the course of events."

Again there fell a silence.

"'We count on you to put people off. Miles off,'" Pelham murmured suddenly. Pointer had given every fact, as known to him so far, with the most meticulous care. It was only his conclusions that he had kept to himself. "That's a most extraordinary letter under the circumstances!"

"I don't know about Mrs. Orr, but Mrs. Clifford is absolutely incapable of murder," General Brownlow said firmly, "or of being connected with a crime of any kind. I've known her off and on since she was a child. Nor is there the slightest motive here. She has a life interest under her father's will that must bring her in a clear thousand a year. A thousand to Mrs. Clifford is like five thousand to most people. More than ample for her needs. You might as well suspect Sir Edward of having had a hand in Julian Clifford's horrible end."

And with that the conference broke up.

Pointer's next objective was the Hampstead branch of the St. James Bank. Before leaving Scotland Yard a few inquiries over the telephone at all the branches near Thornbush had told him that Mr. Clifford had a town account there. And Pointer was always interested in the banking account of men who died suddenly, let alone of men who were murdered.

The reason for that cut-off head might lie quite near home. Clifford was not a racing man, or Pointer would have thought of a horse. But was there any large cheque outstanding of his which his death, if known of, would have invalidated, or at least held up?

In that case, since Julian Clifford was killed last night, any such cheque would have been presented to-day as soon as the banks opened. This did not oust Etcheverrey from his place in the heart of the mystery surrounding the death of the great writer, but Pointer believed that mystery to be complex, not single.

Pointer had his private doubts as to whether it was quite fair to the bank manager to let him cash a dead man's cheques, for others might be presented, innocently or not. But the Chief Commissioner had decided that nothing should be done for the present which would let the world at large know that England's foremost author was dead. Pointer rather deprecated that decision, but it had been made. Though by now it was past banking hours, a telephone message to the manager had found him still on the premises, and Pointer was shown in at once on his arrival. Detective Inspectors do not ask for appointments every day.

"Do you mind if my chauffeur waits outside in the passage?" Pointer asked, as he shook hands. There was only the one door.

The manager was too full of anxiety to have any room for objections.

"A man's body has just been discovered," Pointer began, "in circumstances that suggest foul play. He was an acquaintance of Mr. Julian Clifford's. We have discovered some notes among his papers which make us think that he had in his possession a large sum of money of Mr. Clifford's. That he was only just in possession of it. A business venture pure and simple, but on a large scale. Mr. Julian Clifford is out at his home. Now this is the point. Was any large sum paid out very recently by Mr. Clifford? We think the payment of which we're speaking was originally by cheque, and probably was presented to you early this morning as soon as the bank opened."

The manager reflected a moment. He had started at the last words.

"It's in strictest confidence, of course?" he asked.

Pointer had to tell him that as the sum might possibly be the motive for an attempt at murder, it was not possible for him to promise secrecy.

The manager reflected a little longer.

"You say Mr. Clifford's away from home?"

"His family tell me he's off on one of those expeditions of his when he leaves no address. Getting up facts for his next book," Pointer said promptly.

More meditation on the part of the manager.

"Well, I'm in rather a difficult position," he murmured.

"Why don't you get into touch with Sir Edward Clifford?"

"He's out of town. Also un-get-at-able."

"A depositor—and such a large depositor as Mr. Julian Clifford," murmured the manager uncertainly.

"Still—murder, you know!" Pointer threw in. And the manager made up his mind.

"Well, a very large cheque of Mr. Clifford's was presented early this morning," he said slowly.

Pointer nodded. "For how much?"

"Seventy thousand pounds."

Having said that much, the manager made up his mind to be quite frank.

"Mr. Clifford had spoken to us of that cheque. About a month ago he had us make the necessary arrangements to pay a hundred thousand into his current account. He told me that he would draw on it by a very large cheque, and that he wished the cheque cashed without any further formalities or delay."

Pointer nodded.

"This morning, as soon as we opened, Mrs. Clifford presented a cheque of Mr. Clifford's drawn to a Mr. Selfe for seventy thousand pounds. It was duly endorsed, and of course we cashed it at once. That is the only large sum which had been paid out of Mr. Clifford's account lately."

"Mrs. Clifford. I see. Was she alone?"

"No. A lady was with her in her car. I happened to be coming in at the moment the car drew up."

"Did you recognise whoever was with her?"

"It was Mrs. Orr."

"You know her?"

The manager hesitated again. "No," he said finally, "but seeing it's you, I don't mind passing on a bit of gossip. My son Gerald is a barrister. Junior to Mr. Robinson. He tells me that they're briefed in a case coming on shortly. Smart society divorce. It's to be heard as soon as the courts open. Mrs. Orr is cited in it by name. No chance of a defence. The wife intends to get her knife into her. Gerald showed me some photographs of Mrs. Orr. That's how I recognised her at once. Odd companion for Mrs. Julian Clifford."

"May I see it? A Selfe is a sort of partner of this man who was shot."

"I see. You think?"

"It's too early to think yet," Pointer returned, as though that were with him always the last resort. "But of course I must have a look at it. If only in the way of routine."

He was shown the cheque. It seemed in perfect order. It was made out to R. Selfe, Esq., and endorsed R. Selfe. The date was last Thursday.

"I must ask you to let me have this for an hour or so."

The manager agreed, provided that it be returned next day.

"I don't want to talk over the finding of this body more than I can help with Mrs. Clifford. It's a harrowing subject, especially if we're wrong, and this money has nothing to do with our case. How did she take the money?"

"In notes of a hundred pounds. Here is the list of the numbers. Mr. Clifford had requested that the money should be held ready for him in just that way. They were handed to Mrs. Clifford in seven packages of a hundred notes. The cashier asked, of course, if she shouldn't send it out to her car by our commissionaire, or lend her the man's services, but she declined both suggestions."

Pointer thanked him and left. He had much to think over. A cheque for a fortune ... an uncrossed cheque ... a cheque to R. Selfe . . . and cashed by Mrs. Clifford as soon after her husband's death as it could be presented . . . with Mrs. Orr waiting in the car outside ... a cheque which Julian Clifford had expected to be presented, and which he wished paid without any trouble being made to the person who should present it.

Not a simple case this . . . complex . . . very.

Pointer had the cheque photographed, and the photograph enlarged. Then he saw what he expected to see. The final e was not continuous with the f of Self, but had been carefully added. So carefully, so exactly, that only the enlarged photograph showed the break and slight overlapping of the strokes. The endorsement on the back presented no breaks. There Selfe was one word, written swiftly and with a dash. Under the camera too the initial R on the face of the cheque showed a certain waviness of line due to slow and careful writing ... so did the Esq. On the back the initial was swiftly penned. In other words, the camera showed that, as Pointer had suspected, the cheque, originally made out by Julian Clifford—for the signature was his without a doubt, hastily and carelessly written—had been to Self ... to Julian Clifford. Some one into whose hands it had fallen, had ingeniously altered it to a not uncommon family name. And the alterations had apparently been made with Julian Clifford's own pen and ink. There was a little peculiarity about the nib used which showed throughout.

Pointer docketed these new and most important facts, then he reached for the telephone. He mentioned to Sir Edward's valet that it was "Mr. Marbury of the Home Office" who was speaking.

"I understood that Sir Edward left yesterday evening to join a commission at Chequers on the Sudan Cotton Areas, but I find he hasn't been there. Do you know where I can reach him over the telephone at once?"

"I am sorry to say, sir, that there is no telephone at Sir Edward's cottage at Weybridge, where he is spending the day."

"His cottage"—Marbury seemed perplexed—"are you sure? When did he leave town?"

"Sir Edward left about nine yesterday evening, sir. He changed into tweeds, and took nothing down with him but a gun and cartridges. That always means the cottage, sir."

"Do you know which gun, and what number cartridges?" Pointer asked in the sudden tone of a man who has a clue.

"He took his old 12-bore gun, sir, and a bag of Numbers 4 and 6 cartridges."

"Did he drive down himself?"

"Yes, sir."

"Well, that certainly seems to settle it," murmured Marbury. "When do you expect him back?"

"In time for dinner, sir. Eight o'clock."

Marbury rang off, after thanking the man. It was now just after five. A wire would be useless. Sir Edward Clifford, Julian's only brother, had taken a gun and a bag of cartridges away with him yesterday about nine o'clock . . . easily identifiable shots in some circumstances . . . under a loose ulster a gun could be strapped to the body with comparative ease, if a man drove his own car. . . .

Pointer hastily got into his gas-man make-up again, looked around for his tool bag that contained other things beside tools, pushed his cap a little farther on one side, touched it to a sergeant coming in at the main entrance, and swung himself on board a Hampstead bus.

The Haslar's house was a bare five minutes' drive from that of Julian Clifford. When the latter had married Catherine Haslar, Sir William Haslar had built the two houses, and given the larger as a present to his new son-in-law. An inquiry of the gas company had told Pointer that on the principle of the shoemaker's barefoot children, the Haslars had gas fires in all their rooms.

Bag on shoulder he lounged up to the basement door.

The butler was appealed to. "Certainly not!" he announced "You can't go making a noise just now. There's illness in the house."

"Well, of course, sir, if you want to be all blown up by a blocked pipe, carry on!" The man spoke nonchalantly.

"You won't make any noise?" The butler was no keener on explosions than are most people.

"Not so much as a mouse nibbling cheese." Pointer came in and looked about him. He chatted as he sorted out his pliers. Chatted of a gas explosion farther down early this morning which he was surprised to learn had not brought in any complaints from Mr. Haslar.

"Ah, well, of course if he came in abaht four in the morning, he couldn't have heard it. It was at three." Then he went on to tell of Mr. Clifford's house, where he had just been. Mr. Clifford had lost his umbrella. One of the servants at Thornbush had said in Pointer's hearing that he must have left it at Mr. Haslar's house last evening ... an insinuation which was loftily repudiated by Wilkins. Mr. Clifford had not been to the house for a month past.

Pointer, who wore the full uniform of the gas company, was allowed to roam the house by himself. He went first of all to Arnold Haslar's bedroom. There he knelt for the briefest of seconds by the hearth, staring at the bed where lay a young man with his eyes closed. Haslar looked very white. But was he really ill or only keeping out of the way? On the mantelpiece was a much-used New Comfort pipe. In a rubber-lined pocket of a waistcoat hanging in the dressing-room was some tobacco of the kind which the head porter at Heath Mansions had noticed was smoked by Mr. Tourcoin last Friday evening.

Pointer tiptoed to the wardrobe and opened it noiselessly. The man on the bed had not seemed to pay the slightest attention. But he suddenly turned over and barked:—

"What the devil are you doing with my clothes?"

"Gas smell, sir," Pointer said, immediately coming up to the bed and taking a good look at the man in it.

"There's a gas leak somewhere. We can't locate it. But if it leaked last night say, and the wardrobe was open, you'd smell it when it was suddenly opened, and think something was wrong again. It smells pretty strong."

He put his head into the wardrobe and sniffed several times. There was an ulster, or some coat of similar texture, hanging on the last hanger. Pointer put out his hand as though to steady himself, and sniffed again. The last coat was an orange and brown check tweed. Without an apparent glance at it, he shut the door and sniffed in a farther corner of the room, working down to the floor in a most convincing way.

Haslar seemed to fall into a heavy slumber. Pointer stood a moment photographing the face on his mind. He noted the big frame, the masterful, rather overbearing jaw, the eyebrows meeting over the bold nose—secretive eyebrows these —and the mouth firm yet passionate. Then he melted from the room and slipped downstairs to the ground floor. Here he found a telephone in what was evidently Haslar's own particular room. One end of the large library shut off by folding doors from the book part proper.

Pointer asked for a number that would have meant nothing to a listener. But it was the secret number used by the officers of New Scotland Yard, and insured instant connection and precedence.

The Chief Inspector murmured a few short sentences. Decoded they meant that one of his men, got up as directed, was to ask the "watcher" outside Haslar's house for a card. It would be one of Arnold Haslar's own cards, that Pointer had just taken from a drawer in the writing table. It was to be used according to instructions.

Pointer wanted that brown and orange ulster at once. If Haslar continued to sleep well, it might be at the Yard by six o'clock.

Then he took up his own work of going swiftly but carefully over the house.

CHAPTER FIVE

While the Chief Inspector was roaming Arnold Haslar's house, Julian Clifford's new librarian and Diana had been looking at some rare books at Sotheby's. Straight was expressing his disappointment at Julian Clifford's absence.

"He has left me neither instructions nor a free hand. Hobbs is too busy to question Mr. Clifford's preferences. He certainly is a worker! And Newman, apart from your warnings, dislikes me. Jealousy, I suppose. No man likes to be supplanted."

"Supplanted? Newman?" There was joy in Diana's tone. She had been looking rather bored by Straight's little outburst.

"So Mr. Clifford hinted in our after-dinner talk last night. He's thinking of letting Newman go. But that's in strictest confidence. What concerns me at the moment far more is when he is coming back. I—"

A passing newsboy waved his papers at them.

"French anarchist killed in Hampstead flat! Headless man in Hampstead!" he shouted.

"Hampstead?" Straight bought two papers.

"Why it's Heath Mansions! The building near us!" Diana said, aghast as she caught sight of a photograph on the front page. Straight said nothing. He was reading. Suddenly Diana gave a low cry. She went livid.

"Here! you're ill!" Dick said solicitously.

"A taxi," she murmured. "I'm all right. Don't come with me."

"Certainly I'm coming with you." He signalled to a taxi, gave the man her home address, and jumped in beside her. But Diana sprang to her feet.

"No! I want to be alone. I must be alone." She spoke in
a strange, wild voice. She looked around for another taxi.
There was none.

"Dick, I want to be alone. You can't come with me."
She seemed unable to find other words.

"Sorry to force my society on you," he said quietly,
"but I'm coming. You've had a shock."

Diana looked at him with dilated pupils. Her eyes
suddenly looked enormous in her pale face.

"You must keep out of this, Dick," she said again in
the same firm tone. "You of all men. I know how you
would hate to be mixed up in anything disagreeable."

"No more than the next fellow," he assured her. "And
when you're in trouble, you don't suppose blows would
drive me from you, do you? What frightened you in that
paper?"

"You're quick," she said in a low tone; "I'm glad no one
else was with me. Dick, something awful has happened. I
knew evil was bound to come of— I must go home at once.
I must see Arnold—" She pulled herself up.

"Exactly!" Dick reminded her. "What was it the doctor
said? He must have no shocks. So Arnold being out of
court, suppose you face the fact that you're driven to turn
to me?"

Diana passed a hand across her eyes. She shivered.

"Murdered like that! Decoyed, and then butchered!"
she said under her breath. "Give me the paper again!"
She took it from him hurriedly, and read as though every
unnoticed punctuation mark might make a difference.

Straight, too, dipped into his sheet. There was enough
and to spare to hold his attention in the columns. When
he came to the description of the man who had taken the
flat, he gave a start. The house agent had remembered
something more than he had told the police. He had now
remembered and described to a reporter an unusual ring
which the man had been wearing on the little finger of his
right hand—a black opal very highly rounded. Two gold
snakes were coiled about it, their coils making the ring,

their heads apparently holding the stone in place between them as they nearly met across it. The serpents were carved in great detail and in the round.

At first the house agent, though he had remembered the ring, had not placed the man who had worn it. He was now sure that it had been on the hand of the mysterious Tourcoin. His clerk, too, remembered it, as well as the check ulster which the man had worn.

Straight felt Diana sag in the corner beside him as she came to the description of the ring and the overcoat.

"We both know a ring like that, but has Arnold such an ulster by any chance?"

"A ring like that. . . . Such an ulster ...!" she repeated under her breath. "It is Arnold's ring and ulster that are described here. As to the ulster—" She drew in her breath sharply, with a shudder.

"It's a damnable business," Straight said, after a moment's deep thought. "All we can do is to keep our own counsel—as long as we can," he added grimly. "What about the name? The name of Tourcoin?"

"Some one in a French town of that name, or Belgian, I don't know which, asked him to advise them about some new electrical plant not long ago. The name would still be fresh in his mind."

"But why in the world should Arnold have given a false name when looking over the flat? What possible connection is there between him and a Basque communist?" he asked, looking bewildered.

Diana sprang to her feet, rocking with the speed of the taxi.

"I can't stand it! I can't stand it!" She turned a distorted face on Dick. "There's another taxi!" She waved to it. "I can't endure to hear it talked about. To speak of it!" She motioned again. But the cab had it's flag up and passed on. Diana sank back into her seat as though her legs gave under her. Straight bit his lip. The incident showed him how little he counted with her in Diana's inner life. "You saw him yourself this morning coming out of the place—Heath Mansions," woman-like Diana could talk of nothing else. "Others may have seen him too!"

Straight looked at her warningly. "Forget that, Diana! I have—completely!" A newspaper boy with a later edition than the one which they had seen ran past. Straight got a copy.

"Who was the Man who took the Flat?" was now the heading. Diana and Straight, heads together, scanned it. The description, pieced together by an able reporter, fitted Arnold Haslar with appalling closeness.

Neither spoke until they turned into Arnold's garden. Newman, Clifford's secretary, was just being admitted. Diana gave a sudden cry, a cry of sheerest terror, and clutched Dick's arm with fingers that hurt. Her hands were colder than he had imagined living hands could be. He thought that she had fainted. Her face with its eyes closed looked so white. But in a second the lids lifted. She squared her shoulders as the cab stopped. She seemed to pull herself together with a great effort. She looked more like sinking to the ground where she stood than walking up the steps, but she went forward very steadily, refusing help. Wilkins came out hurriedly. "Are you ill, Miss Diana? Let me call Alice. Let me assist you"

She paid no attention to him. Newman had gone on into the hall.

"Mr. Newman?" she asked quickly, imperiously.

"Mr. Newman is here, Miss Diana. He insists on being allowed up to see Mr. Haslar for a moment. I told him that the doctor's orders were to the contrary." Wilkins had obviously not yet heard of the murder, nor of the man with the black opal ring and the check ulster.

Diana stepped in swiftly, and laid a hand on the newel post. She still looked as though she needed its support.

Newman turned at her entrance; he was just mounting the stairs. He, too, was very pale. The eyes were far back in their sockets, but they were still as unreadable as ever. He and Diana faced each other in absolute silence for a long minute.

"I didn't expect to see you," she said in an oddly shaken voice.

"I'd like to go up and speak to Arnold for a moment," was his only reply.

"No one can see him," Diana said in a firmer voice. Newman seemed to hesitate.

"He's feverish, I understand. Is he lightheaded?" he asked in a lower tone, though Wilkins had already gone on down the hall.

Diana did not reply at once. Then she asked:—

"Why should he be? You've seen the evening papers?" Newman nodded.

"Hadn't we better talk in here?" He glanced towards a room.

Diana did not seem to hear him. She was speaking in a very low, very stony voice.

"You saw about the murder in Heath Mansions?" she asked again.

Once more he nodded.

"Did you read the description of the ulster the man was wearing? Of the ring?"

"I read them. Yes." Newman was standing with his head bent. His eyes only were raised and were fastened on Diana. As before, Straight could make nothing of their expression. Was it inimical or merely intentionally blank? Then Straight looked at Diana. Never would he have believed her face capable of showing such passion. The girl seemed to be swept by a fury—a fury that was shaking her where she stood— a fury which was in spate but which she was damming back.

"Why?" Newman asked gravely.

"Because Arnold has a coat and ring exactly like them." Straight frowned. Women were the most imprudent of beings.

"Because coats and rings can be borrowed, Mr. Newman."

"You mean—?" Newman still spoke very quietly, rather thoughtfully.

"That my brother had no interest in murdering anybody. But that might not be true of—Sanz Etcheverrey." She spoke the words in a low, tense whisper.

"The man who was killed?"

"No. _Not_ the man who was killed."

Straight looked quickly from Diana to Newman, and back to Diana. What did this scene mean? Newman did not glance at her now. He was looking meditatively at the black and white marble squares of the hall.

Diana swept past him. Her brother's valet came down the stairs.

"Mr. Haslar's asleep, miss. He's been asleep nearly all afternoon."

"Good." Diana hesitated. Straight took a step forward. Could he slip up and get that ulster? He had looked in the cloakroom just now, and it was not there.

"The tailor sent a man for an overcoat of Mr. Haslar's a little while ago, miss. I got it out without waking him," the man continued. "He had a card of Mr. Haslar's, saying that his new check motor coat was to be handed to the bearer, miss. I did quite right, I hope? I didn't wake Mr. Haslar," he repeated.

"Quite right, Smith," Diana said rather faintly. She turned suddenly and came up to Newman, who was moving towards the door.

"A moment! I want to speak to you outside."

When they were clear of the steps she said in a low, bitter voice, "I think it only fair to warn you that I may have to tell all I know to the police."

"Warn me?" Newman asked, as though not understanding her.

"Arnold may have gone to that flat or you may have gone in his things," she went on, "but I am convinced that in some way you are mixed up in the affair. I heard you tell Arnold only last week that that flat was to let. If

Arnold gets drawn into the crime I shall speak out. Please don't go on with the farce of having lost your memory." She looked at him with eyes that seemed to scorch what they looked at.

He looked bewildered. "Farce? I only wish it were," he said heavily.

"You have not lost it," she repeated firmly; "I've known it all along."

Now he gave her a measuring look. The look that a fencer gives another when he steps forward, foil in hand.

"Have you told Mr. Straight as much? Not yet? I see. Not yet."

He nodded thoughtfully; almost, Diana felt, as though she, and what she was saying, had retreated into the background of his thought. Almost she could imagine that he was hearing some other voice speak, and was listening to it rather than to her. The feeling chilled her.

Turning towards her, he made a gesture almost of dismissal.

"Do what you feel you must do," he said coldly, and raising his hat, walked on past her.

For a second she stood with clenched hands, then she turned back to the house. She went into the room where Straight stood waiting for her. It occurred to Diana for the first time, that possibly she had not appreciated Dick at his proper value. There was a certain measured, and measuring quality about the young man which had a little amused her, and a little chilled her, out in Australia. Yet she felt suddenly very glad that he was in England, and at Thornbush just now. Dick was never spectacular, but she felt, a little self-reproachfully, that his was the kind of character to which one turns in moments of trouble. If only he were not at other times something so perilously approaching a prig!

He closed the door behind her.

"What in the world?" he began. She raised her hand.

"That ulster has gone—taken—fetched! But by whom?" There was terror in her face now.

"Well test it. Who's your brother's tailor? Rivers of Saville Row?"

He rang up, and after a moment dropped the receiver back.

"No one was sent from there. But, of course, the fact that your brother gave a card looks as though it might have been some local presser . . . some regular man he employs."

"Dick, do you think it could have been Newman whom you mistook for my brother this morning, coming out of Heath Mansions?"

Dick did not answer for a moment, then he said:—

"Why should it be Newman, Di?"

Now it was her turn not to reply.

"Why did you connect him with this dead anarchist?" he asked again.

She shook her head. Her eyes were closed. He had never expected to see Diana look so broken.

"I'm only groping," she said faintly.

"What do you know of your uncle's secretary that makes you link him with this Etcheverrey murder?" he persisted. "You ought to tell me, Di. If there's any chance of helping Arnold out of this unholy mess it will be that you and I pull together."

"I can't tell you, Dick," she said, after another long moment. "I didn't mean to say as much as I did before a third person. But it welled up. Nothing will make Mr. Newman speak out. Nothing! He's like some creature hiding in his lair. He knows that he's safe there, and won't come into the open."

A passion of hate sounded in Diana's voice. Straight gave her a very searching, not over-pleased look. No man cares to hear the woman whom he hopes to marry speak like that of another. It takes too much to explain it. Diana walked to the window and stood drawing a deep breath.

"If things get worse, if suspicion falls on Arnold, I must go to the police and tell them—what I know. But not to you, Dick—not yet. If that's why Newman has seemed so strangely fond of Arnold—" she stood biting her lip and quivering afresh against the sharp light of the window.

"You won't tell me what the secret is between you and him, then?" There was an edge to his voice.

She did not reply. His face flushed.

"I had hoped that I could be of some use to you and Arnold, Di. I am sorry that I overrated your confidence in me."

"Oh, Dick"—she held out a quivering hand—"be generous!"

He took it—a shade stiffly.

"Let me warn you for both your sakes, to think over every step before you take it. In this affair, you can't accuse Newman without involving Arnold. At least, I'm afraid so. The whole affair is really too grave." He went on in a kinder tone, "You see, it was Arnold whom I saw slipping out of what I now know is Heath Mansions this morning. And"—again he hesitated, but the danger of a misunderstanding on her part was too real—"and the doctor thought he had just had a terrible shock, remember. What about the servants? Are they to be trusted?"

"The butler has been with us since father's days. So has the housekeeper. I think they'd stop any of the servants chattering. But of course it's bound to leak out sooner or later. So many people have seen that ring."

She seemed about to leave him, but he detained her.

"Diana," Dick's eyes were very gentle, "I repeat that I think you ought to tell me what you know about Newman. Evidently you know something very important, very much to the point, in this awful affair."

She looked irresolutely at him. Even though she felt sure that Richard Straight was a good man to go to for advice, Diana was terrified of a false step, for the waters were deep. Yet she knew that the very things in his character which kept her from being in love with him, as she thought, his caution, his imperturbability, a certain coldness in his judgment of his fellow men could be an advantage at times—at such a time as now, for instance.

"I must think things over first," she said finally.

He made a gesture of "as you please."

"But be careful!" he warned. When she left him Richard Straight paced the room. Had it merely been Diana who had connected Arnold and that flat, all would have been well. She might have turned to him, and Dick would have had a magnificent chance of winning her enduring love by standing between her brother and the result of whatever it was that he had done.

He had been proud to marry Diana Haslar as things were. . But how long would it take for things to change? It seemed a far cry from Haslar to a Basque anarchist, but that brown and orange check ulster, that snake ring, might yet bring the whole police pack out in full cry after their owner. So Straight feared. It was an intolerable thought, that because Arnold Haslar should have been such an utter fool as to wear them when taking the flat, because he had been such an utter idiot, Diana was to be mixed up in the business, if it ever came out. Why, he too, Richard Straight, might yet be dragged, through them, into the affair.

This idea came like a blow to him. He was as good as engaged to Haslar's sister. He had arrived but a few hours before the crime had been committed. The police said that the man in the flat had been murdered last night. He, Dick, had no alibi for last night. He could tell people that he had been fast asleep from about ten till he was roused next morning, but would they believe it?

Dick did not share Diana's suspicion that possibly it was Newman who had worn her brother's things and taken the flat. Yet it was maddening to think that if only Diana would tell him the whole of what she evidently knew or suspected, about her uncle's secretary, it might be sufficient to free Arnold from all but the blame of a foolish fancy for taking flats under assumed names.

Diana came back into the room.

"Arnold's still asleep. I didn't wake him but I took his ring out of the drawer where he keeps it, and now I'm going to Thornbush. I must speak to Newman again. What's that, Wilkins? Can a gas man come into the room for a moment? Certainly."

They passed a tall, lanky figure with a shock of dark-red hair as they went out. His bag was in their way, so that there was a second's delay as he moved it more hastily than tidily, for half the tools spilled out, and in his very civility to pick them up Pointer blocked the passage still more, and incidentally got two very good photographs. Straight merely looked very worried, very perplexed, and thoughtful, but Diana's face was a travesty of her usual one. Gone was that effect of radiant youth, gone the cool aloofness of her glance. She had recovered a measure of composure, but in her eyes was something desperate, frightened, very nearly cowed. Neither Dick nor Diana spoke on the way to Thornbush, where Diana learnt that Newman had not yet returned. Diana stood a moment thinking deeply, then went on to her own room with a heavy, dragging step. Dick decided that the best thing for him to do would be to try and get some work done.

Outside, a couple of boys—they looked about fourteen—were hunting through the garden. "Sir Raymond Tirrell's nephews," so they had explained to Trimble, had lost a pet dormouse. The little chap, taken for an airing into the garden, had developed an unexpected sprightliness. The tips of his ears had last been seen disappearing through Mr. Julian Clifford's hedge. Might they search the garden? They would be careful of the beds. Sir Raymond was Mr. Clifford's nearest neighbour, so Trimble wished them good luck, and volunteered to keep the cat shut up. The lads must have been very fond of that dormouse. Inch by inch the garden was searched. Two spots where flowers had recently been changed were noted, and reported later on to the two road-menders outside. The boys went off finally with their recaptured pet, so they told a servant.

Pointer meanwhile was looking through some locked drawers in Haslar's study. They yielded nothing of interest to him except some letters of Mrs. Orr's.

Evidently there had been, if there was not now, an engagement between the two. She wrote as though she definitely counted on becoming mistress of the Hampstead house, even though only to have it sold.

Suddenly the telephone bell rang. A servant entered, making towards the instrument at a leisurely gait. But Pointer had reached it at the first tinkle.

"'Alf a tic! It'll be for me. From the boss. Speaking from the head office." He took the receiver and nodded. "It's 'im all right. Yes, sir. This is Mr. 'Aslar's."

"Who's speaking?" called a sharp voice: the voice of a very angry, or a very excited man.

"Me, sir; Long."

"I want your master at once on the 'phone. Is he in?"

"'Alf a mo, sir." Pointer passed a hand over the 'phone. He worked very hard at the trick. Inside the mouthpiece was now another one that blocked it completely so that nothing could pass through to the ears listening at the other end. Nothing showed. The thin rubber mould fitted easily. "It's my boss all right," Pointer turned to the manservant; "wants the foreman." A touch of Pointer's finger and the india-rubber lining to the 'phone disappeared into his palm. "'E's not 'ere now, sir. 'E's out. What number shall I tell 'im to ring up?" was the next best move to asking who was
speaking.

"Westminster 1876? Oh, very good, sir." Pointer heard the receiver slammed down at the other end, and continued, "You'll be at the works, I suppose, sir? And what about those three-quarter fittings? They don't seem to work quite right. Mr. 'Aslar 'ere seems to've made no complaint, but farther down the road the smell is somethink awful. Very good, sir. Yes, sir. At once!" and Pointer turned away.

"I'll send along my mate to go on 'unting for that escape. I must 'urry. The boss is on his 'ind legs." And Pointer made for the nearest telephone outside the house.

Here he rang tip Westminster 1876. He got the number at once. Pointer was a capital mimic, thanks to hard work and lessons from the best mimic on the London music halls. In a hoarse voice, as like Haslar's as he could make it, he wheezed into the tube.

"Just got back with a damned bad cold. Who's at that end?"

"Me!" came in menacing tones.

"Who the devil's 'me'?" croaked the pseudo Haslar.

"Brown!" came in the same tone. "Now do you understand?"

Pointer coughed into the receiver by way of gaining time. He was doing double-quick thinking.

"I'm in a hurry," he croaked finally.

"What do you suppose I'm in? I want to see you at once. _At once_, understand!" Haslar might have been the mysterious "Brown's" slave. "Same place as before."

"I'm damned if I'll come," Pointer retorted.

"Oh, yes, you will!" There was an ugly menace in the voice. "Oh, yes, you will! I know everything. Understand?"

Pointer did not reply.

"Now do you get me? Come at once. Same place as before."

"Can't. Not to the same place," Pointer said doggedly— and truthfully.

"Why not?"

"Dangerous."

"Where, then?" growled the voice at the other end.

"How about the grill-room of the Savoy?" Pointer asked, as a feeler in that hoarse whisper.

"How about the throne room of Buckingham Palace!" came the retort. "I don't think you quite realise what you're in for, my clever young friend. I've got you in a cleft stick. One shift of a finger and you're crushed."

"I suppose you're aware that this is not an automatic exchange?" Haslar's voice asked roughly, thickly. "Either speak sense, or dry up!"

"I'll talk sense fast enough. Now listen. There's a Spanish feeding place off Shaftesbury Avenue. Fuenta Castellana. I'll be there outside the door at seven to the moment. And look here, Haslar, don't keep me waiting. If I got bored I might stroll into that police station near by. Get me?"

"I've a mind to send Newman," Pointer hoarsely confided to the wire.

"You come yourself!" was the retort, "and don't forget your pocket-book. You'll need it, by God! No cheques, mind."

"I shall get Straight to come too."

"What Straight? Run straight yourself!" The facetiousness did not extend to the voice.

"Oh, all right. But I shall be in disguise. Aged man. Two crutches. Look out for me." Pointer did not dare hang up for fear of the Brown at the other end ringing up the real Haslar. He waited till the other had expressed his burning opinion of such monkey tricks, and repeated the injunction to bring a well-filled note-case with him. Pointer made for his own rooms at the Yard, and turned to his book of disguises.

"Old Gentleman—crutches" was Number Fifteen. In a slit of a cupboard numbered fifteen was the complete outer man of what might have been the Chief Inspector's great-grandfather. Pointer's difficulty was to give himself a touch of Haslar as well. Also his disguise had to look like a disguise. The effect was to be that of an amateur at the game. The bushy white eyebrows palpably put on, the Father Christmas beard obviously added.

He finally took a taxi, driven by one of his own men, and got out at the little bit of Spain indicated by the mysterious "voice."

He could almost have smelled his way thither. Gazpacho of true Iberian strength was evidently one of the dishes of the day.

Outside the door four men were waiting. One was thin. The voice over the telephone had not been that of a thin man. One was young. Nor that of a young man. The third, though stout and getting towards middle-age, was obviously Spanish. The man speaking had not been a foreigner. The fourth was —good Heavens! It was Cory! Major Cory of the Holford Will Case. A case fought out some dozen years before, where the major had been accused by the daughter of undue influence in causing old Mrs. Holford to leave every farthing to him and nothing to her only child, a middle-aged spinster. In spite of his expressed sympathy with the prose- cutrix, the judge, as well as the jury, had had to let the major bear off the spoils. Pointer had heard with great joy that they did the man no good. Racing and Monte Carlo had helped to run through the money in a couple of years.

Cory was one of those men in whom our police take an abiding interest. For the Metropolitan Police have still a great deal to learn when it comes to appreciating those who, like certain rare orchids, seem able to live on air.

So Cory had wanted Haslar on the telephone all morning. Cory gave his name as Brown. Cory knew Newman, but did not seem to know Straight. Humph. . . . Pointer tottered out of the taxi and hobbled up to him.

"Here I am, Cory, where shall we go?"

Cory eyed him, as a dog eyes a man before biting.

"Think yourself clever because you're got up like an organ-grinder? Your voice gives you away, Haslar, though. I'd know you anywhere."

"Would you?" Haslar's voice asked in chagrin.

"Anywhere. But now—" The other, who seemed in a very high and mighty mood, steered Pointer to a table in a corner. He ordered a bottle of 1896 port, mentioning gracefully that there was no point in not having the best that the house kept, as Haslar would foot the bill.

"And now look here, Haslar," Cory began, as soon as
they were alone. "I know all! _All_. Get me?" Cory bored a
pair of bold eyes into the old gentleman's. "Now, how
much is it worth to you not to have me—" Suddenly the
"gallant major" stopped, shot one glance at Pointer that
made the latter get his right hand ready, and slipped
with extraordinary swiftness out of the place.

Pointer looked about him. A man, a police officer by
his smart, alert bearing, had entered in company with a
com- panion who looked like a needy artist in search of
copy. The two had taken a table not far from Pointer. The
Detective Inspector wondered whether ever any of his
criminals had more regretted meeting Inspector Bradly
than did he at that moment.

Pointer caught his eye and gave the signal of the
C.I.D. as he threw a match away. Rising, he handed a
bank note to his waiter and said he would be back for the
change in a moment. Bradly strolled after him.

"Mr. Gaskell, I believe?" Bradly said politely, touching
him on the arm, "Mr. Gaskell from Leeds?"

Pointer shook hands with the air of a countryman
over-joyed to see a familiar face in a strange town.

"You saw Cory leaving?" he asked under his breath.

Bradly nodded.

"Saw one of your men after him too, sir. Did I frighten
him away? Too bad! Mr. Tindall wanted to see if he
couldn't find out something down here about a Spaniard
who has been to the mortuary to identify this Etcheverrey
who's just been found killed. Thank Heaven, if I may say
so! He said he couldn't identify him at all. Might be him,
might not. But Mr. Tindall was told that he looked at that
foot as though expecting to find a scar on the sole. Mr.
Tindall thought he might have come on here. So he
might. But 'a tall, slender, dark young man with a big
drooping moustache' would fit a dozen chaps in that very
room. Still, Mr. Tindall asked me to come along and point
out a couple of dagoes who are ready to sell any one to
either side."

"You were in that Holford Case, weren't you, Inspector?" Pointer asked presently.

Bradly nodded. "Yes, sir. Before your time, wasn't it?"

"Ever heard the name of Haslar mentioned in connection with it?"

"Haslar?" Bradly thought hard. "I don't remember that name cropping up."

"Nor Clifford?"

"Oh, Clifford was one of the chief witnesses against Cory. He all but dished him. Mr. Julian Clifford, the great author, I mean. He was a friend of old Mrs. Holford's. He maintained that Cory had stolen a later will and burnt it. Knew the very hour he stole it. But he couldn't prove anything. Though he saw to it that every one knew what he thought, so that there should be no hanging on to clubs or society afterwards for Cory. It did me good to hear him in the witness-box."

Suddenly Bradly clicked his fingers. "Mr. Clifford's nephew! Australian boy. Yes, Haslar was his name. It was in the holidays, and he used to come into court with his uncle, Mr. Clifford, and ask me no end of questions in between whiles."

"You're keeping an eye on Cory, I suppose?"

Bradly said that during the twenty-four hours about sixty police orbs were more or less focused on the major.

"He's evidently up to no good," the police officer went on, "he never is, of course. But I mean that he's evidently up to something he can get into trouble over, or he wouldn't have faded away like that when he saw me. I don't deny that I would give a year's pay to jug him, and he knows it! That poor old Miss Holford in an Institute sticks in my crop."

Pointer let Bradly return to Tindall, and walked off. That telephone message from Brown . . . the whole. tone of Cory's conversation with the supposed Haslar ... a previous grudge against Clifford ... a boy, now a man, who knew of that grudge. ...

Pointer walked on deep in thought, leaving his change for some other time.

Clifford—Haslar—Cory. . . . Linked, though but loosely, by the old crime of the stolen will. Clifford as principal witness, Haslar as a young, eager listener, with the retentive memory of a boy for what interests him, Cory as the accused man. Were these three once more linked closely, for all time, by a new crime, by the most terrible of all crimes?

Pointer returned at once to New Scotland Yard where he learnt several things. No one could be found who had seen any stranger entering or leaving flat fourteen, where, according to the head porter, some silver ornaments had been stolen.

Nothing of any importance had been listened to along either Mrs. Orr's, Clifford's or Haslar's telephones, except his own conversation with "Brown."

The woman detective who had been sent to Mrs. Orr's house reported that that lady had an impeccable bill of health as far as last night went. This morning she had left for Paris by the eleven boat train from Victoria, and Mrs. Clifford had been among the little group of friends to see her off.

Inspector Watts sent in word that no packages of any kind had been delivered at Wellwyn and Co.'s warehouse in Thames Street after closing time yesterday, until a vanload of wireless masts had arrived this morning about ten. Detective-Inspector Watts had been assured that no mistake was possible.

Finally came the account of a very pretty bit of wizardry that had been performed in the office of the house-agent while the Chief Inspector had been finishing his investigations among Haslar's effects. Arnold Haslar's voice had been reeled off by a tiny microphone phonograph which had been in the gas man's bag. The house-agent had identified the "What the devil are you doing with my clothes?" as undoubtedly the voice of Monsieur Tourcoin, who had taken Marshall's furnished flat on Friday last. The same performance had obtained the same result from the head porter. So Tourcoin was now fairly well proved to be Arnold Haslar. Was it quite true that no packages whatever had been left at the warehouse? There could be no question of a "burglary" there. Every building in that street had its night watchman. Pointer's ruminations were interrupted by still another piece of information. It was from the man who was trailing Cory. The wily major had taken a bus to some flats, had walked up to the third floor, had shot down in a lift for one storey, and there caught another on its way to the roof garden, while Pointer's man was covering the door nearest to the first shaft. After the roof garden all trace of Cory was lost.

Pointer had given his man very strict instructions to lose him rather than let him see that he was followed. He did not want the major to leave London. The police had half a dozen funk-holes of his on their list, to one of which he was sure to return once he believed that no one was trailing him.

CHAPTER SIX

It was eight o'clock. Pointer began to think that he might waste a few minutes of the case's time in eating a dinner, when a message that reached him along his telephone wire whisked that prospect away once more.

"Is that Chief Inspector Pointer? Police-Constable Caldicott speaking. Acting in accordance with instructions received at the station, I am reporting directly to you, sir, that Mr. Haslar has just been murdered."

Pointer's lips tightened. He had not expected this. Yet, at the same time—

"I was called in by the butler at four minutes past eight, sir. Just two minutes ago"—P.-C. Caldicott was evidently an accurate young man—"Mr. Haslar was shot in his study. Don't know yet how it happened, sir."

It was not many minutes later when Pointer was hurrying with the speaker up the winding drive.

"Left a man in the house, I hope?" the Chief Inspector asked.

"Yes, sir. P.-C. Bacon. I whistled for him at once."

Bacon stood in the hall waiting for them. The servants were evidently battened down below hatches.

"Mr. Haslar isn't quite dead, sir, as we thought at first. The doctor found some signs of life. He insisted on having him carried to his bedroom."

Pointer ran upstairs, and with one constable went thoroughly, but swiftly, over the house and through the garden. No one was in hiding. Then the Chief Inspector turned the handle of Haslar's room very gently.

A young man looked up as he entered without a sound.

"Medical man?"

Pointer laid his card on the table.

"You'll have to be quick, Chief Inspector," the doctor whispered. "We've just sent for Sir Hercules Hawkins. Not that he can do anything. Bullet went in here and is still in." He pointed to a spot just above the right ear. The injured man lay on a table pulled between the windows. Sheets had been spread on it, sheets covered him. Pointer did not waste more than one long look at the head and face. The doctor had cleaned the wound too carefully for him.

"Singed hair?" he asked.

"Singed hair and blackened skin," the doctor assured him. "Revolver must have been fired pressed against the head."

"No hope of his speaking?" Pointer asked.

The doctor shook his head.

"I don't say that for some brief moment consciousness may not come back. It often does just before the end. The final flicker. But that's the merest chance. Ah, here's Sir Hercules, with a couple of nurses!"

A gray-haired man entered hurriedly. Pointer slipped from the room as silently as he had entered it.

"Who's he?" the surgeon muttered; "splendid-looking chap! Knows how to put his feet down. Boxes, I'll bet."

Downstairs Pointer went into the study, the room where the injured man had been found. He stood with his back to the door closely eyeing the whole before he took a step forward.

Suddenly he heard the front door open. Stepping into the hall, he saw Diana come hurrying in. Straight was with her.

Both stopped appalled as they caught sight of the constable who rose from his seat in the hall. Diana's face, already pale, grew ghastly. Then she saw Pointer at the study door. She took a step towards him. Something in its swift motion suggested the pathetic effort of a mother-bird between her nest and a robber. She knew at once that this man with the sun-browned face and the steady, very clear, gray eyes was in command. As she looked at him, she felt a sudden sense of his power, of his ability to surmount difficulties that would stop a smaller man. And with that sense came a sickening knowledge of her brother's danger.

"Miss Haslar? I am Chief Inspector Pointer of New Scotland Yard. Can I have a word with you in the next room? This gentleman is—?" He eyed Straight as though he had never seen him.

"Mr. Straight. My uncle's secretary," Diana said swiftly. "He merely accompanied me to the house when I could not make out a telephone message just now. But please don't wait." She turned to Dick very resolutely. She did not intend to involve him in her brother's disgrace, for she feared that an arrest had been made.

His answer was to open a door. The three stepped in.

"What is wrong?" Diana asked in a toneless voice.

Something in the grave kindness of the face looking at her frightened her more than any words would have done. She read Pointer's look rightly as profound pity. Pity for this young life caught up into the swirl of dark passions, she who should have been a creature of sunshine and happiness. Somehow, Pointer felt that so far the lines had not fallen unto Diana in very pleasant places.

"Miss Haslar," Pointer broke the painful silence, "your brother has met with an accident. The doctor and a surgeon are with him upstairs. He has been shot in the head."

"Shot!" Diana wheeled. She made for the door, but Pointer stopped her.

"No one is allowed to enter his room. They are trying to extricate the bullet."

"He's not dead?"

"Not when I was there a moment before the surgeon came. He's very badly wounded, but he was not dead."

"Who shot him?" Diana asked, putting out a hand and grasping the back of a chair. Whom did she suspect? The dread in her eyes told the keen eyes that barely seemed to glance at her that she suspected some one.

"I know nothing about the case yet," Pointer said quietly. "You probably can tell me who was Mr. Haslar's enemy?"

"He has no enemy. No open enemy," Diana said slowly.

"A so-called friend, then," Pointer said swiftly. He hoped to get some name out of her in her agitation. But she only turned away with a weary, yet resolute, gesture.

"He has a host of friends whom I don't know."

Pointer glanced inquiringly at Straight, who promptly passed the look on to Diana. But she met his eyes stonily.

"Who sent for you?" Pointer asked, after a pause.

"I don't know. A telephone message just reached me at my uncle's, Mr. Julian Clifford's house, saying that something had happened to Mr. Haslar. I couldn't make out what."

She had not tried to. She had guessed an arrest, not a fresh crime. Whose crime?

"If you and Mr. Straight could wait for me in the, drawing-room, I should like to come on up in a few minutes, and ask some questions," Pointer went on.

She looked at him like a creature caught in a snare. Then she nodded, and followed by Dick mounted the stairs as Tindall arrived hot-foot. The Chief Inspector had telephoned him the news before starting out

Tindall, like Pointer, looked keenly about him. There was no sign of a struggle except that one chair had been pushed violently back against the table behind it—a chair on the farther side of the big writing table which only a couple of hours ago had been the object of Pointer's own interest.

The Chief Inspector opened the door and said a word to the constable. A moment later and Wilkins came in. He looked what he was, a dependable, honest man. He was pale now and trembling.

"Who telephoned to Miss Haslar?"

"I did, sir. Just before you arrived. Or rather I got the constable to telephone her something guarded."

"Where did you find your master's body? I see. You heard no shot?"

Wilkins' face twitched. His eyes filled.

"No, sir. But of course with the noise that cars make nowadays, one bang more or less—" Wilkins waggled a shaking hand helplessly. "I've been in service here since Mr. Arnold was a boy at school, and to think that I sat reading the paper! To think that not one of us downstairs raised a hand to help him! Just up from a sick-bed too!" Wilkins quite broke down for a minute or two.

"And Mr. Haslar—was he tidy? careful about cigarette ends, matches, and so on?" Pointer asked to steady him.

"Remarkably so, as a rule, sir."

"Who are Mr. Haslar's enemies?" Tindall asked suddenly.

"Why, he hasn't any, sir." Wilkins spoke with dignity. "Why should he have? At least, he's none in England. I can't, of course, speak for Australia."

That was all that was wanted of Wilkins for the moment. As soon as the door closed behind him, Tindall wheeled.

"So Haslar was remarkably neat and tidy, eh? Just so. And I thought you hadn't yet seen that burnt paper under the desk, while— Hallo!"

Pointer had lifted the flounce of a chair cover and both men now saw a revolver lying under the seat near an open window. Holding it in place with one gloved finger, the Chief Inspector ran a chalk outline around it. Then he lifted it with the greatest care. It was a .25 automatic. From some faint marks in the barrel, Tindall thought that a very light silencer might have been used. They found no finger-prints on the metal. Two shots had been fired.

"Two shots!" Both men looked carefully around the room again. They found no bullet or blood spatters.

"Went wide, probably out through that window, or the other man has the bullet. Carried it away in his body, though that's unlikely, as there's no blood trail. Look here"—Tindall was down on his knees—"that revolver was flung. Flung so as to look as though the murderer had got out into the garden." He pointed to a long streak on the polish of the parquet floor which had stopped at the little snub-nosed thing Pointer was now wrapping in tinfoil.

"It wouldn't have been flung here, from where Haslar was found lying. That disposes of any idea of suicide. Besides, two shots were fired from it. No. Haslar must have fired the first at his opponent, and then had the revolver wrenched from his hand and got the second in his own head, practically killing him. That done, the murderer stepped away from the falling body, and flung the revolver towards the window from about here." Tindall stood "here." "And then left, either by the front door or by the other window. I believe there's a connection between this murder and Julian Clifford's. Uncle and nephew. What do you say, Chief Inspector?"

"A connection? Oh, yes; I, too, think there may be one. Probably a close one."

Tindall joined Pointer, who, after strolling around the room again, touching this, feeling that, even testing the earth around a palm, and lifting the pot up and down in its brass jardiniere, was now bending over a small heap of charred remains of paper which lay under the desk, a match among them. Both stood up after a long scrutiny. Not even the magic of modern science could reconstruct that black dust.

"Some one ground it into the carpet after burning it," Tindall murmured.

"Haslar. His right heel shows it. I looked at his shoes upstairs," Pointer replied. He was down on his knees minutely examining the carpet in front of the pushed-back chair, running a tiny but very powerful vacuum cleaner over it. The gadget was barely the size of his hand, but it did its work well.

Tindall watched him with secret impatience.

"The eyes of the mind, Chief Inspector, are the ones that see farthest. As soon as you've done sweeping, I'd like to question the servants again."

"By all means." Pointer put the little patent back in his case. They called the butler in again and then the valet. The rest of the servants knew nothing.

At half-past six this afternoon Arnold Haslar had rung: said he was fed up with bed, and intended to get up. He was in a very grim mood; but he had been tending that way for a fortnight past, both men agreed.

The butler thought it was due to the coming attack of the 'flu, but the butler, under Tindall's careful pressure, was inclined to connect it with the arrival of a couple of letters by this morning's post. Wilkins had a nephew who collected stamps, and he therefore kept an eye on envelopes from abroad. One of the letters, in a very odd, bold writing, had come from Spain. He had not noticed the other.

"Spain!" Tindall cocked an eye at Pointer. "What place in Spain?"

But Wilkins could not say. The butler connected that Spanish letter with Mr. Haslar's illness because, after breakfast, he had found a letter scattered over the table and floor, torn into tiny shreds, and his master sitting as though stunned beside the table. He had had to be helped into bed, and the doctor summoned. No. The butler had not spoken of this to any one, not even to Miss Diana. He had "thought it better not." The later letters which had come from Mr. Haslar today had been sent down to the office.

The valet had more to tell. About seven, after saying that he would dine out, Mr. Haslar had gone downstairs. About half-past, or perhaps a quarter to eight, he could not be more exact, Smith had heard his master's voice in the north library, which was his own study, raised as though in anger. The words, "You've got to do it, and do it at once!" reached Smith, but he was too far up the stairs to catch anything but that one passionate roar. On that had come what he, as well as Wilkins below, had believed to be a motor-cycle starting up its engine outside with a set of terrific bangs. A few minutes later, Wilkins, coming into the library to see if all was well with his young master, found him slipped to the floor by his writing-table chair apparently dead, a little red wound still trickling blood above his ear. No one had seen or heard any one enter or leave the house. But Haslar's friends generally let themselves in and out with careless ease. The latch of the front door was caught back by day. Questioned as to strangers who had been to the house lately, Major Cory's photograph, among six others, was picked out unhesitatingly by Wilkins as that of a man who, giving no name, had first come to see Arnold Haslar last Thursday evening. He had come on Friday, and also last night, and had then for the first time given the name of Captain Brown. Wilkins' eyes met those of the Chief Inspector and the man from the Foreign Office with a certain dignity.

"I'm telling you the exact truth, sir. Things can't be worse"—which incidentally spoke volumes for Wilkins' idea of the police.

The man had arrived each time at about the same hour on Thursday and Friday and yesterday. Somewhere around nine. Questioned closely, Wilkins said that there had been no signs of any trouble between his master and the man whose photograph he had identified, but he had noticed that on no occasion had Mr. Haslar offered to shake hands with his visitor, who had stayed over an hour on the first two occasions, though but a bare half-hour last night. On the first occasion, at any rate, the conversation must have been of a very private character, because he, Wilkins, had had some business that took him to the library at the same time, and had only caught a low murmur.

"A very unusual thing with Mr. Arnold Haslar talking in his study, sir. As a rule, you have to hear every word, whether you want to or not. It and the library are really only one room, partitioned off."

Pointer referred to some coolness between Mr. Haslar and his uncle, Mr. Julian Clifford. But obviously the butler knew nothing of any such feeling.

Both he and Smith unhesitatingly identified the automatic found by the window as Mr. Haslar's. More important still, the valet swore that it had been in its usual place when his master was having his bath. He had opened the drawer to drop a penknife into it. Smith had an idea that he had heard Mr. Haslar come up and go into his bedroom while he, the valet, was tidying up in the dressing-room. He must have taken the weapon then. As far as Smith knew, Mr. Haslar had never taken the automatic downstairs before.

"So Mr. Haslar expected trouble," Tindall mused. "Knew when it was coming, and got ready for it. Was he a good shot?"

"He was apt to get over-eager, and spoil his aim." And just out of bed, he, Smith, wouldn't be surprised if his master had missed the man entirely, worse luck. Smith knew nothing about any caller last night, but he did know that about ten Mr. Haslar had driven off in a great hurry, telling Wilkins not to let any one sit up, as he would not be back till very late. Smith had an idea, only an idea, that Mr. Haslar had rushed off in answer to a telephone message that had seemed to vex him very much.

"Any one in the house who knows more than you and Wilkins do?" Tindall asked, pulling on a glove.

"No. None of us knows anything really. It's tough! . . . not knowing . . . not being able to do something." And Smith left them.

"Strange case!" Tindall mused; "strange and deep. Etcheverrey like a spider in the middle of the web. I wonder what Sir Edward Clifford will say. He must be back by now. It's close on nine. There's the devil of a lot to do. To bridge the gap between Clifford and Haslar, and link both with Etcheverrey!"

Caldicott, the constable, came in.

"Gentleman of the name of Dance to see you, sir. Mr. Haslar's manager. Said you just telephoned him."

Pointer had.

Dance was a stout, frank-faced man with a strong Australian accent. He was considerably older than Haslar. Just now he looked consternation personified. He was of no help, except that he scoffed at the idea of a business enemy of Arnold Haslar's.

"This has nothing to do with business," he maintained. "Search for the dame! Fortunately at the office Haslar's supposed to be still ill with 'flu. He'll stay ill with it too. We're a good firm. A darned good firm. But shootings—whew!"

"There's a strong-room built into one end of this study," Pointer said finally, "would you open it for us? I want to see inside it." He did—very much indeed.

Dance hesitated.

"You know the code word?"

"Oh, yes, I know it. But"

"The butler told me Mr. Haslar keeps no valuables on the place."

"That's right. Still, you see, after all, a code word"

Pointer and Tindall stood with their backs to Mr. Dance who, even so, held his hat over what he was doing. Finally he called to them.

"Door's open."

The opening showed a fairly large strong-room, large as a big cupboard. Dance glanced at the shelves, on which dusty deed boxes were stacked.

"Nothing's gone. Haslar keeps six-year-back accounts, and papers, and so on, here. Like his grand-dad. The boxes are unlocked. There's nothing else in them."

Pointer found that there was nothing else in them. He looked very, very carefully. So did Tindall, catching his idea.

"And about a package," Pointer went on, after the door had been locked with the same coyness on Mr. Dance's part, "a package that Mr. Haslar, or a friend of his, sent, or brought down, to the warehouse late last night"—Pointer ran over the possible times and sizes— "will you inquire for it and send it along to me?" He gave his name and home address, for Pointer believed that Watts might have been deceived. "We think it will help us, give us a line about this affair. I should expect the parcel to be marked 'to be kept in a cold place.' You haven't a furnace, have you?"

To his relief he learnt that the warehouse was only a between-station for electrical parts and material on its way to or from Australia. There was no furnace.

Mr. Dance would obviously have liked a fuller explanation of many puzzling points, but this was a very busy evening with him, and as all Pointer's hours came under that heading, the meeting quickly broke up. Tindall too shook hands and hurried off.

Pointer looked at his boot-tips for a long second. Then he had Smith in again, and offered him a cigar and a chair.

"There's a confidential question I want to put to you," he said slowly. He waited.

"Confidential it is," the ex-Anzac said cheerfully.

"What was the quarrel about between your master and Mr. Clifford?"

"Mr. Clifford?" For a second Smith stared as a man does who is suddenly, unexpectedly, wrenched around to face another way. Then he looked a little dubious.

"Though you may not see the connection, that quarrel may give us a line on who it was who shot Mr. Haslar," Pointer said very quietly.

Smith eyed him with respect.

"That so?" He straddled his chair and clasped the carved back in a meditative embrace. "That so," he repeated thoughtfully. "Well, I don't know what it was about, but it was a pretty hot affair. You're referring to last Wednesday evening, of course?"

Pointer nodded.

"You didn't hear anything?"

"Nope. I never was much of a listener-in," Smith said carelessly, and Pointer regretfully believed him. He did not look it.

"Only as Mr. Haslar flung the door open he nearly caught my toe, and I had to step back to let Mr. Clifford pass out. Mr. Clifford looked very calm, I must say. Quite unruffled. But Mr. Haslar called after him, 'If you do do it, look out for yourself!' That's all. Not much of a clue there, is there? But it's funny"—Smith sat up straighter—"it's funny that then he threatened 'If you do do it,' and to-day he was shouting that 'You've got to do it!' " He looked keenly at Pointer, who shook his head.

"No, Smith. It wasn't to Mr. Julian Clifford that he spoke to-day. I wish it had been," he added cryptically.

Smith got up rather sheepishly. "Of course, sleuthing can't be as easy as that, I suppose. And, of course, Mr. Julian Clifford had nothing to do with any shooting."

He went away to make other and more startling combinations yet, of the two sentences, while Pointer went up to the drawing-room where Diana and Straight sat waiting for him.

Straight looked as though he very much wished himself well out of it all. Murders, or shootings, were not at all what he had expected when he had landed in Portsmouth only yesterday as Julian Clifford's librarian. Straight felt that he had a grievance against fate. Here he was, a plain, common-sense sort of young man, only desirous of doing well in the world, of getting on, being drawn into a very black, deep, and dangerous affair. What was the reason for that bullet which had all but killed Arnold Haslar?

"You have no idea who fired that shot at Haslar?" he had just asked Diana.

She only stirred as though in pain.

What did Arnold know? Had he learnt something? Did he guess something? Was it because of some incautiously shown curiosity that—these were the knives at which she was staring, wondering which of them was about to be plunged in her heart.

The door opened and Pointer came in.

"Did you ever hear your brother speak of a man of the name of Cory?"

She shook her head. Straight, too, shook his when Pointer turned to him.

"And you, Mr. Straight, have you by any chance ever heard Mr. Haslar speak as though there were any especial person with whom he is on bad terms?" Straight never had.

Pointer next ostensibly asked each about the other persons at Thornbush this afternoon. In reality he was obtaining from Diana and Straight a time-table of their own actions. They were simple. When Wilkins had telephoned to Diana they had ostensibly been having tea together. In reality Dick had had the tea, and tried in vain to coax Diana to have some.

After another careful glance in every room, Pointer drove away from the house to stop and question his watcher at the corner—a taxi-driver with a cab that would not go, tinker though he might.

The man had seen no one enter, or leave, Arnold Haslar'?. house, but he was not a picked man. The coming royal visitor kept every good man busy combing through the aliens' quarters of London. Also, nothing is harder than to watch a place for hours on end. Especially if, like this man, he had to pretend to attend to other interests as well. Doubtless he had done his best, yet Pointer knew that at least one person—a man probably—had come, and therefore gone, from Arnold Haslar's house. This person had left a plentiful sprinkling of yellow sand on the carpet in front of that dashed-back chair. Now the paths in Haslar's garden were gravelled with red gravel. The roads and pavements around showed only the usual town dust. At Thornbush, however, the paths were all of yellow sand, rolled for the most part into compact ribbons. But one little walk, cutting off a corner of the drive—a corner that shortened the distance to Haslar's house too, was freshly sanded, and soft as a country lane. It looked, therefore, as though a person from Thornbush had been the man —or woman—who had pushed back that chair.

Diana and Straight had been in each other's company. They were out of the question. Mrs. Clifford was at a Spiritualist meeting. Hobbs was located in the Ritz dining with some South American film magnate. There remained Newman. . . . Newman . . . Pointer had a theory of what had happened in that study. But his theories were always subject to modification, should facts not fit them without having to be twisted. Had Major Cory, after he had given his trailer the slip, made his way to Haslar's house? Pointer thought that he had.

He himself drove to Thornbush and stopped in the garden. In his hand was what appeared to be a stereoscopic camera. It was an uncommonly good binocular. He chose a position against a plane tree and donned dark gray gloves. His cuffs, too, were tucked well up out of sight. A casual eye from the house could hardly notice him at this hour of gloaming against the snake markings of the trunk, as he carefully studied a certain open window facing him.

Newman was bending over a well-lit table on which a paper sprawled, by its ungainly size an English paper. He was reading it avidly. Pointer recognised a picture in it. Newman was reading an account of the "Heath Mansions Mystery," as it was now called. A moment, and he had tossed it to the floor and spread out another from a pile beside him. Suddenly he stopped, turned his head towards the door, and called cheerily, "Come in!" Pointer could hear his voice easily through the open window. As he called, Newman, working with noiseless speed, shoved the several papers into a drawer of his writing table with an amazing stealth. Not a crackle reached Pointer; not a crackle could reach the door of the room.

Newman now called, "Oh, is it locked?" in a tone of great surprise, closing the drawer. All without any noise. Then with an "I'm so sorry, I'd no idea!" he strode to the door. A servant entered. Pointer went around to the front and rang the bell.

He sent in his name as Pointer, without prefixing his position. Newman saw him at once. Pointer introduced himself to him as of Scotland Yard.

"I've come about the accident to Mr. Haslar," he began.

"Accident?" Newman started, or seemed to.

"He was shot at close range just about the time you dropped in to see him this evening."

"Do you mind telling me what happened?" Newman asked coolly, but his lips had a white line around them.

Pointer told him the bare facts.

Newman sat with his head leaning on one hand. He had an unusual power of absolute immobility.

"Miss Haslar must be in great trouble," Newman said, when Pointer had finished.

"She's not so much in trouble as she's keen on getting the man who shot her brother. She thinks he was shot, you see."

"Don't you?"

"Not necessarily. Haslar might have meant to commit suicide. Might have all but succeeded," Pointer said, apparently not looking at the man.

Newman's hand gave a little quiver before it steadied again.

"Why should he do that?" he asked without raising his head.

"Ah, why! Can't you suggest anything?" Pointer asked. "You were the last person seen with Mr. Haslar."

"Was I indeed?" Newman seemed lost in thought. "No, I can suggest nothing."

"What time exactly did you see him?" Pointer went on.

"Somewhere around seven, or a little after."

"Did you see any one coming or going to the house?"

"No one."

Newman did not mention that he had called earlier and had been refused permission by Diana to speak to Arnold.

"How about some one having shot him who has a grudge against him? A man of the name of Cory, for instance?" Pointer suggested idly.

"Cory!" Newman repeated reflectively. "I seem to've heard the name before. But where"

Newman was no fool; Pointer had not thought him one.

"And you think this same Cory—?" Newman queried, as one at sea.

"One or two things were told us that show that he had a grudge against Mr. Haslar. That he felt that he had been drawn into something," Pointer said vaguely. As a boxer, he watched always the feet of the person to whom he spoke. Newman moved no part of his body above the table, but his feet shifted now.

"According to what was told us," Pointer went on in his quiet, ruminative way, "this Major Cory was acting for Mr. Haslar in some way."

"Indeed!" Newman looked politely interested, but no more.

Pointer rose. He had met a wall. For the moment he thought it best to retire. It would be sheer waste of time to ask this man of what he and Haslar had talked, or why he had called on him.

At the nearest telephone he learnt that a message had just reached the Yard asking the Chief Inspector to come to Sir Edward Clifford as soon as possible. He also listened for a minute to the report from one of his men concerning the same gentleman. Then he hurried off in his swift gray car.

CHAPTER SEVEN

It was close on ten when Pointer was shown into the room where Sir Edward sat talking in low tones to Tindall. The Chief Inspector found a man who, under his surface calm, looked as though he had had a tremendous shock.

For the rest, Sir Edward was a typical diplomat in appearance. That is to say, a man who kept his real self completely out of sight. Urbane, courteous, non-committal, he was a pleasant talker who could speak for hours without betraying one private opinion—a man who never made a positive statement in public in his life.

Pointer's police glance sought the man behind the arras. He seemed to see a gentle and affectionate nature with a strong sense of duty, of right and wrong—not a man of hot blood, nor one given to swift action. Tindall was with Clifford. He had been waiting for Pointer.

"Sir Edward has a very striking theory," the F.O. man began, as soon as Pointer had sat down. "He thinks that though Etcheverrey would not commit an ordinary murder, yet he might if he thought he was being spied on, or if, even more, Mr. Clifford had ever—say for some literary purpose in the future—got into his organisation in some way. You see? You remember that while the Cliffords were at St. Jean de Luz two years ago, Etcheverrey's name was in every paper?"

Pointer nodded. The anti-royalist Basque had given a sort of free pardon to the ex-Empress Zita through the press. And the effrontery of it had amused, or infuriated, the whole of Europe.

"You think Mr. Clifford had some such literary interest in Etcheverrey?" Pointer asked.

"I do"—Sir Edward spoke heavily—"I do. I have for some time past had a very definite idea that my brother was revolving the idea of using Etcheverrey as material, and in the near future."

"Suppose Mr. Clifford had probed deeper than we know?" Tindall struck in. "He had practically unlimited money, a most inquiring brain, invincible courage, or he wouldn't have gone on a whaler as he did once, as one of the crew, too. Suppose he had actually joined some band of Etcheverrey's agents, and been discovered? Betrayed himself in some way, and been murdered; or, as Etcheverrey would consider it, executed. Beheading is the method of execution among the Basques, you know."

Pointer said nothing, he merely listened with close attention.

"And as to Haslar," Tindall went on, "Haslar may have been a go-between between Etcheverrey and Clifford."

"And Major Cory?"

"Also a member of the band, I think," Tindall said slowly.

"Possibly he learnt that Haslar was weakening, might give the show away, and shot him."

Pointer smoked on in silence.

"How do _you_ account for Cory?" Tindall asked, with a touch of impatience.

"You F.O. men always want so much for your money," Pointer quoted gravely under his breath, though Clifford was obviously not listening.

"You're working on another line?"

"I intend to to-morrow. We were only called to Heath Mansions this morning. To-morrow will see a big step forward, or all the signs deceive me. I don't think this is a case that can stand still. There's hurry in it, to my thinking. Did Mr. Clifford ever say anything to you, Sir Edward, on which you base your idea of his being particularly interested in Etcheverrey?"

Sir Edward roused himself from a deep reverie which was too deep for Pointer's taste. Men do not usually go off into brown studies when their own theory of their brother's murder is being discussed.

"My brother Julian never referred to Etcheverrey at Thornbush as if he had any personal knowledge of him. Though he seemed, I often thought, amazingly well up in his life story. But then, my brother was well up in so many things." Clifford spoke in a voice of deep regret.

"Who beside Mr. Clifford referred to Etcheverrey at Thornbush?" Pointer asked. "Can you remember any one else who ever questioned you about him?"

"No one but Miss Haslar; and she merely because as a girl she had heard a good deal of him during the war, when she once spent a summer at Hendaye."

There was a short silence.

Tindall rose and took a sympathetic leave. He had many new lines now to follow up. Pointer went with him into the street, and stood a second beside his car.

"How did Sir Edward take the sight of the body in the mortuary? Did he identify.it?"

"It was a frightful shock to him. Naturally."

"He recognised the body quite definitely?"

"He did. Quite definitely."

"Did he recognise it quickly?" Pointer persisted.

Tindall pulled at his beard.

"I pretty well insisted at the Commissioner's on being the one to break the news of Julian Clifford's end to Sir Edward, and on taking him to the mortuary afterwards. . .."

Pointer nodded.

"So I think I owe you the truth. I don't think Edward Clifford particularly wanted to identify that body. I think he wanted to be not quite sure. Natural perhaps. It's a horrible end to the brother you've been good friends with all your life. At any rate, he seemed unable, or unwilling, to be certain that it was the body of Julian Clifford, since the head was missing. But I remembered something he

had told me himself apropos of one of my boys hurting
himself while diving, that Julian had pierced his foot with
a stake once while treading water. I showed him that
scar. Either that clinched it, or that decided him to
recognise the body. I'm frank with you."

There was a short pause.

"You may not have been the one after all who broke
the news of Mr. Julian Clifford's terrible end to Sir
Edward Clifford," Pointer said in his turn. "Perhaps Mr.
Hobbs did that. At any rate, Mr. Clifford's literary agent
was followed into the train at Surbiton, the same train
that brought Sir Edward up to town. He travelled up with
him in the same compartment. They had it to themselves.
That means a long talk. At Waterloo, Mr. Hobbs hurried
back to Thornbush without a word or glance at Sir
Edward, who got out of the train more slowly. By the
way, Sir Edward wasn't apparently expecting any one at
Surbiton. He was buried in a pile of papers, so my man
says."

"Hobbs! but surely you don't suspect—but I suppose
like a good Scotland Yard man you suspect every one!"
Tindall was rather bored by such zeal.

"Whatever it was that brought Hobbs flying down to
meet Edward Clifford has nothing to do with
Etcheverrey, therefore nothing to do with me." He went
on "I happen to know that Hobbs hadn't even heard of the
man's name, except as Sir Edward talked about him at
Thornbush. Of course all of us at the F.O. are full of
nothing else these days. No, what brought Hobbs would
only be some family worry. Or"— he stopped a moment—
"I wonder! Hobbs hinted once to me, not so long ago
either, what one might call his suspicions as to Clifford's
reasons for leaving home every now and then. But Hobbs
had had a glass too much, and I thought nothing of it. But
it's possible that he really thinks Clifford is mixed up in
some scandal. Or may be mixed up in some. And that
would exactly explain Edward Clifford's manner by the
coffin. He didn't want to rush things. He wants time to

think them over. He does, you know. 'Slow and sure' is said to be his motto. But it's not mine!" And Tindall jumped into a taxi.

Pointer was shown in again.

"When you spoke to Mr. Clifford of Etcheverrey, was any other person present?" Pointer asked after a sympathetic pause.

"Certainly. I often spoke of him when all the Thornbush household was there. And this last time— after dinner yesterday—only yesterday!" His voice shook.

"Who was there then?".

"The whole Thornbush household."

"Did you ever speak of Etcheverrey's diagram-signature, or of the name of his refuge in the Pyrenees?"

"Certainly not."

"Do you think Mr. Clifford knew of it?"

"That I cannot say." Sir Edward seemed to be thinking back. "Tindall has told you, I suppose, of my general impression of my brother being much more up in the facts of Etcheverrey's activities than I should have expected. A word or two here and there—I did not notice them at the time— but by them, and by the questions which he did not ask, I now feel sure that he knew more than one would have expected him to."

"Now about Mr. Clifford's will," Pointer went on, "do you know if he had made one? And if so, where he kept it?"

"He made a will only a couple of years ago. It's at Thornbush. A copy is at his bank, I believe."

"I'd like to see that will. If possible I'd like to have a look at it to-night. My car is outside, may I drive you to Thornbush?"

Sir Edward hesitated.

"It's a terrible position—to know what I know and— However, I believe she is out to-night. Yes, I know she is."

"She?"

"Mrs. Clifford, of course. You shall see the will, Chief Inspector, if it's still there and still addressed to me, and if I can get it without letting Mrs. Clifford know. I understand that she has no idea"

"We've told her nothing," was the guarded reply.

"The shock may kill her. She and my brother were a most devoted couple." He led the way out.

"Have you any idea as to the contents of Mr. Clifford's will?" Pointer asked, when they were off.

"He read it to me. If it's still the one which he made two years ago, as I think it is, I'm sole executor and residuary legatee. There are a few legacies to relatives; ten thousand to Hobbs; nothing to Mrs. Clifford, at her express desire."

"I've been wondering," Pointer said, "whether Mr. Clifford had any unexpected valuables on him. Any large sum of money. ...",

Sir Edward seemed to sit rather still for a second. Pointer felt as though in some way he had given the other a jar.

"My brother never mentioned such a thing to me," he said finally, with his eyes now intently fixed on the Chief Inspector.

"Can you hazard a guess as to any dangerous thing that Mr. Clifford wis on the eve of doing?" Pointer went on.

"You mean those words of the palmist's—though it's hardly fair to call Mrs. Jansen that. I think Julian referred to something connected with Etcheverrey. Obviously, one might even say."

"I'm always rather distrustful of the obvious," Pointer said quietly. "You didn't see Mr. Clifford yesterday after dinner?"

"No, I left Thornbush about nine and went to my rooms here, where I changed, and drove down to my cottage at Weybridge. The wood pigeons needed thinning out if any of my blue peas were to be saved."

Now Pointer was a country boy. The gun taken, the cartridges chosen, were such as a man would choose for this purpose. But, as a rule, wood pigeons come and go between the hours of five and nine of a July evening.

"Did you shoot many?" he asked carelessly.

"You mean this afternoon? I forgot to take my long-distance glasses down with me. I'm as blind as a bat a couple of yards off. So, though I blazed away for half an hour or so, I only succeeded in hitting one of my own decoys."

"But did you meet any friends at your cottage, Sir Edward?" Pointer did not disguise the fact that he wis questioning the other, asking for his alibi.

Sir Edward did not seem to notice what he must have known lay behind the questions.

"No, I never take friends down with me to Weybridge. I only go to my cottage when I want to be alone. Driving down a tyre burst. I had no spare wheel. By jogging along slowly I crawled to the cottage on the rim, getting to Weybridge nearer one than ten. I slipped in without waking my housekeeper or her husband, who acts as my butler-valet. Everything I need is always put up ready for me in the dining-room. Cold supper, electric kettle. So, as so often before, I went to bed without any one in the house being the wiser, after leaving a note on the hall table telling them at what hour to serve breakfast."

"And the car?"

"My chauffeur put on a new wheel."

They drew up at Thornbush. Sir Edward Clifford rang the bell. Mrs. Clifford was out, he was told, with Mr. Hobbs. Mr. Newman was out too; so was Mr. Straight.

"That's all right, Trimble. I shall be in Mr. Clifford's library with this gentleman." Sir Edward led Pointer quickly into the room and tried a drawer. It was unlocked. From the back he drew a sealed envelope addressed to himself. It was marked "The Last Will and Testament of me, Julian Clifford."

"You think I had better open it?"

Pointer looked the envelope over with his glass. It had not been tampered with. He handed it back.

"Please."

Again a quiver passed over Sir Edward's face. It looked like intense emotion as he read the address to himself. In other words, it was just the look that a clever man would assume at such a moment. And Sir Edward was considered clever in a quiet way. He glanced it over. "This is a new will. Made only some six months ago. I'm still the sole executor and residuary legatee, but the bequest of ten thousand which my brother told me he was leaving to Hobbs is halved. Five thousand goes to Newman. And only five thousand to Hobbs. To Newman 'if still unmarried' is the wording. A thousand pounds he asks Mrs. Clifford to distribute among the servants as she thinks fit. He adds, after some very moving words of gratitude to her, that he leaves her nothing at her express wish, as she strongly objects to inheriting anything from him on his death, and is otherwise amply provided for."

He handed the will to Pointer, who read it through.

So Sir Edward was his brother's heir. And both he and the dead man were believed to have loved the same woman, a woman whom her husband's death would set free. . . .

Pointer did not suspect Sir Edward Clifford, but no position, however worthily won, no reputation for personal integrity, could undo these facts.

"Five thousand seems a lot for Mr. Newman," was his only comment.

"Umm. ... I don't suppose Julian ever expected it would be handed over. There's not so much difference between them in years, you know."

"There was no ill-will between Mr. Clifford and Mr. Hobbs, you think?"

"None whatever. Simply Julian knew that Hobbs is doing uncommonly well out of his literary commissions, and so on."

"May I copy out the gist of the will?" Pointer asked. He wanted to stay on at Thornbush until Mrs. Clifford should return.

Sir Edward nodded and sank heavily into a chair in a dark corner.

Head on hand he sat there, apparently deep in thought. Pointer too was thinking hard. He was busy with the will. So Mrs. Clifford was left out of the will, and knew it. She did not benefit in a monetary sense by her husband's death. Not in the ordinary way. But Mrs. Clifford had cashed a cheque for seventy thousand pounds as soon after her husband's murder as the banks were open. To that extent, merely going by the facts, she had benefited to the tune of a large fortune.

And the will gave Newman as well as Hobbs five thousand pounds. Seeing that that young man was, as far as was known, unmarried.

Curious proviso that. Yet both men lost their legacy, or could not claim it, as long as Clifford's death remained uncertain. Whoever had cut off Julian Clifford's head had believed that he had rendered recognition of the corpse impossible. And Pointer, though he had not an ounce of vanity in his nature, knew that with nine out of ten detectives the ghastly device would have succeeded.

He asked Sir Edward a few questions about the papers in the desk as he looked them over. The other gave rather absent-minded but apparently carefully truthful replies.

It was not far short of eleven when a ring came at the front door. A voice, it sounded like Straight's, but if so it was tense with excitement, asked if by any chance Sir Edward Clifford was at Thornbush. The servant showed him in, Straight's usually impassive face was working. He looked intensely, painfully stirred.

"Can you get a message through to Mr. Clifford, Sir Edward?" he asked in the same eager voice.

"No," Sir Edward said dully; "no, I can't. Why?"

"Miss Haslar wants him fetched if it's humanly possible. She's just had an awful shock. Haslar's spoken. He's recovered consciousness. I've come from his house. I had walked over to find out if anything fresh had been found out. They fetched Diana, who had gone to bed early—" Straight seemed to be unable to continue.

"And what did Mr. Haslar say?" Pointer asked quietly, in that steadying voice of his. He guessed what the injured man had said from the perturbation which Straight showed.

"I was in the room, asking the night-nurse how Haslar was doing, when he suddenly opened his eyes. 'Fetch Diana,' he said quite rationally, only very feebly. The poor girl came on the instant: she thought she was to receive some last word or message of affection. But when she knelt down beside his bed Haslar only gave a fearful cry and struck at her. It was like a ghost trying to strike. And he shrieked out, 'I did it all for nothing! I've killed Julian Clifford! There's his head. Take it away! Bury it!' And with that he fell back dead. At least I think he's dead. I rushed off for you, Sir Edward. They told me at your flat that you were here. Diana insists that Mr. Clifford must come to Arnold at once. She thinks it's the only thing that can save her brother. Heaven knows why!"

Edward Clifford had risen and stood facing this unexpected visitor.

"Arnold Haslar! Arnold Haslar!" There followed a silence short but poignant. "Did _you_ know this?" he asked, turning on Pointer. "Did _you_ know that it was Haslar who had killed my brother? But what reason? What motive?"

It was Straight now who jumped.

"Mr. Clifford isn't killed. Haslar was delirious." The new librarian at Thornbush looked as though the whole world had gone mad. Pointer eyed his shoe-tips for a full second.

"We believe that the body found with its head cut off early this morning in Heath Mansions is the body not of

Etcheverrey, but of Mr. Julian Clifford," he said finally. Straight collapsed into a chair.

"Then—then—!" He stopped and stared first at Pointer, then at Sir Edward. "I _knew_ it was delirium!" he said, as though to himself. "For, of course, the man who murdered Mr. Clifford murdered Arnold Haslar too!"

"There is a man who might have tried to kill both men," Pointer agreed, "a Major Cory."

"Cory!" Edward Clifford recognised the name on the instant. "He certainly hated Julian, and with reason. You mean, of course, the Major Cory of the Holford Will case. But where would Haslar come in?"

"We know that Cory and Haslar knew each other," Pointer said cautiously. "Here's his picture." He pulled it out of his pocket and handed it to Straight. "It was taken some years ago, but it's a good likeness. Did you happen to see this man at Mr. Haslar's last night?"

But Straight had not seen whoever it was that had been closeted with Arnold Haslar in his study when he had walked over to Haslar's house after dinner at Thornbush. He explained that Haslar had come out and asked him to wait a few moments, adding that the caller wouldn't stay long. After the man left, Arnold had spoken of going to a music hall and a dance club afterwards, but he, Straight, thought his friend was looking ill, and would be better for a quiet evening. As Haslar was indignantly denying either looking ill, or any intention of staying in, the telephone bell had rung. His friend had gone back into his study—they were in the library—and had listened to a rather long message. He had hung up the receiver after saying grudgingly, "Very well; I'll be there. But it's damned inconvenient." To Straight he had explained that a very urgent business summons would take him out of town for some hours. They arranged to postpone what had been intended as a sort of welcome-back-to-England celebration for himself till to-night.

"And to-night—" Straight began, when he turned to the door. They heard the swish of a car driving up. A minute more and Diana came flying in.

"Uncle Edward, where is Uncle Julian? You must tell me. I must find him. If you don't know, Alison must speak."

"Why, Miss Haslar?" Pointer asked.

"Tell him, Dick." For once Diana was not equal to a task.

"I have told them. They believe with me that the same—" He stopped short.

"Uncle Edward, Arnold's raving! But if we could only find Uncle Julian and bring him to his bedside— There she is. That's Alison!" She ran out of the room again. Those inside, openly listening, heard the front door open, heard Diana's quick, feverish sentences telling Mrs. Clifford of what her brother Arnold had just said.

"Of course Arnold was delirious. He was shot just after reading that awful account in the paper about the headless man found near us, and Uncle Julian being away, he has confused the two all up as one does in a nightmare. But if Uncle Julian comes at once"

"Diana dearest!" Mrs. Clifford was speaking in a very kind tone as she came on into the room.

"You here, Edward? What have you been saying to frighten Diana? Julian's safe and well, thank God. But I can't reach him, Di. He gave no address in that note he left for me. But he said he would be home in time for lunch on Thursday."

Her eyes went to Pointer.

"This is Chief Inspector Pointer of New Scotland Yard," Sir Edward introduced him.

Pointer bowed.

"I'm afraid you must prepare for bad news, Mrs. Clifford," he said very quietly. "We of the police believe that an accident has happened to Mr. Clifford."

"An accident?" For a second her colour, always pale, grew whiter still. Then she recovered.

"Oh, no," she said confidently, "I should have known of it at once. When do you think this—accident— happened to my husband? Why do you think it is to Mr. Clifford?" She spoke with an air of bearing with the stupidity of a child.

"The accident happened last night," Pointer said gravely. "It was a mortal accident." Then he added, after a little pause, "The body has been identified beyond any possibility of doubt, Mrs. Clifford, by the finger-prints."

"But not as my husband's," she said with certainty.

"We believe," Pointer went on, "that a body found near here at Heath Mansions this morning, and taken at first to be that of a Basque anarchist, was really that of Mr. Julian Clifford. There is no possibility of a mistake this time, I am sorry to say."

"Uncle Julian!" Diana gave a cry. "Uncle Julian!"

Mrs. Clifford stared at Pointer, her head held very high.

"A body? Anarchist? You don't mean that headless body of which the evening papers are full?"

Pointer said that he did mean that. Her eyes darkened to green.

"What appalling nonsense!" she said indignantly. "Do you think that I shouldn't have known immediately—felt it at once—if anything had happened to him! How abysmally ignorant you people are of the things of the spirit!" She turned on her brother-in-law.

"You too, Edward! You too think I wouldn't know! Julian will laugh when he gets back on Friday!"

"Mrs. Clifford," Pointer said solemnly, "from where he is, there is no coming back."

Alison flushed a deep rose flush. She drew herself up.

"It's incredible! It's almost as though you all wished— " Then she checked herself. "Forgive me," she turned to Edward Clifford, "poor Edward, you look so worn! But your grief is all for nothing. Julian is alive ... is well ... is happy."

"Where is he?" Pointer asked, with something of sternness in his voice.

She gave a careless twitch of her slender shoulder. "You will know all in good time."

"I am afraid we must take our own measures then," Pointer replied.

"You mustn't do anything that Julian wouldn't approve of when he gets back," she said quickly. "Edward, I trust you to see to that."

"I want to look into his money matters," Pointer said slowly.

Alison Clifford started palpably.

"Certainly not! That is my cousin, Mr. Hobbs', affair. He is my husband's literary agent. Julian would never forgive such a thing. You must wait, Edward"—she spoke with urgency—"Julian will be back by Friday."

"May I see the letter left for you this morning?" Pointer asked. "I understand that a note was left for each person in the house."

"I have destroyed my letter," the answer was instant, and Mrs. Clifford left the room with an air of deep displeasure.

"How about you, Miss Haslar?" Pointer turned to the slender figure shrinking, almost cowering back away from the others.

"I—I don't know where mine is," Diana said in a strangled voice.

"Could you give us an idea of its contents?"

She seemed to force herself with difficulty to speech.

"It was only a line to say that Uncle Julian wanted to verify some topographical point, that he would be back on Friday at latest, and would I meanwhile go on with my grandfather's letters."

"And dated?"

"It was dated yesterday." Diana had turned to Edward Clifford while speaking. He avoided her eye.

So he believed that his brother was dead. He believed that Arnold was responsible, that those wild words . . .

Suddenly she stepped up to Pointer, laid her hands on his arm, and looked dumbly up into his face. An agonised question was in her eyes. It would have been touching had it been any woman, but from Diana Haslar that mute appeal was very moving.

"I see," she said hoarsely. "There is no hope. He is dead. Oh, God!" It was a prayer, not a mere ejaculation.

Straight stepped forward as she made for the door and took her hand. Sir Edward looked on with no softening lines of his set mouth.

"I'd like a word with you, Mr. Straight, as soon as you've seen Miss Haslar into her car," Pointer suggested.

Straight came back, looking years older than the young man whom Sir Edward had met for the first time only last Saturday.

"Now, Mr. Straight," Pointer began, "we know you've only just landed in England, but it seems that Mr. Julian Clifford had talked with you after dinner last night"—the gas man had learnt that from the butler—"his last dinner. Did he seem to have anything on his mind?"

"Well, I think he had," Straight said judicially. "Of course I thought then that he probably was always a little _distrait_."

"Julian was _distrait_ at times," Edward Clifford murmured, with what struck Pointer as a rather wary look at Straight.

"At any rate he was so then. Long silences. Just a word now and then."

"And those words were about?" Pointer asked. And Edward Clifford's face grew blankly inscrutable, as though he were preparing to hear something which he might not like.

Straight did not reply on the instant. He looked as though he were trying to think himself back to yesterday's quiet talk with the man now lying dead.

"About my work. A little. He left an impression on my mind that he would be shortly going away from Thornbush for a while, though he didn't say so in so many

words. He said something about working out my own
ideas. Especially not continuing exactly along Newman's
lines. Newman had been librarian as well as private
secretary, you know." Straight paused. "It's awkward to
say now that murder's been done, but Mr. Clifford struck
me as—" He paused, hesitated.

"Well—as what?" came from Edward Clifford sharply.

"As afraid of Newman," Straight said simply.

"Julian afraid of Newman!" Sir Edward echoed
incredulously.

"It wasn't what he said," Straight said slowly, "it
was—his face? his voice? I don't know. But I thought so.
Yet, as far as I can remember, all he said was, 'I shouldn't
go to Newman more than I could help, if I were you.' I
said something about Newman seeming very willing to be
of help, and he gave me a queer look. A very queer look,"
Straight repeated solemnly. "Struck me even then as
such. 'Let's hope you'll find him so to the end,' he replied,
and again it was the tone that was odder than the words.
I repeated 'to the end, sir?' And after a long silence he
said very curtly, and in a very low voice, 'Mr. Newman is
leaving me. But that is strictly confidential. But now you
see why I should prefer you to find your own feet?' I forget
what I replied. And then he rose and joined Mrs. Clifford
in the walled garden. But just as he stepped over the sill,
I thought he was going to ask my advice about
something—or wanted me to help him in something"

"Julian!" repeated Edward Clifford, in palpable
amazement.

"I'm only giving my impressions. And the impressions
of a stranger may be all wrong. But that's what I thought.
I was going to say something like 'Is there anything I can
do?' But of course I thought that if there was, he'd have
said so."

Straight stopped. He looked as though half minded to
say no more, half inclined to add something to what he
had said.

"Well?" Pointer prompted.

Still Straight hesitated. "It's rather difficult to go on. You don't know me. I might be an imaginative chap . . . given to romancing. . . . I'm not. I'm the opposite. But you don't know that."

"Well?" Pointer asked again.

"You'll think I've fear on the brain—but I thought Mr. Clifford not at all keen on the short absence from Thornbush of which he spoke. Or rather, to which he referred. The first time was in the course of some directions as to what he wanted done. He said—as nearly as possible—'I've a lot of foreign books, most of which I don't care about, yet some of which are quite worth having. Pick out those you would propose to keep. Then leave the rest for me to look over. I may be away for a short time from Thornbush, but I'll glance them over when I get back.' There he stopped. There was a long silence. Then he said to himself, '_when_ I come back.' And his face and voice sounded like a man very doubtful of his coming back. That was all then. Another moment came in the course of a few words about Australia, and travels in general. He said—after another long silence— 'Yes travelling is pleasant. If you want to go, and are sure you'll get back safely.' That's all I have to go on. Just those two remarks. But both, and especially the latter, sounded to me as though Mr. Clifford was nervous of something that lay before him. I thought at the time, until just now, in fact, that he must be a poor traveller, bad sailor, and so on."

"Julian! Well, Straight, thank you for telling us this. You certainly have surprised me." Sir Edward sounded genuinely amazed and also a shade relieved, Pointer thought. "It's as unlike my brother as though you had been talking of a stranger. I suppose it really was Julian? You saw his face?"

"Oh, yes." Straight laughed at the idea of a substituted Julian Clifford. "He sat on after dinner and went out into the garden . . . joined you. ... I heard your voices dimly."

There was a little pause.

"And here," Straight rose, "is the note which I received, ostensibly from Mr. Clifford, this morning." He handed a folded piece of paper to Pointer.

"Did you keep it for any especial reason?" the Chief Inspector asked, reading it.

"I—don't—know," Straight said slowly. "I suppose I should have kept it in any case, but—well, the note struck me as odd."

"In what way 'odd'?"

"Well—unlike his words of the evening before. Here he tells me to turn to Hobbs and Newman."

Edward Clifford looked the letter over very carefully. It
was dated yesterday.

"Dear Mr. Straight,—A passage in my novel needs verifi-
cation on the spot. I expect, however, to be back at Thornbush
by Friday. I should like you to begin with the subject index
as you planned. Newman will give you any help in his power. So
will Hobbs, of course.

"Faithfully yours,

"Julian Clifford."

"You think this is Mr. Clifford's writing?" Pointer asked Sir Edward.

"I should say so. Certainly. The very way the punctuation marks are made is his. And that signature. It's on his own paper, too."

It was more than that, thought Pointer. Like the additions to the cheque, it was written with Julian Clifford's own pen, or its exact mate. But as to whether the dead man had written it—

"Did you see Miss Haslar's note?" he asked Straight.

"Yes. She showed it me. Hers and mine were lying on the hall table when I went out for a walk before breakfast. I noticed them lying there along with two for Hobbs and Newman."

"She expressed no surprise at her letter?"

"None." Straight did not add that she had looked very uneasy and had scanned it in silence more than once. Instead he said good-night.

He left a profound silence behind him.

"His conversation with Mr. Straight—the tone of it—was very unusual on Mr. Clifford's part?" Pointer asked.

"My brother must have been deeply disturbed," Edward Clifford replied in the tone of a man taking swift mental soundings. Pointer thought that some little part of what he had heard fitted in, perhaps very badly, with something else. Edward Clifford, supposing him to be honest, had not exclaimed at the idea of Julian Clifford dreading his journey as he had at the idea of his being afraid of his secretary.

"Afraid of Newman," he repeated again. "Amazing! Under ordinary circumstances I should say Straight was romancing, but as it is—!" He sighed profoundly. "Well, I have always known that my brother's secretary is a queer fish. But this throws a new, and a most sinister light on his queerness."

"In what way queer?" Pointer asked, as though Newman had struck him as a type of the commonplace.

"In every way. Of course I know about his lost memory, and so on, but I used to watch him very closely after Julian first took him up, and I came to the conclusion that he didn't want his past to come back to him. There are exercises, founded on the Freudian theories, of getting into touch with the submerged half of the mind. He never would allow them to be tried on him. I— Well—frankly I sometimes doubted whether his memory was entirely gone. And I'll tell you another person who more than doubted, and that's Miss Haslar. She never said so, but I'm sure of it. She distrusted

Newman from the first, and insisted that Julian was doing a foolish thing to keep him on. But Julian was one of those men who, when they back a side, can only see that side. He never backed it lightly, I'm bound to say. But once his stand was definitely taken, nothing could shift him."

"Could I speak to Mr. Newman?" Pointer asked. Sir Edward rang the bell. But Mr. Newman was out. When had he left? Directly after "this gentleman" had called to see him. About half-past nine.

"This gentleman," otherwise Chief Inspector Pointer, rose as soon as the door shut behind the servant.

CHAPTER EIGHT

"I think we had better have a look at Mr. Newman's rooms. Will you show me where they are?" Pointer asked.

Sir Edward took him up. The secretary's bed-room presented a scene of wild disorder. Coats and clothing had been flung here and there. A bag stood half packed, and then abandoned. A gaping suit-case too had been apparently discarded at the last moment as too hampering.

"Flight!" Edward Clifford looked about him with a slow pallor creeping over his face. "Does this mean that we're standing in the room of the man who murdered my brother and mutilated his body so horribly? If so, it'll be"

Pointer said nothing. He was looking intently about him.

"If so"—Edward Clifford's tone changed: it hardened— "if so, Chief Inspector, then that legacy was the motive." He spoke in a quiet but authoritative voice. Pointer wondered what other possibility he was definitely shutting out.

"Five thousand pounds might tempt a poor man," Pointer agreed.

"And, as you know, Newman has a salary of only two hundred and fifty pounds a year. Ample, but not if he were of extravagant tastes. If Newman killed my brother, there is no other motive possible."

"It will be a shock to Mrs. Clifford, I'm afraid," Pointer murmured, "I mean this apparent flight."

"A frightful one. She believed entirely in the man's good faith. So much of a shock that I think it should be kept from her for the present."

"If possible," Pointer said non-committally.

"I think it will be quite possible. But—if Newman is guilty, what are we to think of Haslar's cry?"

"It's a very intricate case this, Sir Edward," Pointer said thoughtfully, as he too glanced all around the room. "One step at a time is all that we can hope for."

"I suppose Newman will be followed if he really has tried, as this room suggests that he has, to escape?"

Pointer set his mind at rest. One of his best men was in charge of Newman. He swiftly made up a parcel of the absent man's clothing—a very complete parcel.

"They give us his measurements," he explained in answer to Edward Clifford's inquiring stare. "Part of the regular routine. You knew Mr. Newman well?"

"I lived at Thornbush for five months after he first came to Mr. Clifford. While Cleave Ford was being fitted with central heating."

"What about his time off? Regular time on which he could count, I mean," Pointer asked.

"His evenings were generally his own. So were Saturdays as a rule. And Sundays always."

"Do you know what he did in the evening, or over the week end?"

"Evenings—I think he never went anywhere except to Arnold Haslar's. He became tremendous friends with him from the first. But on Sundays he vanished utterly and completely. We used to chaff him about it until we saw that he didn't like it much." Sir Edward stopped.

Pointer had stepped to the fireplace. All the grates at Thornbush were concealed by handsome, wrought-iron double doors like small casement windows inset within the marble of the fireplace. It was the neatest way of dealing with small stoves, or grates, that Pointer knew. He believed it to be a Belgian idea. At least, he had often come across it in Brussels. He now opened the little doors and stooping down, felt the bars. Then his eye travelled up the wall. He stepped quickly into the bathroom, and came out with a small nickel shaving-cup in his hand. He detached a water-colour picture from the wall. Then he dragged a table across the fireplace, placed a chair on it, and stepping lightly up, held the picture, glass-side up, as a tray, while he gently blew something on to it off the picture rail—a small wisp of charred paper, so black that no writing showed on its thin film. Then he drew out the cup from his pocket and carefully turned it down over the fragment, holding it all very level as he stepped down on to the floor, and put it on the table.

"Mr. Newman burnt something in that grate. The bar is still warm. Nothing big. He crushed it all into fragments, but this one bit must have escaped his notice and blown up there. I'll send a man with it and Mr. Newman's clothes to the Yard at once. We may learn something from them."

From below came the sound of a banged door. And then another.

"That must be Hobbs." Clifford listened for a moment. "He must be told, of course; about Newman, I mean. But I think Mrs. Clifford should be kept in ignorance of what has happened. After all, Newman may return to the house. It's just possible that this room does not mean what it seems to mean. Don't you think so, Chief Inspector?"

"I don't think he'll come back," Pointer said thoughtfully, following Clifford down the stairs and into the library, after handing his parcel to his chauffeur, and placing the cup and picture with extreme care in an attache case which he strapped over an air cushion on a collapsible table in the car.

Julian Clifford's literary agent was standing with his legs far apart, swaying slightly. He looked savagely up at them as they entered.

"Well, what d'ye want?" was his greeting. "What's up now?"

Clifford looked at him with thinly veiled disgust. The man had been drinking.

"Something has happened to Julian," was Sir Edward's short reply.

Hobbs stared. White streaks like dead fingers showed on his cheeks. He seemed trying to pull himself together.

"What d'ye mean?" he asked a trifle less surlily. "I thought I told you . . ."

"He's been killed—murdered." Edward Clifford could be terse too. "This is Chief Inspector Pointer of New Scotland Yard. He's investigating the case."

Hobbs's dropped jaw all but prevented his nodding to Pointer. He certainly looked an amazed man.

"It was his body that was found near here in Heath Mansions this morning. That headless body." Edward Clifford gulped at those last horrid words.

Hobbs seemed sobered. His face grew mealy white. He was a handsome enough man in a big, burly way. He seemed to shrink a little now.

"I say, this is going too fast! How do you know—if it has no head—how do you know it's Julian?"

"There is no doubt possible," Pointer assured him. "And now Mr. Hobbs, would you mind explaining just where you thought Mr. Clifford was when you assured an official of the Home Office this morning that he was collecting local colour, probably in Liverpool?"

Edward Clifford was looking intently at Hobbs. Hobbs looked back at him. A blank, non-committal look. And yet he sent a message to the other.

"I thought he had gone, as he so often does, for literary material. But I can't grasp this awful news! It's incredible. Surely there's been some mistake. If his head is off, I repeat how can you be sure it's Julian's body?"

Pointer explained about the identified finger-prints.

"And the thickened finger-joint is his. So's the scar on the sole of the foot," Edward Clifford finished.

"You're absolutely certain it's Julian?" Hobbs asked, biting his lip.

"Certain? Absolutely," the dead man's brother assured him.

Hobbs grew paler yet.

"I can't believe it!" he said thickly. "I can't realise it."

Suddenly he straightened up.

"My God! Haslar was all but murdered too!" He turned a white, wild face from one to the other. "What does it mean? Why these two?"

"Mr. Hobbs," Pointer asked again, instead of replying, "where did you think that Julian Clifford was? Have you no idea where he might be expected to be, supposing he had really gone away of his own free will yesterday morning?"

"None whatever," Hobbs said promptly—a shade too promptly. He looked hard at Sir Edward.

There was a silence. Pointer noticed that Edward Clifford did not seem any more anxious to question Hobbs than he had been to question Straight, though he listened with an even more strained attention.

"Have you had any unusual visitors at Thornbush lately?" Pointer asked.

"By Jove!" Hobbs looked this time hard at the detective officer. "There was a man—refused to give his name—asked for Newman. Saturday morning around twelve. Newman was out. He then asked for me by name. I had him shown in, of course. Didn't care for the look of him. Wrong 'un, if ever there was one. Ex-cavalryman type. He talked on about his admiration for Clifford's works and that. I thought he wanted to sell me a typewriter, or get some translation rights for nothing, he was so vague. Finally he asked to see Clifford himself. I said Clifford never saw any one without an appointment. He said, 'Tell him I'm come from Haslar. Mr. Arnold Haslar. Then he'll see me.'"

There was a pause in the narrative. Hobbs looked as though he were trying to be very exact in his account.

"Did Julian see him?" Edward Clifford asked at last.

"What! Disturb him of a morning! I didn't send in any message, of course. I went out into the dining-room and marked time with a sandwich. Then I reported that Mr. Clifford regretted that he was unable to see Mr. I waited for the name. None came. So I went on, 'Unless Mr. '—

another pause, but still no name forthcoming— would state his errand. 'Did you say I came from Haslar?' he asked. I assured him I had forgotten nothing. He looked rather taken aback, I thought, gave me a look over as though he was about to propose something shady. If so, he decided against it. Hesitated for another moment, and said sneeringly, '_You_ don't seem to be much in Mr. Clifford's confidence,' and left, knocking his hat over one ear."

"Was this the man you saw?" Pointer produced the photograph of Cory.

"That's the man."

"Did he say nothing else?" Pointer asked.

"Nothing of any importance. Nothing I remember. But the emphasis on the 'you' made me wonder if he thought some one else knew more—of whatever his errand was."

"Newman?" asked Edward Clifford sharply. Hobbs said nothing, but his silence was a "yes."

"But you know," he went on, after another pause, during which he stood again jingling some change in his pocket, "I don't think a shady caller had anything to do with Clifford's murder. We have too many of them. I think"—he hesitated, and drummed on the mantel-shelf—"well what I told you in the train, Edward. I met Sir Edward in the train by accident this afternoon," Hobbs explained to Pointer, "and told him that I think Julian Clifford has a separate establishment somewhere."

Edward Clifford looked intensely indignant.

"Impossible! I repeat, quite impossible!"

"Why so?" Hobbs jingled some keys in his pocket. "He was away from home pretty frequently. Why impossible?"

"The idea is quite untenable to any one who knew the plane of life on which Julian lived." Edward Clifford spoke with apparent sincerity.

"And where do you think this establishment was?" Pointer asked quietly.

"Not an earthly," was the prompt reply. "But I've thought it for some time."

"Any reason for the suspicion?"

"Human nature. My cousin Alison would bore any husband stiff," Hobbs said in a contemptuous undertone to Clifford, who looked at him as at a reptile.

"We'll discuss this matter to-morrow when you're more yourself," he said in an icy tone, turning away as though hardly able to trust himself to look at the insolent grin on Hobbs's face.

"Mrs. Orr is a widow, I understand?" Pointer said, apparently out of the blue.

Edward Clifford looked, if possible, more indignant than ever; but he listened for Hobbs's reply. It did not come for a full minute. And then Hobbs said in a thick, low voice, hoarse with passion:—

"What's Mrs. Orr to do with this? I was speaking of a possible separate establishment of Julian's. Not of friends of himself and his wife."

"And now, Mr. Hobbs, one question," Pointer went on coolly, "where were you last night from, say, ten onwards?"

"I went out to post a letter at ten or half-past," Hobbs said easily enough. "I was talking with Mrs. Clifford and writing at the same time, till my cousin went up to bed. Then, as I said, I went out to post a letter, found it a marvellous summer night. Came back and sat on in the garden for a while, then went to bed. It was just short of twelve when I wound up my watch. This morning I found I'd caught a chill out under the trees. When I got down about eleven I found a letter for me from Julian"

"You kept that letter?"

"Don't think so. I'll look, of course; but, as a rule, I never keep any but important letters."

"Did you hear or see anything of Mr. Clifford before you went to bed?"

"Yes, I heard him in his library, I thought. I feel certain I left him there when I went out to post the letter. Afterwards I didn't come through the house at once. By the time I went up to bed all was dark downstairs."

He was not able, or appeared not to be able, to add anything more except just as he was turning away. "Wait a bit—I seem to remember a telephone ringing in the library as I sat talking to Mrs. Clifford. I have a fancy that I heard Clifford reply. That's what made me certain he was there when I went out."

"You can't remember any words of his reply?" Pointer asked.

"Not a syllable. We were talking at the moment."

"Though you may not remember the words, have you no idea of the manner of his reply? Was it friendly? or was it business-like? or was it annoyed at all?"

"Well, I couldn't swear to it, but I have a hazy notion that he was rather impatient. Not like Julian to be that. But I don't think I've mixed it up with any other time." He rubbed his face wearily.

"I think I'll go for a walk now, and see if the fresh air won't help my head. This has been an awful shock. What about Alison?"—he was speaking to Edward Clifford.

"Frightful!" Sir Edward said under his breath. "When she's convinced of the truth it may well kill her."

"What will kill her will be not having known that anything had happened to Julian, when she was seeing him alive and well in her crystal," Hobbs said callously, and turning, left the two together.

Pointer thought that Sir Edward would have liked to follow him out, but if so, the latter checked the impulse.

"I must let Tindall know at once of Newman's flight. He'll be in his rooms at this hour." Sir Edward reached for the telephone and passed on the news.

"He's coming as soon as he can get here." He hung up the receiver. "But a word about Hobbs. You don't suspect him, do you?"

Pointer did not reply.

"Well, I don't," Clifford said firmly. "Hobbs is far too shrewd a business man to be a criminal. As a literary agent my brother considered him unequalled."

He was not too good a business man to drink, nor to have a very dangerous temper, was Pointer's private comment on that. But he said nothing.

"Unfortunately he's developing a habit which will be the ruin of him unless he checks it," Edward Clifford went on, "a habit of taking more than is good for him. But he's not a criminal. On the other hand, he's a man who lives a fast, careless life. That idea of his about my brother's absences"— Edward curled his lip—"put it quite out of your head, Chief Inspector. Anything dishonourable would be impossible to—" And then Edward Clifford came to a full stop. He flushed scarlet. "Er—er—his private life was absolutely exemplary." He finished hastily, and getting up began to walk up and down the room, apparently getting deeper and deeper into a brown study.

Pointer was certain that Julian Clifford was engaged in something not strictly legal when he had met his death. It had seemed a strange thing of which to suspect the great author. But there was his odd question to Astra. There was Hobbs. . . . Hobbs knew something, or thought that he did. So did Mrs. Clifford. Edward Clifford's flush of just now, all bore out the same idea. Besides, though he was apparently grief-stricken at his brother's terrible fate, he also seemed absolutely without any ideas as to how, and where, the search for the murderer should be started. He was as one lost in bewildered helplessness. Pointer had come to the conclusion that Sir Edward did not want the circumstances of Julian Clifford's death probed, except as they concerned Etcheverrey. He either knew, or feared, that any other line of inquiry would open up painful details—painful to the living. He must have some reason for this. It was not one that would have occurred offhand to any reader of Julian Clifford's lofty books. He had turned down Robbs's idea of an intrigue with scorn. But what other idea did he hold himself?

Pointer had believed at first that if he could find the head of Julian Clifford and establish the identity of the murdered man beyond question, that he would get all the members of his family to speak, and so come on the clue to this most strange death. But not if this idea were right. In that case, even then, he could look for no help from the Thornbush circle. Nothing would bring back the dead, they would argue. Pointer knew how egoistic people can be when it is a question of a family scandal. Better, they would think, that ten murderers escaped than that one just man should have cause to wince. Pointer did not agree. But that being the case, the whereabouts of Julian Clifford's head faded into the second place beside the question of what the writer had been doing, what planning, what other interests he had, besides his interest in Etcheverrey?

How could he, Pointer, locate the place where Clifford was supposed to be, if he were honestly supposed to be alive? That vision of him in her crystal which Mrs. Clifford had thought that she saw, or had pretended to see. . . . Houses with "gables like steps" mounting into heaven. He believed that those words had really slipped out. If so, they might help to orient the search. But how could the Chief Inspector get on the track of those gables? Where were such gables? English they were not. Nor Basque. Nor French. Nor Spanish. Pointer ran through a long list of the impossibles. Yet apparently they were in the street where Mrs. Clifford thought that her husband was—supposing her to be innocent.

Tindall was shown in.

"So the secretary's run away! Being trailed, of course."

Pointer said that he sincerely hoped so.

"Can I see his room?" Tindall surveyed the wild scene thoughtfully. Then he returned to the two men in the library. He closed the door carefully, even though a detective was on duty in the hall.

"Sir Edward, a thought has been growing in my mind since you 'phoned. What about Newman being the man we're after? Being Etcheverrey himself? This idea would link Clifford and Haslar for certain, and doubtless Cory.

We have learnt that worry and depression were common to both Mr. Clifford and Haslar these last weeks. It was common to both of them, because it sprang from a common cause—from Newman. You know, Sir Edward, you believed that Etcheverrey might be hiding in some quite commonplace identity. How about that identity being your brother's secretary?"

Sir Edward had wheeled, and now stood staring at him.

"What a possibility!" He seemed to consider it. "It's a brilliant guess. What ghastly irony, if so, that I myself should have spoken of my idea before him. Let me see. . . . When Etcheverrey was in Persia, Julian was in Australia. Just he and Mrs. Clifford—over six months away. Hobbs worked on as usual, but Newman took a holiday for the whole time. It was the winter. He was supposed to be in Rome looking up facts for Clifford about the Fascist suppression of newspapers. . . . And then that time when the Prince was in South America . . . that wouldn't fit Newman, but, of course, he may have worked through an agent more often than is believed. The attempt on the King of Spain—yes. Newman was free then. Julian thought him climbing in the Lake district. I must go into this in more detail with Hobbs, and check dates. What do you say, Chief Inspector?"

"'If I thought Newman were really Etcheverrey himself," Pointer said slowly, "I should be inclined to wonder if Mr. Clifford were not trying to bring him into some book of his, and in trying, had not got nearer to the truth than Etcheverrey liked. . . . Nearer to publishing it, I mean. Just now, Sir Edward, you told me that the central drawer of his writing table contained Mr. Clifford's work of the day, the finished chapters being in the left-hand drawers, the notes for the future parts, or for the whole, in the right-hand ones. I took the liberty of glancing at the contents of the middle drawer"—for the second time, he might have added. "Mr. Clifford has apparently stopped at the very last line of a page and in the middle of a sentence. Of course I don't know, but I should have thought that an author would finish a sentence, especially this one. It runs: 'Roberts felt that the'—I can't imagine even a boy in school of a summer day when the bell rang leaving a sentence hung up like that. And Mr. Clifford has a pile of untouched manuscript paper in the same drawer."

"My brother would have finished writing down his thought while the boat sank beneath him!" breathed Edward Clifford tensely. "But the remainder of the sentence—the next page—may be in a blotter." Hurriedly he led the way into the room where he had handed Pointer the will. He pulled open the central drawer.

There, in a neat pile, lay Chapter nine of _The Soul of Ishmael_. There lay the third page with its typing running down to the very margin of the lowest edge. As Pointer had said, it ended with the unfinished sentence. Beside it was a carbon copy. It, too, showed no further pages.

Tindall and Sir Edward hunted skilfully, minutely, as men hunt who are used to searching for papers. Neither they, nor the Chief Inspector, found any completion of the phrase. Apparently Julian Clifford had stopped his typewriter at "the" and never touched it again.

"Some one has taken the page, or pages, following!" Edward Clifford muttered, as he straightened the piles again; "Newman probably."

Pointer was examining a sheet of carbon paper in front of a mirror.

"Here's proof or at least strong presumptive evidence of the fact that there were more pages on that pile. That sheet there is page three. Here are a whole bunch of superimposed numbers, that's certainly an eighteen. Mr. Clifford is hardly likely to have torn up so many pages?"

"Certainly not. He worked page by page, not leaving one until it was perfect in his eyes. I wonder"—Sir Edward tapped the table nervously—"if it was his next chapter for the _Arcturus_. If so, it would be nearly finished by now, I fancy. He was never behind with his work. Where's the last _Arcturus_?" He spun round on his heel and pulled the monthly in question out of a revolving bookstand. "Yes. Chapter eight was the last. What can you make out on the carbon sheet, Chief Inspector?"

Pointer explained that chemicals and photographs would get the full value. As it was, he could only read a few sentences. Tindall, more experienced at such work, did a little better, but he soon flung it down.

"That all takes place in England! That's no good!" Then a moment later he gave an exclamation that brought Pointer and Clifford to his side. He held up a slip of paper with some sentences scribbled on it. They were in Julian Clifford's small, close writing.

He read them aloud.

"'Have Roberts next go to Capvern, and meet E. Join E.'s band—England having become dangerous. Get necessary details as to organisation of E.'s band.' There we are!" Tindall waved the paper in front of Sir Edward, who nearly snatched at it, and then tried to read it upside down. He nodded when he had scanned it.

"Get necessary details as to organisation of E.'-s band," he repeated. "Julian's way, when a thought occurred to him, was to jot it down on the 'first thing that came to hand which he would drop into that drawer. Unfortunately he never made any rough drafts. Still, I think your discovery, Chief Inspector, about the unfinished sentence, is vital. Vital! How did you come to look for it? For, after all, these sheets were under a pile of unused paper."

"It was only natural," Pointer said diffidently. Praise always made him shy. "When a jeweller's been killed, you think at once of jewels in his possession. If it's a banker, you turn to his bank first of all. Or a statesman—you think of state papers. In each case you ask yourself, what was peculiar to the man. In Mr. Julian Clifford's case it was his books, his writing; so, merely as a matter of routine, I looked at his manuscript, or rather his typescript."

"It was a master-inspiration!" Sir Edward repeated. "Let me see," he mused, "I wonder if Bancroft could help us. He's Julian's publisher. I'll see him at once to-morrow. I'll explain that I'm worried about Julian"—Sir Edward's face twitched—"and that I wonder whether in his talks with Bancroft he suggested going to any particular spot."

"Ah! that's where Mrs. Clifford thinks her husband is!" broke in Tindall, with the air of a man who has solved the riddle to his own satisfaction. "Investigating some part of the Basque country. He would, of course, ask her not to speak of his whereabouts. Pointer, well played again!" He turned to the detective officer with the words that used to echo from one side of the football ground to the other in the days before Pointer joined the Force.

"And the gables that I think may have been in Mrs. Clifford's mind, the gables that she therefore 'saw' in the crystal? The gables that climbed into heaven like steps?" Pointer asked.

"Basque houses have so varied an architecture quite apart from their own," Tindall reminded him. "Many of them, they return home, build something in the style of the country where they made their money. But now about this idea of yours. I think we shall score this time. Team work does it. That, of course, was why Mr. Clifford asked Mrs. Jansen the question about possible danger. Playing with dynamite wasn't in it with probing too deeply into Etcheverrey's organisation, or into his past."

There was a pause.

"I wonder if Julian suspected the truth, or what we believe to have been the truth, at the end?" Clifford said, coming out of a deep reverie. "If so, that would explain why he wanted quietly to get rid of his private secretary, why he warned the new librarian of Newman. He might well! Poor Julian, he might well! And if only suspicious, Julian would not speak of it to any one—least of all to me—about a man who might be innocent, who might really have lost his memory."

"That lost memory was a master-stroke," Tindall murmured appreciatively. "Now I'll confess something that's been disturbing me not a little." Clifford shot a glance at Pointer. "Julian asked me about"—he seemed to think a moment—"about two months ago, how one could best make a large payment to a foreigner in such a way that it couldn't be traced back to oneself. I naturally showed surprise. I suggested letters of credit, but he insisted that the money must be untraceable. I couldn't help him with any advice. Bonds to bearer seemed the only way out, since he said that a large sum of money might be in question. But when I pressed him as to what he was up to, he looked at me thoughtfully and finally said that I had better know nothing whatever about the matter.

"I confess I asked no more. I was startled, uneasy. No one likes to hear a member of his own family put questions like those. No one occupying a responsible post in the country, that is. Not with the Labour Party always ready to sling mud at us. I confess I thought of a subsidised paper for distribution in Italy—to be printed in Switzerland, independent of Fascist censure. Julian had some such idea in his mind, I know. I was, of course, strongly opposed to it. But now I see that he was probably thinking of Etcheverrey or some lieutenant of his. Perhaps that was partly in Hobbs's mind when he talked to me this afternoon in the train. He told me that he believed Julian was away on an errand which it might be as well not to investigate. He told me that, apropos of a man from the Home Office who had called at Thornbush this morning. A man called Marbury"

Pointer bowed with a faint smile. "I was Marbury."

"Hobbs said that he hoped he would not insist on investigating where Clifford really was. Warned me that he was afraid that Julian had got mixed up in something—well, something of which it might be as well not to speak in the market-place at the moment. Then he even suggested, as he did again before you, that Julian was mixed up in some vulgar intrigue."

Edward Clifford took a turn up the room and back.

"That discovery of the Chief Inspector's about the page—his idea about the coming revelations in Julian's novel— they do indeed open up vistas. Julian lunched with Bancroft only last week, I know. I know too that he talked very freely with his publishers. Bancroft may have some precious piece of information to give us to-morrow. You'll come with me, of course, Tindall, and you too, I hope, Chief Inspector."

But Pointer could not promise. He arranged for a telephone report in case he were detained.

"Was Mr. Clifford in the habit of talking over what he was writing? In his own home, I mean?"

"As far as I know, never. He liked to get away from his work in his leisure hours. But, of course, to his secretary he would doubtless refer to his work. Probably discuss it—dreadful thought—with him."

"And the person who took the remaining page or pages of the chapter that Clifford was writing"—Tindall was deep in conjectures—"would be that same private secretary, who, if we're right—as we most certainly are— was the very character that Clifford was about to introduce. Newman may have sent that telephone message to Clifford which Hobbs thinks he heard. The message might easily have asked Clifford to come to Fourteen Heath Mansions to meet some one whom Newman might have assured Clifford was an expert Basque scholar. But an invalid, say. Yes, that all fits in quite well into the known facts."

"And Haslar?" Edward Clifford frowned, "what was Haslar's role?"

"Haslar," Tindall replied thoughtfully, "was, we know, or rather is, supposed to be a great friend of Newman's. He may be, instead, merely his tool or his prisoner. But Haslar, we may take it, acting according to his instructions, takes the flat." Tindall paused, evidently getting together some more straw for his next brick. "Cory—like a vulture, his presence with both men means that something's wrong, he's the very emblem of death throughout—Cory who was to figure as Captain Brown ... as the Basque expert, perhaps"—Tindall's cheeks were flushed as he reconstructed his scene—"Cory, we learn from Hobbs, was sent on Saturday morning to Thornbush to get a general idea of Mr. Clifford. Perhaps he was to invite Mr. Clifford to Fourteen Heath Mansions then. At any rate, that fell through. Etcheverrey miscalculated there. Or Cory outran his instructions. But about Haslar—are we to take Haslar's ravings as merely empty words? Or have they a substratum of fact?" He addressed this directly to Pointer.

"Not as empty words, merely," Pointer thought decidedly. "I believe the relations between Mr. Clifford and Mr. Haslar have been a little strained of late?" he asked, turning to Sir Edward.

"They have seen less of each other," Edward Clifford allowed. "Like Hobbs, Haslar is prone to put the worst construction on the most innocent things. My brother was interested as a character in a coming novel, in a friend of the Haslars. In the Mrs. Orr whom you mentioned, and whom, for once, Hobbs had the grace to defend. Arnold Haslar took it upon himself to resent my brother's interest."

"Perhaps Mr. Haslar was in love with the lady," Pointer suggested artlessly.

"Very likely. But as my brother was in love with his own wife, he need have had no fears on that score," Edward Clifford replied curtly.

There was a short silence broken dreamily by Tindall, still at his weaving. "Was Newman's the hand that actually fired the shot at Haslar? What do you say, Chief Inspector?" He wished that Pointer would join a little more freely in the discussion. After all, though not the

Foreign Office, the Yard does good work—quite good work.

Pointer told the facts of Newman's probable visit to Haslar's house as revealed by his tiny vacuum sweeper. But he made no comment on them. Instead he seemed to change the subject.

"Apart altogether from his own work, did Mr. Clifford have any papers or letters in his possession which Mr. Haslar wanted, or may have wanted?" he asked unexpectedly.

Sir Edward stared.

"Papers? Letters? I don't quite see. . . . Oh, yes, of course, Cory made you think of that! No, I don't see how there could be any such question here, Chief Inspector," Clifford said decisively. "Certainly I know of none such."

"I think Etcheverrey may have played one of his very clever games. May have got Haslar to choose Cory without explaining why he wanted him," Tindall said now. "Etcheverrey would count on Cory exceeding his instructions. Suppose Clifford were handed over to him, as it were."

Sir Edward made a gesture that looked like uncontrollable anguish.

"Etcheverrey may have counted on Cory taking his revenge," Tindall went on gently but remorselessly, "being a Basque, revenge would be the first thing he himself would take in Cory's place. I think—so far—that Haslar took the flat with no intention of harming Clifford, simply acting under orders. Who knows what trumped-up reason was given him. That of the Basque friend, say. Haslar takes the flat, Etcheverrey as Newman lures Clifford there, Cory is told to kidnap Clifford. He does just what Etcheverrey counts on his doing: he shoots Clifford. Shoots him, as Cory would shoot him, from the back. Haslar falls ill. When he sees the evening papers to-day with the account of Etcheverrey's supposed murder, he guesses the truth. When Newman comes in he knows it. He tells Newman that he must confess. Newman tries to murder him and practically succeeds. I think that is a workable hypothesis. Even those torn-up pieces of paper with Etcheverrey's signature on it which you boggle at"— he turned to Pointer—"fall into line. Etcheverrey, safely ensconced at Thornbush, left them as a true, yet false trail. For they led directly away from Thornbush. As for the head —my new hypothesis may be a trifle weak there yet." Tindall looked almost wistfully at Pointer, who was staring at his own shoe-tips.

"I wonder," Pointer said suddenly, "if you would allow a chartered accountant to go through Mr. Clifford's accounts, Sir Edward?"

Clifford stared. "You think—?"

"I think they ought to be very carefully looked into," Pointer said, rising, "merely as a matter of routine, of course."

"Oh, yes, I see. Of course. I heard my brother say, by the way, that Straight was a chartered accountant before he took up librarian's work."

"Good. Perhaps you would see him about it. I would like it done as soon as possible. The thing can't be done secretly, of course, since the accounts are under Mr. Hobbs, I believe?"

"Entirely. As I told you, Julian was more than satisfied with him. Besides having a splendid knowledge of where to place work, he's a wonder with figures. He was Third Wrangler, you know."

And on that Pointer took his leave.

"Fine fellow, Pointer," Tindall said, as the door closed. "One of the best brains at Scotland Yard. Quite a marvel for his years, but the police routine sets its seal on a man's mind. They can't get away from it." And he plunged into the necessary steps to be taken to follow up and prove his theory.

Pointer meanwhile drove back to his own rooms at Scotland Yard. Night and day were but figures of speech to him when need was. Various men had been routed out of bed and some modern magic as soon as his car had reached Scotland Yard.

When Sir Humphry Davy saved the papyri of Pompeii, he blazed the trail for the treatment of all charred papers, though that trail has turned many a corner since then.

In this instance the paper was heated again and photographed the second before it crumbled to a white ash. Charred paper so heated gives off minute quantities of gas which fog certain specially prepared plates. Ink, however invisible to the naked eye, acts like a screen between the paper and the camera, shutting off the action of the gases, so that when developed the plate is foggy except in the places marked with ink.

Pointer was finally handed a photograph of that small island of salvaged paper, which a touch would have turned into black dust, on which now he read

I know the danger
discovered your secret
                    wife

The last word was very doubtful. It might have been _knife_ or _life_. The writing and the paper and the ink were all those of Julian Clifford.

Pointer sat for a second lost in meditation. Tindall would he pleased to see this. He had a copy sent over to his flat.

Compared with this feat, the deciphering of the carbon paper was child's play. Heated, treated, rolled, photographed, enlarged, one of Pointer's men had typed page after page from it—ten pages in all—with only here and there a blank word. Evidently Clifford used a very good brand of carbon paper. It showed that there had been twenty pages in all, finishing the chapter. As Tindall had thought, they were entirely concerned with England, but copies would none the less be sent to him and Sir Edward, along with the copies of the two sentences extracted from the burnt paper that had flown up on to Newman's picture rail.

Then Pointer turned to another report, concerning Newman's clothes, which he had sent to the Yard at the same time. These had one by one been put into as many paper bags, sealed, beaten, and the dust then microscopically examined.

A certain gray waistcoat had yielded, among other usual trifles such as cigarette dust, lead pencil dust, quite a knob—microscopically speaking—of fiddler's rosin, more properly called colophane; a rosin, that is, which is used by violinists to give their bows more bite on the strings. The analyst had added a note to say that this special rosin was "black rosin," such as is used exclusively by players of the double bass.

The microscope had also found on the knob several bits of very fine quality Wilton carpet wool of a deep, soft blue. In other words, the waistcoat had been worn by some one who played the double bass in a room where there was a blue Wilton pile carpet. The same message came from one of the coat sleeves.

So Newman played the double bass. It suited his grave face, his slender hands and wrists, that Pointer thought looked made of whipcord.

Double bass and blue carpet. . . .

It was not an address, but it was something.

An inquiry over the telephone brought confirmation of the terrible words gasped out by Haslar to his sister. Words heard by the night nurse as well. But Haslar was not yet dead. He still breathed. Pointer's plain-clothes man added that he himself was sitting in the room behind a screen. And finally there came yet another message for the Chief Inspector before he left the Yard.

It was from a very unhappy wight, who explained that he had lost Newman—lost him hopelessly.

"Clever of you, Black," Pointer murmured. "How did you manage it? Or is it a patent process?"

"_I_ didn't do it, sir," the man breathed apologetically, "it's not the first time that chap's given a trailer the slip. Not by a long chalk. He left Thornbush immediately after you. I followed him on to a bus. He got off at Charing Cross post office, and posted two letters. Then he went into a cinema."

"Ah," said Pointer, "just so!"

"But he didn't try the usual trick of walking in one door and out another," the detective explained resentfully. "I was prepared for that. No. He must have doubled back on his own tracks in some way. Sat down for a second and then slipped out by the door he came in. All I know is, he has gone. Gone completely."

Pointer was not pleased. But no man, not even a detective, can do more than his best. And after all, the Yard had the blue carpet and the double bass to cling to.

He wrote out a description of Julian Clifford's missing secretary for insertion in the _Gazette_, the police daily paper which no civilian may read. In it, and over the telephone to all police stations, orders were given that the constables were to report any place, where they heard, or had heard in the recent past, stringed music regularly played, especially on a Sunday.

They were told to pass on the request to all milkmen and postmen on their beats or in their neighbourhood. The stringed instrument especially suspicious was given as the double bass, but as Pointer was not sure that a constable's ear could be certain of distinguishing it properly, he also included the whole range of riddles, preferring to sift all information later.

A snapshot of Newman was enlarged for the paper and printed on a grating so that every deviation from the absolutely regular was at once noticed. They were very trifling, very few.

Ordinary enlargements of the snapshot were got ready to be taken to-morrow by detectives to all musical societies, all instrument dealers, and musical supply stores. A double bass presupposes chamber music, or membership of some orchestra, or musical society. A telephone call was sent to all taxi stands and garages asking any men to report at the Yard who had recently carried a double bass. It was barely possible that they had carried one to-night. Newman, even though he thought his home address undetectable, might have changed it, and his instrument, to a fresh place. Here was one of those points that no amount of reasoning could settle. No deductions in the world would discover where that place was. But the dust beaten out of his waistcoat pocket and examined under the microscope might yet find it. Then Pointer called it a day, and went to bed.

But at dawn he was up again, and out at Thornbush, watching with the two road-menders the summer sun wake the garden. Nothing on earth is more lovely. When it grew light enough to see, the men shook off the spell, and fell to work on the places which had been marked by the two "lads after their dormouse," as having been recently disturbed. They found nothing, let alone a tin box with plaster—and a head—in it.

Then Pointer whizzed along to Haslar's garden. The same dormouse had escaped there too, it seemed. Places of disturbed earth had been marked. So the same search took place here too, with the same negative result.

CHAPTER NINE

Pointer was at breakfast at eight o'clock when he received a letter rushed up to him by a motor cyclist from Scotland Yard, where it had just been delivered. It had been posted the previous evening at Charing Cross. It was signed A. Newman, and ran:—

"To Detective Chief Inspector Pointer.

"Dear Sir,—I know that you have had your suspicions of
    me, and that it is only a question of days before the trap closes
    if I stay at Thornbush. I prefer to slip away while I can. The
    headless body found in Fourteen Heath Mansions, and iden-
    tified—publicly, at any rate—by the police as Etcheverrey, a
    Basque anarchist, is Mr. Julian Clifford's. I killed him last
    night for reasons which concern no one but myself. I took the
    flat for a month, under the name of Tourcoin, and induced Mr.
    Clifford to come there late last night. The rest you know.
    Haslar guessed what had happened when he read the description
    of his coat and ring, borrowed by me; as well as from some
    things that I let slip. I shot him to prevent his going to the

police. I did not intend to hurt him severely. My intention was
  to inflict a slight wound to disable him until I could make my
    arrangements.
    "Faithfully yours,
    "A. Newman."

Pointer had barely finished this when his telephone buzzed. It was one of the men whom he had left at Arnold Haslar's house. He was speaking from a near-by telephone. He read out to the Chief Inspector the letters which he had just taken from the postman. None interested Pointer except one from Newman. Practically a replica of his own letter, informing "Dear Miss Haslar" of the same terrible facts and ending up "yours very truly."

The letters were duly re-fastened and delivered.

Newman evidently believed that he had got clear of the police, or this letter would not have been written—not yet. So Pointer read the situation. But had Newman really escaped? Time alone would tell. As for the telephone message to the taxis, no information was brought in overnight that fitted Newman, nor was his portrait identified by any of the men.

Pointer himself drove at once to Thornbush and had a short talk with Sir Edward, who had spent what remained of the night there. Clifford read Newman's letter with a puckered brow.

"It fits in with our idea of last night, and with that deciphered bit of burnt paper. 'I know the danger,' Julian wrote. But that was evidently just what my brother did not know. Of course the last word on that fragment is either _knife_ or _life_. Certainly not _wife_. I see no necessity of even suggesting that third reading."

Pointer agreed that until they knew more, either of the two words might be substituted.

There was a silence.

"This confession of—we will continue to call him Newman —is an extraordinary document. Is it a genuine confession, do you think?"

"Very difficult to say, Sir Edward."

Mrs. Clifford came into the room at that. She looked very composed. Yet Pointer thought that she had not slept well. He handed her the letter from Newman. Sir Edward had decided that that ought to be done. She read it, and let it fall to the ground. For a second she stared at him with eyes dilated by horror, then she sat motionless in the chair which Clifford brought forward. So motionless, that she scarcely seemed to breathe. Finally she looked up, outwardly at any rate quite calm.

"This is all some wild mistake. Arnold began it with his ravings, and now Mr. Newman writes this with some idea of saving him from suspicion. Suspicion of—oh, it's too horribly grotesque! I wish I could make you understand, both of you, that Julian is perfectly well, and never has been in any danger, at least not in danger of his life. I had a letter from him only this morning. I kept it to show you, Edward. Though he expressly asks me to destroy it. I'll get it."

"It's not possible that Julian wrote that letter, Alison," Edward Clifford said sadly. "My dear, there's no doubt whatever that our Julian is dead—none."

Mrs. Clifford bit her lip.

"I'll get his letter. That'll convince you. . . ."

A minute later she returned looked rather flushed. "I must have dropped it somewhere. I thought I had locked it in my bureau, but it's not there."

"What was in it?" Pointer asked bluntly.

"Just vague generalities," Mrs. Clifford said casually, "except that he repeats that he'll be back for certain on Friday at latest."

"Still no address?" Pointer asked, raising an eyebrow.

"Still no address," she said coldly. Pointer stood looking down at her. His face was very grave.

"Mrs. Clifford, I don't think you realise the position at all," he said finally. "We at Scotland Yard believe that your husband was murdered. I believe that he was murdered by some one in, or closely connected with this house. We know that he is dead. I'm sorry to say, we know it. You yourself are not free from suspicion. No one who is in any way connected with Mr. Clifford can be. Yet you persist in an attitude which cannot but be considered suspicious, for it true its best to hold up the search—to put it off. As Sir Edward says, that letter of which you speak is a forgery. We must see it—if it is to be found. It is most unfortunate that it should have been—lost."

Clifford listened as though each word hurt him. He all but interposed once, then he caught the Chief Inspector's warning eye and kept silent.

Mrs. Clifford looked absolutely unmoved. Her rather rabbit-like mouth set itself perhaps A shade firmer.

Clifford leant forward and took her hand.

"Alison, I wish I could spare you. If there were a doubt possible. . . ."

Mrs. Clifford looked at him very pleasantly, but apparently she was not to be shaken from her attitude of absolute conviction that Julian Clifford was well, and would return by Friday evening.

"That's only the day after to-morrow," she pointed out, "do wait till then, Edward, before doing anything. Anything whatever."

Trimble came in. Chief Inspector Pointer was wanted on the telephone. It was Richard Straight's quiet voice this time.

"Is that you, Chief Inspector Pointer? Could you come at once to Mr. Haslar's? I walked over before breakfast to hear how he is. He's still alive. But Miss Haslar is in trouble. She's just had a letter from Newman, and has something to tell you about him that she thinks you ought to know. She may change her mind. I've had a great deal of difficulty. . . ."

Pointer could not fly to the house, but he did his best to get there before Diana should have done anything so unkind.

He was shown at once into her sitting-room. She sat in a big chair looking oddly small and pinched. Her face was very white and still. Before her was an open letter. Straight was pretending to read the morning paper. He jumped up and shook hands.

"Miss Haslar wants me to stay. . . . She has something to tell you"

"Have you had a letter from Mr. Newman too?" Pointer asked her.

"Yes." Diana spoke tonelessly. Her voice was the tired voice of one wearied with a long, long struggle. "Mr. Newman is really Sanz Etcheverrey, Chief Inspector."

Straight jumped.

Pointer only looked at the toes of his shoes.

"You're sure?"

"I was engaged to him. It was a secret engagement. But I was engaged to him."

There was a silence.

"Do you feel like telling me more about it?" Pointer asked. "Except the mere fact of your identification, I think the details can be kept quite confidential."

Diana seemed wrapped in some cloak of remembered sorrow. Even when Straight went over to her and took her hand, she quietly but firmly disengaged her own. Just now she was locked among her memories. No one could enter. "It was the second year of the war," she began again.

"Why, you were only a kid, Diana," Straight interjected.

"I was nineteen. He was twenty-one. I was at Hendaye with some relations called Riply. Mr. Riply enlarged the harlour at Melbourne," she explained to Pointer.

"Sir Karri Riply, the engineer?" he asked.

She nodded. "He was dying. The ship he came over on had been torpedoed and exposure in a boat for three days had given him pneumonia. All the hotels were being used as military hospitals along the coast. But we finally took a villa, his wife and I, at Hendaye. Just this side of the Spanish frontier which was practically unguarded just there. Even long after the Bolo affair, a five-franc or peseta note, as the case might be, would get you over the line and no questions asked. There were lots of Spaniards swarming everywhere as far as Bordeaux. Sanz Etcheverrey was one of them. He called himself Senor Rosa. But he told me in strict confidence that his real name was Sanz Etcheverrey, then an unknown name to me, and to everybody outside a very small circle. Well, he and I—" She gave a half shrug. "I adored him. He seemed to adore me, though he refused to have our engagement made public. He said that as he was on a very private and dangerous mission it would injure him if it became known that he was attending to anything else but his orders. He never pretended—to me—not to be a secret service agent. But I didn't guess that what he was after were the Melbourne Harbour plans which Mr.—he was Sir Karri only the night he died!— Riply always kept with him. Sanz used to ask me all sorts of questions about those plans too. Where Mr. Riply kept them, and so on. I, like a fool, used to consult him as to the best place." Diana gave a hopeless gesture of her hand, then she let it fall back into her lap. "Karri Riply died quite unexpectedly. I hurried home from the hospital where I helped, to find Mildred, his wife, holding him up in her arms while he fought for his last breath. Suddenly I thought of those plans. Sanz Etcheverrey had been talking about them only that day. And at that moment, as though I at last had a ray of sense, I remembered that he had got the password to the safe out of me—oh, very cleverly! But for the first time I had, as I say, a ray of sense. I hurried to the room where the safe stood, opened the door, and there, working with an electric torch, with a beret pulled down over his eyes to his cheek-bones, was Sanz. I knew him at once, though I had never seen him in his Basque dress before. I screamed at him. But he—he hit me!" Diana covered her face with her hands. "I suppose he meant to kill me. He knocked me senseless. He must have picked me up and carried me to my room and locked me in. When I came to I had an awful pain in my head, but I got out through the window. There was no use trying to get help. The servants could not be spared at such a moment. I saw the marks of a car, two cars to be exact, which had just left the villa. They were both going the same way. I knew Sanz's tyres. I got out a motor-bicycle and followed them. I followed them all night until dawn found me in Spain, at Pamplona. There I caught up with him in a sort of locanda—a strange little place. And Etcheverrey was in the midst of the wildest-looking lot of brigands! He was giving them their orders, I think. I asked for the plans back. I still never dreamt that he wouldn't give them to me." Diana's smile told how she judged that action now. "They tied me up and carted—it wasn't carried—me to an upper room. After about an hour Etcheverrey climbed in from the roof. He told me that the others wanted to kill me because I had found out their meeting place, and because they thought I had heard their passwords. He wanted me to come with him. I refused. When I should have distrusted him I had trusted him. Now when, as it happened, he was honest with me, I distrusted every word. He got me out by carrying me on to the roof and letting me down, bound and gagged, to the ground. Then he put me in a car. And at that I did believe him, for some of the men caught sight of us and fired. It wasn't what I should call a car at all. It was a sort of motor float that carried oil to the coast for the submarines. He laid me on the floor and covered me with a rug and drove like mad. How we bumped and swayed! Another car went after us, but Etcheverrey hit its tyres when it gained too much. They only hit one of our petrol tins and set it on fire. We just beat them into France. He had a British passport, it seems—a military passport! And I had mine! It was our papers that got us over the border. Because, after all, when it came to shooting, the French guards turned out to a man in a solid line across the road, on their side of the bridge. Etcheverrey ran me on to Bayonne, where he dropped me at our consul's. Then he turned the car and dashed off. I never saw him again—until I saw him come into the drawing-room at Thornbush in the wake of Uncle Julian, and heard that his name was Algernon Newman, and that he had lost his memory in the last year of the war while fighting on our side in a Surrey regiment at Saint Quentin!"

Again there was a silence.

"Why didn't you tell us this before," Straight asked stiffly, "when first you heard that Etcheverrey was supposed to have been murdered?"

"I don't suppose I can make you understand." And she turned to Pointer as though there was more chance with him than with Richard. "If he _had_ really lost his memory, it seemed an awful thing to bring up a past when he was a spy against us. . . . And he saved my life. . . . Whatever he did as well, he saved my life that day at Pamplona. He was wounded saving me."

"Did you ever tell Mr. Clifford about your belief that Mr. Newman was Sanz Etcheverrey the Basque anarchist?" Pointer asked.

"No. If he had really lost his memory—that was the dilemma. Had he lost it, or had he not?"

"You couldn't be sure?" Pointer was looking at her apparently casually but in reality very keenly.

"Not for certain—though I doubted it. But though I tried him over and over again, I could never trip him up. He never gave himself away in all these many years."

"Did you ever tell Mr. Clifford who you thought his secretary was?" Pointer repeated.

"No. I did my best, without telling him, to get him to let Mr. Newman go."

"And Mr. Clifford?"

"He thought I was prejudiced."

"When Sir Edward spoke of Etcheverrey, did you tell him what you have just told us?"

"No. I told no one."

"Did Mr. Newman know you suspected him?"

"Yes. He used to treat it as something funny. I never accused him in so many words of being Sanz Etcheverrey, but I as good as told him that I didn't believe he had lost his memory. Or that he was an Englishman. Or that he had ever fought on our side in the war."

"And he?"

Diana flushed. "He used to jeer at me. It amounted to that. He used to beg me to tell him of his past, not to tantalize him with vague hints. You know Mr. Newman's gibing way. A way that he never had at Hendaye," she ended on a soft note.

"Was Mr. Etcheverrey musical?"

"Very. He could play anything with strings—'Cello, violin, anything with strings."

"Did he ever play the double bass?"

She could not say.

"And Mr. Newman. Was he musical?"

"No. He always insisted that he couldn't tell whether they were playing Wagner or Blackpool."

"Was Mr. Clifford interested in Etcheverrey—I mean, of course, as distinct from Mr. Newman, his secretary?" Pointer asked next.

"I thought so. Lately it seemed to me that he was always talking of him, to Mr. Newman of all men! Uncle Julian spoke as though he got all sorts of ideas about him from Mr. Newman."

"Do you think Mr. Clifford intended to make any literary use of the knowledge. Expected to put Etcheverrey himself in a book?"

Diana stared in horror.

"That thought would have been the last straw!" she said in a low voice. "Reckless as Sanz Etcheverrey—as

Mr. Newman is, he wouldn't dare to chance that! Yet—"
She bit her lip.

"You think it would appeal to him?" Pointer finished.

"It might," Diana agreed, "he loved to play with
danger."

"But you yourself had no idea of any such intention on
Mr. Clifford's part?"

"None whatever. Nor have I now, I'm thankful to say."
The answer came with convincing sincerity. So she had
not taken those missing pages of Mr. Clifford's unfinished
chapter. A suspicion that had crossed Pointer's mind just
now.

Pointer turned to ask Straight the same question, but
the look of absolute stupefaction on that young man's face
was answer enough. Obviously he had not heard of any
idea of introducing the anarchist into the author's work.

"Good Lord!" he breathed, "what a coincidence that
Mr. Clifford should have been murdered by the man! I
suppose it _is_ a coincidence?"

"More probably Mr. Clifford stumbled on some truth,"
Pointer explained.

"I see," Straight still looked amazed, "and
Etcheverrey, finding himself discovered, killed him."

This was Tindall's and Sir Edward Clifford's
suggestion too. And like a warning notice not to keep to
the wrong side of the road, two sentences stood out before
Pointer's mental eye. Two sentences that had been burnt
to a brittle cinder: "I know the danger"; "discovered your
secret."

"Oh, no, no, no!" Diana burst out, with a sound to her
voice as though it came tearing from her very heart itself,
"not that! Etcheverrey would never have killed Uncle
Julian for any personal reason. If it's true that he killed
him, then it was for some other, some political end."

"I believe you love him still," Straight said harshly,
looking at her in open indignation.

"And if I do—can I help myself?" she asked
passionately. "Can you cure yourself of cancer by wanting

to be cured? Don't you suppose I've told myself all the facts over and over again? Of _course_ it's glamour and only glamour. Of _course_ I've had a lucky escape—but I can't tear it out." She was all but whispering. Tears stood in her eyes as in a child's, but these were the tears that scald.

"And I thought you loathed the chap!" Straight looked bewildered and hurt. "You always said you loathed him," he repeated accusingly.

"Of course I said so, because I didn't," Diana retorted indignantly.

"Well—women are the devil," was the morose and very feeling reply. "And only now that he has murdered Mr. Clifford and tried to murder your brother, you think the time has come to speak out?" Straight snorted. "And I thought it was love of justice! To tell me to my face that you still love this murderer—"

"He's not a murderer." Diana was white but decided. "He's a man acting for his government. If he—if he—had anything to do with Uncle Julian's death it was as an agent; as a secret service agent"—she hid her face in her hands—"obeying orders as a soldier does."

There was a pause.

"And now, Miss Haslar, to pass on to another point"—the Chief Inspector looked very grave. "It was not Mr. Newman who took that flat, 14 Heath Mansions; it was your brother, Mr. Haslar. He has been identified beyond any doubt."

"He was all muffled up," Diana began quickly.

"Mr. Haslar has been identified by his voice—an unusual voice," Pointer said quietly, inexorably.

Diana gazed in dumb misery out of the window. A lovely day seemed to mock human suffering. A thrush, even though it was July, the month of flowers, not of birds, tried a few notes. Then he fell silent, as suddenly as though he were a friend and had seen her face. But the calls of the gold-finches flashed to and fro across the roses; and on a sudden, sweet and clear, a wren's song rang out like a silver bugle, as gay, as spiritually alive, as in spring. The little brown singer popped back into its shady nook, but something in the gallant strain had helped Diana. She turned around.

"When you first read in the papers of the murder of Etcheverrey, what did you think?" Pointer went on. "You could not then have thought that it was Mr. Newman who had taken the flat, since you say that Mr. Newman is Etcheverrey?"

"I thought it was Arnold then, of course, who had taken it," she agreed. "I thought—he had learnt of Sanz's treachery —and had—killed him."

"Because of you?" Pointer asked gently.

"Because of me, and because of the taking of the Melbourne Harbour plans."

Straight understood that drive back to Arnold's house now. That cry of fright when she had seen the man, of whose terrible death she had just read, standing on the steps."

"And when you saw Mr. Newman?" Pointer pressed.

"I knew then that it was he who had killed—not been killed. I thought that he had taken Arnold's ulster and ring. But I never guessed that the unknown, murdered man was Uncle Julian! And in spite of what he writes in those letters, I can't believe it. I can't!" Diana ended on a strangled cry.

Straight jumped as though something had stung him.

"I can't stand your grief for this anarchist," he said hotly. "You're not even pretending to—to cast him off. If you were disgusted with him, it would be different. But, as it is—I told you that I loved you. I told you that I wanted nothing better than to make you my wife. That I would wait years for you to say yes." He paused dramatically.

"Well?" Diana—it is regrettable to record the fact— snapped at him.

"I won't trouble you any more," he said coldly. "I withdraw any pretensions to winning your affections. I could hardly hope to carry the day against such a rival as this Basque murderer evidently is."

He stalked from the room. Diana burst into an unmirthful, cackling laugh.

"Jilted by the second man," she murmured. "Really I seem to be most unfortunate!" But her laughter died out as suddenly as it had come. Her head resting against her folded hands, she lay quite still in the chair, looking very forlorn all of a sudden. She had counted on Dick Straight. She had not loved him. She had known he could be severe, but she had counted on him.

The door opened again. Straight held it shut behind him.

"But if ever you should need me—" he began a little sheepishly.

"I don't need you. I never have, and never shall," Diana retorted. And this time Straight banged the front door behind him in earnest.

Diana turned to Pointer, who had apparently been looking at his shoes as a man does when two people forget that they are not alone.

"You had no idea that your brother and this Mr. Newman were concocting any scheme together in which your uncle, Mr. Clifford, figured?" Pointer asked.

The blood seemed to leave Diana's face.

"I—I—knew they were together a good deal," she temporised.

"Did Mr. Newman ever seem to you to take a high hand with Mr. Haslar?"

"With Arnold? On the contrary, he always fell in with everything—" Diana started. She had spoken too quickly.

"I couldn't say what went on when the two were alone together," she corrected herself.

"You had no idea of anything being planned which concerned Mr. Clifford?"

"No." It was an obvious lie. So something was on foot which she had noticed!

"Miss Haslar, your brother is in a most dangerous position," Pointer said in a low and gentle but very decided voice. "I'm not trying to trap you into some admission. During this interview I'm really only trying to see if he might not have taken that flat for some other reason—for a quite different purpose—than what seems the obvious one."

She was silent.

"You know of none? You can think of no reason?"

"None," Diana said firmly—much too firmly. Real ignorance would have hesitated, have cast about. ... So the reason of which she knew, or at which she guessed, told against her brother, and probably did concern Julian Clifford, her uncle.

"What papers were they which Mr. Haslar wanted taken from Mr. Clifford?" Pointer asked immediately.

He had hit some mark. Diana's eyes widened, as do the eyes of a man before he drops, who has been struck over the heart.

"I don't know what you mean?" She was gone, before Pointer could intercept her, slipping out of her chair and through a door like swift running water.

Pointer had had an outline of the Holford Will case hunted up at Scotland Yard, and had read it through—once. What was there in it which had made Haslar pick out Major Cory? What purpose could such a man serve? Supposing always that Haslar had selected him of his own free will—and Cory, in the few minutes when he talked to Pointer, had not spoken of any common master. He had, indeed, seemed to feel for Haslar the resentment a man feels for one who has personally tried to dupe him, to entangle him.

Why, then, had Haslar selected Cory? All that was shown of the major by the evidence at the trial, was that he was an unscrupulous blackguard who would have sold his grandmother to make glue were he offered a good price for her. He had stolen a will very cleverly though—for that Cory had stolen old Mrs. Holford's will Pointer did not doubt after he had read the inside police information—and he had stolen it so cleverly that the best brains in England had not been able to bring the crime home to him. He had done it by a trick. He had returned what purported to be the new will to the family solicitor, but when the envelope was opened, it showed quite another, relatively unimportant paper.

Yes, Pointer had decided, Cory was the last man whom any one who had sat through that trial would pick out for a capable assassin. He had shown up as a white-livered whelp. But if any one wanted a paper stolen . . . Clifford's missing manuscript pages did not affect this. They were taken to be destroyed, not preserved. They were not stolen in Pointer's sense; nor, if it was anything to do with Clifford's work, would Haslar have had need of an outside thief or furnished flat, so that if, as he believed, Haslar had deliberately chosen Cory, Pointer thought that he held one end of the very tangled coil which surrounded the murder of Julian Clifford.

Back at Scotland Yard, Pointer had not finished his swift notes on the latest development of the Clifford Case when yet another telephone message reached him.

Thirty-three constables, five milkmen, and seven postmen had already reported stringed enthusiasts along their usual beats. One postman even claimed that the instrument in question had been most certainly a double bass. It proved to have been a piccolo, but at one of the addresses—a block of chambers off Gray's Inn—Newman's portrait was recognised as that of a Mr. Pollock, Mr. Algernon Pollock, who had had rooms in the building for some five years now. Mr. Pollock was a country gentleman, the porter said, who only came up to town now and then, about once a week it might be, and always over the Sunday. Great musician, in the sense that he was very fond of music. Many a ticket for a concert, or the opera, had been bestowed on the porter. Pointer had arranged that each of his men should represent himself as a buyer of old stringed instruments, who was trying to locate the contrabasso used by the great Domenico Dragonetti, which was believed to be in private hands in London. Each of the detectives went on to say that a gentleman had been described to him by a musical-instrument mender as the possessor of this particular treasure. And he in his turn described Newman. In this case the description fitted—fitted perfectly. Could the collector of musical instruments see Mr. Pollock? Mr. Pollock was away; he had telephoned up yesterday evening late to say that he would be out of England for a few weeks.

Pointer had a very curious volume in his library at Scotland Yard. He turned to a chapter headed Window-cleaners. Every reputable firm supplied him with a list of the houses for which they worked. A little later, and the head porter of the chambers was called up by a man who told him over the wire that he was the manager of the particular window-cleaners company who had a contract for the building. There was talk of a strike. Rather than incommode their most valued customers, the Window Association were sending out a couple of their best men to do the windows this week, so that, should there be any question of trouble, the Gray's Inn flats at any rate would not suffer.

The hall porter told them to send the men along, and within a quarter of an hour a tall, lanky, bearded man, with another smaller companion in the well-known uniforms, carrying the proper appliances, arrived. The one had been a regular window-cleaner, at least for a while. Pointer had picked up tips from him as they came along—the best of which was a bottle of methylated spirit. Even so, he was no speed-fiend at the work. A glance at the board told him that Mr. Pollock had one of the top flats. Pointer promptly left his assistants to begin with the ground floor, and started up the stairs. A maid unlocked the little suite. There were three rooms. The gray music room had a harebell blue Wilton carpet; a fine piano was in one corner, a double bass stood against one end.

The bedroom, the next room into which Pointer stepped, was painted to represent an opening in a beech forest. It was beautiful in colour, but it told Pointer nothing. The third room, the living-room, was furnished with a luxury which made him stand a few minutes considering it very carefully. Those Heppelwhite chairs with their carved wheat ears, and shaped rail backs were genuine. They were not to be picked up for a song; nor that sideboard to match; nor those Waterford tumblers; nor the Spengler Chelsea figures standing on both sides of an early Worcester jar, whose green tinge spoke for its honesty. A rare old Pretender goblet faced Pointer. Its crowned cypher I.R. had an Amen engraved below it. Behind it was a beautiful piece of Beauvais tapestry. Or was it from Mortlake? In either case, it was a lovely though sombre thing, and far beyond most purses. Pointer stepped to some candlesticks on a superbly carved writing-table, and looked at the hall mark. York silver, and a Paul Lamerie tray, on the table of a man whose salary was £250 a year! And then Pointer saw something coiled on the wall over the writing-table which kept even him rigid in his place for a second. It was a hangman's noose. . .

CHAPTER TEN

Pointer knew that especial twist of rope, and knew that knot. He stared at it fascinated. What was its meaning? He examined the top of the rope with his lens. Its dust suggested many months in the same position. An ice-axe had been thrust through the loop. On each side were snapshots of glacier climbing, but that was not a climber's rope. Nor a knot used for any other purpose in the world. Nor in any prison but a British prison. What did it mean? Placed where the eyes of the man at the desk would always see it—must always see it— in that room where everything else was a joy to look at.

Pointer went over the many books. Mr. Pollock had not come back here to "tidy up" last night. Evidently he was afraid of his hiding place being discovered, and preferred to make yet another.

One whole wall was given over to Spanish works alone. Many of these were political. The books were mostly blank as far as name went, but here and there was an Algernon Pollock in Newman's very characteristic writing.

Pointer found three names in an address book, which skilful telephone inquiries soon showed were the names of the other members of a musical quartet which met every Sunday afternoon at Pollock's flat for chamber music. Each had known his host for a varying length of time, but all only since the end of the war. A few more well-planted questions showed that Mr. Pollock had by no means lost his memory of what went on during, or before, that great event. The Chief Inspector next unlocked the drawers of the writing-table. He found nothing that bore on his hunt, until he fished a roll of pink tape out of a drawer. It was wound around a postcard to serve as a core. Unrolling the tape, Pointer smoothed out the card. The top had been cut off at some time to permit of its going into a frame. So at least Pointer thought from the little marks on the edges. At the back, one line of writing alone survived the shears. A rather faded "you an idea of the place." The words were in Mrs. Clifford's writing, but that was not why Pointer stared at the card.

"Gables like steps running up into heaven," that was how these roofs were built. The picture was of a street in some town—not an English town—and those peculiar gables.

Pointer put the card carefully into his letter-case. Then he glanced over the bathroom, and went out into the hall, told the porter that he was feeling ill and that his mate would carry on, and hurried back to New Scotland Yard. Here he changed and went in his own person to interview the proprietor of the flats, and to explain to him that Scotland Yard feared, "from information which had come to hand," that a

robbery was being planned on some of the rooms in the chambers. He wanted, therefore, to introduce two of his men in the guise of a night and a day porter. They would require no pay. The proprietor was enchanted with this proof of the wide-awake attitude of our great detective force, and Pointer's men were accepted on the spot. Only the proprietor and the head porter were to know the truth.

In his car he studied the little picture postcard again—studied it through his glass. The architecture, all brick, was new to him, and was quite charming. It was a definite style, Pointer saw, and an old style—one that had grown. A house or two showed it in its entirety, but all of them in some particular. In every case the gables were high, and rose in steps, generally seven or nine, on a side to the peak, another step. The windows were high. Some of the houses showed each window enclosed in vertical mouldings crowned with arches, which were again enclosed in one large moulding carried up into the gable. The doors were many of them of slatted wood. Some were studded. Pointer the man quite forgot Pointer the detective-officer as he came on item after item of charming design and work. Where was this place where the builder was still a craftsman? He studied each detail anew. The houses were all of brick—small Tudor bricks, and all the courses— Pointer got his first clue.

"Flemish bond," he muttered to himself.

That is to say, the rows did not, as in "English bond," consist of bricks laid alternately longways and endways, "stretchers and headers," as a builder would call them. But each row was alternatively composed of all headers or all stretchers. And the whole of every house all down the side of the curving street which the postcard showed, was built in this way. Only Flemish bond . . . those fireplaces at Thornbush had told Pointer that probably some one there knew Belgium.

Pointer took the postcard and went to see one of his many friends. He had them in all walks of life. It was to a priest that he turned now. Father Warbury had given a lantern lecture to some of the young plain-clothesmen only a little while ago, which Pointer had attended. He had lectured on the architecture of Holland, and at one point in his very interesting address, he had made a little leap into Flemish styles before pulling himself up, and saying that that was a subject in itself, and a most fascinating subject.

Pointer found the priest in, and showed him the postcard. He looked at it for a bare second.

"Bruges. Charming town. Don't know it? I'm pained. I thought you knew all that we ordinary mortals do 'and then some,' as the boys say. Yes, Bruges." He looked again at the little piece of cardboard. This time the word seemed a talisman. Bruges to the good father meant but the fifteenth and sixteenth-centuries, and stood, not for a town of misery and horrors, but only for a little square which, running from the Pont des Augustins to the Pont

Flamand and the Porte d'Ostend enclosed a world of art
and genius the like of which could not be matched then,
or later. To him it meant van Eyck painting in the Main
d'Or, Menlinc in the rue St. Georges, with Bourbus and
Gerard David near by; and Caxton bending over his
presses. At any other time Pointer would have been
delighted to be conducted into this submerged city of old,
but now he was only anxious to get away. The priest
noticing this, picked up the card again and turned to
modern times.

"Yes. This is a picture of the rue de l'Aiguille in
Bruges. There's no other architecture in the world quite
like it—not even in Belgium. Leopold II. had sense when
he wouldn't let the modern mason spoil his Nuremberg . .
. 'the Venice of the North,' as some call it . . . ridiculous, of
course. Bruges hasn't the colours of Venice, but neither
has Venice such skylines."

Father Warbury again lost himself in a disquisition.
Beginning cheerily this time with broken, redented bows,
to pass on over perpendicular string courses, brick lace
work, decorated key stones, and relieving arches, to the
gloom of disappearing timpans, rounded frontons, and
plastered door cases.

Pointer hurried away as soon as the last word was
said.

Bruges? What could be supposed to be taking Julian
Clifford to that town? . . . supposing that Mrs. Clifford's
slip about the gables that climbed into heaven was a
genuine slip, and it was so slight that Pointer believed it
to be genuine. He got a guide-book, and soon saw that
had she wanted to direct his attention to Bruges, she
would have described the beffroi, or the cathedral, or the
canals. Yes, Pointer believed the slip to have been a true
one. What illegal action then could Clifford have been, or
have been supposed to be, engaged in at Bruges? Bruges
is very near Ostend—a few minutes by train or car. Could
Ostend be the real objective? But Ostend has no streets

where the gables climb into heaven in converging sets of steps that meet at the gable point.

Pointer called Ward in again.

"Anything going on in Bruges to draw such a man as Julian Clifford there, and have him want his presence kept secret?" he asked.

Ward pondered.

"Plenty to draw any lover of the beautiful to Bruges. In spite of its trippers, and its drinking water that may, or may not, be typhoid. But to have Julian Clifford want his presence kept secret"—his face lightened—"of course! Mrs. Orr! Her mother, Lady Winter, married a Belgian. Baron van der Bracht. They live just outside Bruges."

"Family respected? The van der Brachts, I mean?"

"Very much so. Tremendously hit by the war, but he's one of the Court Chamberlains. Mrs. Orr is supposed to be over there, I've heard to-day."

Pointer pondered over the idea after Ward had gone. Mrs. Orr? Mrs. Orr and Julian Clifford? That idea might conceivably be stretched to explain Clifford's murder by some one, Haslar or another, who was in love with Mrs. Orr. But it would not explain Mrs. Clifford's attitude. There were plenty of things to take an artist or a collector to Bruges. Collectors walk in very dark places sometimes. Did Julian Clifford collect? His house did not show any such taste. His wife, so Ward had told him, professed a dislike of most old things.

Still—Pointer decided to try another "friend." Mr. Aronstein was back in town to-day, and Aronstein was the buyer for the great American millionaire and collector, Wallend Seaborn.

"To a collector," Pointer began over a lunch to which the other had insisted on carrying him off, and whose amplitude made the abstemious Chief Inspector shudder, "is there anything now going in Bruges which is really worth while— worth while on a large scale, I mean?"

"Bruges," Aronstein toyed with some more foie gras, "relic of the Holy Blood, of course. That's unique. Brought back from the Holy Land by a crusader, but apart from the money to buy it, which would run into several fortunes, the town would rise as a man if the authorities even hinted at such a sacrilege, and tear buyer and sellers to pieces. The same is more or less true of the crystal shrine in which it's shown. Diamonds and sapphires and solid gold figurines. Then, of course, there's the Chimney of the Frank. Marvellous piece of carving. That, too, the town would never sell."

"Anything it would sell?" Pointer persisted, "in some roundabout, secret way?"

Aronstein shot a long, lazy but very keen glance at Pointer. "You're far from being a _little_ pitcher, but you certainly have the longest ears of any man I know."

Pointer looked very astute.

"One hears things," he murmured modestly.

"This talk is strictly confidential, of course? Oh, I know you, Chief Inspector; I haven't forgotten the Josephine necklace. Still, I'd like your word."

"Would anonymous be sufficient?" Pointer pleaded, "any information I get will be for use, not show. That do?"

"Perfectly. Now what do you want to know? Open out."

"Is there anything buyable in Bruges that would take, say, three or four days to get hold of, would cost a pot of money, would be risky to get out of the country, or at least get the purchaser into serious trouble if he were found out?"

"There is. More properly there are. Several things. Bruges, like many another Belgian town, wishes to sell a few of its treasures—but you know all this, of course."

"Just assume that I know nothing whatever. Why shouldn't the town sell?"

"The government doesn't want the nation's treasures cast out wholesale. It's passed a very stiff law to that effect, and it's very much on the alert. I've had several things offered me, from this very town we're speaking of, provided I would take all responsibility if things went wrong."

"All responsibility if things went wrong," murmured Pointer thoughtfully. "How wrong could they go?"

"Prison. Long term. Theft. And theft of church property," Aronstein said briefly. "The agent who approached me, made it quite clear that the town council would disown all part in the affair—would never have heard of any offer. But privately I would be put into touch with the right people who would let me have the various articles—at a price, mind you— if I would take all risk of the government getting on the track of what was going on. It wasn't good enough for me. I don't need to do things in that style. _Caveat emptor_ in an ordinary way, yes. But prison! Though I don't say that if _l'agneau mystique_ from Ghent—"

"Could you tell me in detail what was offered from, or by, Bruges?"

"Several pictures. . . ."

Pointer shook his head. He did not think that pictures would account for the mystery at Thornbush. Mr. and Mrs. Clifford had sent a large number away to homes, and down to their brother's place at Cleave Ford.

"A couple of tapestries well worth having from the cathedral. A gold monstrance. Possibly—doubtful that— but possibly the St. Ursula shrine. A missal. . . ."

Pointer shook his head at each item.

"And, low be it spoken, the Charlemagne Crystal."

"The Charlemagne Crystal?" Pointer pricked up his ears.

Aronstein lit a cigar nearly as fat as himself. He loved to lecture.

"Genuine Charlemagne. Genuine crystal. Supposed to have been the reason for Charlemagne's successes . . . saw things' in it. Saw Ronceval, but too late. Eginhard, his secretary, mentions it. So do all the _Romans de geste_. Charlemagne willed it to Luis of Aquitaine, his third son, who took it to Aquitaine. The legend runs that

Joan of Arc is supposed to have consulted it at Rheims and seen her awful end, and that was why she tried to give up politics. Unfortunately for the legend, before her day it had left France. How did it get to Bruges? Well, after the _Bruges Matins_, when the town rose against the French, and the gutters ran red with his soldiers' blood, Philippe-le-bel, the then King of France, took the crystal with him as a talisman to aid him in the great reprisal against the city. Though one would have thought three to one would have been sufficient preparation without magical aid. Anyway, when he was defeated at the Battle of the Golden Spurs, the crystal fell into the citizens' hands and became Church property. So did the king, pretty nearly. The crystal has remained in Bruges to this day. Unless it's been sold secretly, since it was offered to me for Mr. Seaborn. The town took charge of it after they dissolved a Dominican monastery. But, mind you, it would still rank as Church-owned."

"When was it offered to you?"

"Nearly two months ago, on June first or second."

"How would any one set about purchasing the crystal?" Pointer asked.

"Very cautiously, if he were wise," laughed Aronstein. "But Bruges at last has built a splendid new museum. The great West Flanders Museum, and appointed a new director. A Mr. de Coninck. He's willing to deal, if the purchaser can get the stuff out of the country, and will take the risk of prosecution should he be caught. Some men might be tempted. I'm not."

"How much is the crystal worth?"

"You'd have to pay something around sixty, or possibly seventy thousand. Even I should have to fork out fifty."

"Mr. Julian Clifford collects, doesn't he?"

"Not that I know of. But Sir Edward attends a sale now and then. He has some good things down at Cleave Ford."

"Ah, yes, I understand that Mr. Julian Clifford's secretary, a man called Newman, buys for him."

"Newman? I've met Newman. Wonderful chap on Spanish bindings. But I've never seen him at a big sale."

"Would Julian Clifford be likely to hear of these things on offer at Bruges?"

Aronstein laughed.

"I wondered how much of this you already knew!"

"The agent's name?" Pointer suggested trying to look omniscient.

"Mrs. Orr. Ah! I thought you knew it. Yes, she's a sister-in-law of Coninck's—or at least her half sister is Madame de Coninck."

As soon as the lunch was over, Pointer wirelessed an inquiry to Bruges as to the Charlemagne crystal. The reply came back at once. The crystal was very well, thank you, Why shouldn't it be? Could the Chief Inspector have a look at it? Was it on view? It was. Case number sixteen. First room on your right as you entered the museum. Yes, that fitted quite nicely into Pointer's mosaic. It was the answer that he expected.

So there was a great prize to be bought at Bruges. Did Julian Clifford's mysterious secretary know this too? Did the collector in him—for the chambers near Gray's Inn were those of a real collector—covet that crystal as well?—for himself? Or as a gift to some one who would prize it highly?

A complex case this.

By hurrying up his work, Pointer was able, after all, to accompany Sir Edward and Tindall to Julian Clifford's publisher. On the way he told them of the alteration in the cheque cashed by Mrs. Clifford early yesterday morning.

Sir Edward hurried on for a moment in silence.

"I'll look the matter up, of course. Thanks for mentioning it, Chief Inspector. I'll look it up. But I have an idea as to what it refers. In strict confidence I was told something last night which explains that cheque. In any case it had nothing whatever to do with my poor brother's awful end. It was a purely family matter."

"Of seventy thousand pounds?" Pointer echoed in a surprise which he made very obvious.

Clifford changed his step.

"And what about the fact that the cheque was made out originally to Self? That the e and R and Esq. were added afterwards?"

"I understand your natural anxiety to clear up every point," Sir Edward spoke soothingly, "but in this case there is no need to worry. I can assure you that the cheque was altered by Mr. Clifford himself, and that it, and the reason for it, have nothing whatever to do with his death."

"But have they nothing to do with his head having been cut off?" Pointer asked, without apparently glancing at Sir Edward.

The man he was questioning almost tripped.

"I—how could it be connected with mat terrible mystery?"

"If the cheque were not yet presented when Mr. Clifford was murdered, his death would delay, or prevent, its being cashed. The only way to get that money quickly would be to avoid any suspicion arising until after the money was paid out by the bank, that the man killed was Julian Clifford. Given certain circumstances, it is not easy to think of a better way of preventing that identity being known than the one taken here. Given the circumstances of a murder, for instance, or a death in town, where a body is hard to dispose of."

They were in the empty, quiet Temple Gardens, and Clifford stood still. Tindall, too, stopped and tugged at his beard.

"A very natural thought, Chief Inspector," Sir Edward said at last, "But one which does not apply here. I can assure you that the money was not needed in any particular hurry. On the contrary, had those at Thornbush had any idea that my brother was dead, it would never have been presented at all, and a great deal of trouble would have been saved." Pointer looked unconvinced.

"I should like to hear the explanation given you of that cheque," he said finally. Pointer generally got his own way. His was a compelling personality, perhaps because it was so quiet as a rule.

"Suppose we take a cab for a few minutes' talk. We're before our time." Clifford lifted his stick to one passing on the embankment. As they settled themselves, Pointer asked: "I suppose that Mr. Straight is at work on Mr. Clifford's accounts?"

"Well—not to-day. No. I think I must talk the matter over with Hobbs first. In fact—in fact the accounts are rather connected with the affair of which I was informed last night."

"By Mr. Hobbs, Mr. Clifford's literary agent?"

"By his cousin, Mrs. Clifford, in the first place. She confided to me her belief that my brother has got himself into some trouble—abroad. I can't be more precise. She would not give names of places, even supposing that she knew them. It's not exactly an illegal thing which he intended to do, and which, therefore, she and Hobbs believed he was actually doing over there this week. But, on the other hand, it's one which would perfectly explain her and Hobbs's attitude. You see they thought, and she still thinks, that in Julian's own interest, by his own express commands, nothing must be said of where he is. She told me enough to let me see that we must go very carefully indeed. For unfortunately certain negotiations have already been opened up. It's a question of the purchase of something which is not allowed to leave the country —openly. Hobbs, whom I immediately tackled, assured me that he is putting things right, and that by the end of this week, all danger will be over of my brother's name being mixed up in any scandal, provided we do nothing to make a scandal inevitable. That cheque is quite in order, Chief Inspector. It's for the purchase of this—object; a huge sum, but I understand not beyond the worth of the object, and after all, Mr. Clifford could afford to gratify the only request of the sort that his wife has ever made. Hobbs cabled last night to stop the deal. He thinks he was in time to prevent its actually leaving its own country, and that being so, he has every expectation, certainty almost, of having the money refunded—in time. The money was sent off to an intermediary yesterday morning. But any investigation on our part, Chief Inspector, would do irreparable mischief just now. Quite irreparable. My brother's name would be brought into a most deplorable prominence. Hobbs went so far as to assure me solemnly that were he alive—and were the facts to become known—my brother, Julian Clifford, would be liable to imprisonment! Of course, I myself would have to resign at once at the mere whisper of such a thing. Now, this whole affair has nothing whatever to do with Julian's death, nor with the terrible taking away of his head. As I say, Hobbs believes that he sees his way to put things back exactly as they were. Mrs. Clifford will not get her wish—for the moment. But if only matters can be adjusted, she, when she knows the facts, as she must very soon, will look at the mat- ter exactly as we do."

"And the alteration on the cheque?" Pointer asked rather dryly.

"Hobbs spoke of it to me. The cheque was first drawn out to Self. Then, when Mr. Clifford decided not to appear so directly in the matter, and learnt that one of the—ah—intermediaries was called Selfe, he himself merely added an e, and so on. The alterations did not show, and Julian did not initial them."

"I see," Pointer said. "Mr. Hobbs seems to've thought of everything." He spoke in a tone of real appreciation.

"Our aim now," Sir Edward went on, "is to uncover the reason for Etcheverrey's murder of my poor brother, and how far Haslar was guilty, or accessory to the fact. It's a hard enough task without adding other tangles to it.

That discovery of yours points to the only solution of this riddle, I do believe—the discovery that my brother was going to write something which Etcheverrey felt that he must stop. Add to that Mr. Tindall's remarkable guess as to the identity of Etcheverrey, and I think we may safely feel that we are on the right road."

There was a little silence.

"What was it, what _could_ it have been that my brother was going to write which caused his death?" Edward Clifford repeated ruminatingly.

"I've a notion that only a betrayal, real or fancied, would have made Etcheverrey kill a man," Tindall said, "unless it was all a ghastly mistake."

Mr. Bancroft proved to be a pleasant, business-like man, an old acquaintance of both Tindall and Sir Edward.

"Necessary to reach Clifford at once . . . and you think . . . yes, I see the idea. I know he is away from home. Mrs. Clifford told me as much when I 'phoned to her yesterday.

For Clifford had made an appointment. He was going to bring us in the next chapter of _The Soul of Ishmael_ himself some time during yesterday morning. We had been discussing it last time he and I lunched together. We're bringing it out in parts in our monthly magazine as you know. We suggested a little more—eh—well, adventure—incidents—"

Bancroft looked apologetic at having to mention such words. "The public taste is so depraved nowadays that it insists on high seasoning. Over-seasoning. And even such a giant as Julian Clifford who leads the masses, has to take account of it."

"'I _must_ follow the mob, because I lead them.'" Tindall quoted the French revolutionary's words.

"Ex—actly! As it happens, Clifford was turning over in his mind a very dramatic idea. His—I really cannot call William Roberts a hero—his chief character, let us say, being forced to leave England, was to go abroad and find an outlet for a quite unsuspected side of his character with a notorious Basque anarchist. The anarchist was to be drawn from life if possible. Clifford gave me an outline of what was to come." Bancroft here unlocked a drawer. "I think he meant to take these notes with him, but he jotted them down at my house and left them behind him, and I confess I could not resist the temptation to keep them. They are so exceedingly interesting—so clear. But possibly you may find in them some suggestion as to where he would be likely to go first. He refers to Capvern once or twice. And to a place called Guizep— really these Basque names are worse than the Welsh."

Bancroft laid an envelope in front of Sir Edward, who took it gladly.

"Let me have it back when you've done with it. Cliffordiana, you know," the publisher said smilingly, "and Clifford may yet ask me for it. By the way, when, or if, you do reach him, ask him to let us have the next instalment as soon as he can, will you? Newman says that no chapter was handed to him to be sent on, so he prefers not to risk a mistake. So do we! And as Clifford is expected back by Friday—Mrs. Clifford seemed certain of the day—at a pinch we can wait till then."

"When did Mr. Clifford leave the notes behind him?" Pointer asked.

"When? About a fortnight ago. Week ago last Friday." Bancroft flipped some pages over in his engagement pad.

Finally, after nearly an hour, the three took their leave.

"Well," Sir Edward said, as they stood a moment before the house. "Bancroft has been very helpful. Some of those suggestions he remembered—and that precious envelope with Julian's own notes. They, I think, had better be photographed at once. Three copies, please, Tindall, tell the clerk. And let each of us have one to pore over as soon as possible. There may be nothing in them. But one can but hope."

Pointer shook hands. He had left his gloves in the publisher's private room. Mr. Bancroft was still alone. Pointer found his gloves, and stood a moment chatting.

"You're bringing out a life of William Haslar shortly, I understand?" he asked.

"We hope to. But the proofs are still at Thornbush. As a rule, Mr. Clifford is most prompt in returning them."

"Interesting book to write," Pointer rambled on in the tone of a lover of books, which he was. "Still, for even a distant connection, there must have been some difficulties. What letters to leave out . . . what incidents to suppress. . . ."

Mr. Bancroft agreed. But he only agreed. He added nothing to Pointer's knowledge.

"Miss Haslar is helping him with them," Pointer went on. Mr. Bancroft again agreed.

"Arnold Haslar came down with flu yesterday," Pointer went on. "High fever. Odd thing is, he keeps calling out to Julian Clifford to let him have 'the paper.' Implores us to 'take the paper' from him. We don't know what paper. No one knows what to make of it or what to do. The doctors seem to think we're keeping something back. But how on earth can any one tell what paper, or what letter it is, which Haslar wants to get away, or get back, from Clifford?"

Mr. Bancroft was interested, but he could not help. He could only instance a distant relative who had also behaved in an eccentric manner during a high temperature. So a disappointed fisherman had to leave, with no fish, large or small, of the kind that Pointer thought would alone explain the choice of Major Cory by Arnold Haslar.

The photographed copies of Julian Clifford's notes were quickly sent on to him, and Pointer glanced them over. Then he went on with his telephoning—telephoning that took him all the rest of the afternoon and evening.

It was past midnight when he was disturbed by a report from one of his road-menders.

"Hobbs has just left, sir. Walking. Direction of Haslar's house. Wright's following."

Pointer was off in his car within a few minutes. He stopped it a little to one side of the house and went on on foot. Outside the gate he lit a match, and tossed it away in a peculiar curve.

A second later a hand touched his arm.

"Wright speaking, sir. He's inside. Came straight here."

Wright melted away, to return to his post outside Thornbush, and Pointer let himself into the house with a latchkey which he had slipped off Arnold Haslar's own key ring. Below the door of the library a light showed. The room was locked. The key blocked the key-hole completely. Even with his sound accumulator on, Pointer could only hear low voices —a man's and a woman's voice. At last they came nearer. The door was very cautiously opened. Diana Haslar put her head out and looked up and down the hall. Pointer stood just inside the door of the next room, which he held ajar.

"Weren't you seen coming here?" she asked fearfully.

"No. No one's on the look-out at Thornbush, and I crept in too quietly here to be heard. I'll leave you to shut the front door after me. Till day after to-morrow then, at Thornbush. If the boat's in on time, you'll be back by half-past five at latest."

She nodded, and closed the door with infinite caution behind the man, looking like an Eastern page in her short cherry silk dressing-gown and slippers. Pointer followed her upstairs at a safe distance. She went into her brother's room. The door was shut, but he found another door leading into the bathroom open, and peeping in he saw Diana sitting by her brother's bed with a book on her lap. But she was not reading. On her face was a look of intense excitement, intense joy. One of Pointer's men was in a distant arm-chair by the window, ostensibly as an assistant nurse. Round the leg of his chair was a cord, the colour of the wood, which ran through eyelets in the wainscoting to each of the doors. In the day-time it was taken away, but slipped on at night by the man on duty.

Pointer stooped down and gave it two quick tugs.

A minute later, and the man stepped out with an empty glass. He followed Pointer to his own room and closed the door.

"Has Miss Haslar left the room at all?" Pointer asked.

"Yes, sir. She went down about twelve for a snack. She's taking the watch till two, as I reported to you, sir. She came back just now, at ten to one. I suppose she dosed off a bit."

"You didn't hear any sounds at all just before she went down?"

"No, sir. No sound at all."

Pointer melted away. Merely as a matter of routine, genuinely so this time, he stepped into the library, shut the door, and switched on the light.

Sometimes people in a very engrossing conversation left odd things behind them, and the low voices which he had heard had sounded very absorbed.

The room looked as usual, except that a couple of chairs had been moved from one side to the centre of the room. They were not very near each other. Neither they, nor their position, suggested intimacy.

Pointer looked beyond them at the place where they had stood. Moving them had left free an old knee-hole writing-table, which, so Pointer had found yesterday, was used as a hold-all for odds and ends. Just now the table too stood a little away from the wall at one end. Pointer eyed it curiously —closely. Something caught that keen eye of his lying between one of the feet of the table and the wall—something

that had prevented that end of the table being rolled back true as it had stood yesterday and this morning.

It was the ferrule of an umbrella—rather new-looking. Now umbrellas are not much used in libraries at any time, let alone in a dry July. Pointer turned it over very thoughtfully. Hobbs had not carried an umbrella when he left here just now, nor when he left Thornbush. His trailer had told Pointer that he was carrying nothing in his hands.

But Julian Clifford had taken his umbrella with him when he left his home night before last. The butler was certain of this, for on going up to bed he had noted its absence as well as that of his master's soft felt hat. Besides, Clifford was one of those men who always carry an umbrella. Pointer had sent one of his men to the house with a gamp this morning which purported to be one that Mr. Clifford had left in the post office. The butler had rejected it promptly. The detective, by clever doubts and beliefs, had obtained a close description of the author's umbrella—a fairly new one, a recent present —among other more praiseworthy peculiarities it had a loose ferrule, one that threatened to drop off at any moment. Mr. Clifford had caught it in tram points the first day of carrying it. Trimble mentioned that Hawkins meant to have it seen to, but Hawkins never saw to anything before he had to.

Pointer laid the little thimble down on the writing-table and studied that piece of furniture intently. The chairs moved away from it meant that the whole table had been swung out. He swung it out. Behind it, the papered wall showed no opening, nor did the carpeted floor. The wainscoting ran unjointed past the spot. There remained the table itself. But to open any of its drawers it would not have been necessary to move the chairs away. Pointer took out the drawers and laid them on one side. Then he examined the remaining skeleton. Yes, there was a place running the width of his hand all along the back. Pointer promptly up-ended the table. There are not many ways of opening secret places in such pieces. He finally found that by screwing one of the feet around twice out jumped the back of a panel like the door of a cuckoo clock. He put his hand in and pulled out an umbrella, and then its handle, then a couple of letters tied with red tape and addressed in a faded handwriting to a Mrs. Walton in Yorkshire. The date was nearly thirty years ago.

The umbrella handle exactly tallied with the description of Julian Clifford's which had been given to Pointer's man. The umbrella looked as if it had been violently treated—possibly in the effort to cut off the handle—possibly before. The handle had been hacked off with some blunt instrument, the cane crushed and splintered.

Yes, with such an instrument, for instance, as a sharpened spade.

He took his finds away with him, and but for them, left everything as he had found it. Then he went home.

So Miss Haslar and Hobbs were to meet the day after tomorrow at Thornbush after a boat got in, and had met tonight in the library of Arnold Haslar's house!

Intricate case this! He decided to watch Diana Haslar himself to-morrow, for the hour of the rendezvous and some- thing in the tone of Hobbs suggested that it was to be the finale, or the wind-up of, or, at any rate, the report on some piece of business on which Diana would be engaged. Mrs. Clifford's cousin, Julian Clifford's literary agent, had spoken in the tone of a man who would be waiting, but the look on the face of the dead man's niece was that of one who has promised another that he can count on her, of one who is to do something.

Pointer was sorry. He had planned a very busy and very early morning at her brother's warehouse as a rat-catcher, with a wiry-haired marvel from the Yard—a champion ratter. No night watchman and no warehouseman in Britain could resist the offer that he intended to make.

However, after due reflection, he decided on "ladies first."

CHAPTER ELEVEN

And that was why, on the morrow, when Diana got down at Bruges, a chauffeur followed her out of the train and into the town—a chauffeur who had crossed to Ostend with her, had taken a ticket to Bruges just after her, who had arranged with the Bruges police to have a taxi-cab waiting for him outside the station. But Diana was walking, so he made a sign to the man at the wheel and walked on after her.

Bruges, ringed and intersected by canals, is interesting, and can be charming; but not in July, when it is crowded with British trippers who surge noisily in serried ranks along its main streets, avoiding its art treasures but crowding its cake shops.

As it happened to be a saint's day, or a wedding, or a funeral, the bells of all the churches, above all the great bell of Saint Sauveur, the massive cathedral, were shattering the air with swift, jarring peals. The bells of Bruges are now rung by electricity, and need not even pause for tired muscles.

It was the half-hour. And the _beffroi_, that beautiful tower that lifts its coronet high into the air above Bruges' big _place_, was giving one of its quarter-hour selections of carillons. Melodies may sometimes be suitable for being played on bells; this one certainly was not. Barrel organs were grinding merrily within a few feet of each other. Trams banged their gongs all down the curving street.

Diana, who looked a little dizzy with the clamour of Bruges-la-morte, turned into the rue Sud de Sablon. Being July, her English ears did not miss the songs of birds in this country that eats them.

The roof lines of the constantly winding streets were enchanting. Dentellated, crenellated, they rose against a sky whose colours told that the waves of Zeebrugge, the harbour of Bruges, or Brugge, as the Flamand calls it, were very near. She walked on, glad of the exercise.

"_Pas op, mejuffroww!_ (Look out, miss!)" a white-hatted gendarme, who was regulating the traffic, said quietly.

Mistaking the Flemish word for the equivalent of "Pass on," Diana stepped forward. She nearly "passed on" altogether. A car, dashing around the corner, taught her the perils of ignorance. But a long arm swept her back into safety. A chauffeur, a tanned man in a trim uniform, with a pleasant flash of white teeth below his drooping moustache, touched his cap with a "Pardon, Madame!"

She turned at the French, for Bruges is Flemish speaking. She saw him step towards a taxi from which a man had just slipped, and take the wheel.

"Is that your taxi? Can you drive me to the Beguinage?" she asked in the same language.

"Certainly, Madame!" and shutting her in the cab, he drove off into a side street, where he pulled up, and got off, apparently to do something to the back of the hood; in reality to open a map of Bruges and take a long look at _Ten Wyngaerde_, The Vineyard, as the town calls its Beguinage.

The Beguinages of Belgium are peculiar to this corner of Europe. From the thirteenth century on, women solved the question of domestic difficulties and dangers by living a community life which gave them all the protection of a convent, but where they could have almost the liberty of the world. The Beguines, who dress at a glance like other nuns, in white and black, sometimes take no vows, sometimes all but that of poverty. Their money is their own to use and leave. They dwell, not in narrow cells under one roof, with every hour of the day mapped out for them, but live, if they so prefer, in little houses, alone, or with another Beguine friend, set in the encircling,

protecting wall of the Beguinage. In the centre of the
Beguinage at Bruges—a small affair compared with that
of Ghent—is a quiet green. Tall elms, elms that saw men
set out on the last crusade, give it a thin, elderly shade.
Orchards and vegetable gardens lie behind it. Inside the
little houses a simple austerity must nowadays reign, just
as all the inmates are women of the highest character.
For the rest, they live pious lives under their chosen
Superior beloved by the poor, given over to good works.
The chauffeur drove the car to the arched entrance over a
bridge that spanned one of the canals. Here he had to
stop. Before them, like a city within a city, lay the
Beguinage, its little red roofs dotted among the greenery.
In front the water mirrored the curve of its gray wall.
Artists sat sketching it. To one side was the Minnewater,
Bruges' much overrated beauty spot. For though the town
has charming corners, they lie in quiet nooks, off the
main roads. But here at least was peace. Softly the
carillon floated down, melodious sounded Saint Sauveur's
tireless majestic bells.

Diana got out. No carriage may mar the silence of the
Sister's home. She made to pay her driver.

"I'll wait for Madame," he said promptly.

But Diana told him that she had no further need of
his services, paid him, and walked on quickly under the
domed gate, past the crucifix where the Beguines kneel,
coming and going. A sister met her going swiftly towards
their church.

"Mademoiselle van Bracht?" Diana asked.

"Over there. The white house with the geraniums in
the green windows, Mademoiselle," and the Beguine
hurried on.

"But she's at service just now," she added over her
shoulder.

Diana did not seem to be put off her intended call. The
chauffeur, who had lounged in after her, with the vacuous
air of a man staring at unfamiliar sights, saw her step on

as swiftly as before. He saw her rap at a little green-painted door.

"Baronesse van Bracht? Sceur Therese?" Diana asked.

"I am Sister Therese. Won't you come into my sitting-room?" the sister said in French. Diana followed her into a little back room on the ground floor, furnished plainly but comfortably, and so dark that the light had to be kept switched on beneath a statue of Sainte Begge.

The chauffeur tried the latch of the door. It opened under his careful hand without a sound. In his rubber-soled deck shoes he passed into a tiled passage with two doors on either hand. A door at the end of the passage showed the canal, quiet and deserted. He turned, and softly opened the first door on his left. He stood in a neat kitchen. As he hoped, a door led into the next room, where he could hear the two women. Noiselessly he drew the curtains shut over the window, then he cautiously opened the communicating door. Diana was just handing an envelope to the Beguine, who was saying:—

"I will see that it is passed on at once to my sister, Madame de Coninck. She will do the rest. By this evening all will be put right. I will give you a receipt if you will step into this balcony"

At that instant the light went out. Sceur Therese called out in English, and in English English too.

"Who's that? Who's holding my hand?" Then she screamed.

"What's wrong?" Diana called quickly. "I'm here, Sister. What's wrong?"

There came a knock on the door leading into the passage. The same moment the Beguine switched up the light. She glared at Diana like a mad woman. The knock came again. Her white headdress awry, the sister tried to pull it straight; she tugged at the black veil which shadowed her face and which, as a rule, is laid aside indoors.

The door opened, and the chauffeur looked in shyly.

"Pardon, Mesdames, but is anything wrong? I was knocking to ask the young lady whether she left this scarf in the cab, when I heard a cry—"

The sister looked from him to Diana and back to him with the swift, ferocious look of a panther.

"It's a plot, is it?" she said in a low, dangerous voice. "I see!"

Diana stared at her. The chauffeur stared too. His hair seemed to stand up with surprise. His mouth open, he looked from the sister to the English girl.

"She's mad," he said in French. "Come with me, Madame. She's quite mad, eh?"

"Stop!" The Beguine held out her hand. In it was something that glittered.

"Make a move either of you, and I shall shoot. I want that package back. I intend to have it back, so—"

Diana was quick of eye, but just what happened she did not see. The chauffeur did not seem to move a finger. Yet something shot across the room full into the sister's face. It was his cap. The man sprang after it. He seemed to use no force whatever. He only put out one hand, but the automatic fell with a smack against the opposite wall.

"We must go for help. She is evidently quite mad." He spoke pityingly as the woman turned and twisted in his arm.

"Go on to the car below, Mademoiselle. I will follow in a little minute. _Pardieu, la pauvre sceur!_ I will notify the police on the way to the station."

"No," Diana said quietly, "I don't leave her like this. What package is it you miss, sister? The one I brought?"

For a second the sister stared at her, then she said, "I thought you were in it. I see you're not. This man has that letter you brought. I'm sure of it. I'm certain he opened the door from that next room, switched out the light, and twisted the package from my hand before he pretended to knock at the other door. It's only a step between them."

She spoke in English. The man goggled stupidly.

"_Quoi?_ She says?"

Diana translated all that was necessary.

"A letter has been lost? Then why not telephone to the gendarmerie at once? There is a telephone at the portress's lodge. I saw the wires as I passed it. We can all three go there if the sister doubts me. But she is mad. The poor lady!"

Diana looked at the sister, whose face was white with red circles on the cheek-bones—circles of fury. She looked like a horrible clown.

Diana, with an odd look of uncertainty in her usually self-possessed glance, did not move.

"If you will be so good as to open that wooden shutter over there we could see better," the chauffeur said again. "I do not like to let her go. She may do herself a mischief. Throw herself out of that window, for instance." He gave the sister a look in which there was something mocking and something very stern. "The window that is open," he went on, "the window of the little balcony. A slip, and one would be in the canal. And the canal just here is choked with weeds, and quite deep enough to drown the sister, especially if by any chance that sort of iron raft were to fall down which I see is only stood against the window just below, so that a push from an outstretched hand would send it in too. It could so easily pin any one who had fallen in down among the weeds; and it is quite a deserted stretch."

Diana did not stir, but her jaw tightened.

"This man is a government spy," the sister said fiercely. "We must get that letter back. We must act!"

"You are acting, Mrs. Orr," the chauffeur answered blandly, "and acting very well. But I don't think you'll get that package back."

Diana jumped. It was the voice of the Chief Inspector from Scotland Yard. And what was that about "Mrs. Orr"?

"I am Sister Therese," the Beguine said very calmly now. "Mrs. Orr is my half sister. We are rather alike.

Miss Haslar, you know what hangs on recovering that envelope."

Diana seated herself.

"I'm going to understand this," she said, and she meant it.

"I'm afraid that would take longer than you think. But this"—Pointer dived into an inner pocket and held out something—"is what you brought, isn't it?"

"Why should you take that?" Diana asked indignantly. She looked prepared to snatch it from Pointer herself.

He gave her an apparently swift but very searching glance. "Miss Haslar, I think you know that I'm not tricking you when I assure you—_assure_ you—that it is where it should be. Who gave it to you?"

Diana did not answer. She looked at him. She looked at the Beguine whom Pointer still held by one hand on her arm. It was unlike Diana to let things drift. But she made no move, and she turned very pale.

Again he looked at her, with a rather enigmatic look.

"A train back to Ostend leaves in half an hour. I want you to take that, Miss Haslar."

She intended, he knew, to spend the night in that flamboyant resort. Her telegram to the Royal Hotel there for a room had been read this morning at Victoria before it was sent off. Two rooms, adjoining, and with a communicating door between had been engaged instead. Though this she would never know. A woman detective, who had accompanied Pointer, would be beside her. New Scotland Yard was doing its best to watch over Diana.

"I suppose you are crossing back to-morrow?"

She was.

"When you get back to town go straight to your brother's house. Don't go to Thornbush until I have had a talk with you. And don't telephone to any one there that you are back in London." She started. He looked her squarely in the eye. "Don't, on any account, go to or communicate with Thornbush, Miss Haslar," he repeated, "until I have called. I will try to get to you as soon after you reach home as I can. You have been in greater danger to-day than you quite realise." His eyes went to the window overlooking the canal, to the Beguine, and back to Diana.

"Danger—to me? I don't understand." She didn't.

"When a murder has been committed, and a head cut off, those who have gone as far as that are not likely to be playing for low stakes. You mustn't come between a tiger and his kill, and expect mercy," was the Chief Inspector's only explanation. His manner was very grave.

Diana shivered. She was looking very different now from the girl who had taken the cab.

"Will you tell me the truth when you come to-morrow?" she asked, not as one making a bargain, but desperately.

"What I tell you will be strictly the truth. And I expect from you strictly the truth," he said quietly. "And now, I think you had better start."

"But this—this sister"

"Ah!" Pointer gave a queer little smile, "this lady and I have a few things to say to one another."

Diana left the little cottage where all should have been peace, and where she had just spent a most violent few minutes. Something seemed to have given way in Diana. She looked as though something vital had been taken from her.

After an uneventful but sleepless night she left by the boat next morning, quite unaware that the rather severe-looking young woman beside her on the deck had anything to do with her. Her train was to the minute. She had nothing but a suitcase for the Customs, and five o'clock found her quietly letting herself into her brother's house. She peeped into his room, and saw with infinite relief that he was drawing deeper breaths than when she had left him yesterday morning.

She decided to have tea in the library. Its doors were practically sound-proof. No sound from there could possibly disturb the sick man. The room was empty, but from the other end, Arnold's study, she heard a stir.

She stepped towards the communicating door. As she did so, she accidentally clicked her bag against a chair. Instantly all was silent. Opening the door, she saw to her surprise that, though she could see no one, yet the strong-room was open. Had some one been tampering with the deed-boxes ranged along its shelves? She had a vague idea of their number and position. She stepped into it to look closer. On the instant the door slammed shut. She heard the click of the locks falling into position. She was a prisoner in a sound-proof, all but air-tight metal safe.

It was at that precise moment that Mrs. Clifford was very much bored. She was at a concert. The Albert Hall was stuffed from stall to roof. A great violinist had given of his best, and the enthusiasm had been delirious. Encore after encore had been demanded and generously given. It was long past the usual time when the last item was started. It was a Vivaldi Concerto. Mrs. Clifford disliked Vivaldi, even when played by a master.

The concert room was quiet and not too bright. Idly she pulled out her crystal ball and sat looking into it, her arm pressed against her neighbour's, for a voluminous lady overflowed from the other seat. Suddenly she gave a little gasp, and leaning still more to the right, got a better view of the crystal. The players were attacking the Rondon. Mrs. Clifford turned to the man beside her, a man who had twisted around in his seat when she had taken the one beside him, and buried himself still deeper in his music folios, so that his back was practically turned to her.

"Mr. Newman! Something is happening to Diana Haslar! She's in danger. Can you telephone to Mr. Straight? I can't use telephones, you know."

"Sh-h-sh!" hissed the music-lovers around them indignantly.

The man beside her flung his music books on to his seat, and swiftly, with a hand under her arm, led her out into the corridor outside.

"Go at once! Or telephone to Mr. Straight, he's nearer." Mrs. Clifford seemed quite unmoved by Newman's presence, as he was by the fact that she had known her husband's secretary in spite of a very remarkably good disguise—a very professionally made-up disguise.

"What did you see? Where is she?" he asked swiftly. Mrs. Clifford sank on a settee and went on staring at her ball.

"I've lost her! No, there she is!" Newman was behind Mrs. Clifford. He, too, was bending over the ball, his arms on either side of her.

"She's locked in an iron cell. There's very little air. She's pounding on the wall. She seems to be calling for help. It's all dark. Outside some one is standing listening. He's in the shadow, yet he seems familiar. Why, it's Arnold's study! Then that cell must be his strong room. And the word that opens the door must be lost. But what—" Newman had gone.

Pointer came over on the same boat and train with Diana, heard her give her taxi driver her brother's address, and then turned into the buffet for a hasty sandwich. He telephoned to the Yard for the day's reports. There were several. From parcels addressed to non-existent streets and people Mr. Clifford's clothes had practically all been retrieved. Along with them was a blood-stained and beplastered hand towel. The clothes had been identified by Mr. Clifford's tailor.

Pointer felt as though his boat were drawing in, drawing in all the time.

Last of all he learnt that ten minutes ago Hobbs, Mr. Clifford's literary agent, had left Thornbush and had been followed to Haslar's house. He was still there.

On the instant Pointer was out of the telephone booth, and speaking to the sergeant in charge of the station-police. In another he was on one of their motor-bicycles which are fitted with silencers as perfect as expense can make them.

He whizzed off for the Haslar's house at a speed which only his steering made possible. Even so, one tabby never returned to its home.

Arrived at the house, Pointer looked at the gravel of the drive. It showed that a car had just turned at the front door a car with the same tyres as the taxi which Diana had finally captured at Victoria. Driving away, the car had been lighter than when coming. Probably, therefore, it was empty and all was in order. He let himself in with his annexed latchkey. Noiselessly he ran up to her bedroom and listened. All was silent. He tried the door. It was unlocked. The room was empty. So was her boudoir.

He glanced in at the sick room in passing, through the door into the bathroom, but he gave his man no signal. Diana was not there, nor in either drawing-room. On the ground floor, dining-room and morning-room and library were all empty. Remained only the study. As he jumped for the communicating door, it opened, and Hobbs came out.

"Miss Haslar's in there," Pointer said swiftly but very easily. "I've followed her here from the station. I must have a word with her."

Hobbs fell back. His face turned green, his jaw slackened. Pointer's unexpected appearance, his swift yet casual words, his absolute certainty as to where Diana was, seemed to rattle Hobbs.

"I–eh—"

Pointer did not wait. He stepped in and glanced once around the room. Then he was at the safe door. He knew the password, thank God. Pointer had connected up the safe dial with a certain well-hidden burglar's dial before sending for Haslar's manager last night. It had marked every letter he set. The word had been Visit. Pointer now turned the five letters—tried the word. The door refused to budge. So some one, Hobbs probably, had changed the password.

Pointer, his ear to the safe, tapped with the end of his watch chain, sharp swinging blows. He caught a faint tap-tap from the inside.

"She's in there! Good heavens, man, you must have locked the door on her, never guessing that she was inside. Quick, Mr. Hobbs, the password!"

Pointer was throwing the man a rope. But the colour was coming back into Hobb's face.

"Miss Haslar's upstairs in bed, I take it. I haven't seen her, nor do I know anything about the safe or the combination lock. I dropped in to look up a technical point in one of Haslar's electrical books. I was in the library when I heard a tremendous thud. It took me a second to realise that it was the door of the strong room that I heard. At least, I suppose it was. I'm not certain even of that much."

He rattled off the speech at top-speed. His words were not exactly blurred, but there was a thickness about them that made Pointer's heart sink. Hobbs was the worst for drink, and the only chance for the girl locked in would have been a clear-headed, shrewd Hobbs, a Hobbs who would have known when he must cut his losses. Pointer knew from yesterday what Hobbs could be like when he was not sober, and to-day he was more nearly drunk than yesterday—much more nearly.

Pointer gave a whistle like a blackbird's when a poacher blunders too close at night. A man clambered in through the open window. He said a word to him. The man moved to Hobb's side, who looked as though he were watching something awful come up to him.

Pointer jumped to the telephone. He was taking no chances. He might yet get the password out of Hobbs, but meanwhile he was telephoning the Yard to send him the safe-expert with his most up-to-date tools to open a strong room door, which was—Pointer gave the makers' name and the size of the door. But the master-cracksman was away. No one knew when he would be in. Another man would, of course, be sent, but there was no second Cockerell.

Pointer felt certain that it was Hobbs who had altered the code word, but he might be wrong. He tried for Haslar's manager, but Mr. Dance was out. Then he got Thornbush. No one there was in. Mrs. Clifford was out. Mr. Straight was out; it was believed that he had gone to Sir Edward Clifford's. Mr. Hobbs was out.

Pointer turned again to Hobbs.

"Come, Mr. Hobbs, try and think if you can't remember the code word. It would mean a lot," Pointer's eyes dwelt on the other. "I was over in Bruges yesterday with Miss Haslar. I have the letter, by the way, safe and sound, which you gave her to take to Mrs. Orr."

Hobbs's face twitched as though an electric shock had passed through him.

"She might have had a bad time in Bruges. . . . But a good turn cancels a bad one—sometimes. I'm sure she wouldn't remember Bruges if she got out of that strong room at once. . . . Nor would I!"

Pointer was exceeding the law, and doing it most unwillingly, but the need of the entombed girl was paramount. Hobbs looked as if a terrible struggle was going on within him. The sweat stood out on his white face. But he set his teeth.

Pointer turned away. Was Hobbs gambling on the chance that Diana Haslar would never speak? But Hobbs was no fool. Whatever Diana knew could not be equivalent to rejecting the life-line that the Chief Inspector had thrown him. There was a greater reason than fear of what she might say, might suspect. Suddenly Pointer guessed it.

He turned and gave the man in the chair a long look. Hobbs caught it, read it, leapt in his seat, and then sat rigid, his eyes staring glassily.

The door burst open and Straight rushed in. Behind him, hesitating, as though disliking to set foot in Arnold Haslar's house, came Sir Edward.

"What's this about Haslar's strong room and Miss Haslar?" Straight asked.

"Know the password?" Pointer asked, but without any hope. Straight only shook his head with a look of horror.

"You mean to say it's true? That she's been locked in there?" he asked under his breath. "Isn't there a way of telling the right word by listening to the fall of the tumblers?"

"Not with this safe," Pointer said gravely, "but there's still time." His eyes rested for a fraction of a second on Hobbs— "Still time."

Hobbs half stepped forward. Almost, Pointer thought, his hand went towards the dial, but the neat brandy that he had drunk made him wheel about and return to a chair in the shadow by the window.

The safe-breaker arrived from the Yard. He set to work at once with a pneumatic drill. Chemicals were out of the question because of the girl inside.

"How did you hear of what had happened?" Pointer asked Straight above the roar of the drill.

"Mrs. Clifford got some one to telephone me. A commissionaire at a concert hall, I understand. She seemed quite certain of what had happened. . . . But surely Miss Haslar can be got out all right?"

"We must hope for the best," Pointer said none too encouragingly. "If the safe had been standing wide open for a little time before it was closed, she may have a better chance. Our man is quite good as a rule. Sir Edward was with you, I suppose?" Pointer finished.

"No, I ran into him in the garden outside," Straight explained absently.

"I had something very important to say to Miss Haslar," Sir Edward explained at once, retreating with Pointer to the farthest end of the room; "I will tell you about it later, Chief Inspector. A fact has come to my knowledge which makes me wonder. . . . However, Miss Haslar had not returned when I asked for her at half-past four."

"You waited in for Miss Haslar?" Pointer asked, watching his man try another way of tackling those immovable tumblers.

"No, I decided to call again later."

"Did you think the servant who let you out looked as though he had just come in from outside?" Pointer asked next.

"I let myself out, so I cannot say. Looked as if he had come in—?" Sir Edward began to repeat Pointer's odd question, a question which had served its turn of learning that Clifford had not been shown out.

Sir Edward looked round. Hobbs was out of earshot if he spoke low.

"Hobbs is under arrest? So you know?"

"Know what, Sir Edward?"

"Straight came to me about it. It seems he _did_ go through the books yesterday and to-day. Straight suspected Hobbs's accounts from something that Diana told him about a letter which she opened by mistake. Straight says the books are cooked: cleverly done, but he's certain they're cooked. He wants another chartered accountant to go through them with him. He speaks of something like fifty or sixty thousand not

accounted for. Of course in ten years. . . ."

The man from the Yard approached Pointer.

"I'm beaten, sir. This latest pattern is beyond me. There's a chap in Bermondsey, Silly Billy, he might do it. He's just out of a stretch. Not a bad sort."

Bermondsey! From Hampstead to Bermondsey and back! And to find Silly Billy. Meanwhile what of Diana? Pointer too was very pale. It was an awful thing to be standing there helpless and think of the agony just beginning so close beside them. Must they chance gray powder, and the effects of it? Death by chemicals was no worse than death by suffocation.

Suddenly a bookish, gray-haired, spectacled man, a typical musician from his appearance, stood in the room. So swiftly, so silently had Newman come in that only Pointer had seen him enter.

CHAPTER TWELVE

Mrs. Clifford hurried in after Newman. For once she looked in great distress.

"Is Diana still locked in?" she asked before she was in the room.

Straight jumped for her.

"The word, Mrs. Clifford! The new code-word. Do you, by any chance, know another word than _Visit?_"

She shook her head in silent horror, then she turned to Newman.

"Do you?"

"I don't know any other code-word than _Visit_." Newman had flung down a box that was all but beyond even his wiry strength. He tore it open, and began to lay out strange, bulky things on the carpet with desperate speed.

"That word won't open it now." Pointer alone had not shown any surprise at the return of the secretary— disguised —accompanied by Mrs. Clifford. "I can't reach Haslar's manager, nor could he help. The word has been deliberately changed. Going to use electricity?"

Newman nodded. His eyes were unmistakably those of the master of the situation.

Mrs. Clifford had turned to her brother-in-law and Straight.

"Mr. Newman telephoned to you? Oh, Edward, what shall we do? What can we do? If only Julian were here, as he will be shortly now, for this is Friday. Adrian, don't look so terrible," she glanced at her cousin's awful face, "I'm sure we'll get her out yet."

"Clear the room, please." Newman jerked out a box full of an odd, gritty powder with a strong rust smell.

"You want no help? Our man, Burton, is a trained engineer," Pointer asked.

"I want the room cleared, that's all."

"Burton," Pointer turned to the man who had tried his hand at the door and been beaten, "go below and stand by the main switch." Pointer wanted no tampering. "Sinclair, you and Mr. Hobbs go into the room opposite. Mrs. Clifford, if you and Sir Edward—"

"We'll wait upstairs. I'll concentrate, and send down my spirit to help."

"Thank you so much," Pointer said gravely, "and I'm sorry, Mr. Straight, but—"

Straight lingered.

"_Can_ you do it?" he asked Newman imploringly, "a blunder would only make it harder for the right man. ..."

"I shall not blunder. I was in the Secret Service, Mr. Straight. You will see Miss Haslar out very soon, I hope." Newman was already running his hands over the door.

"Mind if I watch you?" Pointer asked, when they were alone.

Newman lifted his heavy lids and let them drop. "Rather you didn't. I'm a nervous chap."

Pointer stood with his back to him and did not use a mirror. But Newman did not sound nervous. Quick and sure, Pointer could hear his movements at the safe. Burton had already knocked out the spindle, Newman now began plugging the hole with desperate speed, using the powder which he had brought with him. Then he tested something with an electric apparatus which he put on the table and connected with a wall-plug. It looked like some sort of dwarf thermo-generator.

Next, after some calculations which he made swiftly but very carefully on a little machine in his odd box, Newman started work of a kind that Pointer could not follow. The expert from the Yard arrived breathless.

"Am I too late? Can I do anything?"

Pointer indicated Newman.

"He thinks he can open that door. The code word's lost. Evidently he's not trying to drill holes. What about it? It's beyond me."

Cockerell stepped forward. He asked a few questions. Newman, without slackening his lightning work, answered curtly enough. By this time strange blue flashes were crackling around the dial box, and forked lightning seemed to answer from the edges of the closely-fitting door.

Cockerell looked excited.

"I've never seen this before—or have I? Wait a bit. . . . Where did I see work like this . . . that must have been done on some such method—ordinary electricity was used then, of course, but where . . . when?" . . . The safe-breaking expert went off into a deep study.

"Does he know his job?" Pointer asked.

"Rather! And yet—I should say better theoretically than practically. Where did I once see something that reminds me of this? . . ."

Suddenly Newman gave a little exclamation. His _crickle, crackle_ stopped. The blue and the yellow flashes no longer seemed to fight each other. In the air was still the strange electric smell of an X-ray room, but Newman was now pulling at the door with cloths over his hands. It opened. Diana lay huddled on the floor. Newman darted forward and picked her up. His disguise had gone by this time. Wig and beard had been pulled off in the heat of the work, and the sweat had washed the make-up from his hands and face.

Diana clung to him.

"Sanz!" her arms went round his neck, "I called you, and you came! I called you the whole time . . . with all my heart and all my soul."

Her face was transfigured. Her beautiful hair clung in damp curls to her finely-shaped head as a baby's does. She was pale. Under her lids were purple shadows, but her eyes were like stars.

"If you won't hold me fast, I shall you." She spoke with a strange solemnity.

This was no laughing meeting of lovers. Diana knew what the hand to which she clung might have done. Yet she clung to it.

"In spite of—everything?" he asked her gravely.

"In spite of—beyond—through—everything. Don't put me down, Sanz. Don't let me go again."

He only looked at her—a searching look to which the foreign sharpness of his features gave something rapier-like. Standing there still holding her, he had a dark, virile beauty which struck those watching him afresh.

Suddenly her eyes fell on Pointer. A look of terror swept down upon her face, putting out the light in it.

"I forgot; I betrayed you!" she stepped back from him, "and then I called you and you came! Oh, Sanz, I've lured you into their hands!"

"How do you mean that you betrayed me?" he asked quietly.

"I told them who you are. After your letter I—I thought it was a love of justice, but I couldn't bear that they should think you—it—a murder!" She whispered the last words, her face gray again.

"But supposing it was one?" he interrupted in a hard voice.

Diana made a helpless gesture.

"It's no use. I've tried to hate you for these years past, I've fought till I'm tired. Life wasn't worth living. In there, when the door banged shut, and I thought I should never see it open again, I've learnt the truth."

He stopped her. He was as pale as she under all his dark colouring.

"You forget that I'm wanted for murder. You forget the murder of your uncle—the shooting of your brother." He spoke almost roughly.

And at that Diana broke down.

He came across to her and took her face for a second between his slender dark hands, gently, as one takes a flower. Then he turned away.

Diana looked at Pointer.

"I must see him before he goes."

"You shall."

"Alone?"

"Alone." Pointer passed her and went on into the strong-room, carefully scrutinizing the boxes. It was dark inside here, except for his lamp. The work on the door had put the lights inside out of action. But there was something in here which he expected to find. . . . Suddenly his hand actually trembled for a second, when his long, lean fingers felt over a well wrapped-up tin marked in a scrawl:—

A. Haslar.
Not wanted forward. To be stored in a cold place.

There was a dent in one side. It was heavy for its size, and the size was that of a seven-pound tin.

Pointer carried it out. Then he saw that Mrs. Clifford was back in the room, her arms around Diana. Pointer put the tin on a table behind him, but his thoughts did not leave it. Inside it was, he knew . . .

Alison Clifford would have helped the girl up to her room, but Diana refused any help. Mrs. Clifford, smiling a little, moved back. She caught her foot in a rug. To steady herself she laid a hand on the tin which Pointer had just set down. There came the oddest sound from her—a gasp, followed by a sort of strangled cry. She fell forward across the table grasping the tin in her arms.

"Julian! Oh, Julian!" She gave a frightful scream and tore at the wrappings with her fingers, shrieking like a demented woman.

"Hush, Mrs. Clifford," Pointer said firmly but very gently, "for the sake of the sick man overhead, for your own sake, you must not scream like that."

She had her hands still on the box, and the look in her eyes frightened Diana, who had run to her. She thought that her reason had gone.

"It's Julian's head!" Mrs. Clifford said in a strange, horrible whisper to Sir Edward, who had come in hastily. "In there! In that tin! His!"

This time Diana screamed—a low, horrified cry. "Is she mad?" she whispered in mingled terror and pity.

"Mrs. Clifford," Pointer said gravely, "I'm so sorry for this horrible shock—"

"His eyes are closed," Mrs. Clifford was murmuring now in a wild whisper.

Pointer forcibly lifted the box out of her grasp. He could not let her continue to "see" what that face must look like now. Not yet earth—no longer flesh.

"You know the truth now," he said gently.

Alison knelt on trembling violently.

"Mrs. Clifford," Pointer said again, "I must take this away for a little while. You shall see your husband's body shortly, believe me. But not like this! Not—" She did not seem to heed him. Pointer thought that she had fainted. He would have left her to the care of Diana and Sir Edward, but when he turned away she clutched his sleeve. She almost tore the stout cloth of his cuff.

"Give me that back! It's mine! Mine by every law of God and man!"

"It is yours," Pointer said with real emotion, "but you must let me put it where it belongs. You must give us"— he glanced at the clock then at Sir Edward—"just one hour. Then you shall see your husband's body, if you still wish to do so, to-night."

She let him go at that and sat staring in front of her with a terrible expression on her face. At once wild and lost, as of a woman who felt the very foundations of her soul rocking within her.

"I'll bring her. To the mortuary chapel, I suppose? Where exactly is it?" Clifford asked. He himself was a ghastly white.

"I'll leave my car. My man will know." Again Pointer turned towards the door, that precious tin clasped in his arm. This time it was Newman who stopped him.

"Aren't you forgetting me?" he asked shakily, "your prisoner?" Like every one else in the room, whether they understood it or not, he looked profoundly moved by what had just happened.

"No," Pointer said easily, "oh, no, Mr. Newman, I'm not forgetting you. I must ask you to return to your old rooms at Thornbush until I have an interview with you." Newman would be better watched this time, Pointer knew.

Outside he saw Diana talking to Wilkins, her face convulsed. He motioned to her to come into an empty room. She all but refused.

"How did that tin come to be in this house at all?" he asked her.

"It came from the warehouse early this afternoon," she replied in a quiet, dull voice. There are points beyond which sensation becomes numb. "Wilkins put it on the hall table thinking it was sent up by mistake, or that I had asked for it. That is all he knows about it. And all I know about it."

The Chief Inspector gave a few more directions to the man in charge of Hobbs. Then he drove off with his precious tin—the tin for the sake of hiding which, so he believed, a half-sober Hobbs had been willing to let Diana Haslar die a frightful death.

The Commissioner and Major Pelham were present when the tin was opened. The plaster was carefully sprayed away until that appeared which they had expected to see, and which Mrs. Clifford had apparently already seen in some strange way—the head of Julian Clifford.

It had a bullet mark behind one ear.

An hour later, Mrs. Clifford followed with Sir Edward. The head had been carefully joined to the severed neck, and a cloth laid over the juncture. The face itself was made as little repulsive as possible. The plaster had done much to preserve it, and the warehouse chill had helped.

Sir Edward brought her in finally when word was sent out. She tottered to the coffin, and stood bending over it for a long time in silence. Then she dropped to her knees beside it.

"Ferryman, take me across? Oh, Ferryman, take me across!" The choking cry brought tears to the eyes of a very stolid-looking young policeman who was on duty in an unobtrusive corner.

"Poor soul! Mad, quite mad!" he said to himself; "talking about ferries here."

Pointer could not let this tormented soul gather itself up in peace, if tormented it really were. For Duse could have acted as Alison Clifford had done here and at Haslar's house. Sarah Bernhardt equalled that cry of pent-up passion bursting all efforts at control. Gently he touched her arm.

"Mrs. Clifford, who fired that shot?" he said insistently. "Who killed your husband from behind— without giving him a chance to save himself?"

She did not seem to hear him.

"I was wrong," she murmured under her breath, adjusting the sheet with what seemed like loving fingers. "'For here rolls the sea, and even here lies the other shore. Not distant. Not anywhere else.' " She turned and faced Pointer as though he had not spoken, looking at him as at a strange and rather meddlesome stranger.

"Mrs. Clifford," Pointer repeated quietly, "no one admires Tagore more than I do. But he would be the first to say that here lies duty as well. 'Here in this everlasting present.' And duty, your duty to your dead husband, to the civilisation which has sheltered you, which gave him the chance to become what he was, is to aid us—or rather Justice"

The widow sank into her chair. She covered her face with hands that looked almost translucent. Edward

Clifford watched her, his own face drawn and haggard. When she finally showed hers again, it was serene.

"I cannot help you, Chief Inspector. Please don't misunderstand me." Her eyes on him, she paused. Keen, searching, were the last words to apply to their gaze. Yet Pointer felt as though she could see far—were seeing far. But he knew his own face to be an impenetrable mask when he chose. It was so now.

"I cannot help you," she said again, almost as to a child. "Or rather what you stand for—the law, man-made law— man-made and therefore to me blind and cruel. My husband has passed into another phase of life. Had he 'died,' to use your expression, by what is called an act of God, you would not have me try and avenge his death. Then why now? The result is the same. All your efforts cannot light the empty lantern. The light is shining where you cannot see it—for the moment. Julian would say the same."

"And the man who killed him?" Pointer asked coldly.

"The man who did it will suffer—will pay in another way. I will not help you to make him pay in your way."

"Then the next murder he commits will be on your soul, Mrs. Clifford," Pointer said very gravely.

Sir Edward started as though to speak, but checked himself. "Justice is necessary," the Chief Inspector went on, "and human punishment is necessary. Or we should be back among the head-hunters in no time. The wheel won't turn forward unless we put our shoulders to it." He spoke intentionally in a matter-of-fact voice: "Your husband was murdered, remember. Slaughtered as a beast is slaughtered."

He paused. Her lids flickered and her eyes widened. She drew in her breath sharply.

"He lies there crying to you for justice," Pointer ended passionately.

"His body lies there, Chief Inspector," she corrected, but apparently with an effort. "Julian Clifford _is_ as much as ever he was; as near! as dear!" Suddenly two large drops rose and hung on her lashes. They gave the finishing touch to her face. Even Pointer felt his anger melt within him. Surely this woman was what she seemed.

"What was the reason for which Mr. Clifford left his home on Monday night? Why were you so sure he was in safety?" he continued.

She gave a cry at that and wrung her hands.

"Did you think he was in Bruges buying the Charlemagne crystal?" he persisted.

She interrupted him. "To think I believed him safe! To think I thought I saw him in the crystal! Then what did I see? How did I see?" She stared wild-eyed at Pointer.

She looked shaken to the heart. Pointer said nothing. If this were not acting, then he realised that the woman must have had such a shock as to be near the confines of what could be borne.

"I who thought I could see further than others!" she murmured. "But I _did_ see Julian in the crystal . . . just as I saw Diana a little while ago. She was there where I saw her. Then why not Julian? Why not my husband?" she asked wildly.

"You have very wonderful gifts, Mrs. Clifford," he said quietly, "but you could not see what was not there, the dead among the living. I think your own imagination, your own belief as to where your husband was, projected itself into that crystal."

She was, or seemed to be, too exhausted to be questioned further, and he helped Sir Edward put her into her car and take her home to where a "nurse" from Scotland Yard was waiting to look after her—with a most vigilant eye.

Her objections to helping him find the criminal, were they solely as she represented them?

Pointer's profession, one he greatly respected, led along so many dark and twisted paths of the human heart. As a doctor spends his days at sick beds beside diseased bodies, so did the Chief Inspector's work take him among diseased minds. It was inevitable that he should distrust appearances as much as any mystic. Given hesitation on the part of the angel Gabriel, Pointer would have distrusted him. What, then, of Mrs. Clifford? She had cashed that cheque for notes, some of which Diana Haslar had taken to Mrs. Orr. Pointer believed that Diana had been given them by Edward Hobbs, Mrs. Clifford's cousin.

Tindall came hurrying in. The telephone had brought him the news. Both men were waiting for the police surgeon to make a summary examination of what had been hidden in the tin.

"Amazing about Mrs. Clifford," the F.O. man said tensely. "Did she know beforehand what the tin contained? Or did she 'see' into it? If the former, she knew that it would be opened within a very few minutes."

"She may have seen what I was seeing, and seeing tremendously keenly," Pointer suggested. "My mind was full of what I felt sure was inside that tin, what I guessed I should find on the shelf in that strong room. Just as sitting close beside Mr. Newman at a concert she got the message which Miss Haslar says she was sending him. Certainly she could not have known by any ordinary means that Miss Haslar was locked in that safe. I shouldn't wonder if whenever she reads a sealed letter, as they tell me she can do at times, or sees into a locked box, if there were some one in the room who knew what the letter or the box contained. She saw through Newman's disguise apparently, but then Newman would have recognised her at once, and must have been very conscious of her presence beside him."

"Thought-reading, in short?" Tindall asked dubiously.

"Always supposing it's not guilty knowledge," Pointer agreed. "I noticed her cousin Hobbs walked away to the window while she looked into the crystal, and 'saw' the stepped gables—saw her own thoughts, I take it, supposing she's innocent."

"This is going to be a slow, intricate case," Tindall said thoughtfully.

Intricate, certainly, but Pointer did not think it would be slow. He made no reply.

"How did Miss Haslar come to be locked into the safe, and who in the world put the head there?" Tindall asked, almost tearing his hair.

Pointer only turned to take the doctor's report which a man had just brought in.

The bullet had just failed to pass entirely through the lower part of the back of the head from left to right and was easily taken out. It was the kind to fit a .25 automatic, and had been fired from too far off to singe or blacken the skin.

"It fits Haslar's automatic," Pointer murmured. "No one else at Thornbush seems to own a weapon of any kind, except Sir Edward Clifford. He, too, has a .25—a common enough type."

"Haslar's warehouse—Haslar's revolver!" murmured Tindall. "I've taken the liberty, by the way, of putting one of our men as well on guard outside Thornbush. I confess I expected Etcheverrey to be detained. Or are you leaving him to me?"

"I'd like nothing done about him till to-morrow," Pointer said thoughtfully, "just as I want to keep my own counsel for that time."

"After his accomplices, eh? Good! So Etcheverrey's under our hands again. Rather fine of him coming back to save Miss Haslar, after that confession of his. Sort of thing he might be expected to do, though. Twisted nature his, with odd streaks of generosity in it."

Tindall accompanied Pointer to his rooms in Scotland Yard. Sir Edward had spoken of going there as soon as he had seen Mrs. Clifford home. Evidently he had something important to say, and something important to ask. He did not keep them waiting long.

"Now Chief Inspector, how did you learn about the Charlemagne crystal and Bruges?" Edward Clifford began at once. "Mrs. Clifford only told me that in strict confidence last night. Hobbs had hinted at it in the train, and obviously Julian had had it in his mind when he questioned me about paying over large sums so that they could not be traced. But how did you learn of it?"

"In the course of some routine work," Pointer said evasively. "I expect, however, to get fuller details from Mr. Hobbs presently."

"Hobbs!" Sir Edward made a wry face. "You certainly let no grass grow under your feet in his case either. Straight had only just told me of the defalcation. Straight found"— Sir Edward now turned to Tindall—"Straight found that Hobbs has cooked the books for the last ten years or so. And to the tune of a large fortune. He wants a first-class man to go through the books with him. The Chief Inspector was right in his suspicions of Hobbs."

They had not been suspicions with Pointer. The belief in the existence of heavy defalcations was the bed-rock of one half of Pointer's theory as to what had happened to Julian Clifford.

"And what about that cheque?" Sir Edward again addressed himself exclusively to Pointer. "Did Hobbs pay it over? He handed it to Mrs. Clifford to cash yesterday morning, telling her that Julian had enclosed it in the note which he had left for him. Hobbs's story is that in that letter Julian wrote that he had received word too late of some urgent necessity, some hitch, which only his own presence over in Bruges would smooth out, and that he was leaving at once, shortly after midnight on a returning fruit-cargo boat. Julian had all sorts of odd friends. The boat would get to Zeebrugge at eight Tuesday morning, and my brother would be at de Coninck's house by ten. He had to leave the cheque for Hobbs to cash and forward the money. Hobbs had a very busy morning ahead of him yesterday, and asked Mrs. Clifford to go to the bank for the money. She knew what was on foot. My brother intended the crystal as a surprise for her, but she had, it seems, overheard some words of

his to Mrs. Orr which had told her what he was about.
But as he had set his heart on surprising her, she kept
up, before him, the pretence of knowing nothing. So Mrs.
Clifford cashed her husband's cheque at once on Tuesday
morning, and handed Hobbs the money. He assures me
that there really is a Selfe assisting Mrs. Orr at the
Bruges end, and that the cheque is perfectly in order.
Mrs. Clifford, when I asked her a few questions, she
cannot talk much about it yet, confirmed all this. She
added that Mrs. Orr pressed her very hard to let her take
the money over. She, too, was going to Bruges, and was,
as I suppose you know too, acting in the affair for her
sister, the wife of the newly-appointed director of the
West Flanders Museum, that great building that's just
been built outside Bruges. The director was not to appear
in the affair at all. But Mrs. Clifford preferred to carry
out what she believed to be Julian's instructions. Were
they his instructions?" Sir Edward looked hard at
Pointer, who only stirred his tea thoughtfully.

"If not," Clifford's hand shook a little, "the murderer
must be— But I confess I find Julian's death a deeper and
deeper mystery the more I study it. I, too, found out a
piece of evidence yesterday—not bearing on Hobbs,
however, but on Haslar. Mrs. Clifford handed me Julian's
diary when I pressed her for dates and hours. In that
diary there's an entry about the discovery in an old
bureau that belonged to Sir William Haslar's private
secretary, or at least was always used by him, of two
copies of letters which had been sent to the writer's wife,
some thirty years ago now. He was killed in a carriage
accident. She died shortly afterwards. In them this man,
Walton was his name, accuses Sir William of very terrible
things. Subversion of party funds, and what practically
amounts to blackmail. They're poisonous imputation
though there have been whispers at times that Sir
William did sail very close to the wind now and then. My
brother makes a note to say that he intends in fairness to
the public to have these letters inserted as an appendix in

his coming Life. He notes down the indignation of Diana, but especially of her brother Arnold. Diana, according to Julian, was certain after the first shock, that no one would credit the allegations. But Arnold Haslar took it differently. There is an entry only this last Thursday in which Julian records that Arnold practically threatened him with violence if he dared to defame a dead man by printing those libels. My brother apparently was quoting Arnold's exact words. I have no idea where the letters are. I asked Hobbs, and he told me the very disquieting fact that Julian had had them on him when he left Thornbush—carried them on his person. He distrusted Miss Haslar, believed that in spite of her apparent acquiescence, she might steal the letters. And after all, family pride is a very strong chain. Now, Chief Inspector, where do we stand? I confess I am puzzled. Here are the defalcations—not yet proven, it is true—but Straight says he'll go bail that he's right, and believes it's not far short of a hundred thousand pounds has gone. Julian never lived up to his income, I knew. Here's the fact of these Haslar letters with the fury of Arnold Haslar at the idea of their being published—Arnold Haslar, who called out that he 'did it for nothing!' Arnold Haslar, who knew about the missing head, and who the murdered man was, when the only printed information was that the corpse was Etcheverrey! But then, what about Etcheverrey himself?"

Still Pointer did not reply. He only nodded thoughtfully.

"Are we wrong about those destroyed pages in my brother's manuscript: the pages pointing straight to Etcheverrey—to Newman?"

This time Pointer did look up.

"It's a very intricate case," he agreed, "but I think—I think —that the pages of Mr. Julian Clifford's coming novel were taken and destroyed because of what was in them. And I think that because of the information shortly to be published through them, Mr. Clifford was murdered." And Pointer inhospitably rose and with an apology ended the few minutes' talk. He was at work before the door closed behind them. The paper in which the tin box had been wrapped was of an unusually good quality. It matched some which Pointer had seen at Thornbush—paper in which his publishers sent Julian Clifford his proofs. Who would open Mr. Clifford's proofs? Newman probably. And the string . . . Pointer found within the half-hour that the string was the same as the ball on Newman's writing table.

Pointer drove on to the warehouse. He found the night watchman just closing shutters and gates. From him he learnt that the box had been handed to a pensioned-off night watchman very early Tuesday morning. The man was only called in for extra duty when, as then, the regular man was busy on some especial job. This extra watchman had put the box in the cellar, but had forgotten to mention the fact to any one. It was only by chance that to-day, Friday, he had learnt of Mr. Dance's inquiry, and by that time, unfortunately, the foreman had mislaid the address given him by the manager to which any such parcel was to be sent. The men preferred not to mention this fact to Dance, but sent the package to Mr. Haslar's house, believing that though down with the flu, he could still see about his own parcels.

Pointer went to interview the ex-night watchman. He left him not much the wiser. A car had driven up to the gates of the warehouse about three on Tuesday morning. The driver had got down and handed him a parcel, saying that Mr. Haslar wanted it taken care of according to instructions which he had written on it. But he did not want it entered on the books, as it would not be left for long. With that the man had clambered back into his seat, turned the car, and driven off. Stanley, the man who took the tin, had marked it K for the cold storage, and, after putting it in the appropriate cellar, had forgotten all about it until to-day. His belief that it was Mr. Haslar's chauffeur who had called in the car rested on mere assumption. He had too little to do with the warehouse nowadays to know Arnold Haslar's car or driver. He could not even describe the latter. He might have been Arnold Haslar himself, and he might not.

CHAPTER THIRTEEN

Pointer drove to the police station where Hobbs was lodged in a comfortable enough room. The shock of the arrest had cleared his brain. He was quite himself again now, and had ordered, and eaten, a very good dinner.

"Why am I being detained here? Why is bail refused, if it's on any charge for which you have a right to detain me? Why am I not allowed to communicate with my solicitor?" he began in the tone of a man who had determined to take the upper hand.

"Bail is never allowed on a murder charge, Mr. Hobbs." Pointer took a chair.

Hobbs was holding himself in with some difficulty. "Murder? Whose murder? What murder?"

"The murder of Julian Clifford. And, if we see fit, the attempted murder of Miss Haslar through a plan concocted together with Mrs. Orr in Bruges where she posed as her unmarried half-sister, a Beguine there called Soeur Therese. Mrs. Orr was really quite talkative when I explained how things stood over here. She had no idea Julian Clifford was dead."

Hobbs's face twitched.

"You don't think you can get away with this sort of stuff with me, do you?" he asked.

"It's the truth, Mr. Hobbs. Mrs. Orr is not the kind to throw good money after bad. She gave us every help, like the sensible woman that she is. We have, as I told you, the money you sent her by Miss Haslar. Five thousand pounds."

"Ay, yes, the money that was sent to straighten things out, if necessary. Sir Edward told you about Mr. Clifford's proposed purchase of the Charlemagne crystal. Needless to say, the money I sent her, except her own promised rake-off of one thousand, was only deposited with Mrs. Orr, so to speak. She was expected to account for it very strictly. As to her own commission, I saw no reason why she should be the loser because Mr. Clifford's terrible end had cut short the negotiations."

"Especially after she had inserted that personal in the _Times_ of yesterday, Tuesday? 'Hobby. Five needed instantly as promised. No letters. May.' She says a small official in the new museum had heard something about the proposed sale. And the money found on you when you were searched just now! A nice sum, Mr. Hobbs. The remainder of the cheque for seventy thousand, as well as some bearer bonds."

"I was carrying that sum according to Julian Clifford's instructions," Hobbs retorted. "It now returns to his estate, of course. Now that I know, what I did not believe until this afternoon, that he is dead. You know why that cheque was cashed. Whatever happened to Mr. Clifford after he wrote those notes which each of us at Thornbush got Tuesday morning, I was only carrying out instructions."

Pointer shook his head. "It won't do, Mr. Hobbs. We've had an accountant looking into the books. According to him you've had altogether not far short of a hundred thousand pounds already out of Mr. Clifford's fortune."

Hobbs did not question the figure.

"The new librarian, Straight, was the accountant, I suppose? I thought that was his game! But you'll have to have reasonable proof, better proof than that before arresting me for murder."

"We have ample proof of motive," Pointer said tranquilly. "Really quite good. Just let me run the facts over to you, Mr. Hobbs. There is the systematic robbery extending over many years—about ten, Straight thinks. Mr. Clifford evidently made some discovery—you determined to kill him at once. You were already getting ready to leave England with Mrs. Orr. She had determined to throw in her lot with you when she found that her name must be published in a coming divorce suit. But before you both went off to subsist quite pleasantly on the money you had accumulated, you thought that the Charlemange crystal would give you the opportunity for additional loot. You never intended Mr. Clifford to get the crystal. What you did intend was to see that Mr. Hobbs got the seventy thousand which you and Mrs. Orr claimed was being asked by the town for it. You have no alibi for Monday night. You lured Mr. Clifford to Fourteen Heath Mansions, or you took advantage of some one else's having lured him there, followed him, and murdered him. You cut off his head, packed it in plaster in a biscuit tin, wrapped it in some paper in which Mr. Clifford's proofs had been sent home, tied it with string from Mr. Newman's ball, and took it to Mr. Haslar's warehouse, rightly thinking that in the ordinary course it would not be detected there for a long time —long after you had left England. How much chance will you have in the dock against that story, Mr. Hobbs? Remember your palm prints on the spade handle through the opening in the gloves you carefully wore."

That last improvised touch did it. Hobbs sagged down in his chair, his mouth working.

"I'm innocent!" he said at last in a hoarse voice, "innocent of all the charges."

"You _can't_ be innocent of both the charge of embezzlement and the charge of murder, Mr. Hobbs. Your one chance to clear yourself of the capital charge is to prove to me that Mr. Clifford's death absolutely disarranged your plans."

Hobbs sat a moment, then he straightened up. He had feared as much from the beginning of the interview, but had hoped to avoid a confession.

"I warn you, of course," Pointer went on, "that anything you say about Mr. Clifford's death may have to be used in evidence, whether against you or another, but anything that you tell me about other matters will be considered as confidential, except where it touches on the murder."

"What does Edward Clifford say?"

"I haven't discussed the matter with him. The only bargain I can make with you, Mr. Hobbs," Pointer said with steel in his voice, "is that one lie, and you may find yourself arrested on a capital charge. But, on the other hand, if you tell frankly all that you know, we may waive the accusation of attempted murder. I can make no promises, of course."

There was a long silence.

"I'll tell you exactly what happened," Hobbs said finally, "it's my best chance with you, I see. It may help— I think it will. Monday night I sat out in the garden till about ten. When I came in, I found a note on the telephone pad for me from Mr. Clifford asking me to go on after him to Fourteen Heath Mansions, where he would wait for me. No name was given of the flat's owner. I was rather surprised, for I had no idea that he knew any one there. But I went to the address, used an automatic corner lift—I had a friend who lived there once, so I knew my way about. As I stepped out of the lift on to the landing, my scarf caught in the lift door. I stopped to put it right. Had to peel off my gloves, and stepped over to the window ledge to lay them down. That brought me to one side of the landing in the shadow. While I was rewinding the scarf, the door of Number Fourteen opened suddenly, and a man thrust his head out, looked around, and then slipped out and closed the door, standing still again for a moment to listen. I was just going to move towards him when he ran down the stairs as light as a cat. Well, I was startled. I stepped to the door and caught hold of the little brass knocker. It gave—the door was open. Apparently the lock hadn't caught. I couldn't understand the affair at all. But I knew that Clifford had the Haslar letters with him in a letter-case. I called his name. No one answered. I walked into the first room to my right and there I found him—dead—shot—sitting with his head sunk forward on his breast ... he was quite warm. There was no weapon to be seen. Well,"—Hobbs stopped and lit a cigar with a match that quivered—"I was appalled. There's no use pretending that Julian Clifford's death wasn't the end of things for me. Edward Clifford, or any other executor, would run a very careful eye over accounts. I couldn't cover my tracks under a couple of days' intensive work, and I wasn't ready to fly at once—I daren't with a murdered man. Then there was the cheque for seventy thousand pounds which Clifford carried ready to cash when necessary, and which, as you know, we'd been working for. I thought of taking his body off with me, but you can't carry dead people around town. I thought of all sorts of things. Then I remembered that on coming in, I had come by a corner door—I had noticed some workmen's tools and sacking. I thought of a sack, and of dumping the body into the river somewhere. I went downstairs and found that there was no empty sack. But there was an empty tin, a tin large enough to contain a head. I went back to Thornbush, got my car out —by some lucky chance the chauffeur had the evening off— took along with me some paper and string, left the car not far from Heath Mansions, walked in by the same way, still without meeting any one. The porters and people were all in the big, central, well-lit part. I took the tin and a spade up with me. The spade went under a loose topcoat which I had put on at Thornbush when I went back for the wrapping material. I had left the door with the latch caught back. I went in, took off Clifford's clothes, did them up into two parcels, and addressed them to fictitious names—I've forgotten what names, or where, for then I took the head . . His voice shook. "I don't need any punishment for having done that. It's punishment enough. I see it night and day. Shall see it. . . . You can't do a thing like that and be the same man afterwards. However ... I poured plaster into the tin, and so on, as you already know. And after some thought I decided that the best place for it would be Haslar's warehouse. He had once told me how things got snowed under in the cellars, do what they would. Besides, I thought then that there was a poetic justice about it, for I believed that Haslar had killed Julian Clifford."

"But we found the tin on a shelf in Mr. Haslar's strong room," Pointer said doubtfully.

Hobbs swore at himself. "Like a fool I put it there when I went to Arnold Haslar's this afternoon and found it on the hall table."

"And what took you to Mr. Haslar's house?"

Hobbs kept sullen silence for a moment. Then, "I had found the Haslar letters Wednesday night which had been on Mr. Clifford before his death, and for which I had been looking everywhere, letters which only interested Haslar, in a secret drawer in his library along with Clifford's umbrella. I forgot the letters while talking to Miss Haslar, and getting her to take some money across for me to Mrs. Orr. I knew quite well that I was watched by day, but I thought I could slip across at night and get them. They were better destroyed."

"That version won't do, Mr. Hobbs," Pointer said decidedly. "You took those letters from Mr. Clifford's body—from his dead body you maintain—when you took the cheque. Just as you—not Haslar—took the umbrella, hacked it into pieces to get it into a parcel with the clothes, and then found after all that it was too awkward to manage."

This was only the sounding of a pilot going carefully in difficult waters.

"You went out for a walk on Tuesday morning as soon as you came down. You walked over to Mr. Haslar's house, let yourself in, or found the door open and walked in, and put the umbrella in that secret partition. You could easily hide the umbrella on you, or carry it in a roll of maps or papers. . . . Then when the whole affair began to get unpleasantly hot, you decided that the letters which you were carrying on you must be hidden somewhere. Somewhere known only to yourself. Some hiding-place, moreover, that would tell against the person in whose presumed possession they were found, should they be found. Mr. Haslar is not likely to open any of his drawers for a long time, so to Mr. Haslar's old bureau you carried them Wednesday night. Miss Haslar caught you with them in your hand. You pretended, of course, that you had just taken them out of the place where her brother had hidden them."

That Diana had actually seen Hobbs with letters in his hand which it was known that Julian Clifford had been carrying on Monday night, the night when he was murdered, was one of the things that explained why she ran so much danger in going to the Beguinage. Why, once her help was no longer needed, it was not intended that she should return to England.

Pointer reasoned—rightly—that when Hobbs had to send the money to Mrs, Orr by some carrier who he believed was not being watched, he was in a quandary. Whoever was taken into his counsel, however slightly, would be a permanent danger to him and to Mrs. Orr. That person had therefore better be silenced. Hobbs, so Pointer believed, chose Diana both because she could be easily induced to take the letter, and because she would be as well out of the way. She knew too much. She had opened a letter meant for Hobbs, Sir Edward said. One that had made her suspect that the literary agent's entries were not accurate. She was a grave menace. Once let the idea that Hobbs had been robbing his brother take root in Sir Edward's mind, and—supposing that he himself knew nothing of the crime—then, in spite of Newman's confession, Hobbs's chance of getting away with, or without, the money for the crystal would be small.

"You decided this afternoon to get back those letters in order to frighten her into silence if things went wrong," Pointer continued, "that is, if she should by any chance return from Bruges. And that was why you went to Mr. Haslar's house when you fancied yourself unwatched. You evidently have a latchkey. You let yourself in this afternoon, and the first thing you saw was that tin in the hall. You put it in the strong room whose password you knew, like most of Mr. Haslar's friends. And because it was there, Miss Haslar had been locked in by you when you thought she had gone in after it—you refused to say to what word you had set the dial." Pointer bit back with difficulty his comments on what had happened.

"I forgot the word." But Hobb's eyes did not meet the other's. "Besides, I'd had a glass of brandy. Neat too. Who wouldn't, when they found that damned tin resurrected, and staring at them from a hall table? Ever since that night in the flat I've only kept going by—" He pulled himself up and sat biting at his cigarette.

"And the crystal was never intended to be really a sale?"

Hobbs set his teeth for a second. "No, just a plant. We had decided to burn our boats, Mrs. Orr and I. As soon as we got hold of the notes for the cheque, I was to leave England and join her. But I couldn't get off at once, things had come too much in a rush for that. And by Tuesday evening I was told by Edward Clifford and you that the body had been identified."

"Did Newman know about the crystal?"

"Certainly not! He was our greatest danger. Of course had I had an idea of the truth"

"What truth?" Pointer asked casually.

"Why, the reason for which he killed Julian Clifford. That he was in love with my cousin. Mrs. Orr had long suspected as much. I had always laughed at the idea."

"It was Mrs. Orr's notion to get Mrs. Clifford into things too? So that if they went wrong there would be your cousin to fall back on?" Pointer asked in his most colourless voice.

"That was the idea," Hobbs said shortly.

"Mrs. Clifford believed the crystal was to be genuinely bought?"

"Oh, lord, yes! Only thing she had ever wanted. She had seen it in Bruges some years ago, and told Julian then that she would give her eyes to possess it. That was quite enough for him. He wanted it as a sort of peace-offering for his frequent absences, I think."

"And Mrs. Clifford believed that Mr. Julian Clifford left for Bruges on Monday night?"

Hobbs nodded.

"And the letters left in Julian Clifford's name?"

Hobbs hesitated. "It's a bad business. But it's not murder. I wrote the letters, of course, the letters signed by Clifford's name. There's nothing easier than what's called forgery. No one ever thinks of doubting a letter when they see a familiar name at the foot. I had to do something to keep people from suspecting what had happened. I knew about what to say in each, of course. Fondest love to Alison. Poor girl. General directions to Newman to carry on. Same to Diana. Straight was to start on the subject-index I'd heard Clifford speak of. I wrote the notes Tuesday morning after leaving the tin."

"You think Mrs. Clifford had no doubts throughout as to the genuineness of the two she got?"

"None whatever. A baby in swaddling clothes could deceive my cousin."

"And was it usual with Mr. Clifford to leave her like that —with only a written note for good-bye?'

"He had done it at least once before, I knew, when he was at work on a serial. He never worked out his serials before-hand. I remembered that on that occasion he had scribbled her a line, poked it under her door, and been out of the house when she got up."

Pointer nodded. "I see. Now, as to the cheque? We know, of course, that you altered the name to Selfe. But how did you account for the name to Mrs. Clifford, I mean?"

"I told her Selfe was the man through whom the crystal would actually be purchased."

"And the second letter, also in Mr. Clifford's writing, the letter which Mrs. Clifford received Wednesday morning at breakfast? The letter posted in Bruges by Mrs. Orr?"

Hobbs grinned sarcastically.

"Well, naturally, I had to take it from her desk and destroy it. It wouldn't have deceived either of you. It wasn't meant to. It was meant to do what it did. Keep my cousin, Mrs. Clifford, quiet."

Again here was a silence.

"Now about the man whom you saw coming out of the flat at Heath Mansions. Did you recognise him?"

Hobbs gave him a long look. "You're clever, Chief Inspector, damned clever. But you'll get a surprise. The man I saw was Straight."

"The new librarian? The man who has just found out the defalcations?" Pointer murmured equably. "Indeed. You saw him clearly enough to swear to?"

"Quite."

"It couldn't have been any one else? Any one of about his height and general appearance?"

"You mean Edward Clifford? It might easily have been. He's always been in love with my cousin. But as it happened, it was Straight."

Pointer sat on a moment, looking at his shoes.

"One thing more, Mr. Hobbs. Mr. Clifford made some notes on his novel, the novel that is coming out in the _Arcturus_. They're not among his papers. Do you know where they are?"

"I've nothing to do with any notes of Clifford's," Hobbs said impatiently, "if they're lost, it's no use coming to me."

"Would Newman know about them?" Pointer asked.

"He might. But Clifford, as a rule, saw to everything to do with his writing himself. Newman's work was social. Clifford, of course, got invitations and letters by the ton."

"But I suppose Mr. Newman typed out Mr. Clifford's manuscript?"

"No. Clifford did his typing himself. He revised too, constantly. As a rule his work went straight from him to his publishers. Though Newman would have the actual sending or taking of it, after I had settled about terms."

"Would Newman know beforehand what was coming in a novel?"

Hobbs yawned. His face was lined with weariness—nerve weariness.

"Couldn't say. Clifford had taken to discussing his coming book _The Soul of Ishmael_ with him lately."

Again there was a silence ... of utter fatigue on Hobbs's part. Pointer rose.

"Well, Mr. Hobbs, of course I must verify your statements as far as possible. Meantime you're at liberty to return to Thornbush. Sorry, but I must insist on its being Thornbush. Sir Edward has not spoken. Straight can be trusted not to speak when he's asked not to. Until to-morrow, when other arrangements can be made, the household at Thornbush must remain as it is. No restrictions will be put on any reasonable outings."

Pointer saw Hobbs off, and then telephoned to Thornbush. Was Straight there? He was. So was Miss Haslar, who had not yet returned to her brother's house.

Pointer found them deep in talk.

"Maud Gillingham would be just the wife for you," Diana was saying as Pointer stopped for a second outside the door.

"I want you two to see more of each other. I shall never marry. I shall wait for Sanz and another life. But Maud is ever so much sweeter tempered than I am, and she's biddable, which I should never have been. Also she's got pots more money."

"Diana!" Straight protested, without any over-vehemence. After all, Diana had openly chosen the Basque anarchist. Pointer entered and asked Straight for an interview. Diana turned to Richard.

"Please let me stay! Oh, Dick, please let me hear the worst. I know—I know that—that it may be hard hearing, but I can't be kept out of this. For Arnold and Sanz both keep me in it. In its heart. Please, Chief Inspector, let me stay."

"It rests with Mr. Straight," Pointer said at once; "if he has no objection, I have none."

"Stay, then, Diana, but you mustn't mind if I have to say things, and say them in a way that may hurt you," Straight warned her.

"Mr. Straight," Pointer began promptly, "we have just had a piece of information which concerns you."

Straight had not expected this. He sat up.

"You were seen last Monday night leaving Fourteen Heath Mansions after Mr. Clifford was shot, and leaving it in a hasty, almost furtive manner. Can you explain this?"

Diana gave a gasp of resentment, but Straight silenced her with a smile.

"Patience, Di!" He turned to the detective officer. "I left Heath Mansions after Mr. Clifford arrived, but not after he was shot. Your witness is lying there. It's an odd story; but it won't help the case forward at all."

"It should have been told me," Pointer said stiffly.

"And it would have been told you. But I like to think things over. Also, it implicates a friend."

"Arnold?" breathed Diana.

"Arnold," the name came reluctantly.

"And the story?" Pointer asked. Still Straight hesitated. "I'll try not to jump to conclusions," Pointer promised.

"Well, as I told you, I dropped in at Haslar's on Monday after dinner, but found that he was unexpectedly called out of town."

Straight paused.

"Did he give you any idea of why and where?"

Pointer had asked this before. Then Straight had given an evasive reply, now he said, "None. I think he was inclined to, but he finally said, 'You're too straightlaced a chap, Dick, my son. We will not blacken your innocent soul with the night's dark deeds.' I decided to go for a walk, it was a heavenly evening, and turn in early. I had only landed that morning. I walked about the heath at random, and then made for Thornbush. Passing what I now know to be Heath Mansions, I ran into Mr. Clifford. He stopped me, asked me if I'd mind dropping a couple of letters in a pillar-box for him, and then coming on after him to flat Fourteen in the building to which he pointed. He added"—Straight looked at Diana as though asking her to forgive him—"he added that he expected to have rather an unpleasant interview with Arnold Haslar. Would I mind coming up? He had left a message for Hobbs, but Hobbs mightn't get it in time. I wasn't very keen on an unpleasant interview between my friend and my employer. Mr. Clifford evidently read as much in my face, for he said, 'It's all right. I only want to borrow your eyes. Haslar has just telephoned me that he has a friend who lives there and who can prove that certain letters which I believe to be genuine are forgeries.' With that he turned in at the gates of the flats. I didn't find a letter-box at once. Doubtless I passed several. When I got back, I walked up the stairs and to my surprise found the door of Number Fourteen ajar. I rang, and then, as no one came, I walked in. The door of a room on my right was open. There sat Mr. Clifford at a little side table beside a lamp, reading a letter. He glanced up and said, 'It's all right, Straight. I shan't need you after all. Sorry to've given you the trouble of coming up here for nothing.' I murmured something and went out. As I closed the door, Mr. Clifford said something which I didn't quite catch. But I think—I only _think_, mind you, Chief Inspector, that it was 'Newman's here. I shall be quite all right.'"

"Newman!" Diana echoed in a little gasp.

"I may have heard him incorrectly. His back was to me and he spoke hurriedly. At any rate, I went on out. In the doorway I heard"—again he glanced at Diana—"I heard a sound like Haslar's cough. I stopped to listen. I wasn't sure whether it came from behind me—from inside the flat, that is—or from outside the flat—from the stairs. I looked out of the door, up and down the landing and stairs. I couldn't see any one. I went to the lift-shaft to press the button for the lift, and as I did so, I thought I caught sight of Haslar's ulster below me"

"Going down or coming up?" Pointer asked.

"I couldn't say. I thought I saw it on a landing. I ran on down, but I saw nothing of Haslar. So I returned to Thornbush and bed. Next morning I heard that Mr. Clifford had left. I saw nothing improbable in that. Next I heard of the Etcheverrey murder in flat Fourteen. That did stagger me. But obviously there could be no connection between Mr. Clifford and a murder. It wasn't as if he had been announced as murdered. I should have come forward at once then, of course. Next, I learn that Etcheverrey's body was claimed by you and Sir Edward to be that of Mr. Clifford, but that Mrs. Clifford and Hobbs denied that it was he, and were certain that he was safe and sound. Obviously I had to think things over. I decided that my tale would add nothing to the facts. I found Mr. Clifford alive, and I left him alive. I confess that the thought of being mixed up in a crime— It was a terrible position. ... I would have had to bring in my friend Arnold Haslar. Altogether I decided to wait a little while longer and see."

There was a little silence.

"And one thing more," Straight went on, "I stood outside the door listening, as I said, to see if I had really heard Haslar, and how I could not have seen any one if they had been standing outside the flat, or on the landing—" Straight shook his head.

"You think whoever saw you was inside the flat, not outside?" Pointer asked.

"I don't know what to think," Straight replied, "it's too terrible a case to decide on quickly."

There was another silence. Diana sat with her head resting on her hand, her face shaded, her lips tightly pressed together.

"And you, Miss Haslar, you knew of this meeting on Monday night between your brother and Mr. Clifford?"

She looked at Pointer, tightening her lips still more.

"I'd like a word alone with you if you would let me have it," Pointer said.

Straight rose reluctantly at her glance. He stepped up to Pointer before opening the door.

"Be gentle with her," he murmured under his breath, "she's going through a frightful ordeal."

When the door closed behind him Pointer began again.

"Suppose you chance it, Miss Haslar, and trust me to see the truth through all the maze of misleading events and side issues. I don't see how you can do any harm by speaking out. Nothing can make matters worse for Mr. Haslar, and knowing that, suppose you take heart."

"Then you don't believe in Mr. Newman's confession?" she asked eagerly and yet with dread in her voice.

"Until all the facts are cleared up, it's not possible to be certain who was an accomplice and who not," Pointer said truthfully. "We know your brother took the flat. But it's possible that he may have taken it simply as the first step in a rather elaborate plan to get back those letters blackening your grandfather's character which Mr. Clifford intended to include in his coming biography of Sir William Haslar. We have the letters themselves."

Diana looked sceptical. But her look changed as Pointer drew a note-case from his pocket and took out of an envelope photographic copies of the two fateful notes. She was startled. Yet, oddly enough, it gave her courage. Here was a man who wanted but the truth. A man who had the knack of getting it, moreover. Diana searched his face again. It was the face of a man of high personal character. There were brains in it. But it could be an absolutely unyielding face. She sat through another agonised moment of silence. There was danger whatever she did or said.

"I think he may have taken it in order to lay a trap for Mr. Julian Clifford," Pointer said again, "a trap to get possession of those letters. Am I right? I've thought so all along. But it wasn't easy to get the proof, to find out what he wanted."

Diana surrendered the position.

"I think so too," she said slowly. "I know nothing definite. But I think he meant to—well, keep Mr. Clifford there for a few days."

"Against his will?"

Diana nodded.

"That, at least, was what I feared when I heard on Tuesday morning that Mr. Clifford had left Thornbush so suddenly before breakfast. And when a man from the Home Office called during the morning, and spoke of Uncle Julian's absence as such a riddle. Seemed so amazed at it! But Mrs. Clifford and her cousin appeared so certain that they knew where Uncle Julian was, that I thought how silly I had been. . . But you see Arnold had just been taken ill that morning, at the breakfast table, and the doctor had spoken of some excitement or shock." She bit her lip.

"Suppose you tell me everything you know about your brother's taking that flat," Pointer suggested. "How did he learn of it?"

Diana hesitated. Pale, she grew whiter still. So it probably was, as Pointer thought, through Newman.

"I really _know_ nothing. Not even that he had a plan," she said finally. "It was only that when Uncle Julian refused to promise not to use the letters, when Arnold could not budge him from his intention of adding them to the Life which was already being proof-read, I felt sure that Arnold would try something. He got the position he holds because of his daring plans, and the absolute fearlessness with which he goes ahead and carries them out. You see, I know him so well that I can guess a good deal of what's going on in his mind. Besides, one day when I said I'd steal the letters if I could—and so

I would have"—Diana's eyes flashed—"they were cruel lies about one of the best and kindest men that ever lived. And lies about him when he was dead and could no longer defend himself—Arnold told me not to worry. Just that."

"When did he say that?"

"Last Friday."

"You two were alone?"

She nodded.

"You had no idea of what his plan was?"

"Well, Uncle Edward—Sir Edward Clifford, I mean—was chaffing a friend that night at a dance club where Arnold and I were. He accused the boy of having kidnapped the examiner and taken the exam papers from him. Arnold started, and gave Sir Edward the look of some one who thought for half a moment that his secret had been guessed. I knew then what his scheme was, or at least suspected something of it. There weren't many things you _could_ do to get those letters." She spoke with an unconscious irritation which would have amused Pointer at another time.

"You were on his side, of course? You thought anything fair under the circumstances?

She shook her head.

"Not towards Uncle Julian, no. I wasn't on Arnold's side at all. Uncle Julian hated publishing those letters. But he thought it the right thing to do. When people have to do dreadful things because they think them right, what is there one can do?" Diana's tone was infinitely sad and hopeless. "However dreadful, what can one do? Besides"—her voice changed—"besides, I was afraid that Arnold would overreach himself. You could no more bully or frighten Uncle Julian than you could Arnold himself."

"Did you attempt to dissuade him?"

"Oh, yes. Coming home from the Havana. But he only got impatient, and told me I was all wrong. That there was no question of personal violence in his mind, nor of bullying. He told me to be quite sure of that; said he wasn't an absolute idiot."

"You think he meant what he said?"

"Arnold always means what he says."

"Did you ever hear the flat referred to?"

She did not reply.

"I wish I could spare you these questions," Pointer said regretfully, "but truth is your best course, believe me. The very best course—for every one."

She flashed him an eager look. There was a sparkle of almost painful hope in it.

"You—you mean?"

Something in Pointer's eyes encouraged her.

"I think I must have heard Arnold refer to it over the telephone last Saturday evening. I heard him say, 'He can't come till Tuesday, but the flat's taken for a month, so that's all right.'"

"Do you know to whom he was talking?"

Diana hesitated.

"Was it to Mr. Newman?"

Her silence was answer in itself.

"Mr. Straight is a great friend of yours and your brother's, I believe?"

"Very great."

"Did he know about the letters—I mean about their existence?"

"Not in the least," she said earnestly. "Mr. Straight is the last man to permit himself to be drawn into a family squabble."

"And Mr. Newman?"

"Mr. Newman was with Uncle Julian when they were found. He and Adrian Hobbs both knew of them."

"And Sir Edward Clifford?"

"I begged Uncle Julian not to tell him. Sir Edward has always been most unjustly critical of my grandfather's policy about the Australian navy."

"And now—how did you come to go to Bruges, Miss Haslar? You found Mr. Hobbs at that desk in your brother's study, didn't you—at the secret drawer?"

"He had the letters you've shown me in his hand. And Uncle Julian's umbrella too. He told me that he had only just found them in that old concealed double back, after hunting for them all day. But I hardly cared about the letters, for he told me something else. I thought it too good to be true, and yet, I believed it!"

"That Mr. Julian Clifford was alive after all?"

"Yes, that you had made a mistake about identifying the body found in Heath Mansions as his; that Alison was right, that Uncle Julian was safe and sound only in a most awkward position. I would rather not tell you about that," Diana said, pausing.

Pointer assured her that the police knew it already.

"And you? Did you know that the nun was Mrs. Orr?" Diana asked. "Or did you just suspect it?"

"I suspected it so strongly that I knew it," Pointer said, a trifle grimly, "chiefly from her manicured nails. They positively glittered. And a little from the marks of having worn rings very recently on her fingers, especially the dent of a wedding ring."

"And was it really her intention to—or was that about the window and the canal only to frighten her?"

Pointer did not answer. He thought that the less said about that the better. He had practically had to promise as much to Mrs. Orr before she would speak. He had only his suspicions on which to go.

"And did Adrian Hobbs intentionally shut me in that strong room?"

Pointer did not answer that either.

"And about Sanz," she said, after a pause, in a low voice; "what is going to be done with him?"

A door had just opened in the east library. Pointer had heard it and recognised the step. Not so Diana.

"You would never have known that he was Etcheverrey, but for me!" Suddenly she sprang up. Diana's spirit was ever for action, weary though her body might be. "Chief Inspector, I feel as though somehow you were my one hope. Sanz Etcheverrey _couldn't_ have

killed Uncle Julian. I know he traded on my love for him
to take those Melbourne plans, but that was different—
that was political. He was against us all during the war,
and I thought I hated him. I told myself I did. I lost my
only other brother though he was a chaplain, in the war.
But this is quite different. In spite of all, I know he didn't
kill Uncle Julian."

Pointer looked at her. She read his look.

"You mean that I think that because I love him?" She
seemed to think over that possibility. "I do. And in that
awful strong room last night I learnt that nothing in the
world is more worth while than being able to love. It's a
miracle. To be loved is nothing—that's easy; that's
chance. But to be able to love! And I had been trying to
crush it out of me all these years. I thought hatred finer.
For years I've been trying to think that Sanz was playing
some deep game of his own here at Thornbush. But he
didn't play a game when he came back, in spite of his
confession, to get me out last night. He offered up his life
for mine. Has he—has he given up his life for mine?"

Diana asked the dreadful question with indescribable
anguish.

"That coming back to rescue you stands to his credit
whatever the issue." Pointer would not say more.

"And that confession?" Diana was in an awful
position. Her brother stood on the one side, her lover on
the other.

"It's a good thing to doubt everybody and everything
in a case of this kind," Pointer said vaguely but kindly.

Diana looked at him imploringly. A very strange look
to see on Diana's face. But nothing of the thoughts behind
them were mirrored in the Chief Inspector's inscrutable
gray eyes. He was as usual aloof, remote, and tranquil.

"But if he didn't kill Uncle Julian, then he must have
written that letter to save some one. To save Arnold. Not
that Arnold needs saving," Diana added hastily, "but I've
wondered whether Sanz didn't think he did, and so jump
in to the rescue. I was mad to think Sanz could have tried

to shoot Arnold. I wanted to think anything bad of him, so as to—" She seemed to recollect herself. "Forgive me ranting like an Adelphi heroine. I'm not taken that way often. But what's his fate to be? Mind you," she came a step nearer, "nothing will alter my feelings towards Sanz. Imprison him for life, hang him—I shall always love him, always wait for him! For no matter what his ideas of duty force him to do, however horrible his political opinions, he himself—Sanz Etcheverrey the man, not the anarchist— is a hero!"

The communicating door between the two libraries opened sharply with a jerk. Algernon Newman, as he still signed himself, came in very gravely. He hardly glanced at Diana.

"Chief Inspector, I've come to clear up a few things— no, not directly concerned with what interests you, but only personal matters. No, please stay, Miss Haslar!"

"Miss Haslar? It wasn't 'Miss Haslar' whom you got out of the safe last night, Sanz," Diana threw back at him. There is no confidence in the world greater, no power surer than that of a woman who is talking to the man whom she knows loves her. And Diana had looked deep into the eyes of her rescuer last night. She knew his heart.

"It wasn't Sanz Etcheverrey who opened the safe," Newman said heavily. "Sanz Etcheverrey is a more or less romantic figure, at least in a woman's eyes. There's nothing romantic about me." He paused. Diana said nothing, but she was obviously with him in any change of name or personality which he might be going to make.

Newman looked ill and very tired. Evidently some fierce fighting had gone on within him. "I'm only a crook's son. Worse—a murderer's son."

Diana half rose. He stopped her with a weary lift of his eyes.

"You mustn't sacrifice your life to a sham romantic personage. You are romantic, you know. There's no romance about being the son of Henry Cadby, embezzler, forger, thief, and finally murderer. That was where I learnt how to open safes —at home." He turned to Pointer. "Oh, I know Cockerell recognised my father's invention of packing with powdered aluminum and iron oxides and then using electricity in a totally new way. But it wasn't because of Cockerell I'm telling the truth now. I could have pretended that I'd caught Cadby once, and so on. . . . But you, mustn't go on thinking me anything but what I am: mud; the scourings of the street." He was talking only to Diana now. He came up to her chair. "Thank you for saying what you did just now. It was what Padre Haslar's sister would say. It helped me to do—what's lot harder than coming back last night." He finished with a half smile, an unconscious flicker of his lips that lent the foreign leanness of his face a touch of ironic vividness. In it was experience, suffering, and bitter wisdom. "Then you were in danger," he went on softly. He stopped as though struck by the phrase. "Perhaps, after all, the danger was as great just now. Anyway, you know the truth—the reason why I would never let you become engaged to me. _You_ engaged to _me!_"

"How can I know the truth when I don't understand it?" Diana spoke with unexpected coolness. "Why did you tell me you were Sanz Etcheverrey long ago at Hendaye? And those men at Pamplona, they called you by that name."

Newman sat down.

"I'll begin at the beginning. I learnt to speak Spanish as a baby, for I was born at Barcelona, where my father was a rather well-to-do mining engineer. Cadby and Penfold was the firm. My mother died when I was born. My father had spent several years in the tin mines of Cornwall. That's where he and Penfold decided to start together in the Catalan capital. When the firm got into difficulties after Penfold's death, my father came to England. I believe there was a fire, and he started with the insurance money as manager in a biggish firm.

Anyway he began to speculate, lost, and borrowed the firm's money; to conceal these he forged entries stole more money, and so on—the usual thing. He was convicted and sent to prison. Meanwhile he had married a woman in the set into which he had by this time sunk. Crooks, all of them. My father came out of prison—I was twelve by that time—and went from bad to worse. He now made his living as a safe breaker, a cracksman. He invented a wonderful way of opening safes; had he been honest he might have risen high, I sometimes think. He made a great deal of money, stole it, in other words. Lived in great style. Called himself Baron de Ribiera from Argentina. Then came the war. I was just short of eighteen, but I joined up, thankful to get free. I had tried several times to earn my own living, but something always gave me away. My father would find out where I was, or some friends of his recognised me, or the police warned my employers whose son I was"

"But you weren't a thief!" Diana said with confidence.

"Not I! I'd have starved first. I hated the life, the whole horrible family life—I enlisted under the name of Pollock, my mother's name. Then came the news that my father had murdered one of his accomplices who was about to give him away. He was caught red-handed, and hanged. You remember the case, I suppose?"

Pointer had been looking it up. Cockerell had finally remembered where he had seen a safe that had been opened on lines similar to those followed for that strong room door last night.

"Man called Strachey?" he asked gently.

"Just so. Well, I slogged away at soldiering. They put me into the quartermaster's office because I was quick at figures. No chance to do more than jog along. . . . And then in 1917 I got hold of some information through a friend in the Foreign Legion, a chap who came from Malaga, about Sanz Etcheverrey, a Basque who at that time was rather on the German side. He was against all the countries of the war, but now he would help one, now the other, for his own reasons, his own price. This information was that a certain official high in the Spanish Government had promised Etcheverrey an amnesty for some followers of his who were dying in Spanish prisons, if he would get hold of details about the Anzac troops and troopships. The official's wife was a von Buck, by the way. They had heard of Riply's escape from the torpedoed ship, and they knew of those plans. Etcheverrey had agreed. The chap from Malaga didn't tell me all this, of course. I had to piece things together. I worked out a plan for catching Etcheverrey and laid it before the quartermaster-general. It was turned down. I was told to stick to figures. I deserted. When I went off in 1914 my father—he was always a generous man with money, and always kind to me, put a thousand pounds to my credit in Cox's bank as a parting gift. I told him I was leaving home for good. I hadn't touched the money, and didn't mean to. But I drew on it now, brushed up my Spanish, came down to Hendaye, and started in great style. I let it be known that I belonged to the Spanish Secret Service. I got into touch with two of Etcheverrey's men and more or less induced them to think that I was Etcheverrey himself. He's double my age, but looked only half his years. I looked a lot older than I was. Besides, they'd never seen him. He kept himself absolutely in the background. I didn't claim to be him, of course. I merely didn't deny it. Little by little I guessed that the Melbourne Harbour plans were the objective of these two. But it was only that night, the night that Riply died, that I was certain. I had just half an hour to forestall them. I couldn't trust two women to guard those papers from these Catalans. They'd have cut you both into strips to make you give them up." Newman threw this to Diana over his shoulder. He was talking to Pointer, but he included Diana from now on.

"I had to get you out of the way before they could come. Once let them see you in that room, and they'd suspect that you had the papers. I stunned you and got you into your room. The two Catalans came along before I got clear. I called out that I was off for Pamplona, Etcheverrey's supposed headquarters. I knew Etcheverrey was expected there. Well, the two hung on to me. But they had an accident with their car at a turning when we were almost in Pamplona. I had to go on. As it chanced Etcheverrey was working in Nice, and the rumour that he was coming was spurious. I passed myself off as him with the crew I found there, supplying U-boats with petrol, they were part of a sort of pipe line that ran to the coast. Then you blew in." He looked ruefully at Diana. "However, we got clear. Only unfortunately they hit a petrol tin on our car over which my coat sleeve hung down. Tin and coat went up in a blaze together. You got the fire under, but the Melbourne Harbour plans were smoke. They were in a pocket of that coat. That meant that I had nothing to show for my absence but a very thin tale of adventure; but I gave myself up and decided to tell it, leaving out the purely personal part, of course. There was a court-martial, but—well, the news was just out of my father's execution. They were very decent. They decided to believe me. I asked for a front line job, and this time I got it. I chose a Surrey regiment, because your brother was chaplain to their division, so you had told me at Hendaye." He was speaking only to Diana now. This might be his last talk to the girl, except the tragic leave-taking that the Chief Inspector had promised her.

"That's what you meant by Padre Haslar?" Diana had hardly noticed the reference before. He nodded.

"It was next best to being with you. Life was a bit grim those days. Your brother was a man in a million. He"— Newman made a gesture of inability—"but what's the good, you can't describe a man like him!"

"He was a dear!" Diana said, with a catch in her voice; "he loved the whole world."

"He loved God," Newman said seriously. "It takes a very good man to be able to love God. But he did. You knew he was killed trying to get a couple of wounded soldiers out of a shell-hole that was filling with water? Hit just after he got them through our barbed wire."

Diana nodded. She guessed what was coming.

"I was one of the two. We had been three days in that shell-hole."

There was a long pause.

"When I woke up in hospital—I had collapsed at the wire —I found that no one knew who I was. My identity disc had been cut off when they dressed my arm at a clearing station. So had my few remaining rags. We had all to be evacuated quickly and my things were left behind. I was too weak to be questioned. And I didn't care to talk. I had heard the Padre had been shot helping poor Wingate to make a last effort. Wingate was much worse wounded than I was. I didn't want to live. But in the ward was a chap who had lost his memory. It struck me that he was a lucky devil. And then I pretended to've lost mine. Only to be left in peace, at first. But I began to think what a wonderful thing it would be if I really had lost it—for ever. The memory of that circle of crooks, of the underworld, of all I loathed, of my father whom I secretly loathed too. Though, as I say, he was always kind to me— kind and forbearing. To be rid of it all! To drop it off like a dirty shirt. It seemed a heavenly thought. I played it. It worked. No one suspected me. You see, I had been studying the poor fellow in the ward who really had lost his memory. He wanted it back. Lucky man! Then Mr. Clifford came along, and spoke of Padre Haslar. Spoke of him as a friend. I couldn't claim to've known him, but that made me accept Mr. Clifford's offer to see what he could do for me. What I could do for myself was how he put it. Well—the rest you know. Any one of the name of Haslar could wipe their boots on me for"—he pulled himself up—"for Peter Haslar's sake," he finished hastily. But he had intended to bracket another name with the dead chaplain's.

"And now, Chief Inspector, what are you going to do about me? Nothing of this alters my confession. Diana,

Miss Haslar, is going too far there. I give myself up for the murder of Julian Clifford and the shooting of Arnold Haslar." Newman spoke in a steady, firm tone. "I stand to that."

Pointer said nothing. He seemed lost in a profound conviction that his bootmaker had sent him two rights or two lefts, and that a closer scrutiny of his shoes would reveal the mistake.

"What are you going to do with me?" Newman asked again.

"Have a word in private, I think, first of all," Pointer suggested.

Diana got up. She looked as though she felt the need for thought. This Newman was another man. Son of a crook, son of a murderer, and yet . . . Diana felt that life could be extraordinary difficult. Suddenly she wheeled.

"Then if you're not Etcheverrey, why did you kill Uncle Julian? If it's not political, if you're not—" She did not finish either sentence.

Newman's face hardened. His jaw line showed more clearly. He said nothing, only stared with expressionless eyes out of the window as she left the two men together.

CHAPTER FOURTEEN

"What about Mr. Pollock's flat?" Pointer asked. "Where did Mr. Newman get the money for such furnishing?"

Newman looked fixedly at him.

"Quick work! Yet I haven't gone near the place since all this. I thought you were more than usually clever when I first saw you. Or have I been under surveillance all these years?"

"No, the address was only discovered in the course of some routine work on this case. But about the things there?"

"Ah!" Newman's smile was bitterness itself. "Family traits proving too strong for me might explain them, mightn't it '—to a Chief Inspector? Just as what I might call Home Hints made it easy for me to get away from your men, and to disguise myself afterwards. If you're a criminal it's handy to know the ropes from childhood."

Pointer's eyes were apparently on his shoes.

"I see. Yet with that explanation of your furniture, how was it you worked on with Mr. Clifford as his secretary so long?"

"Thornbush was home to me, Chief Inspector. At least, let us put it that the motive for murder kept me there."

"Mrs. Clifford?" Pointer asked bluntly.

Newman leapt from his chair.

"Who dares say that?"

"It's what people always wonder when a man kills a married man for no apparent reason. And in your case, it was suspected for some time before."

The iron self-control broke in Newman's face.

"It's a lie! A foul, infamous lie! Mrs. Clifford? She's a saint! Perhaps that's why, to my shame be it said, Chief Inspector; and though she has been kindness itself to me, she bores me even more than she does Hobbs. And that's saying something! Mrs. Clifford wasn't the reason why I—killed Julian Clifford."

"Then what was the reason?"

Newman lifted his dark eyes for a second to the window. "Neither to you, nor to any one else, will I give the reason, Chief Inspector." He spoke with absolute finality.

"The prosecution will be based on a clandestine lore affair between you and the lady. There's no other motive possible."

Newman looked darkly at him.

"The reason I killed Julian Clifford was because he had stumbled on the truth about me," he said slowly; "and on something disgraceful in my past as well. Something which he intended to tell." The sentences, came out slowly, as steel is drawn out inch by inch. Newman's face was impassive as ever. The words rose before Pointer, "I know the danger"—"discovered your secret." Words in the murdered man's handwriting found burnt in this man's room.

Pointer said nothing for a while.

"And about Mr. Clifford's general knowledge of Etcheverrey? And his special knowledge of his signature and the name of his home?"

"I learnt all I could while planning to get hold of him at Hendaye. 'The plan that failed!'"

"Because of Miss Haslar?"

"Well, obviously it tore it when she and I fled together." Newman's swift, sardonic smile came and went, leaving his face as grave as ever.

"And you told Mr. Clifford what you knew?"

Newman looked at him thoughtfully. "Little by little. When he began to be so interested in the fellow, I let him think I had a Spanish anti-revolutionary friend with whom I talked over week-ends. Mr. Clifford liked to get hold of something that Sir Edward didn't know. I think he wanted his book to surprise him."

"Was this information confidential?"

"Not in the least. But I'd rather not discuss Mr. Clifford. Not with you, Chief Inspector. Not with anybody, but least of all with you. Your questions aren't always what they seem on the surface." Newman's voice was dry. "I had hoped, of course, to get clear away and stay clear away, after my confession."

"I see. And now, Mr. Newman, Mr. Clifford made some notes on that novel of his that is coming out in the _Arcturus_. They're not among his papers. Do you know where they are?"

Unlike Hobbs, Newman did.

"The only notes I know of were some he left by an oversight about two weeks ago at his publisher's house. But as he afterwards decided to shift Etcheverrey's headquarters to the Spanish side of the Pyrenees, he decided that they would be of no use to him."

"And about the novel itself? You know, I suppose, what he planned to do? You have an idea of how the story would have run?"

"I have an idea of the main outlines. But—" Newman checked himself. "I refuse to discuss Mr. Clifford, as I have already said once before."

"Pity. Well, should you decide to make a clean breast of everything, though I shall not be available, the Assistant Commissioner will always be there. I may have to go away on an investigation at once. As long as you confine your strolls to this neighbourhood, not farther than Haslar's house say, you can come and go as you like—for the present. Of course you'll be followed, and by a good man. I needn't say what any attempt to shake him off would entail."

Newman gave a short and very bitter laugh.

"There are a few more questions I must have answered if Mr. Haslar is really to be cleared." Pointer

went on. "First, who was in the room when you spoke to
Mr. Clifford of the diagram signature of Etcheverrey's
and of the name of the Basque's home?"
Newman seemed to think. "No one but Hobbs. But he
wasn't paying any attention. He was hunting out some
mistake in royalties that he'd just found out."
"And when was this?"
Newman could not say for certain. Some time the
latter half of last week.
"And now about Mr. Haslar himself. We know, of
course, all about his connection with the flat. But was it
you who first mentioned the flat to him?" Newman
thought a moment. Pointer felt sure that he was going to
give an evasive reply, or refuse to answer.
"I hope we can clear Miss Haslar," he said sadly.
"Unfortunately, she seems mixed up in that business of
the flat."
"Miss Haslar?"
"She was heard talking of it to her brother before he
took it. We are sure that he had some helper there. I'm
afraid that that helper could only have been his sister. He
wanted her to get the letters away from Mr. Clifford, we
think, or rather we are fairly certain."
"I told Haslar of that," Newman said briskly.
"Is Marshall a friend of yours?"
"No, a mere acquaintance. But he happened to
mention to me when I met him by chance in the tube last
week, that he wished to let his flat furnished. So, as I say,
when there was a question of a furnished flat being
wanted"
"By Miss Haslar, I suppose."
"By Haslar himself," Newman corrected shortly. "Miss
Haslar knows nothing of the flat. Or, if she knows of it,
it's only been after the event."
"But she was to help her brother about the letters. It's
no use, Mr. Newman, attempting to shield her, we know
that Mr. Haslar had a helper. Had a plan to get those

letters of his grandfather's away from Mr. Clifford. No one but Miss Haslar could have helped him."

"I take back about having thought you more than usually brilliant," Newman said curtly. "There are other people in the world, Chief Inspector, than this little circle here and around Thornbush. There is, or was, for instance, a man called Captain Cory. You asked me about him yourself once. He's a man who has a grudge against Clifford. He's also a man who had showed himself uncommonly skilful at getting hold of papers. Haslar had been present at his trial. When he concocted the plan of the flat, or rather—" Newman waited a moment. Then he said: "I think absolute frankness is best here. I don't want you to think that there was any mix-up between the taking of that flat and Haslar's arrangements about the letters and my part in the matter; that is, the death of Mr. Clifford. Haslar took the flat for one single purpose only—that of getting back the letters with Captain Cory's assistance. I used the flat for my own purpose. That clear?"

"Did you meet this Cory yourself?"

"No, Haslar telephoned me Friday evening that Cory wouldn't get to the flat till Tuesday, but on Saturday morning Cory himself came to Thornbush. He asked for me, but I was out. I rather think he came to find out if Mr. Clifford carried the letters on him. always. Or possibly he intended to double-cross Haslar in some way. Get hold of the letters and sell them at a stiff price. He only saw Hobbs, as it happened."

"Was Haslar going to be present in the flat when the letters were taken?" .

"We both were. We didn't trust Cory an inch further than we could see him."

"The plan was not one that included violence?"

"Haslar's plan? Certainly not. We were to be there to prevent anything of that sort. That at least is what Haslar thought." Newman gave his unmirthful smile. "The taking of the papers was to be entirely Cory's part. I believe the idea was that Haslar would telephone to Mr. Clifford that he had met a man who could prove that the Haslar letters were forgeries, if Mr. Clifford would bring them to Fourteen Heath Mansions. Then Cory, made up a little as Major Brown, would receive him, look at the letters, and—the rest was left to him, as to how he intended to trick Mr. Clifford into thinking he returned the same letters to him."

"When was this plan arranged?"

"I don't exactly know. Thursday and Friday, I think. I wasn't present."

There was a pause.

"I suppose you know that the doctors are as hopeful this morning about Haslar as they were pessimistic up till now?" Pointer asked. "You know they think that he took a most unexpected turn down the right road to-day?"

Newman said nothing.

"They're trying the latest craze, no nurses to-day," Pointer went on half-absent-mindedly. "Once an hour a nurse slips into his room and gives him a capsule. Strychnine. For the rest of the hour he's left in absolute stillness and darkness. Funny thing medicine. One capsule an hour makes for recovery, while three would kill him before he could swallow them. He'll be able to speak to-morrow. To tell us the real story. For, of course, Mr. Newman, until he does that, it's hard to believe that he was not more implicated in the murder than you represent him."

Newman's face had darkened at the good report of Haslar.

"And that rope on your sitting-room wall," Pointer went on; "I recognised it as one of ours, of course. From inquiries I find that the rope that hung Cadby is missing. They are always kept, as you know, together with a death mask of each man. You tipped some out-going sergeant of police a little too freely, I'm afraid. But it belongs to us, Mr. Newman. You must let us have it back."

"You can have it any time you like," Newman said through his teeth. "It's served its turn. I put it there to remind me of who I am. But as Miss Haslar knows the truth now, it can go. She'll be wise and take the respectable side of the road. Oh, life is damnation!" The sudden outburst was repressed as soon as it flashed out.

Pointer looked at his shoes for some moments.

"That rope belongs to us," he repeated slowly. "I suggest that you have a talk with a Superintendent of Police whom I've asked to come here as soon as he can. He's a man who was sent over to Barcelona in connection with the Strachey case."

Newman's face grew more sombre still.

"I don't want any last messages," he said hoarsely.

"You'll want this one. You'd have had it long ago but for your change of name. Pollock was posted as missing, of course. The man who murdered Strachey was not your father. Your father, so Cadby swore in a duly witnessed statement which he made to the governor the day before his execution, was Penfold. The statement was investigated and found to be correct."

'Penfold? His partner?" Newman could hardly speak articulately.

"His partner—a civil engineer—a man of the highest character; of whose integrity there never was any question. You are John Penfold, only child of Henry Penfold, a very honest gentleman, and of Isabelle Treherne, daughter of a solicitor. Both of them of Penzance, Cornwall. She had Armada blood in her, which I think accounts for something in yourself which puzzled us all a bit—though as a Devon man I know a Cornish man when I see one. However, to go on—that fire in Barcelona was Cadby's doing, to cover up some falsifications in the books as well as to get the insurance money. Unfortunately your father, to whom he was sincerely attached, had gone to the office. Cadby thinks he must have suspected him, and gone to have a quiet look at the books. He was burnt to death. With all his bad qualities Cadby was never the same man again, or so he said in his confession. You were an orphan, your mother had died when you were born. Penfold's money was lost with the firm's smash. Lost by Cadby. Cadby took you back with him to England, passing you off as his son. He thought that if people knew that he was bringing up the son of his late partner, some suspicion might arise that he felt himself in some way responsible for your father's death.

"Also, he had a sort of feeling that though you, to you, he might atone. It wasn't a feeling that kept him straight, but it prevented his ever willingly letting you want for anything, or letting you go.

"You never thought of inquiring in the Barcelona records whose son it was that was born there. We did, of course. Cadby had no son. Penfold had one boy who is duly entered on the registers, was duly baptized at the English Church there. Your sins are on your own head. Whatever you have done, now that you know the truth, you will not be able to plead that it was your father's blood that was too much for you, family traits too strong for you. Copies of the papers concerning your parentage will be handed you by the Superintendent when he comes."

Newman stood staring at him. All the colour had drained from his face. Before his mind's eye passed his miserable, desperate, hate-filled boyhood in surroundings from which his honest fibre revolted. He thought of his efforts to get out of them, of the years at Thornbush, happy years had he been leading a true life. And now! He shut his eyes for a second.

"But for your confession you could walk out of this house with a lighter heart than I dare swear you've known before," Pointer went on.

"You're a devil!" Newman said passionately. "What you've told me alters nothing." There was something desperate in the tense voice and in the eyes that stared out at the sunshine. "Alters nothing! I _did_ kill Julian

Clifford and shoot Haslar. But not a word of this news of yours about myself to Miss Haslar, nor to any one."

"Oh, certainly. It's entirely your own affair," Pointer agreed.

Newman, very pale, stood biting his lip, swallowing hard.

"It was Mr. Clifford I understand who wished Hobbs to leave him?" Pointer asked suddenly.

Newman stared for a second as though he could hardly hear the other through the tumult in his head.

"The other way around," he said absent-mindedly.

"I asked, because, but for your confession, Mr. Newman—since you wish me to continue calling you that—we at the Yard would wonder whether he might not have just found out that Hobbs had been systematically robbing him. We could go on to wonder whether Hobbs had not murdered Mr. Clifford to save himself from prosecution, and all that that would mean. Mr. Hobbs, we might say, had learnt of Arnold Haslar's plan about the flat on Saturday morning from Major Cory, who sold him the information, and had gone to the flat Monday night— Cory had been given a key which he might have handed over—and there Hobbs murdered Mr. Clifford after luring him to Heath Mansions. He would have a dozen pretexts. That is what the police might think. They might look on Mr. Haslar's injury as an accident. In fact, but for your confession, the whole case might assume a very simple aspect."

The skin on Newman's face seemed to tighten as a wet drum tightens, till it stretched taut across his high cheekbones—the cheek-bones of a man of action. For the first time Pointer saw his hands shake as he clenched them.

"You're the devil himself!" Newman said hoarsely, in a tone of anguish, and turning, he stumbled from the room as though the floor were pitching and tossing beneath his feet.

Sir Edward looked in. Straight was with him. Seeing Pointer alone, they came on in.

"I suppose you are arresting Newman?" Sir Edward asked. "It's very trying meeting him face to face—at liberty— around this house. The house of his victim."

"Mr. Newman won't be here to-morrow, I fancy. But, Sir Edward, I thought you were doubtful of his confession?"

"I'm doubtful of everything," Clifford said wearily. "This news about Hobbs, frightful! A cousin of Mrs. Clifford's. A member of my brother's family, so to say. He cannot be prosecuted, of course. Mrs. Clifford would refuse to do so in any case and my hands are tied. Why, he would only too gladly broadcast my brother's unfortunate idea of purchasing the Bruges Crystal. My sister-in-law believes that he will surely be punished in some esoteric way. I'm afraid I should find jail more satisfactory."

"It may come to that yet, Sir Edward, and more," Pointer said slowly. Then he changed the subject, and told Clifford the good news of Haslar's expected, or at least hoped-for recovery. Sir Edward seemed delighted at the prospect of hearing from the injured man exactly what had happened.

"He'll at least be able to name his assailant, it was broad daylight when he was shot." Straight said that according to the latest bulletin, Arnold Haslar was expected to be able to both speak and answer a few questions by to-morrow morning. Until then the doctors wanted him kept in silence and absolute stillness. Straight was beginning to look himself again. Diana had known best all along. He did not claim to be heartbroken at her definite turning-down of any idea of marriage between them. After all, there was something to be said for not being engaged to a girl who had a love affair with a Basque bandit, and a brother who, wearing flamboyant coats, took a flat in which people were afterwards found murdered.

About nine o'clock another and a startling bulletin came from the sick room. It stated that Arnold Haslar had recovered consciousness and asked for Chief Inspector Pointer. Unfortunately Pointer was not to be found at the Yard, nor in any of the places suggested by his clerks. So the sick man had contented himself with a few laboured words only, but these were startling enough.

Haslar had been in the flat at the moment when the murder was committed. He had actually seen Julian Clifford shot.

The bulletin finished with the news that he had just fallen back again into a profound sleep which must on no account be broken.

An hour went by. Then another. There was no sound or stir in that darkened bedroom where on a narrow white bed it took keen sight to make out a shape lying motionless. A head so bandaged that it was scarcely distinguishable from the pillows into which it sank. A chalk-white hand lay inert on the metal brocade of the blanket. Light, and slow, and faint, came the breaths from between lips but a few degrees less colourless than the bandages, than the linen.

The nurse had come and gone, the patient had had his hourly capsule, and had immediately seemed to slumber on— if slumber it could be called.

It was past midnight when the door opened slowly— slowly but not furtively. In came a man. He stood a second to get his bearings in the dimness of the one light that shone like a large pearl above the table on which stood the medicine. He stepped up to the bed. Then he moved to the little table and looked at the box of capsules—read the label, the directions, and stood a second quite still. He switched off the light and crossed to the window. Looked out. Rearranged the curtains and turned up the light. Then he went to a huge walnut wardrobe—opened it and felt inside. Once more he came back to the bed. Something in his circling suggested a vulture about to settle. His hand went out to the box. He opened it and counted oat six of the little objects inside. From an envelope in his pocket he shook out six other capsules into the box, the same as the others in appearance. Now he paused, listening intently. Then bending over the bed, he pressed shut the nostrils which a bandage loosely covered. The mouth under Haslar's toothbrush moustache opened. Into it the man swiftly dropped the capsules taken from the box. Instantly the breathing stopped half-way. A faint shudder ran through the body. The hand drew down in a spasm beneath the sheet. The whole body seemed to straighten itself. The head slipped sideways off the pillows' on the farther side. The man waited a second. Then he laid his hand on the man's heart. There is an elementary trick in Ju-Jitsu by which a hand so placed is held by a grip above the elbow, while the body on which it rests bends forward all but breaking the wrist. This happened now. The man screamed like what he was—a trapped animal.

"Take it quietly," said the man whom he thought dead. "Tindall, Doctor Evans, and an Inspector are in the next room watching you.

"Richard Straight, I arrest you for the murder of Mr. Julian Clifford last Monday night." The usual warning was given by Chief Inspector Pointer—in bandages, lavish chalk make-up, and a shirt which fastened up his back by tapes.

"Inspector Watts, you can take away the Japanese cinematographic camera from the top of the wardrobe. It's a camera that works in the dark, Mr. Straight."

"Rubbish!" Straight had some difficulty in getting his lips to shape the words. "Why, I had only met Mr. Clifford an hour or so before—what earthly motive would I have had for killing him?" He tried for a note of derision.

"Motive? His novel The Soul of Ishamel is coming out in monthly parts in the _Arcturus_ magazine. Either you had met Mr. Clifford before, or he had come on your story by some chance, without knowing your name. You might have met without either of you recognising the other again for he often dressed in a disguise when he was on his investigations, and he was very near-sighted. At any rate, in _The Soul of Ishmael_, the reason why the chief character has to leave England, is the same as that which made you leave England. Only you went to Australia, while the man in the book was to go to the Pyrenees and join Etcheverrey's band. And that reason was appropriation of money which the town council thought was properly invested. With a swindle to cover the tracks—a clever swindle. Your tracks were carefully covered, I admit— so carefully that another man went to prison for what you did. But the tracks are there—down in Bedford. And the tale as told in Mr. Clifford's novel is so exact, the steps so carefully given, that any acquaintance on reading it, knowing you of old, knowing about the money which you claimed had been left you as a legacy, could not but link you with the story, had it gone on for but one more chapter. And that linking up by an intelligent reader would have meant prison for you, Mr. Straight—a long term—prison and an end to all your ambitions. You were quite safe so long as the little connecting link could not be brought home to you. Mr. Clifford's novel showed how this could be done."

"Preposterous!" But Straight looked as though his spine were crumbling inside him. "What about Newman's confession? What about his being the anarchist of whom Clifford was writing? And how should I have known anything about the flat at Heath Mansions? Your tale's a tissue of absurdities."

"That flat? You were sitting in the south library downstairs here after dinner at Thornbush, while Mr. Haslar was talking to Captain Cory on Monday in his study. Every word they said must have been heard by you through the communicating door. The whole plot was gone over for the last time. How Mr. Clifford could be lured to the flat by the message about the Haslar letters, of how Cory was to steal the letters, and so on. You heard Cory say that he could do nothing until Tuesday."

Pointer was guessing the unknown by the known facts. But the trial of Richard Straight for Julian Clifford's murder proved that he was right.

"But this is lunacy!" broke in the man under arrest. "I had only parted from Mr. Clifford after my first dinner with him, and on the best of terms, as the servants, as every one at Thornbush can testify."

"Quite so. Therefore it was probably after that dinner that you read the current number of the _Arcturus_. A number in which the story breaks off just before the crucial point—for you. A few more pages and it would be too late. An _Arcturus_ was lying on the table in the library where you sat while waiting for Mr. Haslar's visitor to go. You read it, saw your danger, it's imminence, and heard a plan being finally run through beside you which you thought would save you. That was why you shot Mr. Clifford in the flat to which you lured him by just such a telephone message as you had heard suggested. You doubtless imitated Haslar's voice, or claimed to be speaking for him. And afterwards you took away from his writing-table drawer the typescript pages which would have betrayed your story.

"It was you, not Mr. Haslar, who postponed the planned gaieties of last Monday night. You probably alleged some work for, or talk to, Mr. Clifford. Or your own fatigue after your journey. That telephone call that you told us arrived after you got to the house and which hurried Mr. Haslar into the country, came from you yourself as soon as you left him. You sent another to Mr. Newman. So that neither man could stray into the flat. And also so that if things went wrong, neither man could have an alibi. I think you used Cory's name for that purpose, and let them think they were to meet him for some urgent reason. After the murder, Mr. Haslar would of course think those bogus appointments confirmed Cory's guilt. To Mr. Newman it would look like Haslar's doing. The key to flat Fourteen you took from Mr. Haslar's ulster hanging in the hall before you left the house. You also took his automatic which you know from his habits in Australia he kept beside his bed. You were friends enough to chance being found upstairs. Then you went to the flat. You thought it might be as well to leave some sort of a trail. Little dreaming how Mr. Hobbs would help you by taking away everything that would ordinarily identify Mr. Julian Clifford. You remembered hearing at dinner about Etcheverrey and the hunt for him. You passed the time until Mr. Clifford could get to you by writing a couple of notes which you crumpled up in a way that you always do crumple your thrown away paper, a tight, egg-shaped ball. You could not know, that they would bring the trail looping back to Thornbush, and Mr. Clifford. When Mr. Clifford came, you let him in, doubtless saying that Haslar or the supposed owner of the flat would be back in a moment. You left Mr. Clifford seated by the lamp looking at some book placed there to catch his eye. You went into the bedroom, pushed the door open, and shot him with Mr. Haslar's pistol to which you had fitted a cardboard silencer—an Australian dodge which you had evidently learned out there. Hobbs saw you leaving the flat after the murder. In your agitation you forgot to notice whether the defective catch of the front door shut properly. Your account of meeting Mr. Clifford, of leaving him alive, is of course pure invention. Just as was your tale of Mr. Clifford's fears of Newman, and his dread of his coming journey. You were careful not to overdo it. You only thought you heard Mr. Haslar's cough. But to run on, after you left the flat, you put Mr. Haslar's revolver back in his room. And then went quietly to bed under the roof of the man whom you had just murdered. To-day, when you heard that Arnold Haslar had been present in the flat, and claimed to have seen the murderer, you decided to silence him."

Straight made no further remark except to swear that he was innocent and that this was but the invention of Scotland Yard.

He maintained this at his trial, but when his appeal against the death sentence passed on him was disallowed, he wrote a letter to the Chief Inspector, one of those long, detailed letters that men of his temperament often do write at such a time. In it he confessed that Pointer's theory of the motive; a theory proved up to the hilt at the trial was right; that Mr. Clifford in the course of talking to him after dinner on Monday about his work had let fall that he was going to take the coming instalment of _The Soul of Ishmael_ to his publisher's next morning. This was an item which had meant nothing to Straight at the time but which had spelled disaster, full and complete, when he had read while waiting in Haslar's library the last published chapters of the novel. Straight knew then that he had only a few hours in which to avert discovery —practically only Monday night.

After many digressions, Straight went on to say, in this final confession, that he had probably himself given Julian Clifford one half of his own story long ago,—on a boat going to Corfu,—when he, Straight, had met a man who claimed to be a commercial traveller in dried fruits. It was after a dinner at which Straight had taken too much to drink. The drink and a gorgeous night unloosed his tongue, and half the tale of a clever swindle on the council funds was told to the commercial traveller as a good yarn.

Next morning a very sober Straight found that the commercial had left the ship at dawn. Straight never touched stimulants again. He hoped, and believed, that the part told by him would be forgotten. In any case it was fairly harmless as long as the man to whom it was told did not come upon the other half and put two and two together to make a most unpleasant four—a four that could mean prison. Unfortunately for himself this was what had happened. Julian Clifford had come upon the other half of the story which had been told him by a stranger in the dusk of that Mediterranean night, an unseen stranger who stood to him merely for a base, but intriguing tale. And Julian Clifford, with the flair of the true artist, had welded the two stories together in his yarn as they had been welded in fact. He had even given the swindler a character strangely like Richard Straight's. As to Straight's knowledge of Etcheverrey's signature and home,—Julian Clifford, during the after-dinner talk, had jotted down a few suggestions for some minor headings in the subject index which was to be the new librarian's first task. On the back, as Straight was putting it away in his pocket-book, he called the writer's attention to a V in a tiny outline of a house, and two incomprehensible words.

Clifford had peered at them, mentioned that he was very short-sighted, and explained them with a laugh as Etcheverrey's code signature, and the name of his home in the Pyrenees, something that even Sir Edward did not know.

Straight had the paper in his pocket, when the idea of using Etcheverrey as a trail occurred to him in the flat. A trail that as Pointer had said, he imagined would lead far afield.

"Any time you have another case like this on, let me know, and you're welcome to sign my name again to whatever bulletins you like," Doctor Evans assured Pointer before he hurried off to see to Haslar. The sick man's bed had been secretly rolled into another room. The only truth in the last bulletins, which Pointer had written, was that Haslar was making a wonderful recovery.

On the stairs the Chief Inspector met Tindall hurrying up. Telephone messages had been trying to reach him for hours. Unfortunately the F.O. man had come upon a most promising short cut to Etcheverrey and had taken his Chief with him on a fruitless excursion into the suburbs.

"Straight instead of Etcheverrey!" Tindall could not read just his ideas for a moment. "By the way, you telephoned us that you had absolute certainty that

Newman was after all not Etcheverrey. You're sure of that?"

"Absolutely."

"Why?"

"I'm afraid the reasons are confidential."

"Humph—well—he had a most amazing knowledge of Etcheverrey's secrets if it's true that he was Julian Clifford's source of information on the Basque."

"Mr. Newman checkmated Etcheverrey once during the war." The door opened. Sir Edward came in slowly. Heavily.

"I've just told Mrs. Clifford the news," he sank into a chair.

"And how does she take it?" Tindall asked sympathetically.

"She—she thinks that my brother is giving her a message from the other world to his slayer. A message of forgiveness. A promise that expiation in this world will wipe the slate clean, and that Julian will be there ready to greet him as a friend when he 'passes over.'"

"By Jove!" was all Tindall could murmur.

"It must be a wonderful help to be able to believe that sort of thing," Sir Edward said a little wearily, a little wistfully, nd a little impatiently. "I confess I found it for once hard to empathise."

There was a short silence. Then Tindall turned to Pointer.

"I've heard you say, Chief Inspector, that the game's never lost until it's won. You've certainly won this one. And won it well. Clues versus deduction, eh? Well, for once they have scored."

"I never knew a case where deductions alone could have gone much further afield," Pointer said thoughtfully. "Only clues, pure and simple, could get one out of such a labyrinth."

"So Julian's notes, which to us, seemed to point full to Etcheverrey, to you pointed to Straight? Odd!" It was Sir Edward speaking.

Tindall made a grimace.

"His carbon sheet, rather? Eh, Pointer? The sheet I turned down."

Pointer nodded.

"Still, that phrase in the notes about 'England dangerous' struck me very much. Seeing that I had Straight in my mind as the probable criminal. I wondered if Roberts's past, instead of his future association with Etcheverrey, might not be the danger, the cause of the murder. And the five pages on the carbon sheet gave us just the clue we needed. On the very last page of the chapter as it was meant to be.

"We have two men who are very good at that sort of an investigation. By the help of it, they soon worked back to the truth. Incidentally Newman, who I found knew about the notes left nearly a fortnight ago with Mr. Bancroft, had made no effort to get hold of them."

"You suspected Straight from the first!" Clifford asked, "On what grounds?"

"I suspected everybody," Pointer said a little dryly. Tindall smoothed away a grin under cover of stroking his beard. He knew quite well whom Pointer had included in his suspicions.

"Of course Hobbs' telling you that you saw Straight come out of the flat was a plain enough tip," he murmured, "but I imagined you didn't believe the tale. Hobbs himself thought so."

"Hobbs had to think so. He was going to be under the same roof as Straight, and had a tremendous grudge against him. Which was why I had to question Straight about the incident, for if he had learnt from Hobbs that I knew of it, he would have known by my silence, that he was suspected."

Tindall nodded to each point in turn. "But what set you on Straight's trail in the beginning?" he pressed. "You talk of clues. Surely it was reasoning rather. Reasoning from the facts, not to them. Pointer too preferred the latter way when possible, but it had not been possible in the Clifford affair. In other words reasoning from a clue I found."

"Which clue? Where?"

"The tape pinned across the door catch. If the murderer was one of the narrow circle at Thornbush, in which circle I included the Haslars, that pointed to some very hurried, very improvised, plan.

"Whoever did that, knew that only a short time could elapse between the arrival of the victim and his death. Else so clumsy a precaution would have aroused suspicion. But evidently the man who came was not, and was not expected to be, suspicious. Here was where the oddity lay. For apparently, too, he did not know the flat well enough to roam about it. That tape looked to me very unlike the work of whoever had taken the flat. Let alone the work of Etcheverrey. For, they would have had ample time to silence the lock invisibly. It certainly did not look like the work of an engineer, let alone an electrical engineer of Arnold Haslar's standing. It looked to me like some sudden arrival to the Thornbush circle, and the choosing of Monday night, also made the crime seem the work of a newcomer. For if the criminal knew of the flat, he would probably know that Cory, who never runs two enterprises simultaneously—he had some pigeon-plucking to finish might come in by Tuesday. But why should any one wait until the last night when the flat would be free unless he couldn't help himself? Unless that was his first opportunity? Or Mr. Clifford might have refused to come to Heath Mansions, or some hitch might have occurred. On the other hand, if a new arrival, it must be one who knew that Mr. Clifford is short-sighted, or he would never have chanced that tape. Also, supposing I was right, and those paper scraps in the basket were the work of the murderer, he would have to be some one who could have heard of Etcheverrey. Straight fitted all these provisos. In short all this pointed so directly to him, as the only newcomer to Thornbush, that I very carefully investigated all other possibles for fear lest I had got an idea into my head. Getting an idea into one's head is a detective's nightmare."

Pointer did not add that he had also suspected—in the absence of any other known motive—the new librarian of having known and loved Mrs. Clifford in the past, and that, therefore, he had been very doubtful of her too, for it was only in the last few hours that his men had been able to prove his own idea right, and working by the clues on the carbon sheet, get hold of the real reason for the murder, and so free all the other inmates of Thornbush, except Straight, from suspicion.

"Yet, otherwise, after the crime, Straight never gave himself away?" Tindall thought. "Until just now. When he fell into your trap."

"That trap was the only thing that could catch him. The only thing that would prove who the murderer of Mr. Julian Clifford had been. He had left no clue behind. It might be Newman, after all, or Hobbs, or any one. I might be all wrong. But Straight gave himself away once— badly. When he described to me how Mr. Clifford was sitting beside the little table in the flat. Unless his story was true, the mere fact of his knowledge of Mr. Clifford's real position marked him as the probable murderer. And, too, I think, I should have suspected him anyway after a little scene which I witnessed between him and Miss Haslar. It was a sort of lover's quarrel. At least that was the impression at which Straight med. He acted like an impetuous, quick-tempered young Fellow who was jealous, and intensely hurt by a girl's preference for another. Now impetuous and quick-tempered :hard Straight certainly is not. Even without any previous suspicions, I should have asked myself why Straight should take the trouble to act—before me."

"And why did he?" Sir Edward demanded.

"He wanted to get free. From the man who had worn that ulster and taken that flat. Free because of him even from Miss Haslar in spite of her large fortune. Then came the news that the truth was out. That we knew that the dead man was Mr. Clifford. After that, Straight wanted to be known to be in love with Mr. Clifford's devoted niece and about to enter his family circle. But when he found finally that she definitely turned him down, he was quite willing that she should smother in that strong room. He told me that he didn't know the code-word. Yet when Mrs. Clifford came, he hastened to ask her if she knew of no other word but Visit. No one had mentioned Visit. That was a bad slip."

"He would have let her die? Good God! Why?"

"If she wouldn't marry him she was a possible hindrance—a restraint. Straight knew that he might yet be pushed into tight corner. Hobbs suspected him. And with Miss Haslar and Arnold Haslar both out of the way, he could be free to do what he liked. Just as Mr. Clifford's death left him free to give us that extraordinary improvisation about his after-dinner talk with him. Straight had no intention of murdering either Miss Haslar or her brother, of course. Murder is dangerous. Its advantages must be great, therefore. But Straight could have stood by and let things run their course this afternoon."

"Straight!" Tindall muttered again as one mutters a rid die's unexpected solution. "That little rat! I always wondered what Miss Haslar could see in Straight, even for a short time."

"I think she never saw anything in him but a steady, reliable character, a good guide through life! I think she did her best to like him, and never succeeded because of an inward voice that refused to be told how sterling a character was his."

"Straight must have been slightly bewildered when he heard of Clifford's head being missing." Tindall said under his breath to Pointer.

"When he was told that Newman was Etcheverrey, I fancy he thought that he had only forestalled another criminal by a few minutes."

"You never suspected Haslar at any time?" Edward Clifford asked coming out of a revery.

"If murder were Mr. Haslar's object, I couldn't see why he took a flat. Took it in a way that he might fancy would throw any ordinary inquiries off the track, but which he would know as well as any other man would not put a detective off. That coat! Also like you, Mr. Tindall, I couldn't see why the murderer should set himself the horrible task of cutting off a head, when there were so many easier ways of concealing the body's identity. That looked to me only the desperate resort of some one who found the man dead, and to whom it was of the most vital importance that the death should not be suspected, at least for a time. Once granted that Julian Clifford was the murdered man, then, if not an outsider, Mr. Hobbs was clearly marked as the probable disguiser of the identity, provided there were heavy defalcations in his books—so heavy that the death of Mr. Clifford and the subsequent looking into his affairs would spell ruin for him—a ruin far beyond any legacy of five thousand pounds to put right. The cheque was confusing, of course. So was the effect of Mr. Clifford's supposed endeavour to purchase the Charlemagne Crystal. Then there was always the question of collusion—of helpers. Altogether, it's been a most puzzling case."

"Yet Newman never puzzled you?" Tindall wondered.

"As a personality he did indeed. And also as to what, or how much, he knew. But apart from suspecting Straight at once, I soon saw that Mr. Newman knew too much to have left that Etcheverrey trail behind him on the scene of the murder. For he alone of the Thornbush circle was aware that Mr. Clifford intended using the anarchist in his work, and had talked the idea over with Mr. Bancroft. To Straight that news came as a fine shock. He thought he had been so clever!"

"When did he hear of it?"

"When Miss Haslar told me that she believed Mr. Newman to be really Etcheverrey. A belief that seemed to me to rest on a very shaky foundation."

"Chief Inspector!" It was Diana who burst in on them. "Who shot Arnold? It wasn't Mr. Straight, for he was in the library at Thornbush with me at the time! Horrible, horrible thought!" Her face blanched.

"No, it wasn't Straight. He of course insisted that the same man who killed Mr. Clifford had tried to kill your brother, because he had an absolute alibi during the time when Mr. Haslar was shot."

"But who did try to kill him?" she demanded frantically.

"Suppose you had done what your brother had done," Pointer began gently; "taken a flat for one purpose. Made your arrangements for that purpose. Suppose some one else used those arrangements for quite another purpose. For murder. And you learnt the awful truth. Not the report in the papers. Saw yourself implicated very deeply. Believed that you could not clear yourself. Knew that you had opened the door to life-long blackmail. Suppose you were suffering from an illness which peculiarly affects people's nerve. Couldn't you imagine yourself going up to your room, getting your revolver, and telling yourself that you must use it, and use it at once. 'Do it' were the words Mr. Haslar used. 'Do it, and do it at once!'"

"Arnold does talk to himself when he's very much stirred." Diana was half dazed. "You mean that Arnold shot himself?" There was horror, and there was boundless relief, in her voice.

"Just so. With the second bullet in his revolver. The first had been fired by Straight, who used a silencer. The faint mark is on the revolver still. I think that your brother had but that moment come downstairs and learnt from Mr. Newman, who had rushed in to tell him the terrible truth—the truth he had to know—of who it was that had really been murdered in Heath Mansions. Then Mr. Newman had to leave him for fear lest through his presence that truth be suspected, and Thornbush be connected with the brown and orange ulster. Probably your brother let Mr. Newman out. In the letter-box he saw a letter which Major Cory had just dropped in. I've had a chat, rather unwillingly and one-sided, perhaps, with that gentleman. It was a peculiarly menacing letter from a man who felt that he had been intended for a scapegoat. It was, I fancy, the little heap of charred paper that Mr. Tindall and I found under Mr. Haslar's writing-table."

"But how did Mr. Newman know who the dead man was?"

"When Mr. Clifford left his home so abruptly, Mr. Newman, I think, suspected that Mr. Haslar had had a hand in his absence. And even on being told by your brother that he had nothing to do with that absence, I think he still had his doubts, and had tipped a porter at Heath Mansions to let him know when the new, temporary tenant of Mr. Marshall's flat arrived. The man let out the truth that a murdered man hid been found there, and told him of the taking away by the police of the body. Mr. Newman, I think, stuck on a big black moustache, and going to the mortuary chapel posed as a Spaniard who might be able to identify Etcheverrey. We know that such a man called. I think Mr. Newman recognised Mr. Clifford's very remarkable hands, and recognising them, hurried at once to your brother's house—was met by you and left. Returned again, and had a word with Mr. Haslar. We shall soon learn if my ideas are fairly right."

They proved to be absolutely correct.

"But how do you know—did you suspect from the first—mean, that no one had shot Arnold but himself?"

Pointer looked across Diana at Tindall.

"There was a palm in a pot. The palm had been watered that morning—it was all wet. The brass pot, in which the earthenware one stood, was dry and even dusty. Yet when I tried to lift the inner one out, it couldn't be done because of a deep dent in the jardiniere, a dent that obviously could not have been there when the maid last took out the palm, a dent caused by that revolver crashing against it when it fell from Mr. Haslar's hand. Deflected by the brass pot, the weapon skidded along the floor to near the window. I think Mr. Haslar utilised a moment to fire when a motorcycle outside his house was starting up its engine."

"But those awful words of Arnold's," Diana broke out: "'I did it for nothing!'"

"He had shot, but not killed himself. And when he said he had killed Mr. Clifford I think he believed that by devising that plan for Cory to get the Haslar letters away from Mr. Clifford, he had handed Julian Clifford over to a man who had killed him in revenge for what had happened years ago, —happened and never been forgotten by Cory. The rest was but the effect of the shock of the lurid descriptions in the papers, and of his knowledge of whose that missing head was."

"Straight seemed shocked enough at what happened to Haslar," Tindall pointed out.

"Because he guessed the truth—that Mr. Haslar shot himself. Straight _knew_ that there was no murderer at large but himself. And that meant that Mr. Haslar had learnt who it was that had been killed in Heath Mansions, and did not believe in the Etcheverrey trail. And if Mr. Haslar, then why not others? When Mr. Haslar called out those words that night, Straight saw that his best chance—there was no question of concealing them—was to take his stand beside Miss Haslar. For a while."

Again came one of the short pauses which people need when they are trying to keep up with information that quite upsets their own ideas.

"Then it wasn't my brother whom Mr. Straight had seen near Heath Mansions?"

"I should say not, Miss Haslar. I think that was part of a plan of Straight's to frighten you about your brother's connection with the murder for his own ends. To play the part of the faithful friend."

"But Arnold must have had some shock, so the doctor thought, to account for his state that morning."

"That was probably administered by Mrs. Orr. In our talk at Bruges after you left, I learnt from her that she had written—well—a farewell little note to Mr. Haslar from Paris. It reached Hampstead Tuesday morning. He found it lying on the breakfast table for him. It was a very cruel little note. A definite break. Mrs. Orr did not want your brother coming on after her, and interfering with her quite well-laid plans."

At any other time Diana would have made a scathing comment on Mazod Orr giving up her brother, but now all she cared for was that Arnold was cleared, and that Newman was cleared. Tindall and Sir Edward left the room.

Diana took a deep breath. Her eyes were softly luminous. No one could say that her face was cold now.

"And Mr. Newman took everything on himself!" There was a little pause. "Oh, if only I dared! Does blood—even such blood matter really. After all, we Haslars—he is all that's fine. Surely if he could come unscathed from out of such a home, others could. Under better, happier circumstances."

"Come along and let's see what Mr. Newman has to say," Pointer's tone had something boyish in it, as he led her into a room where Newman was standing, his face like the face of a crusader who has won through to Jerusalem.

"Well, Chief Inspector, I take off my hat to you! Especially after I—I'm glad you know now that I didn't kill Julian Clifford. A man I place second only to Peter Haslar. To whom I owe—all that I do owe him. You are right all along the line. Even as to my being the man who called to see Etcheverrey's body. I never imagined any one could unravel this tangle!"

"Especially"—Pointer spoke grimly—"after you had twisted it up still more by that so-called confession of yours. Oh, I know why you did it. To pay back the debt you owed to the dead brother. For Miss Haslar's sake, too, probably. But I hope the thought that you might easily have gone to the gallows instead of Richard Straight, will keep you from ever doing such a thing again. Your improvised motive to me this evening was really alarmingly pat."

It was a very official eye that looked frostily at the other man.

"I—at the time it seemed the only chance. I knew Arnold would never have done it in cold blood, of course. But I was afraid that some discussion about his grandfather's letters— And when you nearly broke me down with what the police might think but for my confession, I didn't dare speak without thinking it all over. I—well, frankly I thought it might be a trap. Though there was the ghastly chance that it might all be true. It was—it was—"

With a deep sigh, Newman tossed what it had been, away from him for ever.

"It was my duty to break down what I firmly believed to be a spurious confession," Pointer said, inwardly a little amused at the positively ferocious glare that Diana was fixing on him. "Now I really would like to hear your explanation of two things. First, Mr. Pollock's furniture."

Diana stared. But Newman looked faintly self-conscious. "Ever heard of _The Knight's Dream?_" he asked.

"You mean the musical comedy that's been running for a couple of years?"

"I wrote it—words and music. It's a gold-mine apparently. I'm working on another. My agents only know me as Pollock, of course. And the only address they have are my bankers and the Musicians' Club in Wigmore Street. And your second question, Chief Inspector?"

"We found a charred piece of a letter in your room at Thornbush on which we deciphered in Mr. Clifford's writing, 'I know the danger,' 'discovered your secret,' 'wife.' At least I believe the word to be wife. Now those sentences looked rather damning, but wasn't the secret that Mr. Clifford thought he had discovered your love for Miss Haslar?"

Diana gave a gasp. "What a dreadful scrap of paper to find!"

"It was puzzling!" Pointer agreed.

"Yes," Newman said, screwing up his eyes in thought. "Yes, the whole sentence ran somewhat after this fashion. I know that letter by heart," he added turning round with a look new to Pointer—a look that changed him into the lad Diana had loved at Hendaye.

"I know the danger of jumping to conclusions, but I feel sure that I have discovered your secret of hoping to make Diana some day your wife.' And Mr. Clifford went on in the kindest way to tell me, that in justice to Diana herself, that must not be. I might be married already."

"When did he write this?"

"Two years ago."

Two years ago was the time when Julian Clifford had altered his will so as to leave Newman, if still unmarried, a competency.

"And you replied?" Pointer thought it as well to take advantage of this moment to know all that there was to be known.

"I told him he was utterly mistaken in my feeling for you," Newman flashed a grim, yet fond smile at Diana, whose eyes were brimming. "I kept the letter as an additional help to—stick to my guns. But I wonder that such a sentence, found in such a case, didn't hang me," he threw at Pointer interrogatively.

"You were so careful to make your flight look suspicious," Pointer said with a half unwilling smile in reply. "You had gone to so much time and trouble in your bedroom to take down a suitcase, and get a bag off your wardrobe top, and strew so many garments, each of which you had to take from its place, around the room, that it seemed odd you should have burnt this letter if it really was incriminating.

"But Miss Haslar is waiting to hear what it was that Superintendent told you. My best wishes, Mr. Penfold."

And Pointer closed the door behind him.

THE END

Other Resurrected Press Books in *The Chief Inspector Pointer Mystery* Series

MYSTERIES BY ANNE AUSTIN

Murder at Bridge

When an afternoon bridge party attended by some of
Hamilton's leading citizens ends with the hostess being
murdered in her boudoir, Special Investigator Dundee of
the District Attorney's office is called in. But one of the
attendees is guilty? There are plenty of suspects: the
victim's former lover, her current suitor, the retired judge
who is being blackmailed, the victim's maid who had been
horribly disfigured accidentally by the murdered woman,
or any of the women who's husbands had flirted with the
victim. Or was she murdered by an outsider whose
motive had nothing to do with the town of Hamilton.
Find the answer in . . . **Murder at Bridge**

One Drop of Blood

When Dr. Koenig, head of Mayfield Sanitarium is
murdered, the District Attorney's Special Investigator,
"Bonnie" Dundee must go undercover to find the killer.
Were any of the inmates of the asylum insane enough to
have committed the crime? Or, was it one of the staff,
motivated by jealousy? And what was is the secret in the
murdered man's past. Find the answer in . . . **One Drop
of Blood**

AVAILABLE FROM RESURRECTED PRESS!

GEMS OF MYSTERY
LOST JEWELS FROM A MORE ELEGANT AGE

Three wonderful tales of mystery from some of the best known writers of the period before the First World War -

A foggy London night, a Russian princess who steals jewels, a corpse; a mysterious murder, an opera singer, and stolen pearls; two young people who crash a masked ball only to find themselves caught up in a daring theft of jewels; these are the subjects of this collection of entertaining tales of love, jewels, and mystery. This collection includes:

- **In the Fog - by Richard Harding Davis's**

- **The Affair at the Hotel Semiramis - by A.E.W. Mason**

- **Hearts and Masks - Harold MacGrath**

AVAILABLE FROM RESURRECTED PRESS!

THE EDWARDIAN DETECTIVES
LITERARY SLEUTHS OF THE EDWARDIAN ERA

The exploits of the great Victorian Detectives, Poe's C. Auguste Dupin, Gaboriau's Lecoq, and most famously, Arthur Conan Doyle's Sherlock Holmes, are well known. But what of those fictional detectives that came after, those of the Edwardian Age? The period between the death of Queen Victoria and the First World War had been called the Golden Age of the detective short story, but how familiar is the modern reader with the sleuths of this era? And such an extraordinary group they were, including in their numbers an unassuming English priest, a blind man, a master of disguises, a lecturer in medical jurisprudence, a noble woman working for Scotland Yard, and a savant so brilliant he was known as "The Thinking Machine."

To introduce readers to these detectives, Resurrected Press has assembled a collection of stories featuring these and other remarkable sleuths in The Edwardian Detectives.

- The Case of Laker, Absconded by Arthur Morrison
- The Fenchurch Street Mystery by Baroness Orczy
- The Crime of the French Café by Nick Carter
- The Man with Nailed Shoes by R Austin Freeman
- The Blue Cross by G. K. Chesterton
- The Case of the Pocket Diary Found in the Snow by Augusta Groner
- The Ninescore Mystery by Baroness Orczy
- The Riddle of the Ninth Finger by Thomas W. Hanshew
- The Knight's Cross Signal Problem by Ernest Bramah

- The Problem of Cell 13 by Jacques Futrelle
- The Conundrum of the Golf Links by Percy James Brebner
- The Silkworms of Florence by Clifford Ashdown
- The Gateway of the Monster by William Hope Hodgson
- The Affair at the Semiramis Hotel by A. E. W. Mason
- The Affair of the Avalanche Bicycle & Tyre Co., LTD by Arthur Morrison

RESURRECTED PRESS CLASSIC MYSTERY CATALOGUE

Journeys into Mystery
Travel and Mystery in a More Elegant Time

The Edwardian Detectives
Literary Sleuths of the Edwardian Era

Gems of Mystery
Lost Jewels from a More Elegant Age

E. C. Bentley
Trent's Last Case: The Woman in Black

Ernest Bramah
Max Carrados Resurrected:
The Detective Stories of Max Carrados

Agatha Christie
The Secret Adversary
The Mysterious Affair at Styles

Octavus Roy Cohen
Midnight

Freeman Wills Croft
The Ponson Case
The Pit Prop Syndicate

J. S. Fletcher
The Herapath Property
The Rayner-Slade Amalgamation
The Chestermarke Instinct
The Paradise Mystery
Dead Men's Money

The Middle of Things
Ravensdene Court
Scarhaven Keep
The Orange-Yellow Diamond
The Middle Temple Murder
The Tallyrand Maxim
The Borough Treasurer
In the Mayor's Parlour
The Saftey Pin

R. Austin Freeman
*The Mystery of 31 New Inn from the Dr. Thorndyke
Series*
*John Thorndyke's Cases from the Dr. Thorndyke
Series*
The Red Thumb Mark from The Dr. Thorndyke Series
The Eye of Osiris from The Dr. Thorndyke Series
A Silent Witness from the Dr. John Thorndyke Series
The Cat's Eye from the Dr. John Thorndyke Series
*Helen Vardon's Confession: A Dr. John Thorndyke
Story*
As a Thief in the Night: A Dr. John Thorndyke Story
*Mr. Pottermack's Oversight: A Dr. John Thorndyke
Story*
*Dr. Thorndyke Intervenes: A Dr. John Thorndyke
Story*
The Singing Bone: The Adventures of Dr. Thorndyke
The Stoneware Monkey: A Dr. John Thorndyke Story
*The Great Portrait Mystery, and Other Stories: A
Collection of Dr. John Thorndyke and Other Stories*
The Penrose Mystery: A Dr. John Thorndyke Story
The Uttermost Farthing: A Savant's Vendetta

Arthur Griffiths
The Passenger From Calais
The Rome Express

Fergus Hume
The Mystery of a Hansom Cab
The Green Mummy
The Silent House
The Secret Passage

Edgar Jepson
The Loudwater Mystery

A. E. W. Mason
At the Villa Rose

A. A. Milne
The Red House Mystery
Baroness Emma Orczy
The Old Man in the Corner

Edgar Allan Poe
The Detective Stories of Edgar Allan Poe

Arthur J. Rees
The Hampstead Mystery
The Shrieking Pit
The Hand In The Dark
The Moon Rock
The Mystery of the Downs

Mary Roberts Rinehart
Sight Unseen and The Confession

Dorothy L. Sayers
Whose Body?

Sir William Magnay
The Hunt Ball Mystery

Mabel and Paul Thorne
The Sheridan Road Mystery

Louis Tracy
The Strange Case of Mortimer Fenley
The Albert Gate Mystery
The Bartlett Mystery
The Postmaster's Daughter
The House of Peril
The Sandling Case: What Would You Have Done?
Charles Edmonds Walk
The Paternoster Ruby

John R. Watson
The Mystery of the Downs
The Hampstead Mystery

Edgar Wallace
The Daffodil Mystery
The Crimson Circle

Carolyn Wells
Vicky Van
The Man Who Fell Through the Earth
In the Onyx Lobby
Raspberry Jam
The Clue
The Room with the Tassels
The Vanishing of Betty Varian
The Mystery Girl
The White Alley
The Curved Blades
Anybody but Anne
The Bride of a Moment
Faulkner's Folly
The Diamond Pin
The Gold Bag
The Mystery of the Sycamore
The Come Backy

Raoul Whitfield
Death in a Bowl

And much more!
Visit ResurrectedPress.com
for our complete catalogue

About Resurrected Press

A division of Intrepid Ink, LLC, Resurrected Press is dedicated to bringing high quality, vintage books back into publication. See our entire catalogue and find out more at www.ResurrectedPress.com.

About Intrepid Ink, LLC

Intrepid Ink, LLC provides full publishing services to authors of fiction and non-fiction books, eBooks and websites. From editing to formatting, from publishing to marketing, Intrepid Ink gets your creative works into the hands of the people who want to read them. Find out more at www.IntrepidInk.com.

Printed in Great Britain
by Amazon.co.uk, Ltd.,
Marston Gate.